LYNNE PEMBERTON

Eclipse

HarperCollinsPublishers

HarperCollins*Publishers*
77–85 Fulham Palace Road,
Hammersmith, London W6 8JB

This paperback edition 1995
1 3 5 7 9 8 6 4 2

First published in Great Britain by
HarperCollins*Publishers* 1995

ISBN 0 00 649005 0

Set in Linotron Times by
Rowland Phototypesetting Ltd
Bury St Edmunds, Suffolk

Printed in Great Britain by
HarperCollinsManufacturing Glasgow

By the same author

PLATINUM COAST

ECLIPSE

Lynne Pemberton is a founding director of Pemberton Hotels, the group of luxury hotels in the West Indies owned by her husband, Mike Pemberton. Born in Newcastle-upon-Tyne, she had a highly successful career as a model before she met her husband and became involved in the running of his growing leisure company. Ten years later, in 1981, her life took a new direction when she and her husband opened their first hotel in Barbados, an island they had fallen in love with in 1976. Since then their success has been spectacular, and the group now includes some of the most luxurious hotels in the world. Lynne Pemberton divides her time between Barbados and London, where she has a house in Knightsbridge. Her bestselling first novel, *Platinum Coast*, was published in 1993.

From the reviews of *Platinum Coast*:

'A rags-to-riches story with plenty of sun, sea, sand and sex . . . Escapist bliss.'
Tatler

'An ideal light, pacy summer read.'
ANITA BURGH, *Mail on Sunday*

'A tale of glamorous lives and ruthless ambition – impeccable.'
Manchester Evening News

'Romantic suspense, mystery and intrigue in a tropical setting – a terrific read.'
Annabel

'Blockbuster debut novel.'
Daily Mail

To my husband Mike,
who made dreams possible,
all My Love.

ACKNOWLEDGEMENTS

Thanks first and foremost to Colin Walsh, for his constant support, encouragement, and for believing in me in the first place, Keith Miller for his invaluable help and astute comments. Chris Johnson in Grand Cayman, for his generous research assistance. And last but by no means least, my son Michael for his enthusiasm and irrepressible sense of humour.

Book One

Chapter One

A shiver ran through her as the wind outside rose to an agonized howl, rattling the shutters on the chalkstone house with a ferocity that threatened to rip them off their hinges.

The storm had begun.

Feeling relatively secure inside the drawing room of the sturdily constructed beach-house, Lady Serena Frazer-West was quite enthralled by the prospect of experiencing a Caribbean storm first-hand. Overcome by curiosity, she carefully prised open a tiny gap between the louvres of the floor-to-ceiling shutters and, bending forward, strained her eyes to see through the blanket of dark silver rain.

She had never seen such a downpour. A solid sheet of water was teeming out of a sky the colour of charcoal.

Serena remembered the first time she had come to Jamaica on her honeymoon two years previously. It had been raining then. A flicker of a smile crossed her face as she recalled the three-hour drive across the island from Kingston the capital, to the sleepy little town of Port Antonio. She had laughed, and Nicholas had complained loudly, when they had been squashed into the back of a broken down Morris Minor with four pieces of luggage, and a box of rotting paw-paw belonging to the chattering driver. As the old car approached the rushing Rio Grande, the sun had made its first appearance over the top of the soaring blue mountains. Submerging the lush green valley

9

in a translucent pinkish light. The avenue of flamboyant trees lining the roadside, rain dripping from their tightly packed blossoms, had reminded Serena of a mass of scarlet umbrellas.

It was a sight she'd never forgotten.

Now the wind was roaring across the island at more than eighty miles per hour, driving the rain violently, soaking everything in its path. And with it came a veil of mist which seemed to hang over the ground, covering the huge Cannonball tree at the foot of the garden in a ghostly cloak.

Serena's eyes travelled across the covered terrace, then down the garden path, littered now with fallen branches, and on to the dark sea beyond. Through the gloom she caught sight of a huge wave, almost the same height as the ubiquitous coconut palms. Within seconds, it had smashed a small fishing boat to smithereens, the splintered fragments whirling on a great gust of wind before being swallowed up by the blackness of the sky.

Serena was fascinated. She found the untamed beauty of the storm exhilarating and the wildness of the scene stirred her senses. How could she know that for the rest of her life she would always look back on this day, thinking that if it hadn't been for the storm things would have been so different.

Suddenly an involuntary gasp exploded from her lips when, stretching on tiptoe to scan the far side of the garden, she spotted something or someone moving behind the thick trunk of a date palm.

A figure stumbled out into the open. It was a man, his shirt flapping wildly like the wings of some huge prehistoric bird. As the full force of the wind hit him he dropped on to his belly and with his head curled into his chest, he crawled across the sodden ground towards the shelter of the house.

Serena shared his discomfort, afraid for him, as she

watched his painfully slow progress. Every few yards he was forced to lie flat, covering his head with his hands as meagre protection from flying branches and other debris. As he drew nearer he seemed to shout for help, but his voice must have been lost in all the chaos.

She snapped out of her state of mental paralysis and jolted herself into action, running across the large drawing room, down two wide steps and into an internal courtyard that led to the hall.

She could hear the stranger's muffled shouts as she flung open the heavy wooden door. He was slumped against the stone wall of the covered walkway which crossed the front of the house. Staring at him, speechless, she noticed how his broad chest heaved as he turned to face her.

He was panting.

Unable to take her eyes off the man it suddenly struck Serena that she must look totally stupid, standing there gaping. But just as she was about to say something, a particularly ferocious gust of wind lifted him and hurled him forward. She raised her hands to ward him off but the heavy weight of his body fell clumsily, crashing into her right shoulder. She cried out as her ankle twisted and she slid to the floor.

A second later the man was kneeling beside her, his strong hands cool on her bare shoulders. She could smell his wet clothes and a musky aroma coming from his skin, or was it his hair, she wasn't sure which.

'Are you OK?' His voice was very deep.

A sharp pain shot through her ankle. It hurt like hell but Serena forced herself to suppress her tears.

'It's not much, I don't think.' Her voice was tremulous.

'Let me look at it,' he said, gently lifting her right foot.

Supporting her ankle with one hand, he tenderly ran his fingers over her skin, delicately searching for any signs of serious damage. Closing her eyes, Serena sat very still whilst he completed the examination.

'No bones broken, thank God,' he announced, his dark head glistening in the dim light. As he spoke he blinked rapidly, several times, to clear his vision of the tiny drops of rain which fell from his eyelashes.

Serena was shocked by the intense green of his eyes. And when a gleaming smile lit up his dark face, she suddenly felt that she'd known him for a very long time. Holding those eyes for what seemed like an age, she marvelled at the unpredictability of love at first sight.

'Serena darling, what on earth is going on?'

Lord Frazer-West was striding towards them, dressed in a long cotton shirt and jeans; closely followed by Joseph, the butler, in starched white shirt and bow tie.

Reluctantly Serena dragged her eyes away from the stranger.

'I'm not absolutely sure myself,' she responded, glancing briefly in her husband's direction before reverting her full attention to the other man.

It annoyed her that neither Nicholas nor the butler made any move to help the soaked stranger as he struggled to close the solid mahogany door behind him.

Instead they looked on in silence, each gazing at him expectantly.

'I apologize for bursting in on you like this, but my car broke down.'

Serena thought he looked extremely uncomfortable as he glanced from face to face.

'I could have been killed out there,' he added as an afterthought.

'Well, you almost killed me,' Serena commented with a hint of amusement in her voice, glancing down at her ankle which was beginning to swell.

'What happened, darling?' asked Nicholas, stepping in front of the man to approach his wife. 'Are you hurt?'

'I'm fine,' she said casually, not wanting any fuss. 'It's nothing much. I tripped and twisted my ankle, that's all.'

Nicholas immediately spun round, confronting the stranger, his dark eyes clouded.

The man was smiling apologetically. 'It was my fault entirely. Well, the real fault lies with the wind actually. I was literally lifted off my feet and thrown at the good lady. In my opinion the damage is only a slight sprain. Some ice on it, with a strapping, should do the trick.'

For some inexplicable reason Lord Nicholas Frazer-West found the man's perfect diction disconcerting. 'What on earth were you doing out in the storm, man! There was plenty of warning.'

His impatience showed in the tight line of his mouth, whilst he looked the intruder up and down with obvious distaste. Noticing several muddy footprints on the marble floor, he consoled himself with the thought that at least the culprit wasn't standing on the Chinese washed rug in the drawing room.

'I had my reasons, believe me,' came the answer. 'But I've experienced storms like this before. They are capable of uprooting trees, and I thought I should take shelter. You were the closest house.'

'You're soaked to the skin,' said Nicholas matter of factly.

Serena raised her eyes, mildly irritated by the fact that her husband could always be relied upon to state the obvious, whatever the situation.

'Of course he's wet Nicholas! So would you be if you'd just been outside,' she retorted. And without waiting for a reply she spoke briskly to the butler. 'Take the gentleman into the guest room Joseph, find him some dry clothes, and later set an extra place for supper.'

The butler didn't move. He inclined his head and waited, glancing in Lord Frazer-West's direction.

Nicholas was too intent on observing his wife to notice. He was frowning as he recognized the all too familiar thrust of her chin. Her sapphire blue eyes were challenging him, and he swiftly decided it would be futile to argue.

'Do as the mistress says, Joseph.' Lord Frazer-West spoke with the voice of one who'd been accustomed to servants all his life. Joseph nodded, still not saying a word.

'Cat got your tongue, Joseph?' Serena teased.

'Serena,' snapped Nicholas.

The butler lowered his eyes and then mumbled, 'No mistress, ain't bin no cats around here today.'

She grinned in spite of herself, then turned her gaze to the stranger. She guessed he must be feeling increasingly ill at ease, caught up in domestic tensions that had nothing to do with him. And his next words proved her right.

'Listen folks. I can shelter in the kitchen, out of your way, until the storm eases up. I really had no intention of disturbing anyone's evening; I just didn't feel like being injured out there.'

Serena came to his rescue. 'You're not disturbing anyone's evening; is he Nicholas?'

Nicholas didn't reply, but his belligerent body language said it all.

Serena continued unperturbed. 'We were going to have an early supper; play cards and wait for the storm to pass. You might help to break the monotony. We would be delighted to have you join us.'

Nicholas, stony-faced, declined to confirm his wife's insistent welcome and the refugee from the storm was still unsure.

'I've been wet before and it didn't kill me. I really don't need fresh clothes.'

Rivulets of rainwater trickled down the back of his neck as he shook his head. Then, lifting his arm, he raked long fingers through his matted, curly hair and, as he did so, his shirt fell open to expose a muscular torso.

A sudden rush of heat filled Serena's entire body as she watched him. Certain it would show on her face, she quickly lowered her head and stepped back into the shadows before replying. 'Well, it might just kill you this time, and we'd hate to be responsible for that.'

She was unable to keep the teasing tone out of her voice; and, when the man looked at her, she flashed him a smile that was both mischievous and inviting, half woman and half child. It made her look like someone about to embark upon a reckless adventure.

'I'm sure Nicholas has an old tee-shirt somewhere, and a pair of shorts.' Serena looked enquiringly at her husband, who was studying the man's enormous frame.

'I doubt I've got anything to fit you, Mr . . . ' Nicholas paused.

'Fergusson. Royole Fergusson the second, at your service.' Royole bent forward, mockingly sweeping one big arm in front of him in a parody of a bow. He was grinning from ear to ear.

There was an untamed air about him which Serena found irresistible. She stretched out her hand, bubbling with laughter, and responded in kind.

'Lady Serena Frazer-West, at your service, sir.'

Nicholas stepped in front of Royole before he had an opportunity to take his wife's hand. Looking up into the taller man's face, he was as surprised as Serena had been by the intense green of the eyes; eyes which held his own so firmly.

'Come along then, Mr Fergusson. Let's see if we can at least get you rigged out in something dry.'

Nicholas then nodded to the butler, and Joseph led the way out of the small hallway into a fifty-foot square central courtyard, laid in pure white terrazzo. Serena had to be supported by her husband as she limped along.

The house had been designed around the courtyard and all the rooms led off it. It was dark. The windows were shuttered against the storm and an enormous antique brass lantern, hanging on a heavy chain, was unlit. Only a small amount of light, flickering from four carved wall-sconces, cast an eerie glow upon the pale stone.

Royole jumped as a frog croaked loudly, then plopped into the small ornamental pool in the centre of the court-yard, disappearing under a perfect, yellow lotus lily.

A pair of old, stone urns, inlaid with the Frazer-West crest, stood at the foot of a wide sweeping staircase. Serena, leaning against one of the urns, admired Royole Fergusson's broad back as he ascended the stairs holding the curved mahogany handrail.

Only when he was out of sight did she limp barefoot into the drawing room, where the butler had lit several long candles, just in case the electricity failed. They flickered brightly under gleaming hurricane lamps, shadows dancing across the darkened walls.

Earlier in the day Joseph and the gardener had stacked all the terrace furniture into one corner of the room, which now resembled a warehouse. The air felt heavy, with a cloying dampness. It was oppressive and Serena longed to do what she did in the mornings; which was to throw open the tall windows leading on to the terrace, let in a fresh sea breeze and enjoy uninterrupted views of the coastline from every angle.

She noticed that the wind noise had changed. It was deeper now, more aggressive. She was momentarily startled as the large limb of a mahogany tree crashed down on to the roof of the house. But settling comfortably on the deep sofa, she popped a cushion behind her head and another under her ankle. She was thinking about Royole Fergusson, when Nicholas joined her, immediately destroying the moment.

'Was it really necessary to invite a total stranger to join us for supper, Serena?' he complained through clenched teeth as soon as he entered the room.

She didn't reply.

'Serena, answer me! I was looking forward to a quiet evening; just you and I.'

She studied her husband's back as he poured himself a large gin and tonic. 'Might it have been OK to invite him for dinner if he was white, Nicholas darling?' His back stiffened as she pursued her point. 'Or another house-holder perhaps; someone you went to school with; an old chum from your club; even someone who knew someone who went to Eton. If he was someone more . . . how shall I put it, Nicholas, *of our class*?'

He whirled round, almost spilling his drink.

Serena confronted him defiantly, but sank a little deeper into the sofa, anticipating his angry reaction. Nicholas's brown eyes were shadowed, so she couldn't see what they said, but there was no mistaking the annoyance in his voice.

'I hear your contempt, my sweet, and I'll have none of it. How dare you accuse me of prejudice!'

Serena didn't feel like arguing. It was such a waste of time with Nicholas. He invariably overreacted and she found it extremely tedious. She often did it purely to be perverse, but for once she decided to placate him.

'Because, my darling Nicholas, you are a bigot; an absolute snob; insular to the core and I adore you.'

She was smiling sweetly as he crossed the few feet that separated them and sat beside her.

Wrapping her slim arms tightly around his neck, Serena planted a kiss on his cheek and savoured the smell of his expensive after-shave and lemon-scented soap.

'Let's not argue Nicky, please. I felt sorry for the man, that's all.'

She pecked his nose, wetting the tip with her tongue, and watched his anger melt way. Unable to resist, he kissed her on the mouth, whispering, 'And I adore *you*, my Lady Serena.'

They both turned at the sound of an embarrassed cough, intended as a polite interruption. 'Er, will I do?' asked Royole.

He bent his head self-consciously as they surveyed his ill-fitting clothes.

Serena looked at him standing awkwardly at the entrance to the elegant drawing room: he was incongruous in big white tee-shirt, cut-off shorts held together with an old leather suitcase strap, and no shoes.

'You look wonderful,' she said. And she meant it.

Royole responded with a wink. 'Well thank you kindly, mam. I mightily appreciate that.'

He made her laugh with his mimicry of a drawl from the American Deep South.

'Dinner is served I believe.' Nicholas's curt voice cut crisply through his wife's laughter as he stood up and left the room.

Serena shrugged, pulling a long face at her husband's back. 'Don't take too much notice of Nicholas. He's a pussy cat really.'

Royole was certain that Lord Frazer-West was anything but, however he had absolutely no desire to argue with his host's beautiful wife.

Instead he said, a little hesitantly. 'The storm will be over soon, and I can leave. By the way, how's the ankle?'

He walked over to where she lay and leaned forward to look at her foot. Her ankle was already turning a delicate shade of bluish black.

She smiled. 'I'll live. Come on, let's go and eat or risk my husband's wrath.'

'Let me help you.' He offered her a muscular arm and she took it willingly.

Struggling to her feet, she forced herself to suppress the desire that rose within her at the touch of his flesh. Then she indicated the way back through the courtyard; down a dimly lit hallway which ended in a stone archway encased in coral vine.

Together they entered the dining room, where Royole paused on the threshold, his eyes absorbing every detail.

He had never seen such a beautiful room.

Champagne-coloured stone walls rose majestically to a domed ceiling where hummingbirds and yellow warblers flew across richly stocked flowerbeds, alive with colour. Industrious insects, painted in the most minute detail, crawled across the long, swaying leaves of a traveller's palm. For an instant Royole had the illusion that he could actually smell the bright petals of the lilac bougainvillaea that framed the beautiful creation. It was exquisite.

'My father commissioned two Venetian artists to paint the ceiling, they spent several months here in 1958 when the house was built,' Nicholas informed his visitor casually, as if speaking of an everyday occurrence.

A French glass chandelier, ablaze with two dozen candles, hung dramatically above a Regency dining table set with gleaming crystal and antique silver resting on a white linen tablecloth. In the centre of the oval table there was a carved, marble dish filled with sparkling water, on top of which floated pink and white hibiscus. Tall, glass doors covered one entire wall of the room and arched fanlights touched the ceiling. Tonight they were tightly secured against the storm, but Royole could picture them open to the prevailing breeze on a calmer evening – when the murmur of the sea would mix softly with the sound of conversation and laughter.

Royole wanted a room like this for himself.

'It's perfect,' he said in a hushed voice.

'I don't suppose you've ever seen anything like it before.' Lord Frazer-West adopted his most patronising tone.

Royole was aware of the small hairs on the back of his neck beginning to stand on end. It angered him that this pompous man could make such assumptions about him on sight. He looked directly into the eyes of his unwilling host and replied with deliberate courtesy.

'This house is extremely beautiful and you are a very

lucky man to own it.' He paused, allowing Nicholas the satisfaction of a smug smile before continuing, 'I am a well-travelled man, Lord Frazer-West; and I've seen many spectacular homes. I've met lots of different people all over the world,' his voice deepened, 'and I've seen sights you could only begin to imagine. Things for which there are no words.'

Nicholas merely grunted, making no comment. He was disconcerted; irritated by this intrusion into his home. More than that, he felt somehow threatened by the stranger. It made him edgy and bad-tempered.

He turned to Serena who, to his extreme annoyance, was looking at Royole with a triumphant glint in her bright eyes. He muttered something under his breath before picking up a bell from the table and ringing it loudly.

Joseph appeared.

'Pour me some white wine,' Nicholas ordered grumpily.

Serena indicated the chair next to her, patting it. 'Please sit down, Mr Fergusson.'

Royole made no attempt to move. 'I didn't ask to join you for dinner, Lord Frazer-West, and if you would rather I left, please feel free to say so now.'

Nicholas offered a formal smile and spoke resignedly, as if quite bored by the whole thing. 'I believe all men, at any given time,' he paused, staring vacantly over Royole's shoulder, 'are victims of fate. A storm has chosen that we dine together this evening and, on that note, I welcome you to my table Mr Fergusson.'

To Serena's delight and Nicholas's chagrin, Royole Fergusson proved to be a very stimulating dinner guest; both articulate and amusing.

As the Château Margaux flowed, then so did his deep voice. At once intense and passionate when expounding a favourite theory, yet so readily slipping into a frivolous, easy wit when teasing his hosts with an amusing anecdote.

At thirty, he was the same age as Nicholas and had indeed lived a full and exciting life.

'Have you always lived in Jamaica?' asked Serena, holding his emerald-green gaze for far longer than necessary.

He fascinated her.

She was powerless to stop staring at him, even though she was aware that she was virtually ignoring Nicholas. It was just that she had never before met anyone like Royole Fergusson, and as the evening progressed she found herself more and more drawn to him. It was as if he had cast a spell and she was bound up in it.

'No, I was born in St Vincent, in the Grenadines, to a negro father who claimed direct descendancy from a Royal Zulu tribe. Hence my name. My mother's half-French Caucasian and half Guyanese, and at . . .' he paused, calculating in his head, '. . . fifty-three she's still an exceptionally beautiful woman. I have a brother and two sisters. We moved to Port Antonio, when I was three years old, and six years later to Boston, where my father practised as a doctor until his death two years ago.'

Serena said that she was sorry about his father, then continued to listen avidly; learning that Royole had won a scholarship to Harvard, where he had studied law for two years before dropping out in favour of his long-cherished dream of coming back to live in the Caribbean.

'And you, is this your first time in Port Antonio?' Royole addressed his question to Serena.

'No, the fifth trip, the first time was on our honeymoon.' She sighed, 'Our stays are never long enough for me, I feel like I want to become a West Indian,' she laughed lightly.

Royole agreed, his voice impassioned. 'The Caribbean's like that. It kind of gets into your blood, there's nowhere on earth quite like it.'

Nicholas addressed him directly for the first time in little under an hour. 'That I must say is only *your* opinion, yet you do speak with rare perception.'

The compliment was delivered with a feigned sincerity, intended to disguise the disdain Nicholas actually felt for the charming and charismatic individual sharing his table who seemed to threaten everything he stood for.

During the course of the evening Royole had not only dominated the conversation, debasing many of Nicholas's hard-held principles, but he had also captivated the wife he cherished.

In two years of marriage, even in their most intimate moments, Nicholas had never once seen Serena look at him the way she was looking at the animated and handsome face of Royole Fergusson this evening.

After dinner Joseph served strong, Colombian coffee in demitasse china cups. Royole tried gamely to get his finger through the handle but failed, and finally settled for holding his cup in the palm of his hand.

It was exactly ten-thirty when they suddenly noticed that the incessant clattering of the rain beating against the shutters had ceased. 'Listen,' Serena whispered.

A hush had descended. Even the wind had dropped to a dull murmur.

Nicholas stood up and strode across the stone floor to throw open one of the tall windows. He unhooked the shutters and craned his neck outside to look upwards into the overcast sky. It was still raining a little but the calabash trees in front of the dining room were now swaying a lot less violently. The air was damp and it smelt heavily of sea water and sodden earth; that peculiar combination so typical of the Caribbean Islands.

'I think the worst has passed,' Nicholas called out before pacing back towards the table, giving an elaborate yawn. 'I'm exhausted, don't know about you?' He directed his words deliberately at Royole.

Serena glared at him, as Royole stood up, saying, 'I think it's time for me to leave.'

Less than five minutes later Royole was on the doorstep, holding his original clothes in an untidy, damp bundle.

'Thank you both for a wonderful evening. It's been a pleasure meeting you, and I would very much like to return your hospitality.' He looked expectantly between the two dimly lit faces before him; Serena's animated and eager, her husband's incomprehensible and closed.

Nicholas wanted to say that once was more than enough, but he prided himself on being a gentleman with impeccable manners. 'The pleasure has been all ours, albeit an unexpected one. You must call us soon, and we'll see what we can fix up.'

He sounded bored and Royole, as he had done several times that evening, wondered what a beautiful young woman like Serena could see in the obnoxious Lord Frazer-West. Serena held out both her hands. Royole noticed that they were shaking very slightly as he enfolded them securely in his own.

His desire to pull her close was difficult to resist. He longed to feel the softness of her skin again. A sensation he had felt so briefly, but enjoyed so much, whilst examining her ankle. Sensing that she wanted him as much as he wanted her, he was determined to see her again.

'Goodnight Royole,' she said. 'It's been lovely. I really have enjoyed your company.'

It was impossible to read anything in her shadowed eyes, yet her slow smile held a promise. Of that he was certain.

Nicholas quietly inched his way back into the darkened hall, suddenly feeling like an intruder, aware of a strange sort of intimacy between his wife and Royole Fergusson.

Royole was pleased to be alone with her and reiterated what he'd said earlier. 'I meant what I said; I want to invite you to my home.' Dropping her hands reluctantly, he looked around. 'Nothing as grand as this; but my house is full of warmth and laughter. And Caron cooks the best red snapper you ever tasted.'

Serena felt a reaction at the mention of the name 'Caron'. Forcing her voice to sound indifferent, she asked, 'Is Caron your wife?'

She was ridiculously pleased when he shook his head; less so when he went on to say, 'Not yet.'

'Serena darling, Joseph is waiting to drive Mr Fergusson home,' Nicholas shouted from the depths of the house.

There was no mistaking his impatience.

'Goodnight Lady Serena and, once more, thank you. Perhaps you have saved my life tonight.' He kissed his fingertips, placed them softly on her slightly parted lips and before she had a chance to reply, Royole Fergusson turned and strode off down the drive to where the butler was waiting with the jeep.

Serena watched him go, fighting a dangerous impulse to call him back.

Within seconds his tall figure was swallowed up by the dark, velvety night.

Chapter Two

'*No* Serena, I will not go.'

His mouth closed to a narrow line, Nicholas Frazer-West was adamant.

His wife glared at him. 'You're being ridiculously stubborn, Nicholas.'

Serena was experiencing great difficulty controlling her temper; but control it she knew she must, if she was to win the day. They had been arguing intermittently ever since Royole Fergusson's note had arrived two days ago, thanking them for their hospitality, and inviting them to dinner at his house.

Staring up at the sky, she yawned and watched a lone egret wing its way across a cloudless brilliant blue horizon.

Pale pink hibiscus flowers swayed across her vision. She reached out to pick one, almost toppling out of the hammock she had been snoozing in for the last two hours.

Tickling her left ear with the stem of the flower, she sat up; and, with one long, tanned leg lolling over the side of the hammock, she deliberately fixed a cajoling smile on her face.

'For me Nicky, darling.'

She hated herself for pleading, but had no alternative. 'At least think about it,' she added in a hopeful voice.

'I might think about it, but that won't change my mind.'

An exasperated sigh escaped her lips. 'You're impossible Nicholas.'

'I'm sorry, my devious little darling, but this time you

cannot have your own way. I flatly refuse to spend another evening in the company of Mr Royole Fergusson the second. How he has the bloody audacity to call himself *the second*,' he snorted.

'He probably has the audacity because his father was called Royole Fergusson,' Serena quipped.

Jumping out of the hammock, she joined Nicholas in the white-painted, wooden gazebo, where he was stretched out full length on a day-bed with an assortment of cushions stuffed behind his head and under his bare feet.

Serena perched on the edge of the bed and studied her husband. He was pretending to read Tolstoy, but she knew that he would much rather be reading a good spy thriller.

Why not simply admit that he wasn't an intellectual, she wondered. After all, Nicholas had everything that mattered: the advantage of good breeding; the best schools; and a shrewd father who had held on to his inherited wealth before conveniently dying five years ago, leaving everything to his only son.

She knew her parents had been delighted, and relieved, when the newly titled Earl of Ettington, Lord Frazer-West, had proposed marriage to their beautiful yet totally irresponsible daughter on the eve of her twenty-first birthday.

Eager to escape both her boring job in Christie's and the tyranny of her over-protective father, Serena had gladly accepted. She didn't love Nicholas, but had the advantage of knowing that he adored her. And marriage to him meant she could do exactly as she pleased; which she duly did . . . most of the time.

'Anyway, I think that your Mr Royole Fergusson is a fraud. I don't believe all that stuff he told us the night of the storm.' Nicholas spoke from behind his book. 'Joseph told me the man's a philanderer and a notorious womanizer; got girlfriends all over the place apparently.'

'Joseph's such an old woman,' commented Serena. 'Always gossiping about something or other. I'd take anything he says with a pinch of salt.'

'No smoke without fire, darling.' Nicholas dropped his book. 'Hasn't it occurred to you, my naïve little wife, that he probably wants to ingratiate himself with people like us for all the wrong reasons?'

'Oh for goodness sake, Nicholas,' she snapped, irritated. 'Royole Fergusson simply wants to reciprocate our hospitality; no more, no less. Can't *you* see that?'

She stood up. Two angry red spots had appeared on her lightly freckled cheeks. Nicholas tried to grab her by the waist.

'Come on Bunty, let's forget all this nonsense. Come and lie down next to me.'

He kicked a cushion on to the floor and, wriggling to one side, made space for her on the day-bed. Irritated by the use of his pet name for her, usually a prelude to lovemaking, Serena took a step back and out of his reach. Standing with legs apart and hands firmly clasped by her sides, she took a deep breath before she spoke.

'I am going to dinner at Royole Fergusson's house this evening, Nicholas, with or without you. I've made up my mind. Now you can join me if you wish; if not, I do hope you have a wonderful evening doing whatever you choose to do.'

She turned to walk away but Nicholas leapt up and grabbed her by the shoulders. His face had suddenly drained of colour, the muscles around his mouth were taut, and she knew that she had pushed him too far.

'Why is seeing this man so important to you, Serena?' he demanded, as his fingers pressed into the flesh of her upper arm.

'Stop it Nicholas, you're hurting me!' Serena cried out in pain. He didn't hear her. A vacant look had entered his eyes and he began to shake her furiously, uttering a name she had never heard before.

'No Robbie, please don't hurt me Robbie.'

Nanny Roberts was holding both his arms so tight that he thought he would pass out from the pain. He was sobbing and begging her to stop but she continued, repeatedly telling him what a bad boy he had been and how she was going to have to punish him.

'Nicholas, stop it please!' Serena screamed, shaken.

In the two years they had been married she had never seen him like this. Wrenching one arm free, she slapped him hard across the face. He desisted immediately, dropping both hands by his sides.

'I'm so sorry, Serena.' Nicholas hung his head; his long, straight hair fell in a blond curtain, hiding his face. 'Please forgive me.' He had adopted his 'little boy' voice; childish and penitent.

Neither of them spoke for several seconds until Serena broke the silence. 'I do forgive you Nicholas, but only on condition that you take me to supper at Royole Fergusson's house tonight.'

The humid West Indian night was overcast and blacker than black, making the journey down the unmade road towards San San beach all the more difficult. There was no welcoming moon, no twinkling stars to light the narrow dirt-road. Nicholas cursed as the jeep hit a jagged pothole, and he had to swerve violently to avoid careering into a gully.

'This is bloody treacherous,' he swore, and gripped the wheel so hard his knuckles shone white.

'I think we're almost there,' Serena said with more confidence than she actually felt.

Nicholas slowed the car down to a crawl as the road narrowed. Dense vegetation pressed in on them and thick tamarind branches thrashed the windscreen, dropping brown, lumpy pods on to the bonnet.

'I think we might have made a wrong turning,' confessed Serena eventually, looking at him helplessly.

'*Now* she tells me,' Nicholas bellowed.

She was about to tell him not to shout, when the road turned abruptly and the jeep bumped into a clearing, where an old Triumph sports car was parked at the end of a gravel drive leading to a long, low dwelling.

'Is this the place?' Nicholas asked as he cut the engine.

'I think so.' Serena looked unsure, then catching sight of Royole at the doorway she exclaimed, 'Yes it is!' then added quickly. 'Thank you for bringing me, Nicholas.'

Serena grabbed his hand. It was hot and clammy, nevertheless she held it very tight for a few seconds before saying, 'I really appreciate it.'

A raffish expression crossed her husband's pale face, and he winked. 'You know me; I'd do anything for you.' He meant it, and the rangy smile he gave her was full of love.

They both climbed out of the jeep.

Tiny, circular stepping-stones threaded a path through thick clumps of allamanda and frangipani to the entrance of Coralita Cottage, where Royole Fergusson stood, a dark silhouette in the light from the open door.

'Welcome to my home,' he said, holding out his hand to Nicholas, who felt tempted to ignore it.

Serena stood on tiptoe to plant a soft kiss on Royole's cheek.

Built into the side of a bluff and spectacularly, but precariously, suspended 150 feet above Turtle Cove, the entire house was constructed of wood. Intricately carved fretwork, painted bright blue and pastel pink, hung over sun-bleached shutters.

Exposed limestone boulders bordered the living room on two sides, and a deep verandah ran the full length of the house, overlooking the sea. It crossed Serena's mind

29

that she would love to come back during daylight hours, to enjoy what she knew would be a wonderful view of Alligator Head and Monkey Island.

All the furniture was painted white; big, beige cotton cushions in various shapes were heaped casually on the timber-decked floors, next to several low Indonesian carved tables and an assortment of earthenware pots, each containing tropical flowers of every hue. The house was lit by huge candles, flickering under glass hurricane lamps. The air seemed heady with the scent of incense and marijuana.

Royole led them out on to the terrace, where his girl-friend Caron was browsing through a well-thumbed copy of *Vogue*. She rose to greet them; a tall, elegant figure swathed in a long off-the-shoulder dress in cream.

'Caron, I'd like you to meet Lord and Lady Frazer-West.' Royole introduced them formally.

A warm breeze drifted on to the terrace, stirring the flowers and lifting the hem of Caron's flimsy dress.

'Delighted to meet you both! Welcome to Coralita Cottage. Royole tells me you were wonderful hosts the other evening, sheltering him from the storm.'

Her voice, as soft as a caress, had an unusual accent, with only a slight hint of Jamaican intonation, and the hand she held out to them was the colour of dark honey. Her face, especially when she smiled, had an almost feline quality; and her small, even teeth were as white as pure ivory.

Serena thought she was very beautiful.

Caron opened her arms and gestured them to sit on the deep cushions that acted as sofas. Sliding into a cushion herself, she curled long, slender legs under her body, making no attempt to hide the fact that she was completely naked under her dress.

'What would you like to drink?' Royole asked, his voice bubbling with obvious pleasure.

Serena watched him carefully. He seemed agitated or excited, she couldn't decide which, and hoped it was the latter. She sat down next to Caron and asked for dry white wine.

Royole turned to Nicholas, who shrugged and refused the offer.

'Nothing for me, thanks. I've got to try and get us back to Mango Bay in one piece. The road was bad enough sober.'

Nicholas looked stiff and uncomfortable, out of place; like a bit-part actor who'd wandered on to the wrong set. He refused to sit down and, instead, chose to stroll to the far end of the terrace, which was suspended at least twenty foot out from the cliff. He felt slightly dizzy as he looked down to where the Caribbean was breaking below. Suddenly a feeling of vertigo gripped him and, taking a deep breath, he stepped back, almost bumping into Caron who had walked across to join him.

Silver beads gleamed in her long, black braided hair, and a scent of patchouli clung to her. Her amber eyes held steady as she absorbed every detail of Lord Frazer-West's aristocratic face; alien in its insipid colouring, yet extremely attractive in contrast to her own.

His strong chin didn't fit with the rest of his thin, almost gaunt face; and his brown eyes to her revealed a haunted look. Caron had noticed his eyes as soon as she'd seen him.

Nicholas Frazer-West was not what he seemed, she decided. There was a hidden depth; the bland surface, a carefully constructed mask to conceal his dark side. She was quite sure of that.

'Do you smoke?' She offered him the joint she was holding.

He shook his head. 'Like I said, I've got to drive.'

Caron insisted. 'This won't hurt. It'll make you relax; might even help you get through the evening.' She paused.

'Without it, I fear this may be quite an endurance test for you.'

Smiling wryly at her perception, he nodded slowly. Several strands of long silky hair fell across him as she placed the cigarette between his lips, a glazed expression on her exotic face.

Nicholas inhaled deeply. It was strong grass; the smoke burned the back of his throat and his mouth felt dry. She gestured for him to have more.

'I'll be stoned,' he warned.

'That's the general idea.' Caron laughed; a low, throaty sound.

'Go on, finish it,' she urged.

Nicholas nodded and gave her a languid smile, now relishing the attention of this intensely sensual woman. 'I feel much better already.'

Caron returned his smile. 'I thought you might,' she said, before excusing herself to prepare the finishing touches to their dinner; which she then served on a low table, set with an assortment of chopsticks and hand-painted bowls depicting Oriental scenes.

One long-stemmed white anthurium decorated the centre of the table, and the wine was served in pink frosted glasses. They ate Akee soufflé followed by three types of local fish: snapper, grunt and butter fish; each one prepared differently, and each with a distinctive flavour. Warm banana bread accompanied two different rice dishes and baked paw-paw with a subtle hint of ginger. It was all delicious.

Serena struggled with her chopsticks. Royole helped her, and they both laughed as she repeatedly dropped her food.

Nicholas and Caron giggled during the entire meal, much to Serena's annoyance; she was pleased when Caron disappeared into the kitchen to collect the dessert and Royole went to open more wine.

As soon as they were both out of earshot, Serena hissed: 'You're being very silly, Nicholas.'

She had admonished him as a schoolteacher would a child.

He fixed a comic grin on his face and retorted by sticking out his tongue. 'I'm enjoying myself. I didn't want to come here, and now I'm jolly pleased I did, I haven't had this much fun in ages.'

'You're stoned, that's why.' She was angry and a little confused. This was not quite how she'd imagined the evening would develop.

'Are *you* having a good time, my darling Serena?'

He slurred the 'darling', and she glared at him as Royole returned, carrying a freshly opened bottle of Chablis and a bottle of local cane rum. He was closely followed by Caron, bearing a tray of china dishes containing fresh mango and papaya soaked in rum and coconut juice.

'Mmm, this mango is *wonderful*,' enthused Serena, between mouthfuls of the succulent fruit.

'The entire meal was a triumph,' Nicholas announced. His eyes firmly fixed on Caron, he raised his glass in a toast. 'My compliments to the chef.'

In response, a warm flush crept into Caron's face, enhancing the lustrous, honey tones of her flawless skin.

Serena drank silently and looked across at Royole who, to her chagrin, was also looking at his beautiful girlfriend. She stood up and, excusing herself, went to the bathroom. Returning a few moments later, she found Nicholas and Caron curled up together in deep conversation, oblivious to anything but each other.

Serena joined Royole who was leaning over the side of the terrace, staring out to sea. She stood next to him, studying his profile.

The incessant whistling of the tree-frogs mingled with Royole's words, and a scent of jasmine filled the air as he spoke of his surroundings. 'Quite beautiful, don't you think?' he asked, as if he was speaking about his very own piece of heaven on earth. Without waiting for a reply, he went on 'The West Indies is in my blood. I have this great love for the Caribbean and, of course, a dream.'

He turned to face her and she was just about to ask him about his dream when something in his expression made her decide to bite back her curiosity.

His next question came as a total surprise.

'Would you like to go swimming, Lady Serena? The sea's fantastic at this time of night.'

Glancing in her husband's direction, she watched him light another joint; then, throwing back his head, Nicholas burst into private laughter.

'I'd like that very much,' Serena replied.

Before she could change her mind, Royole had ushered her out of the cottage, making no noise. An earlier shower had cleared most of the clouds and a fat, full moon now lit up the sky.

Holding her hand tightly, Royole picked his way down an overgrown pathway towards the sea. He was as sure-footed as a mountain goat and knew the path backwards. Serena was fascinated by the sight of hundreds of fireflies, twinkling amongst the trees like a host of dancing candle-lights. She had never seen so many together at the same time.

At the foot of the hill they had to jump from a grassy ledge on to the beach. Royole went first, and then turned to hold out his hands for Serena, conscious of the ankle that she had injured a little over a week ago.

She landed awkwardly, but fell into the soft sand with no further mishap. Rolling over and laughing, she clambered to her feet and ran into the warm shallows, gasping as the salty sea-spray stung her face, and the wind whipped her long hair across her glowing cheeks.

'I'm not sure this is such a good idea Royole,' she called to him, 'the sea looks very rough.'

He smiled and shouted above the waves, 'Not where I'm going to take you. Come on.'

He led her by the hand to the end of the long white beach, not stopping until they reached a tightly packed rock formation covered in rambling seagrape bushes. Here, they had to turn sideways to slide through a narrow space between the rocks. Scrambling over a few slippery boulders they eventually emerged on to a crescent-shaped cove lying on the edge of a small circular lagoon.

'It's amazing,' gasped Serena, staring at the completely calm surface of the water; so flat that it resembled a sheet of gleaming, black marble.

Undoing the buttons on the thin shoulder straps of her cotton dress, she let it fall in soft folds on to the sand. She then stepped out of it, and slipped her panties swiftly down her legs; hooking them with her big toe, she gave them a little flick. She aimed well and they landed where she had intended, on top of her dress.

She was aware of Royole's probing gaze eating into her naked flesh, yet felt no embarrassment nor, strangely enough, arousal. Instead she felt like a child again; free and uninhibited.

Diving sleekly into the lagoon, her body cut neatly through the glassy surface of the water, sending out ripples in ever-growing circles. The water was very warm and came to just below her neck. She stood very still on the sandy ocean floor, watching Royole take off his cotton shirt and trousers. Unabashed, she stared at his body; he was so tall and perfectly proportioned. His skin, a golden mahogany colour, gleamed in the moonlight.

A moment later he was at her side, towering above her.

She ducked underwater and held her breath, before emerging to his laughter.

With sensitive fingers, he gently lifted her hair up and out of her face, smoothing it flat to her crown. His hand then caressed their way slowly down the length of her

35

back, stopping at the base of her spine; lingering there, as if undecided, before spanning her tiny waist and pulling her body towards his own. He could feel her resistance.

'Don't you want me, Lady Serena?' he asked, and seemed surprised. 'Correct me if I'm wrong, but I thought you did.'

His voice, in soft enquiry, was neither passionate nor pressing.

'Yes I do; but not here and not now,' she replied firmly.

Pushing him gently away, she dived under his arms and with long, smooth strokes swam towards the lagoon's one jagged rock that rose spectrally out of the water.

By the time she reached it, Royole was already there, lying in wait to catch her. As she swam past, he grabbed both her ankles and pulled her beneath the surface.

Kicking and spluttering, she managed to fight free and find her feet. She was still giggling when he burst from the water like a huge whale, letting out a loud roar.

'Careful, you'll wake the neighbours,' she squealed, and splashed him with long sweeps of water before swimming back to the shore and running on to the beach, panting, and shaking with laughter.

'That was wonderful,' Serena told Royole, as she wriggled into her dress, struggling with the awkward straps.

Royole helped her with the buttons. His fingers longed to linger; to trace the pointed tips of her erect nipples, rising and falling under the gauzy fabric. Forcing himself to stifle his feelings of arousal, and holding her chin in the palm of one hand, he moved several wet strands of hair out of her face with the other.

'You must call me soon, Lady Serena. I have to see you before you leave Port Antonio.' He placed a fleeting kiss on her brow, as a father would a child.

She said nothing, not wanting to break the mood, and they both walked back in silence, lost in their own thoughts.

It was after midnight when they slipped quietly into the cottage.

Nicholas was sleeping like a baby, curled up on several cushions, in a cramped foetal position. And Caron had left a scrawled message on the messy dinner table, to inform Royole that she'd call him tomorrow.

'Caron works as a hotel receptionist; she has to get up early,' Royole explained to Serena. 'She rarely stays with me.'

Serena shrugged and, looking at Nicholas, said, 'It looks like I'll be the one driving back.'

Royole nodded and began to clear the dirty dinner plates. 'I think there's little doubt about that.'

Nicholas woke twenty minutes later, whilst Royole was busy making coffee in the kitchen. Serena was sitting on the opposite side of the terrace; her hair, freshly washed, hung several inches past her shoulder blades, shining like newly spun silk.

Nicholas was still trying to focus as she slid down on to the cushions next to him, snuggling close to his warm body.

'So, my darling, awake at last? Royole and I were debating as to whether we should put you to bed here . . .'

Blinking, he noticed how her skin glowed, and a subtle teasing light danced in her eyes. He touched her cheek, tracing a line with his index finger across her mouth and down to her throat. He was about to tell her that she looked beautiful when Royole walked into the room, carrying a tray containing three steaming mugs.

'Coffee is served,' he announced with a flourish, placing the tray on a low table next to them.

Nicholas stood up, a little shaky on his feet. Running his tongue over parched lips, he asked, 'Could I have a glass of water, please. I've got a rather dry throat.'

Serena looked at her dishevelled husband and grinned. 'I really can't think why.'

It was almost one-thirty when they said their goodbyes and left Coralita Cottage. Serena drove slowly and sedately back to Mango Bay, whilst Nicholas snored and muttered unintelligibly for the entire twenty-minute journey.

She was pleased to have the time to herself. It allowed her to think about Royole Fergusson, and the fact that in four days' time her holiday would be over and she would have to leave Jamaica.

Chapter Three

'Do you mind terribly Serena, my darling? Charlie's such an old chum, I'd hate to miss his stag night.'

Nicholas's laugh had a definite lecherous undertone, and Serena groaned inwardly, imagining her husband and his best friend drunk and disorderly, in some sleazy Miami bar. But she answered brightly.

'You know I don't mind.'

They were sitting at a breakfast table positioned on the very edge of the terrace. This spot was shaded by the overhanging branches of a frangipani tree, yet still afforded expansive views of the sparkling waters of the Blue Lagoon.

'Fancy, the old rogue decides to up and marry an American model; just like that, completely out of the blue.' He snapped his fingers. 'Only met her two weeks ago. God would I love to be a fly on the wall when he takes her home to Atherton Hall to meet the in-laws. They had him lined up for The Hon. Arabella Seymour.'

'Oh, not that awful Arabella with the buck teeth and acne?' asked Serena.

Nicholas nodded, laughing. 'That's the one.'

'Well then, I'm pleased he's upped and found this American girl. The best of luck to him,' said Serena, whilst throwing a few crumbs towards a cheeky Doctorbird intent on joining them for breakfast.

Nicholas changed the subject. 'I thought, since we're going home in a couple of days, it doesn't make much sense coming back here.'

Serena, dressed in a simple batik sarong, idly sipped at her orange juice. 'I shall stay and pack up the house, Nicholas,' she said in a firm voice. She could sense his disappointment, and knew she would have to tread carefully.

'But I rather thought you might like to come to Miami with me' . . . He paused, then added hopefully, 'You could do some shopping.'

Her forehead furrowed, dark eyebrows almost meeting above her straight nose. 'I've got lots to do here. I promised to go and see Thomas at Frenchman's Cove. He's got some mail for me to take back to England, and there are some outstanding bills to pay. Et cetera, et cetera,' she sighed.

A playful smile lifted the corners of her mouth. 'Anyway, what would I do whilst you're out on the town all night with Charlie and co?'

He glanced at her over the rim of his coffee cup and noted the obstinate glint that flashed through her eyes. It left him in no doubt that if he forced her to accompany him, she would probably be a bloody nuisance and ruin his entire evening.

'You're quite right. You can pack up the house and sort the staff out, whilst I get thoroughly smashed with Charlie boy.'

'Well, just make sure you behave yourself with all those girls on the loose over there.' Serena chided him, playfully.

'Steady on darling. I'd never do anything like that. There's no other woman in the world that could take your place. You know that.'

'Yes Nicky; but I also know the old West Indian proverb that says "A hot iron will cool in any old dirty water".'

Nicholas shook his head in mock disapproval.

* * *

Serena awoke at six the following morning. Wherever she was in the world, or however tired, she always awoke at the same time.

Nicholas joked about travelling with a beautiful and efficient alarm clock. She had never bothered to explain that the habit had started at the age of seven. After a week at boarding school, she had trained herself to wake early. It had become a ritual, her own space; one solitary hour of peace and privacy before the first bell and the ensuing mayhem.

She was about to slip out of bed for her routine early-morning swim when she felt Nicholas stir, his arms reaching out to encircle her waist. She tried unsuccessfully to wriggle free.

'Stay with me,' he whispered into the side of her neck.

She could smell his hot breath, an unsavoury mixture of spicy West Indian pepper sauce and cigarette smoke. The combination was mildly nauseating.

Pulling her closer, hands gripping her hips, he thrust his erect penis into the cleft of her buttocks.

Serena groaned inwardly, and felt like screaming.

'Nicky please, not now. Later. After I've had a swim.' She tried to make her voice sound promising, at the same time squeezing her thighs together as she felt the tip of his penis pushing, insisting.

He heard the sharp intake of her breath as his fingers struggled to prise her open from behind.

'Open wide for me, Bunty. Please.'

There was no mistaking the urgent demand in his hushed voice; and she knew that if she resisted it would only excite him more.

Facing her back, Nicholas couldn't see the expression of resignation on his young wife's face as she dutifully opened her legs. With an anguished moan he entered her body.

'Tell me Bunty, tell me please,' he implored.

His voice, with its childish undertones, grated on her

nerves. She knew exactly what he wanted to hear. It was always the same. Slightly sickened, Serena complied.

'Nicholas has been a very, very naughty boy, and is going to have to be punished.' She forced her voice to sound stern. 'I'm going to have to . . .'

She didn't finish the sentence. As soon as his thrusting quickened, his whole body shuddered and he shouted her name, before releasing his grip on her hips and rolling away to the other side of the bed.

He lay there on his back; his laboured panting the only sound in the room. After a few moments, he stretched one arm across the bed to stroke Serena's shoulder gently.

'That was wonderful,' he whispered.

'Not for me,' she muttered lamely under her breath, and jumped out of bed.

'What did you say, Serena?' Nicholas lifted himself into a sitting position.

'Same for me,' she lied, from the darkness of the bathroom, where he couldn't see her face or read her eyes.

'I'm really looking forward to this evening, and seeing Charlie again,' he shouted through the open door.

Not listening, she stepped into the sanctuary of the shower where the tepid water drowned his words and cooled her sticky flesh. Washing Nicholas's semen off the inside of her thighs, she prayed, as she had for the last six months, for pregnancy. Serena desperately wanted the security of a Frazer-West heir; and a valid excuse not to make love to her husband, at least for a while.

Nicholas almost missed the one and only flight to Kingston later that day.

Halfway to the airport, he realized he'd forgotten his passport. Serena, who was driving, had to make a mad dash back to the house. By the time they eventually returned, the DC3 was fully loaded and about to take off.

Nicholas jumped out of the jeep, face flushed, looking

for all the world like a very excited teenage boy on his first illicit trip out of school.

'Have fun, and give Charlie my love,' Serena called as he ran across the tarmac to board the tiny, six-seater plane.

He blew her a kiss before he climbed aboard and shouted back, 'Take care. See you in London the day after tomorrow!' His words were drowned in the roar of the propellers.

Serena watched the aircraft taxi down the short runway, and waved until it was out of sight. She then drove slowly and sedately to Coralita cottage, praying that Royole would be at home and alone.

The house looked different in daylight. Much smaller, yet less intimate. Perhaps it was one of those mystical houses that only came to life at night, or in dreams, Serena thought idly as she stepped up to the open front door. A fluffy, black and white cat yawned lazily, and looked her up and down out of eyes almost the same colour as Royole's. She bent down to stroke it, but it moved off with a contemptuous flick of its bushy tail.

'She only likes me,' said Royole, appearing in front of Serena and pointing to the cat.

He was wearing a long, white cotton shirt which barely skimmed his knees. Thick fingers of dusty sunlight snaked across his body, and it was obvious that he was naked beneath the fine, translucent garment. The cat, on hearing his voice, stopped in her tracks and turned, prowling slowly back to where he stood.

She brushed her body against his bare legs. Stooping to pick her up, he patted her head and she nestled into his arms, a contented purring the only sound as he stroked her soft neck.

They both looked at the cat, then at each other simultaneously.

Serena could hear her own heart thundering in her ears.

'Nicholas has gone to Miami,' she blurted out. 'I . . .' she hesitated, 'I came on the off chance that you might be here.'

She noticed for the first time that his eyes, the colour of wet ivy leaves, were also flecked with gold. She became aware of her own vulnerability, but knew she could not turn back now.

'I wanted to see you, before I left Port Antonio.'

'When do you leave?' he asked.

'Tomorrow night.' Her voice was constricted, husky, barely more than a whisper.

Royole dropped the cat. It landed with an indignant shriek, before racing off past Serena.

He didn't speak; just opened his arms wide, and she fell slowly into them. She found the pungent smell of musk overwhelming, an alien smell, yet strangely enough she felt totally at home. She nuzzled close to his neck. It was slightly prickly, and very warm.

'You didn't shave today,' she whispered.

'No,' he shook his head. 'Does it bother you?'

'It depends,' murmured Serena.

He held her at arm's length, then touched the tip of her nose with his forefinger, tracing the line of her full mouth. She noticed his fingers were long and tapered, and the lines on his palm shone white.

'You're very beautiful, Serena.' He nodded emphatically, as if confirming his statement.

'That first time I saw you, the night of the storm, I thought you were the most beautiful woman I'd ever seen.'

Serena blushed profusely and lowered her eyes. She was used to compliments from men, but this man was different. She registered that the hand he held out to her was unusually cool.

As if reading her thoughts he said, 'Cold hands, warm heart.'

'Not always,' Serena responded, thinking of the many

cold hands she had touched with cold hearts to match.

He raised his thick eyebrows, and lowered his voice. 'A cynic, so young.'

'No, just a realist,' she replied, a smile crossing her face.

Suddenly she did look very young, yet there was something in her expression that he couldn't quite fathom; a mixture of maturity and innocence. He found it very stimulating. Dropping his head to one side, he squeezed her hand gently.

'Are you absolutely sure this is what you want?'

The change in her facial expression answered the question for him long before she spoke, 'I want to be with you, Royole. In fact I've thought about little else since I first set eyes on you, but we haven't got a lot of time.'

'Well, in that case let's make the most of what little we have.'

He laughed and she protested with a squeal as he gathered her into his arms, as easily as he'd picked up the cat earlier, and carried her to his bedroom. He laid her on top of his unmade bed. Her eyes roamed around the room. Its floor-to-ceiling shutters were flung open to the late afternoon sun, allowing pale streamers of soft, golden light to dapple the interior. The dull thud of the sea could be heard below the house, and the slow swish of an old paddle fan gently stirred a flimsy mosquito curtain, loosely draped above the low bed.

'This certainly won't deter any little pests,' Serena commented, poking her finger through a hole in the net curtain.

'They never attack me,' Royole smiled, a mischievous twinkle in his eyes. 'My mother always teased me when I was a child; telling me that mosquitoes only liked naughty boys and, if I was very good at night and went to bed when she told me, I would never get bitten.' He shrugged. 'I never did.'

'What? Get bitten or go to bed when you were told?'

He winked; instantly reminding Serena of a film star, she tried to remember his name, a second later it came to her.

'You look like Sidney Poitier,' she said.

He held up his hand. 'Please don't tell me that, I've heard it so many times. In fact when I was living in the States, I was constantly asked for my autograph.'

'I bet you loved it,' she teased.

He grinned, and shrugged his broad shoulders. 'I must admit I was flattered.'

They both smiled, and their eyes locked for a brief yet potent moment. Serena clasped her hands together to stop them shaking, while a hundred questions raced through her mind. What compulsion had brought her to this house, and into the arms of this man, a virtual stranger?

'Are you OK?' Royole's question interrupted her reverie.

'I'm fine,' she said, 'Why do you ask?'

'Because you've suddenly gone very pale, and you look distracted.'

She flinched as he placed his hands on her shoulders.

'What is it, Serena?' He searched her ashen face.

Serena, usually bolstered with confidence, found herself struggling to articulate. She sat up swinging her legs over the edge of the bed, and she took a deep breath, 'To be totally honest, I'm scared. I feel so out of control.'

She searched for the right words as he sat down next to her.

'I suppose it's because you're so different, Royole. You're from another world, so far from mine.' With a shaking hand she stroked his cheek, tracing the line of his jaw. 'Yet, strangely enough, I feel as if I've known you all my life.'

'You're right Serena, we are different, and not only in

46

skin colour. But surely mutual attraction transcends all that stuff. Forget about who we are and where we come from, just enjoy being together. Don't worry about the consequences.'

He lifted a strand of her hair and looped it around her ear.

'You make it sound so simple,' she sighed.

'But that's just what it is. What's more natural than a man and a woman who want to make love to each other.'

He then knelt in front of her, and she watched him intently, her eyes never leaving his face, as he untied the thin straps of her canvas sandals. They slipped easily off her feet. He raised her left foot and tenderly licked each of her toes in turn, before gently nibbling her heel.

'That tickles,' she squealed.

Stopping at once, he stood up and gently placed both of her feet back on the bed, then lifted the hem of her cotton shift dress. It came off in one fluid movement. She was naked underneath.

His eyes slowly travelled the full length and breadth of her body.

He adored the way her hair, a shower of gold, tumbled off her shoulders and fanned across her small, firm breasts tipped with pale pink nipples. He could feel his own response as he focused on her golden triangle of pubic hair.

'I'm almost afraid to touch,' he murmured, staring at her in undisguised awe.

Observing his face, Serena was struck by his obvious sensitivity; so unlike the hunger she had seen on the faces of other men.

He stroked the inside of her thigh, delighting in the warm, soft feel of her skin; finally allowing his fingertips to continue their highly sensuous journey across her flat stomach, between her breasts and on to the nape of her

47

neck. He pulled her head forward, then traced her mouth with his warm tongue.

She bit his lower lip. 'I want to eat you.'

'You can, with pleasure,' he said, and stood up.

Loosening the buttons at the front of his shirt, he pushed it over his shoulders and let it float down his back and on to the floor.

'Stay as you are please, Royole, don't move.' Her tone was urgent.

He did as she asked.

Silently she stared at him for several minutes, before whispering, 'You've got the most beautiful body I've ever seen.'

Right then she knew, with absolute certainty, that she would never forget that moment for the rest of her life. Having acknowledged this, she stroked his hairless chest and taut stomach; her fingers at last teasing the coarse hair curling across his groin.

Royole basked silently in his pleasure, until a loud sigh escaped his lips as she took his erect penis in both her hands. She marvelled at the size. It was very hot, and the skin was as smooth as velvet. He continued to stand very still in front of her, for what seemed an age.

'You can move now. Come on Royole, what are you waiting for . . .'

He touched her hair and a slow smile entered her face, it was both inviting and teasing. He joined her on the bed, biting the side of her ear.

'Tell me what you like, Serena.'

She felt a blush infusing her face. Nicholas had never asked her, nor had the few boyfriends she'd known before him. How could she tell Royole, a virtual stranger, her sexual preferences?

'Tell me Serena,' he urged, 'I can't give you pleasure unless I know.'

Bending her head, she whispered into his ear.

'I would love to,' he said in a hoarse voice.

Her blush deepened as he lowered his head and gently opened her legs.

They made love until the sun, a perfect dark orange orb, had descended from the blue mountains into a darkening horizon and the lengthening shadows of dusk slowly turned to evening.

The hour before nightfall found them sitting on the terrace, naked and wrapped in each other's arms; they sipped Royole's specially made planters' punch, and watched the tangerine glow of sunset finally fade.

Eventually, Serena broke the silence. 'I really wish I could paint. I would so love to capture this particular sunset; or, better still, your beautiful face.'

She sighed, pecked the end of his nose, and continued. 'I can't remember ever feeling quite this content.'

A cool breeze had begun to drift across the terrace.

'Are you cold?' he asked, pulling her closer.

'No, I feel better than I've felt in my entire life.' Lifting his free hand, she kissed the inside of his palm; it tasted of lime. 'I don't ever want to go back to London, or for that matter back to England. I want to stay here with you.'

When he didn't reply, she continued unperturbed, in a calm, clear voice. 'I mean it. I know now that I love you. Given the chance, I'd be with you for as long as you wanted me.'

The sea was calm. There was no sound save the ever-present chirping of the tree frogs and crickets, mingled with a faint rustling from the thick leaves of the Mussaenda trees overhanging the terrace.

After a few moments Royole spoke. 'I would love you to stay here with me, Serena, but I think we both realize it's not possible. Like you said earlier, we're different, from different worlds; and just as I would never fit into yours, nor would you fit into mine.'

'I'm not asking you to fit into mine, Royole. But why can't I fit into yours? It's happened before; we're not unique.'

She looked like a trusting child, and he felt his chest tighten.

'I've got plans and dreams. The Caribbean is changing; I want to be part of that change. There's so much to achieve, such a lot I want to do. This is the dawn of a new era in tourism, and there are fortunes to be made. I intend to make mine, but at the moment I've got very little money, and nothing to offer you.' He paused. Then, eyes darkening, he added. 'Not even time.'

Serena blinked back tears, she looked up as a wispy cloud flitted across the full moon. Half of her was pleased that at least he hadn't mentioned Caron, but as the soft white lunar light touched her face, in a choked voice she said, 'Money isn't everything, Royole.'

He sighed deeply. 'I'm aware of that but it's easy for you to say that when you've never been without it. You're very young, Serena, and if you don't mind me saying, just a little naïve.'

She stemmed any further conversation by covering his mouth with short, wet kisses, murmuring between them. 'Shut up Royole, and make love to me again. Time is running out.'

The following morning Serena awoke to the soft pattering of rain on the wooden roof. She made no sound as she slid out of bed. Not finding her dress close to hand, she quickly slipped on Royole's cotton shirt, tiptoed out of the room, and left the house barefoot.

Her jeep was parked under a huge frangipani tree. Its abundant leaves, heavy with rain, were drooping over the bonnet. Starting the engine as quietly as she could, she moved off slowly down the drive, allowing herself one last glance at Coralita cottage. Now that it was shrouded in ominous, grey clouds, she couldn't help thinking how desolate and sad it seemed.

Not looking where she was going, Serena drove off the track. She cursed the jeep as its wheels spun dangerously in the sodden earth, then ground to a halt. 'Shit! That's all I need.'

She could only ram her foot hard on the accelerator, imploring the vehicle to move. 'Come on, get going. I beg you.'

Her prayers were answered a moment later; the jeep budged an inch and then suddenly shot forward, out of the mud.

Within five minutes she was on the A4 road leading to Blue Lagoon. And by the time she pulled into the drive of Mango Bay the rain had stopped, but the sky was still dark and foreboding. The house looked different this morning; or was it simply that she felt different? Serena wasn't sure.

Wandering around the elegant rooms, she realized for the first time how much there was of Nicholas and his family in Mango Bay, and how little of herself. She wondered why it had never occurred to her before today. Frazer-West family paintings adorned the walls; and a vast array of exquisite collectibles, all chosen by Nicholas's mother, covered several antique tables. Even the fabrics had come from his cousin's country estate.

She had to shower and pack but first she hid Royole's shirt in a drawer at the bottom of her dressing table; consoling herself as she did so, that it would be an excuse to meet him again when she returned to Jamaica in the winter.

She stepped out on to the small terrace leading from her bedroom. A chink of bright blue punctured the otherwise gloomy sky as the sun tried hard to poke through. Memories of the last few hours flooded her mind; memories to be stored, and savoured through the long, boring nights ahead with Nicholas.

Serena had never experienced such lovemaking; so erotic and yet so tender. She even blushed as she thought of her own uninhibited passion. Mr Royole Fergusson had certainly left an indelible mark. She desperately wanted to see him again and, whilst she showered, her mind was occupied with schemes of how she could come back to Port Antonio without Nicholas.

The remainder of the morning was spent on last-minute chores, her mind so preoccupied with thoughts of Royole that she almost forgot to collect Thomas Laynes' mail from Frenchman's Cove, and to cancel the weekly delivery of fresh eggs and vegetables.

Her flight was scheduled to leave Port Antonio for Kingston at four-thirty, and at twenty-five minutes past three she was ready, dressed in black cotton slacks and a short-sleeved shirt, a woollen sweater draped over her arm. The butler was waiting for her at the foot of the stairs.

'Go long, Lady Frazer-West. Don't you worry none bout de house. I can look after every ting.' Joseph accompanied this assurance by puffing out his chest, grinning from ear to ear; looking as if he couldn't wait to be left in charge.

She handed him the leather grip she'd packed – thinking how much she'd love to be a fly on the wall, to see exactly what Joseph would get up to after she'd left.

'I'm sure you can, Joseph. And you know to contact Thomas at Frenchman's Cove if anything goes wrong.'

'What go wrong in Port Antonio, mistress? Nothin'.' Then he added for good measure, 'Nothin' at all.'

They arrived at Ken Jones Airport just as a small island-hopper cut through thick cloud to make a bumpy landing, before taxiing to a halt only a few feet from the terminal.

Jumping out of the jeep, Serena said, 'I'll be fine now Joseph, you can go.' She smiled and, in a firm voice, went on, 'No drinking; and if I hear of you driving the jeep, there'll be trouble. Do you understand?'

He dropped his head. 'Ah don drink de rum no more, mistress.' This time his voice had lost its jaunty confidence.

She knew he was lying, but didn't have the heart to pursue the issue. 'Goodbye then. Thank you for everything. Take good care of yourself and take care of the house.'

The butler waved enthusiastically, before driving out of the airport. Serena watched the jeep until it disappeared from view. She then turned and walked to the far corner of the small terminal, where immigration was located.

Her ears pricked as she heard her name and she recognized his voice instantly, it was unmistakable.

Her stomach turned a sickly somersault as she turned to face Royole. He was dressed in white shorts and a faded powder-blue shirt; and he carried a bundle in his left hand.

'This is your dress and shoes.' He handed her a small package, tied with string.

Their hands met for a split second, yet he made no attempt to bridge the few feet that separated them. Nor did she.

'I couldn't let you go without saying goodbye, Serena.'

'Oh Royole, I'll be coming back to Port Antonio in a few months' time; it doesn't have to be goodbye for ever.' Glancing over her shoulder, towards the plane, she saw a solitary passenger about to board.

'I don't know where I'll be in few months' time though.' He then fished in the back pocket of his shorts and pulled an envelope out, which he thrust into her hand. 'This is my sister's address in America, she forwards all my mail, so if you ever feel like writing, or need to contact me for anything at all . . .'

The co-pilot approached them. 'Lady Frazer-West; if you'd like to board the plane now, please. We're ready for takeoff.'

'Yes,' she nodded, 'I'll be there in a moment.' A nerve twitched in the corner of her eye, and she suddenly found herself chewing her bottom lip; nervous reactions that she thought she'd got rid of years ago.

Royole was looking her straight in the eye. 'Safe journey and take care, Lady Serena. Try to think of me sometimes.'

He smiled. A smile bright enough to light up a whole room she thought, and longed to touch him.

She forced her voice to sound light and frivolous. 'Yes, I will think about you, Mr Fergusson.' She winked, 'If I can find the time.'

He shrugged and took a step towards her, beginning to open his arms. 'By the way, I do want you to know that yesterday was one of the best days of my life . . . so far.'

Serena stepped back. She doubted she could stay in control if he kissed her. 'It was pretty good for me, too,' she managed to say, biting hard on her lip to stop it quivering.

He was about to say something else, when she held up her hand. 'Don't ask me why, Royole Fergusson, but I'm sure we will meet again.' Then, without any backward glance, Serena ran towards the plane.

Chapter Four

ENGLAND, MARCH 1967

Lady Serena Frazer-West checked the clock in her new Range Rover. It was almost ten p.m. She had been held up for the last hour. A quick calculation made her realize that at this rate she'd be lucky to reach Redby Hall, the Frazer-West Wiltshire estate, by midnight. She began to wish she'd rung to let the staff know of her sudden decision to leave London for a spot of country peace; still, at least it meant no one would be expecting her and fretting about her non-arrival.

A serious collision, between a minibus and an oil tanker, had resulted in the bigger vehicle overturning and spilling most of its contents on to the icy road. The consequent mayhem was further exacerbated by freezing fog, so that traffic was now at a standstill, apart from police vehicles and several ambulances.

Suddenly the traffic began to move, albeit slowly; a mass of steel creeping forward, with the artificial eyes of car headlights burrowing through the swirling fog. As the sign for Junction Thirteen loomed into view, Serena indicated left and followed several other cars on to the slip road. Pulling into the nearest lay-by, she consulted a map and decided that it would be simpler to take the road across country towards Swindon, then rejoin the motorway for the remainder of her journey to Castle Coombe.

This plan would have been fine if she had not taken a wrong turn at the village of Lenchwick Cross, becoming hopelessly lost on the Lambourn Downs in a maze of twisting lanes and tiny villages that all looked exactly the same. To make things worse, it was very dark – with only the occasional yellow light from a semi-curtained cottage window to remind her she was not totally alone in the world.

Her spirits lifted as she entered the small village of Letcombe Bassett and spotted a dim light behind the grimy windows of the Plough Inn. Parking at the rear of the pub, she was relieved to hear muted voices and laughter as she walked towards the bar.

The door was locked.

She knocked several times; then, stepping to one side, she peered through the dusty window to see three faces staring back at her. One man was leaning across the bar top and appeared to be the publican.

'I'm lost,' Serena mouthed plaintively.

No one spoke or moved, they just continued to stare.

She shivered, deciding that it might be better to get back into the car and drive to the next village. She was about to turn away when the landlord moved from behind the bar and walked towards the door. He opened it a couple of inches, so that she could just about see a long nose and one dark eye.

'There was a bad crash on the M4. I'm trying to get to Castle Coombe.' Her words tumbled out.

He opened the door a few more inches. 'Yer a long ways off course, miss,' he said, his beady eyes probing every detail of her body before eventually resting on her huge stomach, heavy with advanced pregnancy.

Serena felt uncomfortable; she shuddered, pulling her coat closer to her body. 'If you could just point me in the right direction I would be very . . .'

Her voice trailed off as she became acutely aware of a wetness between her legs; a slight trickle at first, but followed seconds later by a gush of warm secretion, streaming downwards and forming a small puddle on the stone step.

'Oh my God, no! My waters have broken.'

The man stared at her as she cradled her distended belly with both hands. Then the pain came.

The first contraction felt much stronger than she'd ever imagined. She clutched the side of the wall, her hand slipping on the frosty stone, panting until the pain gradually subsided.

'You've got to help me, I'm in labour. Where's the nearest hospital?'

Her desperate appeal finally stirred the landlord into action. 'Come in miss.'

He moved to one side and she shuffled gingerly into the bar. Through a thin film of smoke, she could now see the faces of the two other men. One of them, Tom Bayley, was beside her in a single, long stride.

'Sit yerself down here, miss.' He was a big man and held her as she slid down into the nearest chair. He smelt of tobacco and manure, not a particularly comforting mixture.

'Here, tell her to drink this Tom, it'll help.' The landlord had poured a large brandy.

She swallowed it gratefully, just before a further rush of warm discharge trickled down the inside of her thigh, followed by another contraction slicing across her lower back; this one even more intense than the last. Holding on to Tom Bayley's hand, she squeezed so tightly he winced.

He watched the colour slowly drain from her face, leaving it ashen; and he still thought that she was the prettiest girl ever seen in the Plough, or roundabout for that matter.

'You're going to be fine. I'll take you to Mrs Neil, she'll see to you.'

'Who's she?' Serena panicked. 'I don't want to go to any Mrs Neil, I must get to a hospital. You don't understand!'

Hearing the hysteria creep into her own voice, she told herself to keep calm as no good would come from getting in a state. 'My babies are four weeks premature. I need special medical care.'

'The nearest hospital is more than twenty-five miles from here. With this fog we might not make it at all.'

The publican had spoken with authority and both other men nodded in agreement. They continued nodding as he went on.

'Old Radley's wife had her baby on the way to the hospital only last week; happened in a lay-by. Almost lost the little mite.' He pointed to the big man. 'I think Tom here's right. We'd best get you to Mrs Neil. You'll be fine with her, she's by far the best midwife in the county. All the mothers swear by her. They won't go near a hospital if they can have Mrs Neil.'

If Serena had been able to find the strength she would have screamed. As it was she had to conserve her energy for the next contraction that was about to begin. She realized with growing fear that the contractions were coming every few minutes.

'OK, take me to this Mrs Neil. Anything's better than a damned lay-by.'

'Good girl,' said big Tom, promptly lifting her effortlessly into his arms and carrying her out of the pub.

'I'll call Mrs Neil and tell her you're on yer way,' the publican shouted after them.

Tom settled Serena gently into the passenger seat of her own car, took the ignition keys from her, and then adjusted the driver's seat to accommodate his long legs.

'It's not far,' he reassured her, as the car purred into life. 'No more than about half a mile down the road. Can you hang on?'

'I don't have much choice,' she mumbled, relieved when the Range Rover pulled smoothly away.

The road to Mrs Neil's was a treacherous, unmade lane,

and Tom had to swerve suddenly to avoid a pothole. Careering off the road he bumped along for few moments, the overhanging branches of a huge sycamore tree slashing the windscreen and obscuring his view.

'Sorry 'bout that,' he apologized in his thick Gloucestershire brogue.

Serena thought the pothole would have been preferable, but said nothing. Holding her stomach, she ground her teeth together, half in discomfort and half in anger. She was thinking about Nicholas. He was out of the country on a business trip. She had begged him not to go but he'd insisted, reassuring her that it was only for a couple of days. But the thought of how guilty and remorseful he was going to feel at least made her feel marginally better.

Finally they reached the end of the lane and Tom stopped the car. 'We're here!' he announced, jumping out and running round to the passenger side with the agility of a sixteen-year-old.

He helped her down to the ground, bearing all her weight, and then opened a three-bar gate at the bottom of the pathway to Saddlers Cottage. 'Lean on me,' he urged, as they struggled towards the front door, their feet crunching on the gravel path.

'Mrs Neil!' hollered Tom, rapping sharply. 'Mrs Neil!'

There was no reply; the only sound being Serena's laboured breathing.

He tried again. 'Mrs Neil, are you there?'

A neighbouring dog barked, then stopped abruptly. A few moments later they could hear a voice, muffled and thick with sleep, speaking through the letter box.

'Who is it?'

'It's Tom Bayley, Mrs Neil.'

'What on earth do you want at this time of night?' she demanded. 'It's gone twelve, man!'

'Did Jack from the Plough not call you?'

'No, he did not!' she snapped, then added grudgingly, 'Well, he may have tried, but my phone's been playing up the last few days. I can dial out; it's in-coming calls that are the bother. Still waiting for the blasted engineer to come; the rate they—'

Tom interrupted. 'I've got a woman in labour with me, Mrs Neil. I don't think she's got long to go.'

With that the door was flung open and the midwife appeared in her nightclothes.

'This lady,' Tom glanced in Serena's direction, 'came into the pub earlier, asking for directions. She was lost.' His eyes opened wide. 'She started her labour right there and then in the bloody Plough.'

A stupid grin covered his face, making Serena think he looked slightly simple. Just my luck, she told herself, to get stuck with an ageing midwife and the village idiot. Then she felt the now familiar pain beginning its steady rise. Gasping for breath, she grabbed Tom's arm, her hand as white as bone upon his black donkey jacket. The contraction peaked and small beads of perspiration broke out on her brow. Struggling to stay on her feet, the panic in her voice was obvious.

'I think you'll have to be quick, the contractions are coming fast.'

Instantly alert, Mrs Neil took charge. 'Come on, let's get the poor woman in out of the cold Tom Bayley, instead of you standing there like a big oaf,' she ordered briskly.

Tom nodded, ushering Serena inside.

'Take her into the back bedroom, you know where it is.'

'I should do.' He grinned again, this time in Serena's direction, and by now she was convinced that he was simple.

'Mrs Neil here delivered my boy last year. Nearly lost him an' all,' he added.

'Thanks Tom,' Serena commented sarcastically, 'that's very encouraging.'

He dropped his head on one side to concentrate before helping her upstairs, and into a sparsely furnished room that smelt strongly of lavender and damp. It contained a washbasin, a high delivery bed and battered medical trolley.

Serena couldn't suppress a shudder at the sight of the antiquated trolley holding an assortment of ominous-looking instruments. Tom sat her down in the one and only chair. Seemingly reluctant to leave, he held on to her hand.

'You're shaking,' he said, 'Can I get you something warm to drink?'

Serena shook her head. 'I'm terrified. I don't want to give birth here.'

Catriona Neil entered the room at that point. Over-hearing what had been said, she addressed her patient in a businesslike tone, 'First time is it? Well, I'm afraid you may not have any choice, my dear. How often are you having the contractions?'

'Every few minutes.'

'When you have the next one, tell me,' instructed Mrs Neil as she walked to the small sink in the corner, where she washed her hands vigorously.

She had changed from her nightdress and dressing gown into a more suitable outfit: tailored blouse; tweed skirt and court shoes, all in exactly the same shade of donkey brown.

'Tom, now that you're here, you might as well make yourself useful. Go and boil some water, and get fresh linen from the cupboard under the stairs.'

Tom looked helpless. 'I've got to be off Mrs Neil, my missus will be worried sick, and it's a long walk from here.'

'It's Friday night Tom Bayley; your Lucy will be fast asleep, confident that you're holed up in the Plough as usual. So go on, do as you're told.' She pushed him towards the door.

Serena watched with a kind of morbid fascination as Mrs Neil lifted a small scalpel off the trolley and placed it in a kidney bowl. Shifting in her seat, she suddenly gasped.

'The pain! It's coming again.'

The thickly set midwife, who looked cumbersome but was actually extremely agile, reached her side in an instant and placed her hands either side of Serena's stomach. There they remained until the contraction had subsided. At that point Mrs Neil stood bolt upright, with a knowing look in her eyes.

'Is this your first?' Serena nodded as Mrs Neil went on. 'I see you're carrying twins.' After a slight pause she continued. 'Don't worry lass, you're in good hands. I've been delivering babies long before you were even a twinkle in your daddy's eye.'

There was something about Mrs Neil that instilled confidence. For the first time since her labour had started, Serena felt a little less afraid. A faint smile crossed her face.

'I'm just a bit scared, that's all.'

'Well, I'm sure you didn't plan to have your babies in the middle of the country, with a couple of strangers in tow. But you're young and healthy; I foresee no problems whatsoever. Now, let's get you out of those clothes and into bed.'

When Serena didn't move immediately, the midwife had to click her tongue.

'Where do I undress?' Serena scanned the room.

'Well, here for heaven's sake! No point in being shy, you're about to give birth.' Rummaging in a cupboard to her left, Mrs Neil pulled out a long, cotton nightdress. 'Here, put this on, and get into bed. We've got work to do.' She chuckled, and went downstairs to chivy Tom.

Serena could've sworn the midwife was enjoying

herself. Well, I'm glad one of is, she thought.

She pulled her woollen maternity dress over her head. Dropping it on to the floor, she was standing in her bra and panties, shivering, when Mrs Neil came back.

'Not ready yet, miss? And by the way, hadn't you better tell me your name?'

For some reason Serena did not want the midwife to know who she really was. She muttered the first name to come into her head, that of her housekeeper in London.

'Mrs Boyd. June Boyd.'

When she looked up into Mrs Neil's eyes they held the same knowing look she had noticed earlier. For a split second their mind's met; Serena could see that the midwife knew she was lying.

'Come on then, June, let me help you out of your underwear and into the nightie.'

Serena smiled meekly as if she were a child, when she heard Tom's footsteps approaching the door.

'Don't you be coming in here yet, big Tom,' Mrs Neil shouted. 'Just wait a minute.'

She lifted the nightdress above Serena's head and pulled it roughly over her naked body, leading her towards the bed. 'Now young lady, you've got a tough job to do, so you'd better pull yourself together. You and I have got to bring these babies into the world.'

Mrs Neil's obvious authority soothed Serena a little. As she lay on the hard bed with her eyes closed, she could have been listening to her first housemistress at boarding school, the much loved Mrs McKenzie whose bark had always been far worse than her bite. For some reason, not knowing that she couldn't have been more mistaken, Serena suspected that Catriona Neil was the same type.

Stretched out on the bed, she stared up at the ceiling and submitted herself to an internal examination by Mrs Neil. A fringed, floral lamp-shade covered the over-head bulb. She tried to concentrate on counting its faded rosebuds, while the midwife probed inside her, pressing hard into her groin. She'd got to fourteen when the intruding fingers slipped out.

Mrs Neil pulled off her transparent gloves and announced: 'They are well on their way; it won't be long.' Serena sighed and muttered a relieved 'Thank God!' under her breath.

A knock interrupted them, followed by Tom's voice.

'Shall I come in now?'

Even Serena managed a weak smile as Mrs Neil opened the door, chuckling, 'Sorry Tom, we almost forgot about you in all the excitement.'

Squeezing her eyes tightly shut, Serena prayed for her babies and herself; in that order. She had read somewhere that it helps if you focus the mind on anything but the pain. She tried thinking about the new curtains in the nursery at Redby. She imagined herself floating in the warm Caribbean sea; reliving the day in Port Antonio when Nicholas had capsized their hired catamaran, and she had lost her bikini top. But nothing worked. For the next five hours, the excruciating pain banished every other thought and eventually she gave herself up to all of its agony. Wild, dislocated noises tumbled into her head – her own moans – and she thought she might die.

'Push harder, June, *push*!'

Serena wished she had the energy to yell back that she was already pushing as hard as she could. She really felt like telling the other woman to fuck off; but when she did manage to speak her voice found the right words.

'Please help me.'

'Come on love. I can see the head, you're almost there. One last push.'

Big Tom was holding her hand, constantly whispering encouragement, for what it was worth. His voice, with its strange accent, didn't help; she actually longed for him to shut up. The pain inhabited every fibre of her being, it was all she could register. Finally, taking a deep breath, she summoned a new surge of energy and pushed as hard as she could. Then she gathered every last ounce of strength and pushed again.

One minute later the first of her twins was born.

Ten minutes later the second baby followed.

'You have twin girls,' shouted Mrs Neil in triumph.

Serena, panting, soaked, gave a final push to expel the afterbirth which slipped out easily.

'Thank God,' she whispered. Aware only of a profound rush of relief, she made no attempt to stem the tears that slipped down her cheeks, trickling across her parched lips.

Mrs Neil was visibly bubbling with excitement, smiling joyfully at Tom – who looked equally delighted, his face beaming with such pride that he could have been the father himself.

'Are they all right?' Serena asked the question that all mothers ask.

Mrs Neil nodded emphatically. 'They're very small, but absolutely fine,' she confirmed, smacking each baby's bottom in turn.

With the first cries of her offspring filling her ears, Serena sat up. Turning to Tom, she pointed in the direction of the sink.

'Could you pass me some water, please.'

'Of course miss, you must be mighty dry after all that effort.'

She swallowed the ice-cold water thirstily, thinking it tasted better than anything in her entire life. Handing back the empty glass, she turned to face Mrs Neil.

'Can I see my babies?'

It was then that she first noticed a strange look on the midwife's face. She didn't know why, but it frightened her. And Mrs Neil had whispered something to Tom that she couldn't hear. He left the room immediately, and this frightened her more.

'What's wrong?' Serena's panic was echoed in her voice. 'Are my babies OK?' she demanded.

Leaning as far forward as possible, she desperately searched the older woman's face, trying to discover why she was shaking her head in disbelief, her eyes firmly fixed on one particular baby.

'Your babies are f . . . fi . . . fine,' Mrs Neil stammered, 'It . . . it's . . . it's just—' She could not contain the shock registering in her voice.

'It's just *what*?' Serena's own voice rose. 'Is there something wrong?'

The midwife didn't look up. She was still staring at the baby closest to her. 'I don't know how to tell you this.'

When she did lift her face, it was filled with a look of astonishment that Serena wrongly interpreted as fear. Voice faltering a little, Mrs Neil eventually explained.

'You have given birth to one white baby, and one black.'

There was no mistaking her total incredulity. Serena's mouth dropped open; she was stunned. She continued to stare at the midwife whose features were frozen in an expression of horror.

'Have you gone mad!' she shrieked, 'What on earth are you talking about?'

Mrs Neil shook her head and wiped her face with the back of her hand. 'I only wish that I had. I really don't understand what's happened.'

The woman sounded almost apologetic, as if in some way she was responsible. She lifted one of the babies and, cradling her carefully, carried her to Serena. 'Here, look for yourself and you will see that this baby is most definitely not one of us.'

'I don't *want* to look.' Serena was shaking her head, holding her hands tightly clenched in her lap.

'You must. She is your child,' insisted the midwife, holding the tiny bundle right in front of Serena's face.

The baby was still attached to the umbilical cord, her body crouched in the foetal position, with string legs curled up into her chest. Serena stared at the top of the baby's head. It was slippery wet with blood. Suddenly, the newborn infant began to wail, arms and legs thrashing out in every direction. Tiny hands were thrown up in protest and, for the first time, Serena had a clear view of her daughter's face. Instantly, visions of Royole Fergusson flooded her mind.

It was then that she began to scream.

Chapter Five

'I'm Mr Wilcox. I believe you want to talk to me urgently.'

'Yes I do.'

Mrs Neil shifted uncomfortably in her seat. She was wearing the same brown clothes that she'd worn the previous night to deliver Serena's babies. Dressing hastily, she had merely thrown a Barbour jacket over the top and pulled on the felt hat bought for her sister's wedding. She hadn't slept, so her eyes were puffy.

The consultant thought she looked a little odd. He glanced at his watch with obvious impatience. 'I'm due in theatre very soon, please Mrs . . .' The doctor read a note on his desk, '. . . Neil.'

The booming voice was not lost on Mrs Neil who twisted her mouth into a polite smile before she continued, 'What I have to say won't take long, sir. I'd just like to know whether there's ever been a case of a white woman producing twins, where one child is black and one white?'

If Mr Wilcox was surprised he didn't show it. 'Do you know of such a case?' he asked. 'Because if you do, I'd be very interested.'

'Yes, I do; but it's somebody who lives abroad.'

The excuse came out far too quickly, and the consultant knew immediately that it was a lie. But the stubborn set of his visitor's jaw, and the determined ring to her voice, dispelled any hope he might have of persuading her to identify the mother involved. He doodled on a note-pad for a few seconds, pondering his reply.

'Conceiving and giving birth to mixed-race twins – non-identical I presume – is an extremely rare phenomenon. To my knowledge it's been recorded only a few times in Europe. It's very unusual for a mixed-race couple to have twins where one baby is pure Caucasian and the other black. A million-to-one chance in fact.'

Mr Wilcox seemed to warm to his subject and added, 'Actually about five years ago, a Jamaican colleague of mine delivered black and white twin boys to a white woman who had a West Indian husband *and* a relationship with a white man.

'It means, of course, that two entirely separate eggs are fertilized by two men. It can only occur if the woman has intercourse with the men concerned within a period of approximately eighteen hours.

'For this to be possible she would need to be in natural ovulation during intercourse with the first man, and that could lead to fertilization of the first egg. Then, what we term as a "spontaneous ovulation" during orgasm with the other man could produce a second egg, and if that's also fertilized, non-identical twins, or more to the point siblings, could be conceived within hours of each other.'

'Thank you, doctor. As a midwife, I just wanted to understand how such a phenomenon was possible.'

Her chair scraped across the polished oak floor as Mrs Neil stood up. 'And thank you for seeing me at such short notice.'

'You gave me very little choice,' Mr Wilcox replied. Then he offered, 'Are you sure the lady concerned can't be persuaded to come and see me? I'd be more than happy to talk to her. I might even be able to help.'

Mrs Neil had reached the door, and turned to face him. 'I don't think she's ready to see or speak to anyone just at the moment. Goodbye Doctor.'

*　　*　　*

When Serena awoke she thought she'd wet the bed.

Slowly she slipped a hand between her legs, touching her inner thigh, before lifting her fingers to her face. They were sticky and covered in blood. The sedative that Mrs Neil had given her earlier had started to wear off; the realization of where she was, and what had happened, was creeping slowly into her consciousness. She shut her eyes, and replayed the images of the last few hours in her head: Mrs Neil screaming for her to push; her baby daughters covered in blood; one crumpled, dark face; one equally crumpled white face.

She was only vaguely aware of the footsteps on the stairs. It was the sound of knocking that finally grasped her attention. Pulling her blanket up to her ears, she fiddled with it nervously, staring at the door as it slowly opened. A tentative smile flickered across her face when Mrs Neil's red curls appeared.

'I see you're awake.'

The midwife sat on the edge of the bed. She pulled the blanket away, a little roughly Serena thought.

Serena looked at her and said, 'I seem to be bleeding rather a lot.'

'I know, I've got you some sanitary towels, and here's some stuff for the little mites.' She gestured to the occupied cot by Serena's side. 'Look at them sleeping soundly. That's because they're well wrapped up all nice and warm.'

'Thank you so much, Mrs Neil. I don't know how I can ever repay you.'

'Plenty of time to talk about that later, dear. Got to get you cleaned up first. Now . . . let's look lively because it's four-thirty and I've got to make us both some tea.'

Something about her manner placed Serena on her guard, but she allowed herself to be helped out of bed and sat down in the nearby chair while Mrs Neil stripped the sheets.

'I think you should bathe and put your clothes back on now,' suggested Mrs Neil, handing her a clean towel and her own things. 'You can use the shower-room, next door.' She indicated the direction with her eyes. 'Off you go.'

Serena wrapped the towel around her aching body and, picking her way past several boxes on the landing, headed for the shower. She was very weak and her legs shook as she washed herself from top to toe. This left her feeling more refreshed, but not much stronger. After managing to dress, she emerged and almost bumped into Mrs Neil at the top of the stairs. The midwife was cradling the sleeping babies, one in each arm.

'Come on down to the living room, if you can manage, and I'll give us both that tea.'

Serena accepted gratefully, following Mrs Neil downstairs, holding on to the wall for support.

'Sit yourself in that chair, Mrs Boyd, and I'll put the babes in this one next to you. Just rest whilst I get the tea. I won't be a tick, the kettle's already boiled.'

Serena sat down carefully in the overstuffed chair, which was upholstered in dark green brocade, and very comfortable. It seemed as though Mrs Neil had moulded it to the shape of her own ample bottom. She looked at the twin bundles next to her, but then she thought of Royole, thought of Nicholas, and felt overwhelmed, almost panicky. She had to look away again and concentrated on her immediate surroundings instead.

'*Home is where the heart is.*'

Serena smiled sardonically at the mass-produced sampler. There was also a reproduction coffee table which was chipped and badly stained, and a pine cabinet containing an assortment of books. Behind a brass fireguard, the fading embers of a dying fire flickered occasionally. She glanced at a photograph on the mantelpiece. It showed what looked like a young Mrs Neil. It all made her aware

71

that she was sitting in someone else's house; and what she really wanted was to call home and get a message to Nicholas. Except that she'd have to work out what on earth to say first . . .

'There you are, a nice cup of tea! The remedy for all ills,' chimed Mrs Neil as she walked in, and then poured from a teapot covered in a red knitted cosy.

Handing Serena a steaming brew, she sat down in the chair opposite. 'Now, I think we should have a little chat.'

Serena peered over the rim of the cup, eyes raised in anticipation. 'Go ahead, please.'

'First of all, young lady, we both know that you're not Mrs June Boyd.'

Sipping hot tea, Serena considered telling Mrs Neil the truth, then hesitated. Fate had brought her to this anonymous place, and who was she to argue with fate? With warning bells ringing loud and clear in her head, she replied in a firm voice.

'Does it matter who I am? You're a midwife and your job is to deliver babies. You did just that for me last night. I know that I would've been in dire straights without you, and I'm very grateful. Naturally I intend to thank you generously.'

Serena noticed that Mrs Neil's body language had changed, albeit subtly. There was a strange tension in her that had not been present before.

'My dear, you've had mixed-race babies; that's a rare phenomenon, one in a million, have you any idea how it happened?'

Serena smiled wistfully. 'Yes, I've got a good idea.'

'Well, I can tell you exactly how it happens, medically, so to speak. You have to have intercourse with a black man and a white man, within hours of each other.' Mrs Neil made no attempt to disguise the contempt creeping into her voice. 'That, young lady, is how it happens. So, what do you have to say?' she asked.

Serena closed her eyes, rested her head on the back of the chair, and made an effort to compose herself. 'Only that it was the most wonderful day of my life. He was—' her voice trailed off.

Mrs Neil was certain she could see a glimmer of tears in the younger woman's deep blue eyes.

'I loved him, you see. I would have stayed with him, but he didn't want that.'

There was a profound sadness in Serena's voice, yet Mrs Neil felt no sympathy for her. If anything, she was actually irritated by this obviously wealthy and beautiful young woman, who sat twisting her wedding ring as she talked of one-day love affairs. What did she know of life? Real life. Of hardship and loneliness? The aching kind of loneliness that never went away. It clung like shit to a blanket, so her old mother used to say.

Mrs Neil was staring straight through Serena, her voice odd and detached. 'Your sort will never be able to understand my sort.'

Serena shivered, in spite of the heat in the stuffy room. She desperately wanted to go home, back to the warm security of familiarity.

Both women sat in uncomfortable silence, until Mrs Neil spoke again.

'It wouldn't be difficult for me to find out who you really are, you know.'

Serena returned the midwife's probing gaze, a knot of fear tightening the pit of her stomach.

Suddenly Mrs Neil stood up and gestured at the twins. A smile flashed across her face. 'Please don't worry, I'm only trying to help.'

Serena was feeling bewildered now, not sure whether or not she could trust this woman to whom she owed so much.

'Come on, let's give you a good look at them.'

'Yes, I'd like that,' Serena replied nervously.

The babies were still sleeping, each one snugly wrapped in a woollen blanket.

Serena eased herself from her chair and knelt forward tentatively. She was totally unprepared for the rush of love that filled her entire being as she stared at Nicholas's daughter.

The child was perfectly formed. As if on cue, she had begun to stir and her perfect fingers, capped with the whitest nails Serena had ever seen, fluttered in front of her pink, oval face. She had a mass of fine hair, the colour of old gold. Although her eyes were tightly shut, her mouth, the shape of a rosebud, was moving as if she were blowing kisses.

Serena gasped, awestruck by her own tiny creation, and she pulled at the blanket to get a better view.

It was at that moment that the baby opened her eyes. Serena could see that they were the exact image of her own. Transfixed, she held her daughter's gaze, convinced that the little girl could see her.

'She's a beauty, isn't she?' prompted Mrs Neil.

'Absolutely,' Serena whispered, eyes never leaving her daughter's face, voice filled with longing. 'I want to hold her.'

The midwife recognized the wonderment of motherhood. 'Well, I think you should look at your other daughter first; she's a little smaller and . . .'

'Yes, yes of course,' Serena replied sharply, reluctant to move her eyes for a moment, but turning her head towards the second baby with a sense of apprehension.

The baby had sensed the attention and wriggled free from her blanket, kicking her legs furiously. They seemed ridiculously long, completely out of proportion to her narrow torso and neat head.

A wave of nausea swept over Serena. Looking at the child's skin, so dark in comparison to that of the other one, she felt as though she might faint. She breathed deeply, noting the shiny black hair curling on to her daughter's brow. The small features were almost identical to those of her sister, a fact which for some inexplicable reason filled Serena with dread.

Uncurling long, thin arms, the baby reached out towards her mother. But this frail, human gesture was too much for Serena. Clamping her hand over her mouth, she bit her palm so hard that it drew blood. She looked up and stared out of the dirty living-room window, but saw only the image of Royole Fergusson.

Suddenly she knew exactly what she had to do. If it worked, it would be the ultimate solution for her mulatto love-child, and herself.

Chapter Six

'Darling, how are you?'

Nicholas's voice was very faint; Serena could barely hear him.

'I'm fine.' She struggled to keep her own voice light and carefree. 'Can you speak up, Nicky, this is a bad line.'

'Where are you? I'll call you back,' he offered.

'Oh, I'm just about to go out for the day,' she got in quickly. 'Anyway, what I have to say won't take long. Your mother's invited me to one of her boring charity luncheons on Friday. I said I couldn't go because you were due to arrive home, so I just wanted to confirm . . .'

Nicholas interrupted her. 'I'm afraid I won't be back on Friday. I was going to ring this evening and explain. Something important's cropped up and I have to fly down to Brazil for the weekend. I'll probably get back Tuesday, with a bit of luck.'

Serena couldn't believe her own 'bit of luck'. Forcing her voice to sound disappointed, she managed to say, 'Oh Nicholas! I was so looking forward to us spending the weekend together.'

'So was I, darling. You know where I'd much rather be.'

Nicholas sounded depressed. Serena was ecstatic.

'Never mind Nick, I'll have a quiet weekend in the country.'

'So, how are those twins of mine behaving?'

She could hear him chuckling. Serena took a deep breath. 'Still kicking me.'

'Never mind, it won't be long now, only another few weeks. I'm really looking forward to the birth.'

Nicholas sounded so excited that Serena felt a pang of guilt. 'Must dash Nicholas, I've got an appointment with the doc.'

'It might be rather difficult telephoning from São Paulo so, unless it's urgent, I'll see you on Tuesday morning. Judith in the London office has all the flight details.'

A loud crackling interrupted the conversation and the line went dead for a few seconds.

'Nicholas, can you hear me, are you still there?'

'Yes, I can just about hear you.'

Serena had to shout. 'Don't worry about calling me, darling, I'll be fine. See you Tuesday, take care.'

She was about to put the phone down when the line suddenly cleared, and his voice was loud and very distinct.

'I love you Bunty.'

'You too,' replied Serena, hoping it sounded sincere. Replacing the receiver, she caught a glimpse of herself in the small mirror above the telephone table; dark ringed eyes stared back from a face that appeared to have shrunk visibly in the last twenty-four hours. She sensed, rather than saw, Mrs Neil come up behind her. Then one side of the midwife's head appeared alongside her own in the mirror.

'Talking to hubby were we?'

Serena turned sideways, her heart was thumping. She had to overcome an urge to turn and run out of the house.

'Yes, I was as it happens. Overseas, I'm afraid. I'll leave you some money,' she blurted out. 'If you don't mind, I have a couple more calls to make.'

It was then that she noticed something in Mrs Neil's hand.

She gasped as she recognized her own wallet. It

77

contained her driver's licence, passport and credit cards.

Holding the wallet in front of Serena's face, Mrs Neil grinned broadly. 'Make as many calls as you like, dear. I'm sure you can afford it, Lady Serena Frazer-West.'

There was a long silence before Serena, determined not to be intimidated, adopted the voice she usually reserved for her staff.

'Yes, I am Lady Serena Frazer-West, and I can afford to pay your telephone bill, Mrs Neil. That's if I may have my wallet please . . .'

The other woman ignored her and, clutching the wallet, she started to walk down the hall, not stopping until she reached the kitchen door where she turned to face Serena.

'You go ahead, milady. Make as many calls as you like. Take your time, I'm not going anywhere. And later on, why don't you make yourself comfortable in front of the fire. I'll check on the babies and make us a nice, fresh pot of tea.'

The smile on her face was completely void of warmth.

'Then we can talk business.'

'Serena darling, what on earth has happened? You look absolutely ghastly.'

Rachel Sawyer had opened the front door of her mews house, shocked to be confronted by her best friend leaning heavily against the garage door.

Serena's face was as white as if it had been newly cast in plaster. Her usually brilliant blue eyes were dulled and partly hidden under drooping lids, and there was a distinctly dishevelled look about her. In all the years Rachel had known Serena, she had never once seen her look even remotely untidy. Ordinarily she was very fastidious about her appearance.

They had been friends since starting boarding school together at seven, and Rachel knew her as well as she knew herself, if not better. It was therefore patently obvious that there'd been some crisis.

'Come in quickly, and tell me what's going on.'

Serena didn't move, she began to tremble. 'Rachel, I can't even start to tell you.' Her hand, pale and shaking, pushed a lock of stray hair out of her eyes.

Rachel at that point noticed that Serena was visibly slimmer. Pointing excitedly to her friend's stomach, she squealed, 'Why didn't you tell me that you'd had the babies when you rang?'

'I didn't want to talk about it on the phone.' She shuddered. 'There was too much to tell.'

Immediately concerned, Rachel stepped forward into the street, opening her arms wide. 'What is it darling, what's wrong?'

Serena, stumbling on the wet cobblestones underfoot, fell into the warmth of her best friend's embrace. Rachel was secure, comforting, familiar; she felt good.

'Come inside, and I'll fix us both a large drink.'

Serena answered this in a distant voice, 'I've got something in the car I want to show you.' She was glancing towards the Range Rover parked on the opposite side of the street.

Rachel, wearing a fine silk shirt, velvet trousers and open-toed shoes without stockings, was beginning to feel cold. She started to propel Serena towards the door.

'No. It's something that won't wait.'

'OK, let's see what won't wait.' Rachel started to follow her friend across the road.

As they reached the Range Rover, Serena opened the hatchback and handed over a small, cardboard box containing what looked like a bundle of rags.

It was not until Rachel reached the hall and the bundle moved slightly, that the realization of what it actually contained dawned upon her.

'Serena, this is a bloody baby!'

Serena was right behind her. 'Yes, and I've got her sister here. Quickly Rachel, premature babies have to be kept very warm.'

She pushed her astonished friend through her own hall and up the one flight of stairs into a small dining area at one end of a vast space. The whole room was awash with flowering plants, all in an eclectic assortment of pots. A circular, teak dining table and six chairs also filled the room.

Rachel gingerly placed the box she was carrying on top of the table, then waited for Serena to put her own package down next to it. She began to speak, but Serena placed her index finger to her lips and signalled to her, 'Shushhh.'

Very gently she opened the tight cocoon of blankets, slipped her hand carefully inside, and felt each tiny body in turn. Satisfied that they were alive and warm, she turned to Rachel.

'I could do with that drink now.'

'You and me, both!' stressed Rachel, as she disappeared into the kitchen to pour two large brandies.

Serena crossed over to an L-shaped sofa at the other end of the room; here she draped her coat and then finally sat down.

Rachel joined her, holding out a brandy goblet. It was half full.

'I thought you might need it straight. I suspect that I will. Cheers!' She took a deep gulp of the smooth Hine, enjoying the warm glow that quickly followed, and then flopped down into a wing-backed Charles Eames chair opposite Serena.

'Well, come on. How is it you've arrived on my doorstep looking like something the cat dragged in, carting your babies about in cardboard boxes?'

After only her third swig of brandy, Serena had almost emptied the glass. She placed it on the coffee table, leant back and began to speak. She told Rachel the whole story, leaving nothing out at all.

Serena explained how she had fallen in love with Royole Fergusson the first moment she'd looked into his dark green eyes, that night of the storm in Port Antonio. And she described to her friend, in exquisite detail, the one day they had spent together.

Her voice faltered as she came to the finale in Mrs Neil's cottage and her disillusion when the midwife had turned out to be so self-seeking. In fact she'd threatened to go to Nicholas with the truth, arguing until Serena had eventually agreed to pay her ten thousand pounds to keep her mouth shut.

'*How* much!' Rachel yelled, 'Serena, you must be off your trolley. How do you know she won't be back for more?'

'I can't be certain, but I doubt it. She has a daughter and grandchild living in Spain. The money will make it possible for her to sell up and join them.'

'That could be a pack of lies,' protested Rachel.

Serena shrugged. 'I know, but what choice do I have? I had to pay her and hope for the best.' Holding up both hands, she crossed her fingers.

Rachel shrugged her shoulders and sighed. 'But ten grand, it's extortionate.'

Dropping her head, Serena covered her face. 'I was frantic,' she mumbled, 'I didn't know what to do for the best.'

Covering the space between them in one long step, Rachel was quickly beside her friend; placing an arm around Serena. 'Have you thought about putting Royole's baby up for adoption,' she suggested, forcing her voice to sound bright and positive.

Serena extended her hands on her lap in a gesture of hopelessness. 'Nicholas is back in three days, Rachel. Adoption takes months. But I must do *something* . . .

He'd never get over this, I think he'd kill me.'

Her eyes were darting about, wild and frenzied.

Rachel had never seen her friend like this before, and she found it scary. 'I don't think he'd go that far, Serena,' she said quickly, 'though I don't suppose he'll be exactly over the moon.'

She reached for a pack of cigarettes on the coffee table, wondering how she could calm her friend, trying to remember if she had any valium left. Lighting a cigarette for herself, she offered the pack to Serena who took one and inhaled deeply.

After a brief bout of coughing, Serena turned to face Rachel. 'I have a very big favour to ask,' she paused. 'But I want you to know that I'll understand if you refuse, and it won't affect our friendship.'

Serena took a deep breath, whilst Rachel waited in a state of apprehension.

'I want you to have Royole Fergusson's baby.'

She couldn't help smiling at Rachel's aghast face.

'Just for a few weeks. Long enough to give me time to sort something permanent out. I do have a plan, and if it works then she'll be well taken care of and nobody here need ever know of her existence.'

'And if your plan doesn't work?' Rachel asked, her heart thumping.

'I'll have to acknowledge her and face the ensuing scandal.'

Neither woman spoke, both keenly aware of the implications. But Serena fixed beseeching eyes upon Rachel. Suddenly the sophisticated Lady Frazer-West was gone, replaced by a ten-year-old schoolgirl determined not to be caught breaking the rules.

Rachel was aware of Serena watching her every move. A faint glimmer of light entered her eyes, a kind of mischievous anticipation, and she faked a yawn. 'Well, modelling's just so boring at the moment, no good jobs around. And you know I've always wanted a baby.'

Serena stood up, wordlessly, and they both walked to the dining area.

Rachel had to lean forward to see the baby clearly. Expecting to feel detached, she was quite shocked to find herself captivated as soon as she laid eyes on the tiny, dark head and angelic features. She lifted her carefully out of the box, as if she were a piece of precious porcelain, cradling her tenderly.

'Oh Serena, she's so beautiful. Look, she just smiled at me!'

'It's only wind,' Serena declared.

Rachel ignored this information. 'So what do I call her? I can't keep referring to her as "Royole's baby". Or the "other one"; or, worse, the "black baby".' She grinned, giving her friend a playful nudge.

However, Serena was lost in her own thoughts, gazing into space. 'I've already thought of a name for her. I'd like her to be called Loveday.'

As she said the name, Serena watched her daughter's eyes open. And in that instant the previous eight months just slipped away, like thistledown on the wind, and suddenly they were Royole's eyes she was staring into. It was just for a split second, but he was there, holding her close.

A flicker of pain crossed Serena's face, then was gone. Looking up, she spoke to Rachel. 'Yes, I think Loveday is appropriate,' her voice choked. 'Don't you?'

Rachel simply nodded. She fleetingly wondered if Serena would ever get over having to part with her love child.

'And what about you, little Miss Frazer-West,' Serena broke the silence, lifting up the other baby and stroking her sparkling, golden hair.

Unbidden, yet very vivid memories of her grandmother suddenly entered her mind. She had been a great beauty, with a gregarious personality to match. A lady whose life had been filled with laughter and love. Serena remembered her with great fondness.

'Yes, I will call you after my wonderful gran. She would have liked that.' She licked the end of her finger and, making a sign of the cross on her daughter's head, she pronounced: 'I name you Lucinda Jayne Frazer-West.'

The baby wailed. Serena rocked her to and fro, talking to her in a soft, soothing voice until her sobs subsided. Glancing up, she caught Rachel's gaze, their eyes locked.

'Thank you Rachel. I'll never forget this.'

Rachel kissed the top of Loveday's head and the baby made a little cooing sound.

'Everything is going to be OK, Serena. I know it is.'

Serena smiled wryly, 'If everything goes to plan I may save my marriage, you mean.'

She forced herself to face the future. 'I have Nicholas's daughter. She is perfect, and everything we ever wanted. I must think of her welfare and nothing else. If I allow myself just one moment of weakness, Rachel, I'm lost.'

Chapter Seven

Serena awoke as usual, a few seconds after six.

Instantly alert, she slipped quietly out of bed, padded across the bedroom and stopped at the bay window to throw back the heavy drapes. At once the room was flooded with the bright light of spring. It was a beautiful morning. The sky, the palest of blues, stretched cloudless as far as the eye could see.

Everything was still and silent.

Pressing her hands against the cool glass, she looked out over the formal gardens and on to the rolling valley beyond. A flock of sheep, laden with wool, were nibbling at frozen clumps of grass. A narrow lane curved through neat fields to a sprawling farmhouse, where a single spiral of smoke rose into the air.

Turning from the window, Serena walked towards her bathroom, where she showered, then wrapped herself in a huge white towel and stepped into the adjoining dressing room. Three of the walls were lined with floor-to-ceiling wardrobes in highly polished walnut, the Frazer-West crest inlaid in ebony above each door.

The room had been designed for Nicholas's mother, Lady Pandora Frazer-West, in 1934. Her tastes and influence were still very evident in all the furniture: a small, buttoned love-seat; a bow-fronted Louis Quinze dressing table, with a pretty chair from the same period; an ugly mahogany writing desk in one corner, and an ornate, reproduction French Empire chair.

Serena hated the room.

It was dark and claustrophobic; as was most of Redby Park, the Frazer-West ancestral home. Many times she had tried to suggest changes to the decor, but Nicholas insisted that he liked it exactly as it was.

She dressed casually in jeans and a pale blue cashmere sweater; tied her long hair in a pony tail, and applied a quick layer of pale pink lipstick. She felt full of optimism for the first time since she had given birth.

A brisk walk down the oak-panelled hall took her past several stern-faced portraits of Frazer-West ancestors, who always seemed to be watching her every move, and on to the nursery. She could hear her daughter's cries as she pushed open the door to find the new nanny, Elizabeth Barratt, sitting next to a baby bath and splashing Lucinda with tepid water.

'I don't think she likes that,' Serena chuckled, as Lucinda's wails increased and her face turned bright scarlet.

'Come on then baby, that will do.'

The nanny lifted her screaming charge out of the water, on to a fluffy towel which she had already placed on her lap. Quickly and expertly, she wrapped the towel tightly around Lucinda, holding the baby securely in her arms before she stood up.

Serena stepped forward. 'I would like to hold her.'

'Of course m'lady.' Elizabeth's bright smile lit up her face.

Nursing Lucinda in her arms, Serena stroked the side of her soft cheek, studiously examining every detail of her face.

Nanny Barratt chatted as she carried the baby bath to the sink. 'She slept well, only woke twice. That's very good for a baby of her size. I weighed her this morning, she's put on two ounces.'

'That's wonderful, Elizabeth.' Serena spoke without taking her eyes off Lucinda.

She lifted the baby closer to her face to inhale the sweet, fresh smell of new skin, holding it in her nostrils as she planted a kiss on the top of her daughter's head. 'You're going to meet your daddy soon, and I know he's going to fall in love with you on sight.'

Nicholas did.

He was besotted from the moment he tiptoed into the nursery later that afternoon, led by Serena who lifted a sleeping Lucinda out of her crib.

'Darling! She's the most beautiful baby I've ever seen.' Holding his breath, he carefully took Lucinda in his arms, then whispered anxiously. 'But she looks so tiny and . . . fragile.'

'Hold her tighter Nicholas, she won't break,' urged Serena, smiling.

Lucinda opened her eyes, fixing them on Nicholas.

'She has *exactly* the same colour eyes as you, darling.' He sounded wildly excited, as if he had chanced upon some great discovery.

'I know.' Serena was amused. 'For the moment, but babies' eyes often change colour.' She wondered, with a pang, if Loveday's eyes would change or stay the same as her father's.

Nicholas stared at his daughter in awe, barely able to cope with the surge of love swelling in his chest. His breath caught in his throat as Lucinda began to whimper softly.

'Is she all right?' he asked in alarm.

'Let's put her back, I think she's protesting at being disturbed,' suggested Serena, taking Lucinda from his outstretched arms. She replaced her in the antique crib where generations of Frazer-West babies, Nicholas included, had slept.

Husband and wife crept out of the nursery together. Serena followed Nicholas down the broad sweep of stairs, across the stone-flagged hall, into the library – her favourite room. Reading had always been a passion for as long as she could remember.

It was evening, and the last few remnants of light were ebbing away, the lengthening shadows of dusk had already started to congregate beneath the cedar tree at the bottom of the garden. Serena pulled the drapes. They closed with an almost silent swish as Clive, the butler, entered wearing his perpetual 'service smile'.

'You called, sir.'

'Yes Clive. I think a bottle of my wife's favourite champagne would be in order. All right with you, darling?'

'Wonderful,' responded Serena with gusto.

'Make sure it's ice-cold Clive, the last bottle you served was far too bloody warm.'

'Yes of course, sir. I took the liberty of putting a bottle on ice earlier today.'

'That man gives me the creeps,' Serena said, as soon as the butler was out of earshot.

Nicholas snorted.

She was all too familiar with this peculiar sound; it usually preceded one of her husband's incredibly self-opinionated viewpoints.

'I really don't know where you get these silly notions from, darling. He came highly recommended and I think he's a damn good man.'

'I get my "silly notions" from a thing called intuition; and how many times have I been proved right?'

Nicholas snorted again. Puffing out his cheeks, he was about to retaliate when Clive came back carrying a silver tray containing a bottle of Krug in an ice bucket and two glasses.

'I'll see to that Clive, thank you,' Nicholas filled both glasses to the brim as he dismissed the butler.

Serena lit a candle-lamp, and the flickering light illuminated the gauntness of her face.

Chiding himself inwardly for having left her at such a

critical time, Nicholas made a silent vow that he would make up for his neglect. He began by handing her a glass of champagne.

'To Lucinda.'

They both drank, Serena having joined her husband on the comfortable, old library sofa.

Taking her hand, he played with her fingertips. 'My poor Bunty, you've had such an awful time. I'll never forgive myself for being away.'

'Don't be too hard on yourself, Nicky. How could you have known that I'd go into premature labour.'

She sighed, as if bored with the telling of the story. In fact she really had related it so many times over the last few days, to friends, family, staff, her doctor and obstetrician; always careful not to change any of the details that she and Mrs Neil had agreed upon.

The second baby had been stillborn.

The midwife had done her best but, being ill-equipped to deal with any complications, she'd been unable to save Lucinda's twin.

'But to lose a baby in those circumstances, it must have been extremely traumatic.'

The trauma hasn't stopped for a moment, Serena thought ruefully, as Nicholas continued his guilt trip.

'It's just I'm so damn sorry I wasn't here. If I had been, we might have had a different story. I wouldn't have let you drive on your own to start with.'

Serena glanced over at a silver-framed photograph of herself and Nicholas on their wedding day; noticing, for the first time, the expression of benign confusion on her own face.

'Don't blame yourself, Nicholas. It might not have made any difference if you'd been here. I was so excited about the new Range Rover I just couldn't wait to drive it. You know how bloody stubborn I can be. You certainly couldn't have stopped me.'

Serena had successfully lifted the blame from his shoulders, and he felt instantly better. 'That's true. If you really want to do something then, come hell or high water, you do it!'

He grinned, and she hoped he would forget about the whole, dreadful ordeal and shut up. She didn't want to talk about it any more.

Nicholas finished his drink. 'What's done is done. No turning back, eh?'

'My sentiments entirely. We have a very beautiful daughter. Let's not dwell on the baby who died. That saga ended on the delivery bed. Now we must go forward.'

Serena was certain that Nicholas would find a way to eradicate any remaining guilt; he always did. He loved her, and he constantly tried to please her. She suspected that soon, probably within days, an expensive-looking box would appear. She would open it and squeal, feigning pleasure on finding a diamond necklace, or perhaps another antique watch to add to her collection.

Where once this prospect would have filled her with *real* pleasure, it now seemed completely empty. It just meant that Nicholas would be blissfully happy in his ignorance. She almost envied him that.

She would never have the heart to tell him that nothing could ever be the same again. How could she begin to explain the events of the last few days, or to tell him how destiny had driven a wedge between them?

Instead she would play the game for her daughters' sake, because it was too late to turn back now.

Part two of her plan had already been set in motion.

Chapter Eight

Serena stared up at the arrivals board in Terminal Three at Heathrow airport.

The message flashing in bold white print indicated the flight from Kingston, Jamaica had landed.

Although she stood back a little from the gaggle of chauffeurs and families crowding the exit from the customs hall, she was still grateful to be partially hidden behind a very tall man.

She saw him before he saw her.

She watched him closely as he scanned the sea of strange faces, looking for her. He looked different from the last time she had seen him. She supposed it was the dark, ill-fitting suit, or the air of uncertainty that seemed to surround him.

Serena stepped away from her human shield. Feeling considerably more vulnerable, she stood self-consciously in the middle of the noisy concourse. At the same moment that she tentatively lifted her hand to wave, he spotted her.

His face filled with a smile warmer than a West Indian midday sun. 'Serena, it's so good to see you!'

Serena was amazed at how calm her voice sounded when she replied. 'And you, Royole. Thank you for coming at such short notice.'

His smile slipped away, he was at once serious. He looked awkward, unsure of himself. 'It was the very least I could do.'

An uncomfortable silence followed until Serena looked at the small leather grip he was carrying and asked: 'Is that all you have?'

'Yes, I thought it better to travel light. After all, I may be travelling back with a lot more baggage.'

Her mouth dropped; she tried to smile, but failed. 'Come on then, let's get going. I've got the car waiting.'

It was mid-morning and the road into London was quiet. The noise of the wheels turning on the uneven road surface sounded ridiculously loud in Serena's ears. She squinted as a dazzling April sun filled the windscreen, blinding her for a split second.

They were passing over the Hammersmith flyover when Royole at last spoke his mind. He was staring straight ahead.

'When I received your news I was, to say the least, stunned.' He breathed deeply before going on. 'To have given birth to my daughter and your husband's at the same time is . . .' he sighed, '. . . nothing short of incredible. I must admit I found it hard to accept. I even considered ignoring your letter and had to read it a dozen times before I contacted you.'

Her voice tremulous, she asked, 'And what made you change your mind?'

He glanced at her cautiously. 'It was when I rang, and you told me that our daughter had wonderful green eyes, and skin the colour of creamy coffee. I knew that if I didn't come to see her, I might regret it for the rest of my life.'

His voice dropped, he was almost whispering when he went on. 'I was also afraid she might be adopted, or end up in some orphanage. To be honest, the thought horrified me.'

Serena could not contain her anger. 'She would never have ended up in an orphanage; what on earth do you take me for?'

'I hardly know you, Serena. I had one day with you. How could I be sure?'

She realized that he was perfectly right. Only one day to know someone, to know how they would react in any given situation, was not enough. Yet she felt she had known him all her life, longer in fact . . . from another life.

He noticed her mouth was trembling and she had started to chew her bottom lip. It reminded him of how she had looked in Coralita Cottage, only minutes before he had made love to her.

'I had already made up my mind, if you were not prepared to have her I would keep her.' She swallowed, afraid to look at him.

Serena longed to tell him that she would give anything to keep their daughter, and have him as well. She would even give Lucinda up, and her safe privileged life with Nicholas, just to have him. She wanted him now, more than she had ever wanted anything else. It was like a sickness, rendering her weak and unstable.

'Where are we?' he asked, as she eventually stopped and opened the car door in front of Rachel's house in Knightsbridge.

'This is my best friend's place.'

He could see that her mouth was trembling again, only more so. He slid his hand across the seat in search of hers. It slipped from his grasp as she jumped out of the car, muttering something under her breath. He thought he heard her say, 'Loveday is here.'

Rachel Sawyer was opening her front door as Royole alighted from the car.

'Hi,' said Serena brightly, kissing her friend on both cheeks, before turning to make the introductions. 'Rachel, meet Royole Fergusson.'

Rachel stepped forward holding out her hand. She was dressed in a black mini-dress and black stockings.

Her long, shapely legs seemed to Royole to go on for ever. He decided she was extremely attractive in a brittle, almost boyish sort of way. It was not lost on him that her smile, warm and inviting at first glance, changed to cool and unapproachable a second later.

'Delighted to meet you, Royole.' She glanced briefly in Serena's direction. 'I've heard a lot about you.'

'All good, I hope.' He also glanced at Serena.

'Absolutely too good to be true.' Rachel's gaze was steady and challenging. He knew he was being appraised. It made him uneasy.

They followed Rachel inside, Royole closing the door quietly behind him. In the hallway he helped Serena out of her coat. She flinched as their hands met.

He noticed how the pale blue shift dress she was wearing hung on her; the only visible signs of post pregnancy, a rounded stomach and a slight thickening at her hips.

Rachel ushered them upstairs into the vast living room. Waiting there was a tray loaded with a pot of coffee, cups and a basket of toast, Danish pastries and croissants.

'Breakfast à la Sawyer! I even went out this morning to collect the fresh pastries myself.'

'It smells wonderful,' Royole commented.

Sitting in the deep sofa, he took a croissant from the basket. Watching Rachel pour the coffee, he was aware of her interest in him. Interest she made no attempt to disguise.

He ate hungrily, spilling crumbs on the front of his shirt; any excuse to touch him, Serena thought, itching to brush them away. She was about to do so when, laughing, he flicked the flakes away himself.

'I'm not hungry thanks,' she said, pouring herself a cup of black coffee, when Rachel urged her to a Danish.

'You never are these days, sweetie, you're fading away. For goodness' sake have something.'

Serena shook her head. 'Really Rachel, I couldn't.'

94

Rachel shrugged and continued to stuff herself with another Danish; then a croissant, spread with thick butter and black cherry jam. She spent the whole time studying Royole as he slowly sipped his coffee.

Rachel had decided that he was undoubtedly handsome, although not her type. She personally had never fancied black men. But she realized that the combination of his chiselled face, sensuous mouth and green eyes certainly made for a devastating appearance that would make both men and women look twice.

There was something else that Rachel could not quite put her finger on. He had a certain kind of animal quality; an untamed energy, mixed with an underlying sensitivity of an almost feminine nature. Interesting, she thought, then quickly changed that to *fascinating*. She could understand how Serena had fallen madly in love with him.

Serena pricked up her ears as she heard a faint muffled cry. 'Oh, she's crying!'

'I didn't hear anyth—' Rachel cut off her own words as Loveday cried louder and they all heard quite clearly.

'I'll get her.' Serena jumped to her feet, ran to the top of the stairs and returned a few minutes later, carrying Loveday.

The baby was wearing a white romper suit with a Peter Pan collar, beautifully hand-embroidered with pink rosebuds. Her eyes were wide open, inquisitive, watching the light. And her hair had grown longer, curling on the back of the collar.

Loveday would be five weeks old tomorrow.

Royole stood up. His legs felt shaky. He couldn't even trust his own voice.

Serena gently wiped a tiny sliver of saliva from the corner of the baby's mouth. 'Your daughter, Royole.'

Rachel held her breath, looking from one face to the other, as Loveday was handed to her father.

Royole stared into his daughter's dark green eyes, so

like his own. She held his gaze. They remained like that, father and child, unmoving for several moments.

Both her hands were curled into tight fists. He stroked the back of one hand, very tentatively, with the tip of his index finger. Instantly her tiny fingers uncurled, grabbing his finger and squeezing it tight. He was surprised at her strength.

It was then she smiled.

Royole was overcome with emotion. Serena could see this clearly as he raised his head. His expression told her everything she needed to know. Her daughter's future was safe.

'She is absolutely beautiful, Serena.'

'Yes, she is,' Serena agreed, then asked, 'Did you manage to get the birth certificate sorted out?'

'No problem. It was easier than I thought.' Then he grinned. 'And *much* too expensive. I've called her Luna, that was her great-great-grandmother's slave name; and Josephine, after her grandmother, who I am sad to say will never see her.'

For some reason Serena did not want to tell him that she had called her other daughter after her own grandmother.

She searched for the right words, anything that would not sound over-emotional. 'You will look after her, won't you? Give her everything she needs.'

'Don't worry Serena, she'll have a wonderful home with me.' He hesitated, before saying. 'I married Caron six months ago. We're very happy. She's as excited as me about the baby, I know she's going to love her.'

Serena felt the resentment rising through her as she remembered the exotic Caron, smoking dope and seducing Nicholas with her feline eyes. She doubted that the new Mrs Fergusson would care too much for Royole's love child, but perhaps when she saw the baby she would learn to love her. Serena hoped so, pushing any other possibility from her mind.

Stepping to one side, she turned to face Rachel. She was sure that if she continued to look at Royole's smitten expression and Loveday's exquisite, heart-shaped face, she would lose the control she had been practising ever since she'd spoken to Royole and he had agreed to come to England to see his daughter.

With a note of appeal she spoke to Rachel, 'She's a very good baby, isn't she?'

Reacting to Serena's cue, Rachel jumped up quickly to stand next to Royole, saying in an effusive voice, 'She's wonderful, no trouble at all, sleeps through the night already. I shall miss my little Loveday.'

Royole looked directly at Serena on hearing the name 'Loveday'. Serena held her breath, her heart fluttering like a trapped bird.

'Loveday, that's a very apt name. I'm sorry she can't keep it,' he said.

In response the baby scrunched up her face, which was turning scarlet and, puffing out her cheeks, she let out a loud, rasping noise, immediately followed by a muffled squelch. Royole chuckled as a sour smell began to permeate the room.

'You know what they say, Royole,' giggled Rachel. 'Shit for luck.'

Holding the baby at arm's length, he screwed up his nose and Rachel took her from him. 'Come on then little miss, let's get that dirty nappy off. We can't have you smelling like that for Daddy, can we.'

Rachel continued this soothing chat as she carried her charge out of the room.

'Can we sit down, Royole, there's something I want to say.' Serena wasn't looking at him, but was staring vacantly over his shoulder.

They sat down next to each other on the sofa. Serena clasped her hands in her lap, they were shaking.

'As I mentioned to you on the telephone, I want to

deposit a considerable sum of money in your name.' He opened his mouth but she raised her hand. 'Please let me finish. In return, I want you to swear that you will never tell our daughter who her real mother is, that the truth will go with you to the grave. I want your word, Royole.'

'Before I give you my word, I want you to know that the money will be used for Luna, for her education, and the privileges that I may otherwise not be able to afford.'

She waved one hand from side to side as if this was taken as read. But she repeated her earlier stipulation even more emphatically, 'Yes, but I need you to swear on Luna's life,' the strange name sounded alien to her ears, 'that you will never divulge our secret. Just tell me what I need to hear. Then I'll be gone, out of your life for ever.'

He sighed, closing his eyes. 'I didn't plan for this to happen Serena, you mustn't blame me. We had a wonderful twenty-four hours together. I will never forget it. I think I know what you must have been through since, and I feel very sorry, but—'

'You have *no* fucking idea what I've been through, Royole,' she hissed; then added in a hushed, much calmer voice, 'You will never know.' Turning towards him, her brilliant blue eyes blazing, she reminded him, 'I'm waiting.'

Challenging her demanding gaze, he uttered his words carefully, 'I just think that you may regret this later. Who knows what life holds for us; there may come a time when you want to see her.'

'Don't you understand Royole, I've already had to let her go. Have you any idea how difficult that is for a mother?'

At that point Royole was suddenly confronted with the pain she had endured, and felt unable to add to her suffering in any way.

'Yes, I swear . . . I'll never tell our daughter who her

real mother is. The secret is safe with me. I promise, Serena.'

A long sigh of relief escaped her lips. 'Thank you, Royole. I know the sort of man you are, I know that your word is your bond. I can leave now.'

They both stood, facing each other.

'Say goodbye to Rachel for me. Tell her I'll call later.' Serena was now fighting back the tears that had been threatening all morning. She blinked rapidly, 'Remember what I said to you at Ken Jones airport?'

'You said several things.'

'I said I was certain I would see you again. Now I know, with just the same certainty, that I'll never see you again. Goodbye Royole. Take good care of yourself, and even better care of Loveday.'

He was about to say that he would, when she ran from the room. He had to call after her.

'Goodbye Lady Serena.'

Royole Fergusson left Rachel's house later that day, after several lessons in nappy changing and bottle feeding. He took with him everything belonging to Loveday. There was no trace of her left in the house, it was almost as if she'd never been there at all. Rachel knew that her promise to Serena had been fulfilled, that was all that mattered. But before going to bed that evening, she gazed around her room with a pang of regret, staring wistfully at the space where the cot had been. It was only then that she noticed a photograph on the floor. Stooping to pick it up, she wondered if perhaps it had slipped out of Royole's pocket.

It showed Serena and Royole. And another woman with coffee-coloured skin whose half-closed, slanting eyes made her look sleepy, or stoned perhaps. Rachel assumed it must have been taken in the Caribbean.

Serena was laughing, her head thrown back. She looked

relaxed and happy, whilst Royole's face held an altogether different expression. He looked animated, predatory, almost as if he were about to pounce on a long-awaited prey.

Rachel carried the photograph downstairs, popping it into her desk drawer, meaning to give it to Serena the next time she saw her.

But, of course she forgot.

When Royole heard the rap on his hotel-room door, he thought it was the bellboy coming to collect his cases. Instead he was surprised to see a young woman holding a package.

'Are you Mr Fergusson?'

He nodded.

'Delivery for you from Lady Frazer-West.'

Intrigued, Royole took the package, wondering how Serena had known where to find him. He stepped back into the room, closing the door quietly behind him so as not to disturb the sleeping baby. Then sitting on the edge of the bed, he removed a covering layer of brown paper to reveal a square jewellery box. It was old, the corners worn. He turned it over; the name 'Garrard' was printed on the base. And he gasped when he opened it.

Inside was an exquisite diamond-and-emerald necklace, the stones glittering against a lining of dark blue velvet. Also inside the box was a letter, which he tore open. There was no address or date, and no signature. It was typewritten, simple and to the point.

This necklace belonged to my grandmother. She was a great beauty and an exceptional woman. I would like our daughter to wear it on her wedding day.

Please keep it safe for her until then.

Book Two

Chapter Nine

CAYMAN ISLANDS 1980

'Luna, I will not continue this conversation if you insist on being so stubborn.'

Luna watched her father as he paced the floor of her bedroom. She fought back tears, thinking of the last time she had seen him this angry.

She shuddered at the memory. It had been a couple of years before. She had awoken from a bad dream and, unable to return to sleep, had crept downstairs. Surprised to hear her father's raised voice, she had listened with innocent curiosity at the half-open door of the drawing room. Curiosity had turned to interest at the sound of her own name, then her mother had screamed something she didn't understand; something about a 'love child'. Peeping around the door, Luna had been shocked to see Royole's arm raised as if to strike her mother. It had been like looking at a stranger, and she had wanted to shout out to restore the peace. But instead she had slipped quietly away, running upstairs with her father's hot rage still ringing in her ears.

Now, Luna searched Royole's face when he finally stopped pacing, relieved to see that he did not look like the stranger he'd been on that awful night. This bolstered her confidence and, with her neat head held high, she spoke with more defiance than she really intended.

'I don't want to go to school; I don't want to leave home.'

'Luna Luna Luna!' he repeated her name, throwing his

hands in the air, 'What am I to do with you?'

'Let me stay here with you please,' she wailed.

Then turning her back on him, she deliberately closed her mind to the idea of leaving Grand Cayman and going to a school in a remote part of New England that might as well have been Siberia, as far as she was concerned.

Luna and her father were locked in an especially close relationship. He adored her with the sort of unconditional love that breeds great self-assurance in the recipient. Pampered and indulged by him, she was sure she could win him round to her way of thinking and make him understand. Deliberately opening her eyes very wide, she spoke in a breathless 'little girl' voice.

'The truth is Daddy, I can't bear to think of being away from you,' she paused, 'and Mammy. That would make me so unhappy.'

Her eyes were a much lighter shade than his, more like the colour of grass after a shower; he could see that they were beginning to glaze over with a fine film of moisture. This was proving much harder than Royole had imagined.

'Well, your mother and I have decided it's the best thing for you. I'm sorry Luna, but the decision has been made, it's out of my hands now.'

'How do you know what's best for me?' her voice rose.

'Because I'm your father,' he shouted, running out of patience.

Seemingly oblivious to his rising temper, Luna confronted him once more. 'Does that give you the right to make me unhappy?'

'Luna, baby, that's the last thing in the world I want. But you haven't even given this school a chance yet. You might love it. They have wonderful facilities.' He hit the side of his temple with the palm of his hand. 'What I would have given for an opportunity like this at your age.'

'I don't care, I won't go. I'll run away. I'm warning you, Daddy.'

'Luna, I am adamant on this.' He strode towards the door, stopped and turned. Standing perfectly still, he spoke in a tone that brooked no further argument. 'I don't want to hear another word from you about it, do you understand?'

Royole then slammed the door so hard it shook on its hinges. But he waited outside, listening. Her anguished sobs momentarily weakened his resolve. Royole not only adored his only daughter, he also needed her. Upsetting her distressed him almost more than he could bear, but he desperately wanted Luna to have every privilege. She was bright, exceptionally so, and she deserved the type of education that could lead to a brilliant career.

He strode down the sweeping staircase to where his wife was standing by an open french window.

A warm breeze stirred Caron's black hair, causing it to flutter around her stark profile. She was scanning the extensive terrace, awash with flowering plants in terracotta pots, making a mental note to tell the gardener to cut back the Bay Vine before it strangled the lovely Spider Lilies she had planted a few months earlier.

The gardens were especially beautiful at this time of year; richly verdant and in magnificent full bloom after the blessings of the rainy season. They were her own private piece of paradise, and she was still casting an appreciative eye over them when she heard Royole.

Turning round slowly, she smiled at him. The late afternoon sun, filtering through a palm frond, infused her face with a golden glow and for a moment she looked quite beautiful . . . more like the woman she had once been. The deeply etched lines around her mouth were softened in the flattering light. It was only as she stepped out of the sun that it became clear how unkind the years had been to her.

'That girl's so stubborn. I sometimes don't know what to do with her,' complained Royole.

Not needing to ask who he was talking about, Caron had to suppress the reply she would like to have given. Royole had indulged his daughter all her life, and this was the end result; but she knew from past experience that any interference from her with regard to Luna had to be handled very carefully.

He paced the room, agitated. 'Perhaps we're making a big mistake, Caron; perhaps we should wait another year.'

Caron saw his hesitancy; he's weakening, she thought frantically and chose her words with care.

'But if we wait another year, she may not get into Highclaire Academy, then we'll have to start looking all over again. And do you honestly believe she'll be any more willing in a year's time?'

He knew his wife was right.

What he didn't know was how desperate she was to be rid of Luna. Over the last year Caron had planned her strategy with great care, and was not about to be defeated at the final hurdle. She wanted Royole for herself. Being forced to share him with another woman's child for the past thirteen years had been too much of a burden for too long.

In the beginning, Caron had tried to love the baby Royole had brought back from England. And Luna had not been difficult to love. She was a contented infant who had grown into an extremely pretty toddler, causing stares and comment wherever they took her. And now, as a lively, intelligent teenager, she excelled at everything she put her mind to. During the last year she had demonstrated real promise of blossoming into an exceptionally beautiful young woman.

But Caron hated her stepdaughter. And with such force that it appalled even her at times. Tormented with jealousy, she couldn't wait for Luna to leave. The thought of no longer having to compete for Royole's attention was all that kept her going.

'You're right, Caron. I must put my foot down; it's for her own good.'

'You and I both know, Royole, that Luna has great potential. All her teachers have said so. But if she stays here in the Islands she'll only waste it; ending up just hanging out at the beach like all the kids.'

Caron could see she was getting through to him. Encouraged, she pressed on. 'I'm sure she'll be very happy once she settles down. It's a wonderful opportunity for her. Let's not lose it. You seem to forget that she's still a child. She may appear grown up, but at thirteen she can't possibly be expected to understand what's best for her.'

Now, a confident glint entered her almond-shaped eyes. 'Luna will thank you for it later, Royole. I know she will.'

This statement produced a wry smile, 'Yes, you're right about that.'

Inwardly pleased at the positive effect her words had produced, Caron smiled and stroked the side of her husband's arm. She studied his face closely, a face that had barely changed over the years.

Laughter lines crisscrossed Royle's features, only serving to enhance their appeal; a faint trace of silver highlighted his black hair, still thick. He swam every morning and played tennis twice a week. His body was, in her opinion, better now at forty than it had been at twenty-six when she'd first met him.

They'd come a long way since those early, heady days in Coralita Cottage. Yet she still hankered for the carefree life shared in those years, before they'd left Jamaica to settle in the Caymans with a barely three-months-old Luna.

It had been tough at first, but Royole's ambition had been fuelled every step of the way by Caron's own driving force. She knew, even if Royole did not, that she'd been equally instrumental in his spectacular success. Now she was still his most ardent supporter, enjoying prestige as wife of the president of Fergusson Bank and Trust, a highly lucrative, private off-shore corporation located in Georgetown.

'Come, Royole,' she gestured towards the sofa, 'I'll fix us both a dry martini. I've got something important I want to discuss with you.'

'In a minute, Caron.' His tone was dismissive. 'First I must go and placate Luna. I left her sobbing her heart out.'

He walked out without waiting for a reply.

Caron ignored the familiar reaction in the pit of her stomach; she was accustomed to it. 'Thank God she's going,' she whispered hoarsely under her breath, pouring neat vodka into a cocktail shaker.

She couldn't help thinking, as she did so, that perhaps it would have been different if she'd presented Royole with a child of their own.

Caron had yearned for a child. She had dreamed of a son; a tall, handsome boy who would resemble her husband, and carry the Fergusson name. But after miscarrying four times, several consultants had warned her that she was putting herself at risk. She had refused to believe them, refused to accept that she could not have a child; and, with characteristic single-mindedness she had announced that she would keep trying until she had Royole's baby.

A week later Royole had a vasectomy.

The night he told her, she had wanted to die. Nothing could comfort her when she realized that she would never bear Royole a child.

In retrospect, Caron would pinpoint that time as the beginning of a subtle change in her marriage. A distance developed; slowly at first, but gradually widening to become something that she had tried unsuccessfully to bridge.

Royole became withdrawn, spending more time at the

office, immersing himself in business as if his life depended on it. He would return home tired and be uncommunicative with Caron, yet he was always attentive and interested in every aspect of Luna's life. Whatever time he had available, he would fill with pursuits that involved Luna and her friends.

Caron had felt more and more like an outsider; someone living constantly on the periphery, yet desperate to be one of the main party. She clung to the remnants of past intimacy. After all, they had come a long way together, survived such a lot. She had to hold on. Gradually she convinced herself that, with Luna out of the way, her life with Royole could return to how it had been before, or almost. There was no room in her thoughts for the fact that Royole had long ceased to love her. That was too grotesque to contemplate.

Luna was sitting at her dressing-table, writing a letter, when Royole opened the door very quietly and stepped into the room. He tiptoed up behind her. Leaning over her shoulder, he glanced at the letter.

'What are you writing?'

She carried on writing silently for a couple of minutes before saying, 'I'm writing a letter to you Daddy, but it's coming out all wrong.'

'May I read it?' he asked softly.

Luna sighed, handing him the half-finished note. 'If you like.'

Dear Daddy,
I'm really sorry to be so silly, but I love my school here in Grand Cayman and I hate that spooky old place in Vermont. I will miss all my friends, especially Vicki. I love living in Whispering Cay, and can't bear to think of saying goodbye to the dog, but most of all I can't bear the thought of saying . . .

Royle noticed that several of the words were smudged, probably with tears he thought. He kneeled down next to his daughter and wrapped his arms around her tiny waist. Then turning her round to face him, he stroked her cheek; it felt moist under his fingertips.

Several strands of long, dark hair fell on to her face. He wound the curls around his finger and placed them gently behind her ear. He chuckled as they bounced back on to her cheek a moment later.

'Your hair is wild,' he told her, grinning.

She nodded and gave him a wobbly smile in return. 'I know, I get it from you.'

Royole raked his fingers through his own unruly mop. 'I'm lucky it's still all there these days, getting old.'

Luna never thought of her father as old. He was so vigorous, with a vitality that men half his age lacked. All her friends' fathers seemed like old men in comparison.

'You're not old at all, Daddy,' Grinning, she then added a little shyly, 'My friend Nancie says that her sister fancies you, thinks you're really handsome.'

'She must have seen me on a good day,' he winked. But Luna could see that he was flattered.

He took a deep breath. 'Baby, I think I've got us a solution. Well, more like a compromise actually. But this is a secret between you and me; you mustn't tell Mammy.'

Luna nodded solemnly, waiting for him to go on.

'I promise on my life–' he hated using that expression, but it always seemed to carry a lot of weight with Luna.

'Cross your heart,' she interrupted quickly.

He complied and made the sign of the cross on the breast pocket of his shirt.

'—that if you don't like Highclaire Academy after . . . six months, then you can come home and there'll be no more talk of going away to school.' Royole was pleased he had come up with this offer. His voice was lighter, 'Well, what d'you say, is it a deal?'

Luna thought about the proposition and then hit her father with one of his own favourite catch-phrases. 'Can I have that in writing please?'

Royole roared with laughter.

Luna barely spoke on the long drive from New York to Grafton, Vermont.

Royole tried to interest her in the picture-book scenery as the car sped through meticulously restored villages, with perfect, white clapboard homes, and pretty, cherry-red shops. It was a spectacular September day, the sun warm but not too hot. The world outside the car window looked sparkling and clean; it was easy to imagine that it had just been freshly created, and the reluctant schoolgirl began to respond to her surroundings.

But when Royole reached across to find his daughter's hand, covering it with his own, it was very still and cool.

'We're almost there. How do you feel?'

'Terrified.'

He squeezed tightly. 'You're going to be fine. In fact, Miss Fergusson, I think you are going to knock 'em dead.'

A wan smile flitted across her face, joining up a sprinkling of dark brown freckles across the bridge of her nose. She returned the pressure on his hand.

'I'm not so sure about that Pa, but I'll try my best for you.'

'That's my girl!' He liked it when she called him 'Pa'.

The car slowed down and indicated left. Luna felt a sharp pain in her stomach as she spotted the discreet sign, 'Highclaire Academy', set into a curved stone wall sweeping towards imposing wrought-iron gates.

The gates were open and the limo cruised up a wide gravel drive.

Sunlight dappled the windscreen as they passed under a thick canopy of sugar maple. Beyond the trees a herd of brown dairy cows were grazing in an open pasture.

Suddenly the drive veered sharply to the right and a handsome, turn-of-the-century house came into view in its peaceful parkland setting.

Luna had been to the school once before, but it had been on a dark winter's day. On that occasion the house had been snow-capped and shrouded in freezing fog; it had seemed like the most forbidding place in the world.

Today though it looked different. It was much more attractive, inviting almost, as bright sunshine draped the white colonnaded porch in a warm glow.

The car ground to a halt and Luna spotted a tall, extremely thin woman striding down the four-deep steps leading from the front door.

'OK baby, this is it,' announced Royole.

He heard her sharp intake of breath. She was chewing her bottom lip, something she always did when she was nervous.

Using both hands, Luna tried to smooth down her wild, springing hair before stepping out of the car. She hoped that she didn't look as nervous as she felt.

'Good morning Mr Fergusson, delighted to see you again! I do hope you had a good trip?' The tall woman peered past Luna into the car. 'Mrs Fergusson not with you this time?'

'No, unfortunately my wife's suffering from a nasty attack of bronchitis. She's confined to bed at the moment.'

'I am sorry. Please give her my regards.' Roberta Lee-Jones, administrative assistant to the head of the school, extended a birdlike hand, noticeably small in comparison to the rest of her body. 'Luna, very nice to meet you.'

Luna realized she had never seen anyone with so many wrinkles. The smiling face in front of her resembled a road map. She glanced sideways in her father's direction. He beamed on cue, hoping to look encouraging. But Luna had already decided that she disliked the slightly priggish administrator, and if they were all like her she doubted she'd be staying at Highclaire even for the six-month duration of the pact.

Shading her eyes with her hand, Miss Lee-Jones glanced past Royole and Luna as a gleaming red Porsche convertible screeched to a halt in front of them.

A leggy teenager clambered out, followed by someone who looked like her elder sister. The younger girl leaned against the bonnet of the car. She was dressed in white shorts and a navy blue tennis sweater with a logo on the breast pocket. Pulling off dark sunglasses, she tossed her long, blonde hair. It fell into a tangled mass across her face so, using her sunglasses like a hairband, she secured it on the top of her crown.

Luna thought she looked very chic.

The girl smiled warmly in Luna's direction. Her blue eyes, so pale they were almost transparent, were twinkling with amusement.

Luna liked her on sight.

'Welcome back, Susan.'

Miss Lee-Jones called the girl's name, but a look of horror clouded her face as the elder sister sashayed around the car. Her shapely body was clothed in a very short mini-skirt and Roberta Lee-Jones immediately looked in the direction of Royole, who was obviously enjoying the blatant display of long, shapely legs.

In fact the teaching staff at Highclaire had all breathed a huge sigh of relief when Caroline Forrester had graduated last year. Now they only had one Forrester to cope with, Susan, who was less outrageous. They all put it down to the problem of 'Rich kids'.

'Luna's a new girl,' Miss Lee-Jones was telling Susan. 'So you might as well be assigned to show her round after lunch. She's in your house.'

'Which grade?' the girl interrupted.

'Ninth grade,' Luna said hopefully, delighted when Susan exclaimed, 'Same as me.'

113

Luna smiled shyly, inclining her head. She was eager to say how pleased she was that Susan was in her year, but worried that she might sound pushy.

Susan was studying the new girl with interest. '*Luna*, what an unusual name.'

'It was her great-great-grandmother's slave name.' Royole's deep baritone made this announcement with more than a hint of pride. 'And she would have been a very proud woman today, to see her namesake starting at a wonderful institution like this.'

Luna blushed profusely at this, glaring at her father.

Susan observed the unusual-looking ninth-grader from under half-closed lids. Luna's feline-shaped eyes gleamed with an excited warmth, and Susan envied her pale coffee-coloured skin, thinking how wonderful to be that colour naturally, without spending hours in the sun.

'I think it's a cool name. Don't you, Caroline?'

The elder Forrester, who was chewing gum, was more interested in Royole than his daughter. One of her best friends was having a wild affair with a black fitness trainer, and had told her that it was the best sex ever. She wondered where the handsome father was going after he'd left his daughter at school. Because if he wasn't in a rush, she knew a great place for lunch quite nearby . . .

Royole watched the interaction between the two younger girls with concerned interest. He was aware of Luna's vulnerability, and knew how easily she could be influenced by anyone more worldly.

He had an insane urge to march her to the car and drive straight to the airport, back to the safe haven of home, where he could keep a watchful eye on her. But the thought of Caron's reaction was enough to banish any such idea. And with that in mind he forced himself to say his goodbyes to his only daughter.

Gritting his teeth, he pulled her close, stroking the top of her head. 'Remember our promise, baby. Six months.

If you don't like this place after that, then you're outta here.'

With Miss Lee-Jones hovering discreetly in the background, Luna stood hand in hand with her father at the limousine.

'I'm going to miss you, Pa.' Biting her bottom lip, and determined to be brave, she willed herself not to cry. She could do that later, when she was alone.

Royole felt like he'd swallowed a lump of lead, and had to force his voice to sound cheerful as he ruffled the top of her head again.

'Don't forget you get really long vacations here, and I'm up in New York on business such a lot that it'll be no trouble for me to pop up and see you. Hey, how about we go skiing in Vermont this winter? Just you and I. Mammy would hate it, she's such a warm-weather bird.'

'I'd like that.'

Luna's voice was very small. She wanted him to go, and quickly. She wasn't sure how much longer she could hold out without bursting into tears.

'I think that I'd better go now Daddy. I don't want to be late for lunch on my first day.'

He reached out to take her in his arms. He wanted to hug her one last time.

But she stepped back bravely, and began to back away from him, the gravel crunching under her feet as she lifted her hand to wave.

Royole was suddenly struck by an image of Serena, the way she had looked the day he had taken Luna from her. He watched with a surge of sadness as his daughter ran up the path into the house. She didn't turn to wave as he expected, and so he turned to climb back into the hired limo.

'She'll be fine. The first few weeks are hell, getting settled in and all, but after that it's smooth sailing.'

Caroline Forrester was talking to him from her car window.

'Tell me about it,' sighed Royole.

'I'd love to. I know a great seafood place not far from here. I can give you an insight into all the highs and lows of Highclaire Academy over jumbo shrimp and Chardonnay.'

Royole was tempted, it would certainly lighten his mood; but a glance at his watch told him he had to be on the way back to Manhattan for his cocktail meeting with an important client.

'Some other time perhaps.'

'*Any* time,' she responded in a throaty, teasing tone and laughed cheerfully. Leaning out of the car window, she handed him a card. 'Call me next time you're in Boston.'

Ramming her foot hard on the accelerator, she sped off down the drive, long, blonde hair flying in the wind.

Royole arrived at the Carlyle Hotel on Madison at ten minutes to seven after a non-stop drive from Vermont. He was stiff from the journey, and longing for a drink.

He loved the Carlyle. To him it epitomized everything he enjoyed most about New York. And the pre-war opulence that still prevailed in the hotel's elegant suites and distinguished public rooms. In so many of the newer luxury hotels, one just felt anonymous. Here it was almost like belonging to a private club; the service was understated and charming, and never seemed contrived.

After an early dinner, he liked nothing better than to sit in the renowned Café Carlyle sipping a nightcap, whilst listening to the incomparable Bobby Short on piano. Tonight, strolling through the lobby, he waved to Emilio the concierge and stepped into the elevator just before the doors closed. Glancing at his watch, he calculated he had less than fifteen minutes to shower, shave and change before his meeting.

Pushing open the door to his room, he almost slipped on the pile of messages on the floor. He flicked through them hastily. One was from Caron: could he call her back *asap*; another was from Howard Silverman, his lawyer; and the third was from Ken Bowman, the English investment broker he had dashed back from Vermont to meet.

Royole read that message: 'Due to unforeseen circumstances, I have been held up in London. I will call your office tomorrow to make an alternative appointment. Please accept my apologies.'

Royole screwed up the piece of paper and dropped it on to the bedside table. Sitting on the bed, he pulled his tie loose and undid the top button of his shirt before leaning across to call room service. He ordered a large Jack Daniels, on the rocks.

Ken Bowman had called him last week from London, saying he had a client with a very large portfolio. Well, they'd just have to meet in Cayman now, or in New York when he next came up in a couple of weeks.

The ringing of the door bell interrupted his train of thought. He took the small tray from the waiter and signed his bill with an untidy signature.

Propping two pillows behind his head, Royole sipped his drink, trying to decide whether to ring Caron now or in the morning. He was tired and couldn't be bothered with any cross-questioning. *Where was he going to dinner? Who with?* She was convinced he was having a passionate affair with some woman in Manhattan. Royole often wished he was.

There had been a couple of dalliances, but nothing serious. Nothing to match the magic he'd experienced with Serena the day they'd made Luna. And there had been too many times over the years when he'd been forced to admit that he'd been a fool to let her go.

He decided to ring Caron in the morning, when he could make the conversation brief; when there was always another meeting to rush to, or an overseas call to take. His thoughts then switched to Vermont and Luna's face as she had said goodbye. He was vaguely aware that something had come between them when she'd backed away from him, a little bit of her had gone. He had lost his little girl.

He drank the remainder of his whiskey, then whispered into the empty glass, 'I'm going to miss you, my baby.'

His eyelids felt heavy. They fluttered twice, then closed. His head dropped on to the soft mounds of the pillows, and he was asleep within minutes, dreaming vividly. Of Luna and himself.

They were running hand in hand through an endless corridor; dazzlingly white, lit by hundreds of bright bulbs, all suspended at different lengths from the ceiling. There were no doors or windows, and he wasn't even sure where they were running to. But he knew why it was vital to keep going.

Serena was waiting for them. He was certain she was there. But he woke long before they ever reached the end.

Chapter Ten

'You must understand, Lady Frazer-West, that we cannot tolerate such behaviour. If Lucinda intends to continue being so disobedient, then I'm afraid I have no option but to ask her to leave. She has an extremely disruptive affect on the rest of the girls in her year, who are all studying hard for their exams. Lucinda seems to think that work is for fools.'

Miss Hazel Reed, headmistress of Radford House School, was sitting behind a polished desk. The top, inlaid with dark green leather, was scratched and worn; a vase of fresh peonies stood next to a silver framed photograph of Miss Reed's mother and father.

She drummed her fingers on top of a pile of files.

Looking around the small study, with its faded velvet curtains and stained carpet, reminded Serena of her own schooldays and the dread of standing in front of the head-mistress in a room similar to this.

'To be perfectly frank, Lady Frazer-West, we feel Lucinda is unsuited to our school . . . but we are willing to give her another chance.'

Serena, her long legs elegantly crossed, arranged her lovely face in an expression that was meant to look contrite.

'I'm very sorry. Lucinda, as you know, is an only child. Her father has always indulged her, she's become spoilt.'

'I'm patently aware of that Lady Frazer-West,' the headmistress agreed.

Serena could have done without this patronizing attitude and would have derived great pleasure from telling Miss Reed to stuff her snooty school right up her backside. Instead, making an enormous effort, she smiled politely.

'I give you my word that she will improve next term.'

Miss Reed did not leap at this prospect. Leaning back in her wing-chair, she made a suggestion of her own.

'Lucinda is a very talented actress, have you ever considered sending her to drama school? There are several good ones in London, I believe, and her drama teacher would agree, that she would benefit from the more carefree atmosphere of that type of school, rather than the academic discipline of the system we favour here.'

There was no immediate response from Serena, so the headmistress continued.

'And perhaps Lucinda would be happier at day school, some girls are not suited to a boarding situation. Think about what I've said and discuss it with your husband. We all want what's best for Lucinda . . . I'm sure.'

Miss Reed stood up and walked from behind her desk. Every time she met Lady Frazer-West, she had to remind herself that this stylish young woman with the neat figure, flawless skin and glittering blue eyes, was actually the thirty-something mother of a thirteen-year-old.

'I do hope Lucinda enjoys her exeat, and finds the time to think long and hard about her future. I must reiterate that I'm not sure this is the right school for her.'

'I think I know Lucinda better than anyone,' Serena commented in a resigned sort of way, 'My daughter is exactly like me at the same age, not only physically but in temperament. And I hated my boarding school.'

A *well-that-explains-everything* expression settled on Miss Reed's features. 'Oh, I see.'

Fucking self-righteous little prig, Serena thought as a long-repressed memory of a hated maths teacher popped unbidden into her mind. With characteristic unpredictability, her manner changed abruptly.

'Miss Reed,' she said brightly. 'I'm going to save you the trouble of expelling my daughter, because you and I both know that's what you intend to do sooner or later anyway. Take it from me, Lucinda will not be back next term.'

The headmistress replied in a stilted voice. 'I think you have made a very wise decision, Lady Frazer-West.'

'Good. Then you can tell that to your board of governors when my husband withdraws our financial support for the new sports centre. I know they're going to be very disappointed.'

Serena laughed, clearly enjoying herself at last. 'I'll see myself out, thank you.'

She left the study and walked down the deserted hallway to the dayroom where Lucinda was waiting. She was sitting alone, bolt upright in an uncomfortable wooden chair, flicking through a worn copy of the *Lady*.

Lucinda looked up when her mother walked into the room, her eyes wide and fearful. She was biting her bottom lip in Serena's own mannerism. 'I'm sorry Mummy, I really am. I don't know why I do these things.'

Serena knew she should be angry, instead she reacted with a sharp pang of sympathy. It was bloody tough being a thirteen-year-old, constantly being told what to do by a bunch of adults who often got their own lives wrong.

'I know why you do them, Lucinda.' She meant, *because you are my daughter*.

'You *do*?' Lucinda looked bewildered. The warm smile and soft tone of her mother's voice was not what she'd expected. 'Hasn't she expelled me then?' her voice quivered.

'No, she has not. I've told Miss Reed that you are not coming back. This place isn't good enough for you.'

Lucinda couldn't believe her ears. She beamed. 'You really told old Reed Warbler that!'

Serena nodded, 'I've decided that we're going to find another school for you. One where you'll be happy.'

'Mummy, can I go to day school in London? My old friend Charlotte goes to St Paul's now, and loves it.'

Her voice was full of hope.

'Darling, you're not academic enough for St Paul's; but let's talk to Daddy about it when we get home.'

Lucinda was so appreciative it was pathetic. Together they cleared out the study and dormitory in less than half an hour, making several journeys up and down stairs, laden with boxes and carrier bags. Most of the girls had already left for their exeat and the school was deserted.

Within minutes Lucinda was letting out a loud whoop as the chauffeur-driven Bentley sped past the school gates. Radford House School was history, and she, for one, had no regrets.

'You've done *what*, Serena!'

'For the third time, Nicholas. *I have taken Lucinda out of school*. What's the point of keeping a child somewhere she's so miserable?'

'But Radford's a wonderful school! My cousin went there and loved it.'

'Your cousin was, and still is, too good to be true. She hasn't got a spark of life in her. Even her own mother admits as much. Lucinda's a tomboy. And she's creative; I think we should send her to drama school, or somewhere that concentrates on the arts.'

'And what good do you think that will do? Lucinda needs a first-class education if she's to go to university.'

'And who says she wants to go to university?' Serena retorted in exasperation.

She could feel herself losing the situation, and knew that if she pushed Nicholas too far he would overreact. So, treading carefully, she reined in.

'OK Nicholas, OK, I hear you.' She raised both hands

in submission, then walked over to pour herself a gin and tonic from an antique drinks trolley, not asking Nicholas if he wanted one.

He stood with his back to her, looking out of the tall windows on to Pelham Crescent, his collarbone jutting out from under the fine, lawn-cotton shirt he was wearing. Apart from a slight thickening around his waist, Nicholas's body had changed little since they'd first met. He loathed exercise of any sort, and Serena was constantly reminding him how lucky he was to stay so slim – whilst she was forced to join boring aerobics classes to stop adding unwanted inches.

'I only want the best for her Serena, you know that.'

He was beginning to sound defeated already. This boosted her confidence and, taking a sip of her drink, she planned her strategy, knowing that she had to play on the fact that Nicholas would do anything for Lucinda.

She had to make him feel guilty. Changing her tone to sound more cajoling, she smiled sweetly and delivered her lines.

'I know you adore her, darling. So, if you truly want the best for her, please don't send her away to another boarding school. She'll only hate you for it.'

He inclined his head, revealing a small bald patch at his crown, and contemplated the beige-carpeted floor before speaking.

'I don't think she's old enough to know her own mind yet.'

'She *is* old enough, Daddy.'

Lucinda's sophisticated voice belied her thirteen years. She was tall for her age, and puberty had endowed her with hard budding breasts, which embarrassed Nicholas every time he glimpsed them pushing against the thin fabric of her school blouse.

'I was coming downstairs and heard my name. You're not angry with me, are you Daddy?'

His rigid expression relaxed instantly, softened by a smile that was reserved for Lucinda alone. 'No, of course not, darling. It's just that you're still too young to be the judge of your own future.'

Throwing back her long hair, the same colour and texture as her mother's, Lucinda did something out of character. She walked away from Nicholas and grabbed her mother's hand in a spontaneous gesture.

'Mummy understands, I know she does. She hated school when she was my age. She told me she tried to run away *twice*.'

Serena squeezed her daughter's hand, aware that something had changed between them. This was the first time Lucinda had ever reached out to her, she was determined not to let her down.

Mother and daughter locked their eyes in mutual intent.

When Serena spoke her voice was resolute. 'I think she should go to stage school in London, if she can gain a place.'

Nicholas looked from one determined face to the other. 'Over my dead body,' he bellowed at them, hurt by Lucinda's defection.

Then, speaking in a tone that was much quieter but just as adamant, he issued a warning. 'And just you remember who pays the school fees.'

Six weeks later Lucinda went away to Hastings, a progressive co-ed which offered a nurturing atmosphere for those with creative gifts.

It was a compromise.

Nicholas had been opposed to the choice and had fought a long, hard battle to send her to Roedean. He had only conceded defeat when his own mother had intervened in defence of Hastings.

On the morning she was to start school, Lucinda awoke very early to the sound of rain hammering on her bedroom window. She lay listening to the downpour, refusing even to think about Hastings, and what she might encounter there, having already made up her mind that at the first opportunity she was going to run away.

It was the only thing she could think of to punish her father whom she hated with all the fervour of a thwarted teenager.

Yawning loudly, she stumbled out of bed to open the curtains. She was perversely pleased it was such a depressing day, sunshine would have been inappropriate.

She stayed in her room for most of the morning, watching a little TV and not wishing to see either of her parents. She had nothing to say to them, it had all been said.

It was almost noon when she heard a single knock on her bedroom door, then her mother came in. Serena's eyes were red and slightly swollen. Lucinda suspected that she'd been crying.

'Your father wants to see you before you go, Lucinda. He's very upset that you refuse to talk to him. I suggest that you at least say goodbye.' Serena studied her daughter, regretful that her own relentless coaxing had failed to budge Nicholas.

Lucinda still hadn't accepted that she couldn't go to school in London. She loved her home.

She would miss June's wonderful cooking, and her own four-poster bed. She longed to sleep in it every night.

Lucinda's first letter home arrived six days later; five untidy pages full of life at Hastings. It was addressed to Serena.

The dorms were spacious and bright. Her bed was a bit hard, but she was sure she would get used to that. She had made a friend called Gaynor and she had fallen in love with her drama teacher, who had long hair tied in a ponytail. The food was barely edible, but at least she wasn't going to get fat. The atmosphere made Radford House seem like a prison camp.

Serena was delighted to find the letter chatty and cheerful. She wrote back the same day, telling Lucinda how Percy, their pug, had successfully pitted his wits against an Alsatian in Hyde park. She mentioned that Nicholas was going away on business, but would be back for her exeat weekend in three weeks' time. She surprised herself by writing four pages and signed off 'Ciao for now', which was a catchphrase with Lucinda.

Nicholas had refused to discuss Lucinda, and Serena knew it was futile to broach the subject. He would talk about her in his own time.

For her own part, she filled her lonely nights, whilst Nicholas was away on business, with Robin – a young stockbroker who was much too good-looking, and far too aware of it.

Before him there had been David, a sensitive artist type from Shepherds Bush. He was history as soon as he became too possessive, wanting her to leave Nicholas for his untidy studio.

Serena had been quite happy to fuck on his unmade bed, smoke some of the best marijuana she had ever had, and drink instant coffee laced with brandy from cracked mugs. But only once a week.

The mere thought of living like that every day appalled her, even if she had been in love with him.

Love? What was the meaning of love, Serena often pondered, usually after a session of unsatisfactory sex. Was it the lust she found in the arms of other men; telling her how much they loved her, when really only intent on screwing her?

Or was it what Rachel Sawyer seemed to have in the quiet, domestic calm of her new marriage to a very dull poet who struggled to string a sentence together?

It certainly couldn't be what her own parents had gone

through. They had spent their lives in long, dreadful silences that hurt far more than volatile arguments would have done.

And it was not what she and Nicholas had together. Trapped in a marriage of convenience, like so many of her friends, Serena fulfilled the role of mother, hostess, and occasional lover. Nicholas provided the lifestyle she had become accustomed to, and she was loath to lose it.

Yet in her soul, where she had so carefully buried her past, Serena knew that love, the real kind, was something that had touched her only very briefly. So briefly that the memory, like an old black and white photograph, had faded.

One day of love. Was that all she deserved? she sometimes asked herself.

Then wondered with dread if that was all she was ever going to have.

Chapter Eleven

'I can't believe what you're saying, Nicholas. You've sold Redby Hall without consulting me!'

Serena, dressed in her bathrobe, had been about to cut the top off a boiled egg when Nicholas gave her the bombshell.

'You know you've always preferred living in London, Serena,' Nicholas reminded her. 'Now be honest, how many times have you said that you hate both the country *and* Redby Hall?'

She could not deny it.

She did hate the country and all country pursuits; horses, green wellies and boring country-house cocktail parties did nothing for her. But to sell Redby, without even discussing it, made her hot with resentment.

'Nicholas, just because I hate the country, that doesn't mean you can just up and sell a major piece of property that belongs to us.'

She stressed the *us*, then shouted through the open door towards the kitchen, 'June!'

The housekeeper appeared a moment later, face flushed scarlet.

'This bloody egg is under-cooked. You know I can't stand them runny,' snapped Serena.

June quickly whipped the offending egg away, perplexed. Lady Serena rarely lost her temper, and certainly never over something so trivial.

'I'll boil another one straightaway, m'lady.'

'Don't bother, I'll just have some toast.' Serena reached across the table as June scuttled back to the kitchen without another word.

Mildly amused, Nicholas spoke from behind his newspaper.

'Was it really necessary to take out your annoyance with me on poor June, who never has a cross word for anybody . . .'

Serena interrupted, hissing. 'Oh do shut up, Nicholas! You self-righteous bastard.'

He was about to retort when a half-eaten slice of toast came winging through the air to land smack on top of his newspaper, staining his tie, leaving a greasy trail of butter and orange marmalade in its wake.

Wiping his fingers on a napkin and taking a deep breath, he chastised her condescendingly. 'Sometimes you act just like an overgrown schoolgirl, and I can't begin to tell you how much that irritates me.'

'Yes, well I wouldn't dare discuss what irritates me about *you* Nicholas,' she retaliated. 'It would take far too long.'

A slight flicker of hurt crossed his face.

She ignored it and continued in the same biting tone. 'The one thing that springs immediately to mind is your total unwillingness to discuss anything other than the banal. I'm your wife for God's sake. I think I deserve to be consulted occasionally. And what about Lucinda? She loves Redby. She's going to be very upset.'

Serena's voice softened considerably. 'I had sort of hoped she would live there when she got married. It's a wonderful place to raise children.'

Nicholas had not thought about Lucinda. The house as far as he was concerned was a drain on his rapidly dwindling fortune, and had played host to the ghosts of his own unhappy childhood. He had been pleased to be rid of it.

'And it's not even as if we need the money.' Serena now sounded bewildered.

Nicholas lowered his eyes.

This immediately made her suspicious. 'Or do we? Is that it? Tell me, I need to know.'

Standing up, she stepped towards the door, closed it quietly, and walked back across the room to Nicholas. He sat there; only pretending, now, to read his newspaper.

Serena dragged the paper roughly away from his face, 'For once in your fucking life just tell me the truth. Is that so difficult?'

Slapping her hand away, he stood up, folded his paper meticulously and tucked it under his arm. 'I'm going to change my tie. Then I am going to the office. I have an important meeting at nine-thirty.'

He started to walk away.

Serena found the urge to lash out at him almost unbearable. 'At least tell me one thing, who's bought Redby?'

'How many times do I have to tell you, Serena, to keep your voice down. Why let the staff know all our business?'

She took a deep breath and, with great effort, lowered her voice. 'OK, now tell me. *Who*?'

'A Middle Eastern Prince who paid far more than it's worth. I made a very good deal.' He stopped at the door and turned. 'By the way I won't be home for supper this evening, so don't wait up.'

He looked for her reaction, expecting to be questioned.

There was a heavy silence, but no visible response from Serena. He sighed and left the room.

She stayed in the same position, staring at the closed door for a long time. Nicholas was hiding something, she was positive of that. Well, he was going away on business in a few days' time, so she would do a little investigative work of her own. If he refused to tell her what was going on, then she would just have to find out for herself.

*   *   *

It was a warm, early autumn day.

The sun was shining brightly when Serena, elegant in a rust-coloured wool suit and low-heeled shoes in exactly the same shade, stepped out of a black cab in Curzon Street, Mayfair.

She paid the cabbie, giving him a generous tip.

'Thanks a lot, miss,' he shouted.

Serena smiled, flattered at his use of the word *miss*, and walked smartly towards an early Victorian building which had once been an elegant town house. She pressed an intercom switch next to a green door where a gleaming brass sign read 'Frazer-West Properties'.

'Yes, who is it?'

A voice she recognized instantly as Liza the receptionist.

'Lady Frazer-West.'

A buzz sounded. Serena pushed hard and the door swung open. She stepped into a hall decorated in the pale blue and beige wallpaper which she herself had chosen from Colefax and Fowler the previous year.

Liza looked up from her desk, a smile lighting up her friendly face. 'Good morning Lady Serena, good to see you.'

'Good morning Liza, and a wonderful morning it is too. How are you?'

'I'm fine,' she nodded, putting down her pen.

'And how are the family?' Serena enquired politely, regretting the question as soon as she'd uttered it, convinced she was now going to be subjected to a long reply. She had a vague recollection of a baby being thrust in front of her a few months previously on a rare visit to the office.

'Here, I've got some photographs,' Liza was saying enthusiastically, rummaging in her handbag whilst Serena groaned inwardly.

'She's so beautiful,' Serena had got as far as exclaiming

131

in response to a picture of an extremely pretty child with a mop of golden girls. It never ceased to amaze her how plain girls like Liza could produce such pretty babies.

But much to her relief, the phone rang and she was able to slip out of the reception area, waving as she left.

Nicholas's office occupied the entire top floor of the four-storey building. She only hoped as she climbed the curving staircase, holding on to the highly polished banister, that she would not bump into John Lawson, the financial controller – or Douglas Sissons, Nicholas's smarmy partner who never failed to give her the creeps.

It would be better all round if Nicholas never got to know she'd been to the office, so she had deliberately chosen lunchtime, anticipating that most of the staff would be out.

She was right; apart from the conscientious Miss Webster, Nicholas's secretary, who brought a neatly packed lunchbox every day. Usually with the same white sliced bread filled with cheese, ham or egg, a packet of crisps and an apple. Miss Webster was biting into her second cheese sandwich when Serena appeared.

'Lady Frazer-West, what a surprise,' she said, a couple of crumbs flying out of her mouth. Embarrassed she covered her lips with her hand, quickly swallowed and placed the remainder of the sandwich back in the plastic box.

'Good morning Miss Webster, how are you?' Serena had never been able to bring herself to call the secretary by her Christian name, 'Paulette'. It seemed so incongruous in the case of the woman in front of her.

'I'm fine thank you, Lady S. Catching up on all my filing now that Lord Frazer's away for a couple of weeks.'

'Have you been very busy then?'

'Well, the last few weeks have been hectic, what with the increase in the new Middle Eastern investments. Some days I don't know whether I'm coming or going.'

'I know. Nicholas has been coming home every evening of late talking about the Prince,' Serena said casually.

'I just wish they weren't in such a hurry. That Sheikh whatsis name, I can never pronounce it. Anyway, I'm sure Lord Frazer-West has mentioned him to you.'

'Of course,' Serena lied.

'Well, he's impossible. The man needs ten secretaries working for him.' She pushed a strand of permed hair off her brow. 'But I suppose out there in Kuwait they have millions of staff, tending to their every whim.'

'I'm sure they do,' Serena agreed with her, 'but it's very rude to expect people like you to jump through hoops when they're over here. "When in Rome, I always say . . ." She pointed to the half-eaten lunch. 'Don't let me keep you, Miss Webster. I just need to get something from Nicholas's office before he's back.'

'Of course, no problem. Take your time, I'll be right outside if you need me.'

Nicholas's office always reminded Serena of an exclusive gentleman's club with its eighteenth-century oak-panelling. Her high heels sinking into the thick pile of the specially woven carpet, she crossed the room, heading for the handsome turn-of-the-century partner's desk at one end. She was just looking at the photograph of Lucinda and herself on the desk when the phone rang. She jumped, then relaxed a moment later as Miss Webster took the call.

The top of the desk had been cleared of the usual office paraphernalia. She knew Nicholas kept a key to his private filing cabinet in one of the desk drawers. Trying every one and discovering they were all locked, Serena pressed the intercom switch.

'Miss Webster, do you have access to my husband's files? I can't seem to find the key in here.'

'Oh, you should have said. I'll just pop in with it.'

A couple of seconds later, Miss Webster appeared

around the door, waggling a small key. 'Make sure I have it back before you leave, Lady S, I'm responsible for the files, you see.'

'Of course, I'll only be a few minutes,' Serena smiled reassuringly, putting the secretary at ease.

'Well, I've got to pop out to the shops now. If I'm not at my desk when you leave, just leave it with Liza at reception.'

Serena smiled and then breathed a sigh of relief as the door closed, leaving her alone again. She used the key she'd been given and a panel swung open to reveal a double set of filing cabinets. The top cabinet contained property files, in alphabetical order.

There was a file dedicated to Nicholas's Lloyds transactions, and some appertaining to arbitrations and law suits. Scanning through them quickly, she could see that most of them were out of date, a couple going back to the early seventies.

Slamming the top cabinet shut, she tried the lower one. There were only two files there – both marked 'Capricorn', Nicholas's birth sign. Serena lifted them out, placing them on the top of the desk.

They contained several sheets of foolscap with lines of what looked like coded figures; they all seemed to form some sort of sequence, but it meant nothing to her. She was about to replace them when she noticed a letter. It was from an office in Beirut, addressed to Nicholas and dated two months previously.

Dear Nicholas,

Just a quick note to thank you for introducing me to Jeremy Gray. Delightful chap. I really believe he's going to be invaluable to us in the future; long-term perhaps, but I am a patient man.

I look forward to seeing you in London next month.

Meanwhile take care and remember to keep the night of the 24th October free, I have a very special surprise in store.

I look forward to seeing you soon.

Best wishes, and be well, my friend.

Nabil.

Jeremy Gray was one of Nicholas's oldest friends. They had virtually grown up together. He was charismatic, a politician who – according to Nicholas – was destined to be Prime Minister one day.

'*Nabil, Nabil,*' she repeated the name out loud, racking her brain, trying to remember where she'd heard it before.

Serena was perplexed. Nicholas was a dark horse. Just how dark, she was only now beginning to find out.

Replacing everything carefully, she shut the cabinets and locked the panel. Stooping to pick up her handbag from where she'd left it on the floor, something caught her eye. A partially screwed-up and torn piece of paper was lying in the bottom of the wastebasket.

Lifting it out and unfolding it, Serena recognized Nicholas's bold handwriting. It showed the following day's date at the top, and underneath, 'Flight no. KZ 538 from Miami to Grand Cayman. Arrival Georgetown – 2.30 p.m.' Then the name of a hotel that had been scribbled out, and another one written underneath. But the paper had been torn and only two letters remained 'PA'.

Serena carefully folded this scrap and slipped it into her bag. She then left the office, closing the door and leaving the key to the files with Liza on her way out, warning her to give it to Miss Webster as soon as she arrived back.

It was pouring with rain when she stepped into Curzon Street.

'Shit! I'll never get a taxi now.'

She was about to walk back into the office to borrow

an umbrella, when she did in fact spot a taxi pulling up on the other side of the street, dropping someone off. Running swiftly across the road, she jumped into the back of the cab.

'Pelham Crescent, please.'

A planned shopping trip to Bond Street momentarily forgotten, Serena was now intent on returning home to call every hotel in Grand Cayman to see if they had a Frazer-West registered.

The cab driver began to chat amiably about the government. She answered in monosyllables and, thankfully, after five minutes he gave up trying to engage her in conversation. The journey across town took twenty minutes, but she hardly noticed the time, so absorbed was she with working out why Nicholas had gone to the Cayman Islands.

She knew very little about the Caymans except that they were in the Caribbean, British territory, and home to hundreds of off-shore banks. And she had read a novel many years ago about vast sums of laundered money banked in Grand Cayman by the Mafia.

The cab pulled up in front of her stylish, white stucco house. Serena paid the cabbie and walked towards the front door. The name *Nabil* still nagging her, she turned the key in the lock.

It was then she remembered.

A handsome young man from the Middle East had made a brief appearance at her wedding. He was Lebanese and he had been one of Nicholas's best friends at Eton.

Nabil Khoorey was his full name.

Chapter Twelve

Royole sounded his car horn.

A young man in a battered pick-up truck had careered dangerously out of a side street and swerved in front of him, almost causing a collision.

'Idiot!'

Royole mouthed the word. The teenager grinned in reply, raising his middle finger in a défiant gesture.

Royole was in a foul mood and felt tempted to stop and unleash his temper on the irresponsible youth, but it was raining heavily. It had been doing so continually for three days now.

The traffic on South Church Street, trying to get into Central Georgetown, the capital of Grand Cayman, was almost at a standstill. There was only one thing that irritated Royole more than being stuck in a traffic jam, that was waiting in a long queue to check in for a flight. To make matters worse, the air-conditioning in his car had broken down yesterday. Now he was sweating profusely, his shirt plastered to his back. Exasperatedly he selected a tape from the glove compartment. It was his favourite Vivaldi, 'The Four Seasons'. He turned the volume up to maximum.

As the soothing strains of 'Spring' washed over his jangled nerves, some of the tension eased out of him. His thoughts drifted to the telephone conversation he had enjoyed with Luna last night. She'd called him, literally bubbling with excitement at being chosen to swim in the school team. She'd made some good friends, including Susan Forrester, and after just five weeks at Highclaire, she seemed to have taken to the life like a duck to water.

Royole, in a perverse way, had been almost disappointed by her enthusiastic chatter. She had settled down much more quickly than he'd anticipated. Her newly acquired independence only served to illustrate how fast she was growing up. He knew he had to let her go, but he did miss seeing her bright, eager face in the evenings when he came home from the office. The house seemed dead without her presence, or her friends dropping by. It was as if a terrible hush had descended on it.

So by way of compensation he immersed himself in his work, whilst Caron tried frantically to fill their spare time; planning extravagant dinner parties, inviting new people who invariably bored Royole rigid. Last week she had come home laden with travel brochures: 'Paris in Springtime'; 'The Cipriani in Venice'; 'London in June for Ascot and Wimbledon'. None of it interested Royole. The mere thought of trailing around the capitals of Europe with Caron made Royole feel exhausted. His indifference was obvious, yet this did not seem to deter her. Pathetically, she continued to try and distract him. Yet the harder she tried, the more irritated he became.

It was almost ten a.m. when Royole pulled his Lincoln Continental into the car park of Fergusson Bank and Trust – on North Church Street, Georgetown.

As he ran towards the white multi-storey building, a quick glance at the sky showed several patches of blue seeping into the dark, sable blanket that had hung over the island for days. The rain had almost ceased by the time he reached the swing doors, and the foot of the staircase was filled with sunlight.

'Thank God it's stopped raining at last,' Royole said to the pretty, brown-skinned Caymanian seated at the reception desk.

She raised her navy blue eyes. 'But the forecast is bad, man.'

'Don't tell me that,' he said as the elevator doors opened. 'My wife has organized a garden party for over a hundred people on Saturday.' He stepped out of sight, pressing the button for the fourth floor.

Royole had barely walked into his office area when he was greeted by a breezy, 'Good morning, Mr Fergusson.'

The voice belonged to Dawn, his secretary of just two months, 'You have a Mr Bowman and another gentleman waiting to see you. I told them you wouldn't be long.'

Royole beamed at her, 'Give me five minutes to freshen up, then wheel 'em in.'

Royole found her responsive smile inviting, but familiarity with his staff had caused endless problems in the past, and he had learnt his lesson the hard way. Five years ago a beautiful American girl had joined the company as a financial controller. They had enjoyed an on-off affair for almost six months. His lust, unfortunately, had waned more quickly than hers, and he now had first-hand knowledge of the meaning of 'Hell hath no fury like a woman scorned.' She had attempted to destroy his reputation, and had almost wrecked his marriage.

Cold air greeted him on entering his spacious office. He instantly turned the air-conditioning to low, and took a clean shirt out of a side drawer in his desk.

He was still busy knotting his tie when Dawn knocked on the door. 'Come in,' he called, stuffing the dirty shirt under his desk as the door opened to admit Mr Bowman and another man dressed in a crumpled linen suit and a panama hat pulled down over his eyes.

Royole noted that Bowman appeared relatively dapper in his well-cut pin-stripe suit, and what looked like an old school tie, but there was something about him that didn't quite match the image.

'Good morning, Mr Bowman. Please take a seat.'

Royole indicated a chair on the opposite side of his desk, at the same time glancing across the room to where the other man was standing with his back towards him, looking at a portrait of Luna. Bowman took the hint and announced his companion.

'Allow me to introduce Lord Frazer-West.'

Nicholas was grinning, doffing his hat. 'Remember me Mr Fergusson?'

From long ago, an evening at Mango Bay came back into Royole's mind. Nicholas had the same air of arrogance as he'd had then, when they'd first met. And he hadn't changed much physically either. His slightly sunken cheeks were the only visible sign of ageing.

Royole's heart skipped several beats. The shock of seeing Nicholas again after thirteen years must have registered on his face since Mr Bowman became curious.

'Do you two know each other?'

'Suffice it to say, we have met,' Nicholas drawled in his Old Etonian voice. 'I have to confess, however, that I was unaware that the Mr Fergusson of Fergusson Bank and Trust was the same Fergusson I once knew in Jamaica. It never crossed my mind, and had I not spotted your photograph this morning, in the bank's promotional package, then I would have arrived here none the wiser.'

'Do you still have your beautiful home in Port Antonio?' Royole asked, genuinely interested.

'No, we sold up not long after we met you and bought a house in Barbados. Serena has a lot of friends there.'

'How is Serena?' Royole asked politely. As he waited for an answer a nerve twitched in the side of his neck, and he pretended to loosen his tie.

'As beautiful as ever, if not more so.' Nicholas fished in his pocket, producing a photograph out of a worn leather wallet. He handed it to Royole. 'This was taken six months ago.'

Royole felt a flood of emotion as he looked at the picture. His hand was shaking so much he was certain the others would notice. Nicholas was right. Serena was even more beautiful than he'd remembered. The photo showed her with her arms around a tall, slim girl with waist-length blonde hair, who looked exactly like a younger version of herself. They were both dressed casually in shorts and tee-shirts, and were standing in what looked like an English garden.

His stomach knotted as he noticed that the young girl had the same square jawbone, and almond-shaped eyes as Luna. To him, she was easily identifiable as Luna's half-sister.

'That's my daughter, Lucinda,' explained Nicholas proudly. 'She promises to be even prettier than her mother.'

There was a lump in Royole's throat which he had to clear noisily before he spoke. 'She's very lovely,' he agreed softly, handing the photograph back to Nicholas with reluctance, 'You're a lucky man.'

He'd injected just the right amount of approval in his comment without seeming idolatrous. Quickly resuming his brisk business edge he got matters back on track. 'So gentlemen, how can I help you?'

Bowman seemed to be the spokesman and he initiated proceedings. 'Lord Frazer-West wishes to open an account with your bank.'

Royole was about to ask how they'd heard of his bank, when Bowman answered his question before it was asked.

'You were recommended to us by an associate. Apparently you have a reputation, Mr Fergusson, for efficiency, excellent interest rates and, above all, discretion.'

'And may I ask who this associate is?'

Bowman's eyes narrowed. 'That, I'm not at liberty to say.' He made it obvious that it would be a waste of time to pursue the issue any further. 'What I can say is that

Lord Frazer-West wishes to deposit three million dollars today, if that's possible.'

There was an imperceptible movement of Royole's eyebrows; he spoke with a note of caution.

'I do hope you realize, gentlemen, that transactions of this size require a little time.'

'I'm aware of that, Mr Fergusson, it is my business to know these things.' Bowman sounded slightly affronted and retaliated with his own comment. 'I just hope that you, sir, are also aware that there are many other banks in Grand Cayman that would be delighted to accommodate us. We plan to stay here until the business is, how shall we say it, put to bed. Now then, is it possible to make a deposit today or not?'

'I'm sure we can arrange something,' Royole assured him. Three million dollars was not to be sniffed at.

There was a sound of clicking from the direction of Nicholas's briefcase and Royole struggled to conceal his shock as Nicholas turned the case around to face him. He saw rows of $100 dollar bills, all stacked in neat bundles.

'You do accept cash I assume,' Nicholas was smiling.

Three million dollars in cash was a dubious investment. Royole was tempted to tell him to take his money elsewhere, but something stopped him. He felt that the twist of fate which had brought Frazer-West into his own bank could not be ignored. Perhaps it would even lead to a meeting with Serena. 'Of course we accept cash, but I have to ask you how you came by the money.'

Nicholas ran his fingertips over the notes, saying, 'I sold my country estate in England to a gentleman from the Middle East. He wanted, or should I say insisted on, a cash deal. Who was I to argue? And what does one do with large amounts of cash? Invest it off shore, everyone told me. So, here I am.'

He pulled out a bundle of money, throwing it in Royole's direction. 'Lovely stuff, don't you think?'

'It's necessary,' Royole replied lightly.

'Come, Mr Fergusson, do I detect a cynicism? I'm sure you've made a lot of money from money in your time.'

He laughed as Royole, unwilling to be drawn, pressed an intercom switch.

'Yes Royole?'

'Chris, can you come into my office, please.'

'I'll be right with you.'

A few moments later Chris Johnson, Royole's right-hand man, a genial young Englishman, entered the office. Royole introduced him to both his visitors, and then got straight down to business.

'Lord Frazer-West wants to deposit three million dollars cash with us, Chris.' Royole pointed to the case. 'It has to be counted.'

'His lordship also wants to form an off-shore company, if possible,' added Bowman, directing his words towards the Englishman.

'That's no problem, we have a couple of shelf companies I can offer immediately. Amigal Inc. or Halcyon Corp.'

Nicholas looked up. 'I like the sound of Halcyon, I'll take that.'

'Fine sir,' Chris nodded, 'I'll make the necessary arrangements. You'll need one director and a company secretary. I can fill either if you wish.'

A wide, natural smile filled his face, and Nicholas thought he could trust him.

'You look like a fine young man to me, Chris, so a director of Halcyon you shall be.'

Chris glanced in Royole's direction, looking for nodded approval to take the money. 'You're aware, I assume, that the funds once deposited can be transferred anywhere in the world and in any currency.'

Nicholas returned to Chris with a detached gaze. 'I did make that assumption. And interest rates?'

It was Royole who replied. 'We charge one and a half

143

per cent plus accounting fee. You'll be given a code for your account, to be used at any time, should you prefer not to mention the company name.'

'Oh, it's such fun. Like something out of the movies.' Nicholas laughed, transforming his face to that of a mischievous schoolboy. Chris, however, was not amused. He shut the briefcase firmly and walked towards the door. 'It won't take me long to count it so, if you'd like to wait, I'll be able to give you your certificate of deposit.'

'Oh yes, we'll wait. You will look after that money won't you?'

'Don't worry sir, it's in good hands,' Chris assured him before leaving the room.

Royole spent the remainder of the morning with Bowman and Frazer-West, discussing off-shore banking and accounting procedures. This proved to be a difficult task as he found it almost impossible to concentrate properly. His mind was totally preoccupied with thoughts of Serena, as she'd looked in the photograph. As she looked *now*. So beautiful and fresh-faced, like a young girl.

They eventually broke up just before lunch, with a certificate of deposit for three million dollars from Chris, and with a subsequent meeting planned for the following morning.

Royole declined an invitation to join his new clients at the Palm Hotel, feigning a previous engagement. The combination of Bowman's body odour, plus Nicholas's condescending manner and schoolboy humour, had begun to grate. He felt he could easily detest Nicholas.

Alone again he felt drained, then depressed. He asked himself why. Having just taken a huge deposit, he ought to be ecstatic. But he picked idly at a tuna salad sandwich, leaving half of it, before going into a board meeting which lasted until four o'clock. After that, he left his office earlier than usual, a few minutes after four-thirty.

Royole was uneasy.

He didn't go straight home, instead he drove to Cayman Cai, on the tip of North Sound. It was his favourite part of the island. Many times he had considered building a house by the quiet waters of the sheltered cove, overlooking the Caribbean Sea. He took off his shoes and socks to walk along the deserted beach, wrestling with his thoughts. The reappearance of Nicholas Frazer-West had reopened old wounds from the past. He considered telling Caron, then thought about her reaction, deciding it was better to let sleeping dogs lie.

He paddled in the warm shallows for a while. The water was crystal clear, the reflection from the dying sun giving it a silvery quality. He sat for a while on a large piece of driftwood to marvel at the array of colour in the sky, from bright tangerine to the palest of pinks. But by the time he was picking his way back through the leathery leaves of morning glory that encroached upon the shoreline, the sun had already disappeared behind the horizon with a dramatic final flourish.

There were still doubts at the back of his mind. Three million dollars in cash. It had to be dirty money.

He knew he should have told Nicholas to take his cash elsewhere, yet the desire to be in contact with Serena again, after all these years, had won the battle with his conscience.

Royole drove home with Vivaldi on full volume, and it was dark when he pulled into the long drive of his house. Caron was waiting for him in the brightly lit hall as soon as he opened the front door. Her face was anxious.

'Where've you been, Royole? I called the office. I was worried that something had happened.'

'I'm not a child, Caron; for God's sake, do you have to keep permanent tabs on me?' He scowled at her and, suddenly feeling very tired, he started to walk upstairs.

'But you had a call from the office, they said it was urgent.'

'Was there any message?'

Caron could hear her own voice trembling. 'Yes. Dawn asked if you could ring Lord Frazer-West at the Royal Palm as soon as you got home. He's waiting for your call.'

Royole nodded slowly, avoided her questioning gaze and started to make an about-turn in the direction of the telephone in the drawing room.

'Why didn't you tell me he was coming to see you?' Caron's eyes were piercingly bright.

She had followed him and they were facing each other across a low marble coffee table. Royole had refused his usual dry martini, in favour of a Coca-Cola, which he was sipping slowly.

'I didn't tell you because I didn't even know myself until the damned man walked into my office this morning.'

She cut in sharply. 'You must have known! He made an appointment I presume.'

'Well, don't presume. What is this, Caron, the fucking inquisition?' He slammed his glass down on the table, spilling the Coca-Cola.

It dripped on to the white rug, a dark stain forming instantly. He ignored it.

'Why are you so angry, Royole?' Caron looked puzzled now.

'I'm sorry. I've had one hell of a day, that's all. I dislike Frazer-West intensely and, believe me, I had no idea he was coming to see me today. The appointment was made in the name of a Mr Bowman who, as it turns out, is Frazer-West's financial adviser. I really don't know why it should concern you anyway.'

He sounded vaguely contrite.

She blinked several times, as if to fight back tears, yet when she opened her eyes they were clear and focused. 'I would have thought that was patently obvious. The very name Frazer-West makes me feel physically sick.'

At that point all the suppressed resentment and jealousy, for the love Royole had showered on Luna over the years, came rushing to the surface. Love and attention that should rightly have been hers, she thought bitterly. She tried to restrain herself, but couldn't.

'You still care about *her*, don't you Royole. After all these years you still think about her.' It was more of a statement than a question.

'Of course not. Don't be ridiculous, Caron, I had one day with her. How could I care for someone all this time after only one day?'

'She lives on through her daughter though, doesn't she Royole? You see her face every time you look at your precious Luna.'

Caron picked up Royole's glass and smashed it against the marble table. She barely noticed as blood began to seep out of a gash on her palm.

Royole jumped up and, kneeling in front of her, used his handkerchief to bind her hand. She sat very still, silently crying.

Confronted by this display of her long-sufferance, Royole realized with deep regret that she knew he had never been able to love her.

'I'm so sorry, Caron,' he whispered, gently supporting her chin with his hand.

'Don't be sorry,' her voice had softened, 'It's not your fault. We're not responsible for the way we feel, only the way we act.'

Her eyes opened wide, and he could see that their gleam had gone.

'I still love you Royole, and I've got enough love for both of us. We've come a long way and we're still together. I need you. I can't imagine my life without you.'

Her voice drummed into his ears, the words hitting him hard. He knew he didn't deserve such unwavering love and loyalty. It made him feel bound by the very same

things that bound her to him. Or did he mean 'trapped'?
Royole sighed deeply.

Holding her bandaged hand gently, he fought an urge
to walk out, to escape. Drive to the airport, board the
first plane; any destination, as far away as possible. He
wished in that moment, more than anything else in the
world, that he could tell her he loved her and mean it.

'You're right, Caron, we have come a long way. You've
been a wonderful wife, and a great mother to Luna. I
don't tell you very often how much I appreciate that.
Thousands of women wouldn't have done it . . . not under
the circumstances.'

He dropped her hand into her lap and patted it tenderly.
Looking up, he was pleased to see that she was smiling.

'Thousands of women are not married to Royole
Fergusson.'

Chapter Thirteen

Nicholas had been home for exactly six minutes before Serena confronted him.

She had allowed him time to take off his coat.

They were sitting in the small morning room at the back of the house. It was bright and sun-filled, surrounded on three sides by windows that opened on to a small patio.

He had asked how she was; enquired about Lucinda; patted Percy a couple of times; and sent June off to make a nice pot of English tea, commenting as he always did that it was impossible to get a good cup of tea in America.

'What took you to the Cayman Islands, Nicholas? I didn't know that was on your agenda.'

He registered no surprise whatsoever, just as Serena had expected.

He had an inscrutable face. If she had just told him that his mother had given birth to triplets by Mr Cheng from the Chinese take-away, he would have looked just the same.

'Have I been to the Caymans, darling? That's news to me.'

'Don't lie to me Nicholas, please. You stayed at the Royal Palm Hotel, on Seven Mile Beach, in Grand Cayman from the twelfth to the fifteenth of this month.'

At last a flicker of shock appeared in his eyes, followed by a pause during which Nicholas seemed to weigh up his options.

'OK, OK, so I've been to Grand Cayman. It's not a crime is it?'

'No, it's not a crime. But, as usual, by being so secretive you make me think you've got something to hide.'

He poured two cups of tea from the tray June had brought, handed her one, then took a biscuit which he wolfed down in two bites.

'Are you having an affair Nicholas?'

He burst out laughing, the cup shaking in his hand, 'Don't be ridiculous darling, of course not! Then, suddenly he asked her, 'Would you mind?'

'Of course I'd mind. I'd be distraught,' she lied, deliberately trying to get him to drop his guard.

'I'm genuinely flattered, darling, I had no idea you cared so much.' Nicholas held out his arms. 'Come here.'

'Not until you tell me why you were in Grand Cayman.'

A smirk twisted his face. 'Always the same old Serena, eh, nothing for nothing.'

Ignoring his taunt, she sipped her tea in silence.

'How did you find out?' he asked eventually.

'I went to your office last week to recover a file on interiors I'd left there some time ago. A friend wanted some trade addresses. I used your office to make a couple of phone calls and found this.' She pulled a slip of paper from her jacket pocket and handed it to him.

He barely glanced at it before tearing it into minute shreds.

'I then came home and rang all the first-class hotels in Grand Cayman, until I found a Frazer-West registered at the Royal Palm. It wasn't difficult.'

The smirk had left Nicholas's face to be replaced by a smile of genuine amusement. 'Quite the little detective, aren't we? I assume you also checked whether there was a Mrs Frazer-West registered.'

'I tried, but they wouldn't divulge that information.'

'Ha! It's not only the Cayman bankers who are discreet. If I do have an affair I know where to conduct it now.'

She stood up and faced him. 'Are you going to tell me

why you went to Grand Cayman? Or do I have to nag and nag?'

He sighed resignedly, aware of Serena's tenacity. She was like a bloody dog with a bone, she'd never let go. 'I went there to invest money for our future, simply that.'

'Why the Caymans, why not here?'

Nicholas thought about being honest with her, deciding eventually that it was too risky. So he told her a little, hoping it would be enough.

'The Prince insisted on paying for Redby Hall in cash. So,' he spread his hands wide, 'I asked a few people discreetly, and they advised me to bank it off shore. Might as well have all the tax-free benefits . . . Then I was given the name of a bank in Grand Cayman not adverse to taking large cash deposits.'

Serena stared at him closely, watching for signs of deception or blatant lying. She could usually spot both. But his face was open and he was smiling easily. She decided that he was telling, if not the whole truth, then at least the best part of it.

'Darling, I'm telling the truth. Also, I cannot stress just how important it is not to discuss this with anyone. Do you understand?'

She nodded slowly. 'I do understand Nicholas, and I'm pleased you've told me.'

He looked relieved.

'Good! Well, now that we've got that out of the way, what about this?' He produced a package from under a cushion, where he had hidden it earlier.

'*Pour toi, chérie.*'

Nicholas handed her the gift. It was wrapped in ivory tissue and tied with dark gold ribbon. He studied her reaction as she slowly ripped open the tissue to reveal a mysterious box.

'Oh Nicholas! What is it?'

She sounded like an excited child as she lifted the lid

to find a half-open shell. Lifting it out, she then discovered a single, exquisite black pearl, gleaming ebony against the pink interior of the oyster shell.

'Nicky, it's amazing!' she exclaimed, touching the pearl with her fingertip, almost reverently. 'Thank you! Thank you so much. It's quite the most beautiful gift.'

Nicholas was beaming, warmed by her delight. 'Now you know the *real* reason I went to the Cayman Islands.'

Serena grinned and nodded, wondering if she would ever know the real reason. But the explanation he had given was plausible. She was satisfied, relieved to be free of the suspicions that had plagued her for over a week.

Unfortunately, her disquiet returned in full force when Nicholas took a nap later that morning.

She was in the study, sorting through some mail and making a list for a dinner party, when there was a knock on the door.

'Come in,' Serena called.

June poked her face around the door, 'Sorry to disturb you Lady S, but I found these, and some money, in Lord Frazer's suit pocket. Just as well we didn't send them off to the cleaners too.'

'Just as well,' Serena agreed as June handed her a small bundle of papers and left the room.

There was about thirty pounds in assorted notes, four American twenty-dollar bills and some Caymanian dollars. She glanced with interest at a blue bill with the head of Queen Elizabeth on the back. A few restaurant receipts and a hotel credit-card invoice. She was about to place them under a paperweight for Nicholas to look at later, when a card slid on to the desk in front of her.

FERGUSSON BANK AND TRUST LTD
Royole Fergusson – Chairman
North Church Street, Grand Cayman.

She read it, and reread it a dozen times.

By the time her shaking hands dropped the card, her entire body had started to shake as well. 'Get hold of yourself Serena,' she whispered, gripping the edge of the walnut desk.

She had thought that she had succeeded in burying Royole for ever. She had dug a deep enough grave for him . . . and Luna. And now, after all this time, thirteen years later, he had come back to haunt her.

She wondered how he looked now. If Luna resembled him, or her? If she was bright, pretty? She wondered if they were close and, most of all, if they were happy.

The shrill ringing of the telephone broke her trance.

She let it ring. It sounded several times before someone else picked it up. A few moments later she heard a soft rap on the closed door, followed by June's voice.

'It's Mrs Lesser for you m'lady, on line one.'

Serena was delighted. If there was anyone in the world she needed to talk to at that precise moment, it was Rachel.

'Rachel, how wonderful! I thought you were off to Outer Mongolia or somewhere – with the love of your life.'

'No, Saul has gone on his own.'

Rachel sounded tearful, and Serena was slightly irritated. Her wonderful, independent friend had turned into a hopeless mess since she'd married the manic-depressive Saul Lesser.

'He decided at the last minute that I'd just distract him. He needs to be alone to feel the vibes. You know, the usual crap.'

'You sound upset.'

'I am, and mad as hell. That's why I'm calling you. You know, a friend in need is a bloody pest. Well, how about asking this pest out for dinner and lots to drink?'

Serena sighed heavily, frustrated.

'I'd love to, only Nicholas has just arrived back this morning and I don't think he'd be very happy if I went out without him this evening.'

'I thought he was away until the weekend.' Rachel cursed under her breath.

Serena heard her and smiled. 'How about lunch tomorrow?' she suggested.

'I'm doing an ad campaign for a new fragrance, I'm supposed to be seeing one of the prima donnas in charge.'

'Another day?' Serena asked hopefully.

'Oh, she's a boring old fart anyway, and I'd much rather have lunch with you. Don't worry, I'll put her off.'

'San Lorenzo at one.'

'You got a date,' Rachel replied.

Serena replaced the telephone, still absorbed with Royole and Luna. She had never discussed them with anyone since that time in Rachel's flat thirteen years ago, and had deeply regretted sending her grandmother's necklace to Royole. It had been one of those crazy, spontaneous gestures, carried out in an emotional frame of mind. Rachel had never mentioned the subject either, respecting her need for discretion. It had become their unspoken secret.

She had kept a close check on Mrs Neil, learning that she had indeed sold up and left the country six months after she'd delivered the babies. Serena assumed she had joined her daughter in Spain, presumably using her 'silence' money.

Lucinda had been a very demanding baby, and Serena had often wondered how she would have coped with two of her. Over the years she'd gone through difficult phases where she had dreams of herself and Royole and the two girls. Only the girls were both black, jet black, much blacker than Royole, and they had blonde hair and brilliant blue eyes. She hadn't had those dreams recently, and

154

she fervently hoped they were not about to start again now.

'There you are, Serena.' Nicholas was standing in the doorway, smiling, bringing her back to reality. 'I've been looking for you everywhere. Lunch is served darling.'

He turned and she followed him out of the study, downstairs to the ground-floor dining room. And every step of the way, Serena had her hand in her pocket, clutching Royole's card.

'My advice is to leave well alone.' Rachel spooned a huge piece of tiramisu into her mouth.

'You're going to get fat,' Serena commented with a smile, sipping her cappuccino.

Her friend was undeniably plumper but, in Serena's eyes, she was possessed of the kind of timeless beauty that neither fat nor age could ever alter. It came from within.

They were sitting at a small table for two, in the corner of San Lorenzo, a huge potted palm obscuring the diners on the adjacent table. As ever, the clatter of conversation filled the busy restaurant.

'Let's face it Serena, I *am* fat. But, you see, Saul loves cuddly women,' she sighed with contentment. 'When I think of all those years I starved when I was modelling. Now it's so wonderful to eat . . . and eat . . . and eat.'

She chuckled, digging her spoon into the dessert. 'This is delicious, want to try some?'

'No thanks, I'm not hungry.'

'You're never hungry, sweetie. If you lose any more weight you'll fade away.'

Serena groaned with a hint of impatience. 'Rachel, my weight has not fluctuated, apart from during pregnancy, since I was eighteen. I'm the greyhound breed as my mother always says.'

'Thoroughbred filly, you mean,' Rachel commented through another mouthful.

Serena grinned, watching Rachel scraping the plate for the last few drops of double cream. She licked her lips before wiping them on a napkin, leaving behind bright red lipstick marks. Spooning two heaped sugars into a frothy cappuccino, she got back to the main conversation.

'Why open a can of worms? A very nasty can of worms, I might add. What can you possibly gain from it? Remember you were the one who made Royole promise to have no contact with you at all . . . *ever*.'

Serena looked down at her coffee cup. 'I know, I know, it's just that when I saw his name printed on the card yesterday, so official – *Chairman of Fergusson Bank and Trust* – it made him seem real again somehow. I began to imagine what he looks like now.

'Has he aged? How is he? Is Luna pretty? Does she look like me or him?

'Every instinct tells me not to contact him, yet there's this little nagging voice whispering in my ear. It's saying, why not just once, what harm will it do?'

Rachel looked at Serena from out of warm, brown eyes, clearly filled with concern.

'You know the harm it could do Serena. You've successfully buried all that. I have to admit, I admired the way you handled the whole affair at the time. It can't have been easy for you.'

Rachel noticed the flash of pain enter her friend's eyes, and wondered why on earth she wanted to dig up the past.

'It's just that I've asked myself countless times if I did the right thing, if I made the right decision.'

'As I remember it, darling, you didn't have a lot of choice at the time.'

Serena pushed her coffee cup to one side with perfectly manicured hands. She looked down at her nails, then up into Rachel's face, her eyes brimming with tears.

Rachel slid her hand across the table and patted the back of Serena's. 'Look at you, you look terrible. You're

156

shaking, you can't eat. You probably haven't slept. Is it worth it?'

Serena dashed a tear from her cheek.

'You must think about Lucinda. How would she react if she ever found out?'

'You're right, Rachel. I must confess I hadn't thought about Lucinda . . . or Nicholas for that matter. Too busy thinking about myself.'

Rachel was tempted to say that wasn't unusual, but bit her tongue. It wasn't the time or the place to lecture her dearest friend on her vanities and self-obsession. After all, Serena had enough good points, and they far outweighed the bad.

'Fancy another cappuccino?' she asked brightly. She looped her shoulder-length, brown hair around one ear, revealing a few grey strands.

'Yes, I'd love one,' Serena replied, pushing her chair away from the table to stand up. 'I must go to the toilet, back in a tick.'

She was wearing an oversized trouser suit in taupe and a cream silk shirt with a high collar. Rachel thought, as always, how elegant Serena looked. For her own part though, she was pleased that the pressures of having to look immaculate all the time had been lifted from her. Life was infinitely simpler now. She could wear loose-fitting clothes, indulge herself, and had never been happier.

The coffee reached the table at the same time as Serena arrived back. Sliding into her seat, she hissed under her breath.

'Don't look now, but the Princess of Wales has just come in.'

A low, whispering buzz descended on the restaurant as Diana was shown to her table.

'She's *so* beautiful,' Serena sighed.

'Too bloody good for him,' Rachel retorted with a sneer.

157

'That's a bit unfair,' Serena chided.

Rachel slurped her coffee noisily. 'You never did have great taste in men, Serena.'

Affronted, Serena was tempted to say that Saul was not exactly every woman's dream. And the one who'd preceded him had been an obnoxious bore. But she kept her mouth shut in the interest of peace, leaving the stage to Rachel.

'Personally I think Charles is a pain in the arse. Anyway, enough of royals, let's get back to Royole. I really hope you're not going to jeopardize everything for the sake of seeing him again.' She smiled slyly. 'But he must have been a great fuck.'

As soon as she saw her friend's face, Rachel wished she could eat her words.

'That's a bloody insensitive thing to say!' Serena looked hurt.

'Sorry. It just slipped out.' Rachel seemed genuinely repentant.

'He was good though, too bloody good. The best I've ever had.'

Inwardly Serena willed herself to stay in control. She took Royole's card out of her handbag, glanced at it briefly, then tore it into several pieces and dropped them into the ashtray.

'That's my girl!' Rachel applauded with relief. 'I think that calls for a drink.'

Without waiting for Serena to reply, she grabbed a passing waiter and ordered two glasses of house champagne.

It arrived in minutes and Serena drank hers very quickly, only half listening to the latest on Saul's new book of verse, and an article he was writing for the *Daily Mail* on the dying planet.

It was almost three o'clock when they left the restaurant. The two women hugged each other warmly on the pavement.

Rachel was going to the food hall at Harrods, and Serena had a hair appointment.

'I'll speak to you in a couple of days, don't forget you promised to sit on my charity committee next Wednesday,' Rachel reminded her.

'Oh, damn, I had forgotten about that.' Serena thought quickly, she'd arranged to go to a dinner party with friends. She would have to cancel. Rachel's do was more important, even though she wasn't entirely sure what the cause was.

'That's fine. I'll pick you up around seven p.m.,' confirmed Serena, then waved as her friend walked down Beauchamp Place, hips pulling at the seams of a dated wool suit that looked as if it had been purchased from Oxfam.

An hour later, Serena left the hairdresser and took a cab to Green Park.

She sat on a bench under a huge oak tree, watching the dogs snarling at other dogs. And the inevitable joggers, most of whom looked ready for a cardiac arrest. A few dirty old men. And several sets of young lovers, strolling hand in hand.

Serena thought long and hard about herself. She'd come to the conclusion that she was over-privileged, frivolous, extravagant, lazy and without any real purpose. For the first time in her life she felt an uneasy stirring of self-loathing.

She knew she had managed to manipulate Nicholas because he loved her. He truly loved her, and in his own peculiar way he made every effort to please her. He was stubborn, secretive, undemonstrative and withdrawn. But he was also magnanimous, tolerant and relatively undemanding.

She had an extremely generous allowance, a set of interesting if somewhat capricious friends, and had enjoyed several illicit, heady affairs.

So why this sudden emptiness, this hopeless depression that had descended on her since the discovery of Royole Fergusson's card?

Serena rarely questioned herself or her actions. She hated introspection. It always led to guilt, and she had discovered at a very early age that guilt is destructive. She decided to catch a cab home to Pelham Crescent instead of sitting aimlessly in the park.

The house was empty when she arrived.

Serena glanced at the grandfather clock in the hall, it was a few minutes after six. She remembered Nicholas was going out with some American clients for cocktails straight after work. Making her way up the three flights of stairs to her bedroom, she kicked off her shoes then padded into her dressing room and, opening the top drawer of a small, antique French commode, she took out a key. Kneeling down, she opened another drawer at the base of her dressing table. Taking out a piece of paper with a shaking hand, she moved quietly back into the bedroom.

She locked the door.

Sitting on the edge of the bed, she picked up the telephone. Her hand was hot and clammy as she gripped the receiver tightly. The fingers on her other hand were shaking uncontrollably as she dialled the number.

'Fergusson Bank and Trust Ltd. Can I help you?'

Serena didn't reply. There was a short pause.

'This is Fergusson Bank and—'

'Can I speak to Mr Fergusson,' she interrupted, her voice sounding very small.

'I'm sorry, can you speak up, I can't hear you madam.'

Serena cleared her throat, 'Can I speak to Mr Fergusson please?'

'May I ask who's calling?'

'Tell him it's Lady Frazer-West.'

'One moment please.'

The moment seemed like an eternity. Then she heard him. A hint of wonderment in his tone, but the deep voice unmistakably his.

'Serena, is it really you?'

It was then that her courage failed her. She felt physically sick, her throat so constricted she thought she might choke.

Serena slammed the telephone down and fell on to the bed, squeezing her eyes shut and clamping a hand across her mouth in a vain attempt to stop the sobs.

She thought they would never cease.

Book Three

Book Three

Chapter Fourteen

LONDON 1993

Ryan Scott Tyler knotted his black tie for the fourth time. He was all thumbs.

'Shit, this stupid thing is never gonna work.'

He spoke sharply to his reflection in the bathroom mirror, wishing he had a bow tie that fastened with one easy clip, instead of this impossible tie-it-yourself strip of black silk.

It was lopsided.

He tugged at one corner viciously, then made the necessary adjustments to his collar. The gleaming white of the freshly laundered shirt contrasted sharply with his dark skin and long black locks. He touched the front of his hair; it was still damp.

Dark stubble covered his neck and jaw. Designer stubble or just plain unkempt? He couldn't decide, but there was no time to shave anyway. He was late.

He'd been delayed by a phone call from Rick Aronson in Los Angeles; a call which he'd just had to take. A struggling director does not tell an important Hollywood producer that he can't speak to him because he has a hot date.

Oblivious to time, Ryan had listened avidly to Rick, digesting every word said: the money was almost in the bag; just one more meeting with Maxstar pictures and the deal would be put to bed, no sweat; no bullshit this time, Rick had assured him. As soon as he could come up with a British star to play the lead, they had the green light.

Ryan had felt the usual rush of energy these conversations always engendered in him. It was only some time later that the sobering effect of a shower had cooled his enthusiasm, reminding him of the last two years, and the steady stream of producers, bankers, investors, long meetings and promises already made.

Ryan knew that the movie industry was full of hot air. So, as he dressed, he convinced himself that if he was going to get his film project off the ground he was going to have to do it himself. But he was impatient. More than that, he was hungry, consumed by an ambition that left no room for failure. He was convinced he could make the best movie of the decade. He just had to convince the men in suits of the same thing.

A few minutes later he left his apartment in Chelsea Harbour, taking the lift downstairs to where a car was waiting.

'Evening, Mr Tyler,' the driver greeted him pleasantly, holding open the back door of the Jaguar XJ6 saloon.

'Evening Tom,' replied Ryan, sliding into the dark, comfortable interior.

'Where to, sir?'

Ryan fumbled in his pocket for the address, straining his eyes to see in the dim light. 'Draycott Place. Can you step on it, I'm very late.'

'Certainly, Mr Tyler, we should be there in less than ten minutes.'

As they drove up Lots Road, Ryan began to think about seeing Farrell. She was a twenty-year-old model, destined to become a supermodel; or so she had informed him within minutes of meeting him two weeks previously in Tramp Nightclub.

As the car pulled up she was stepping out of her mews house, dressed in a long, fringed cashmere shawl, draped loosely around her shoulders. It fell open to reveal her ankle-length black sheath dress with contrasting white collar and cuffs, and a white gardenia brooch gleaming at her throat.

A streetlight illuminated her fine-boned face as she walked towards the car, clearly agitated. Fixing Ryan with an icy stare, she sat herself beside him.

'You said to be ready at six-thirty. I was!' she snapped.

'I'm terribly sorry, I had a call from a heavyweight producer in LA.'

'You don't look the slightest bit sorry.'

A slow smile softened his face. 'Well, I am, but what more do you want me to say?'

Determined not to let him off the hook that easily, she continued. 'How long does a fucking phone call take? At the very least you could've called to say you were going to be late.'

Ryan winced visibly. It was all right for men, but he hated women who swore. His eyes fixed straight ahead as she went on.

'Ryan, you're almost an hour late. Not only have we missed the champagne reception, we'll probably miss curtain-up as well, and then have to stand through the whole first act.'

He stared out of the window, regretting his hasty decision to ask Farrell to join him this evening. Beautiful, indulged models were not his thing as a rule. Their self-absorption generally bored him rigid, and this one was proving no exception. Ryan Tyler had no need of a trophy girlfriend. He knew lots of attractive, intelligent women, most of whom were great friends.

To take his mind off his own rising bad temper, he thought about the play they were going to see. He'd been as surprised as everyone else when Peter Ruddock, the highly acclaimed and notoriously temperamental stage director, had cast an unknown to play the lead in *Burden of Deceit*. The story of one woman's rise to power in the US senate after World War Two, her subsequent betrayal of her country and conviction for spying – and all for the love of a man – it was heavy stuff for a young, inexperienced actress like Lucinda West.

Ryan had read a feature about Miss West only last week in *The Sunday Times*. She was an aristocrat who'd dropped her title and her double-barrelled name. A début performance in *The Taming of the Shrew* at the RSC had won her rave reviews.

He liked the name, and if her acting was as good as her looks, she would be perfect for the part of Nancy in *The Mitford Papers*; the film he was busting a gut to finance.

Eventually Ryan broke the cool silence. 'Have you seen Lucinda West in anything before?'

Farrell lifted her long, dark hair, flicking it to the other side of her face; a habit which irritated him immensely. He had to move his head quickly to avoid being hit in the eye.

'No, I've never heard of her.'

Farrell sounded vague, but Ryan was saved the effort of continuing the conversation when they pulled up in front of the Dominion Theatre on Tottenham Court Road. He got out first, whilst she swiftly applied a thin coat of lipstick.

It was five minutes to curtain-up when they entered the theatre. An excited air filled the auditorium, and they both waved to several people they knew before taking their seats.

'It's a full house out there,' commented Jamie the make-up artist, as he applied the final touches of translucent powder to her flawless skin. 'All waiting to see the new star.'

'I'm not a star, Jamie,' Lucinda protested shakily.

'Not yet. But after tonight, you will be.'

She didn't reply, a nerve twitched in her temple and she chewed her bottom lip. The way she felt at the moment,

168

Lucinda doubted she would be able to utter her opening line. Jamie stood back to admire his handiwork, flicking powder off the end of a sable brush.

'Darling, you look divine.' He dropped his brush. 'Absolutely divine.'

She raised her eyes in Jamie's direction. 'Divine' was not the adjective she would have used to describe herself. It was a more suitable description for her mother, whom she had looked exactly like as a child. But adolescence had been unkind; at fourteen she was fat and had developed pimples, not losing either until she was almost eighteen. Now her skin was an unusual, warm beige colour and she was a willowy five foot ten inches – with the majority of her height in her long, slender legs. She hated her ankles, which she thought were too thick, and detested her bosom, which she knew was too big. But she had inherited her mother's wonderful silken hair, the colour of antique gold, and the same enchanting smile. Together with her paternal grandmother's regal, high cheekbones.

'You have an interesting face Lucinda,' her grandmother informed her frequently. 'Much better than beauty . . . beauty fades.'

The dominant Frazer-West nose and narrow lower lip prevented her from being truly beautiful in the classic sense; yet she was possessed of an unusual attractiveness that most people, meeting her for the first time, found captivating. No one knew her face better than she did. Hours spent practising facial expressions had taught her every nuance, every flaw and every good point.

Lucinda stared at herself now in the dressing-room mirror. She was unrecognizable. Her dark brown wig was fashioned in a mid-forties style. Her eyebrows were plucked to a fine arch; her face a mask of pale, almost white foundation, accentuating her brilliant blue eyes and scarlet lips. The transformation was complete. At last she was Sally Lawrence.

'That's wonderful Jamie! You've excelled yourself.'

'It's not difficult, darling. With your face, anything is possible.'

Lucinda stood up, her legs were trembling uncontrollably. She had to sit down again. 'I think I'm going to throw up.'

A knowing look entered Jamie's eyes. 'All the greats feel exactly the same way. Now, I know you're going to be superb.'

She wished she shared his confidence.

But from the moment Lucinda West walked on stage, her presence was riveting. The audience were rapt, and by the second act she had them eating out of the palm of her hand. Her voice soared through the theatre, reaching their hearts, stirring their senses on behalf of Sally Lawrence; to believe in her, share her dreams. When Lucinda took her fifteenth and final curtain call to deafening applause, there was no doubt in anyone's mind that she was destined to become a big star.

Peter Ruddock had taken over The Ivy Restaurant for the first-night party. The paparazzi were out in full force when Lucinda, dressed in a white bead-encrusted evening gown reminiscent of the forties, stepped from a Daimler into the cold January air.

She paused on the threshold, producing a gleaming smile as the cameras flashed; inside, the restaurant was packed shoulder to shoulder with the glitterati of London stage and screen, plus anyone else who had been able to wangle an invitation.

Lucinda was congratulated from all sides as she floated past.

'Wonderful performance!' cheered one notorious theatre critic. 'Absolute magic!' heralded another . . .

'*A triumph*,' the booming baritone of the great man himself, Peter Ruddock, hushed the general acclaim. It fell to a muted ripple as he took his leading lady in his arms, kissing her elaborately on both cheeks. 'You exceeded my wildest dreams darling. The part of Sally Lawrence was made for you.'

The champagne arrived, and he proposed a toast to the new star. 'To Lucinda West and Sally Lawrence,' hailed one hundred and fifty people in unison with him.

Lucinda took a sip of champagne as everyone pushed forward to talk to her. Craning her neck, she searched the sea of faces for those of her mother and father.

She spotted her mother first. There was no mistaking the slim, elegant figure of Lady Serena. She was swathed in an off-the-shoulder black crêpe dress, slit from ankle to knee to reveal part of one long, shapely leg. And her recently cropped hair emphasized her swan-like neck. She was with a tall, very good-looking man; her head was thrown back and she was laughing at something he'd said, her still-youthful face full of vitality.

Lucinda tried to catch her mother's eye, but she was too engrossed. Then she noticed her father, standing alone; she waved to him as a theatre critic from the *Evening Standard* pushed his face in front of hers.

'Did you find Sally Lawrence a difficult character to get into?'

Lucinda had been asked the same question dozens of times, but she smiled sweetly and tried not to sound bored as she gave him a rehearsed pat reply.

'Sally is a complex personality. When I first read the script I found her difficult to understand, yet as soon as I started rehearsals I began to know her better. I even started to like her.' She paused, before saying with genuine feeling. 'Tonight on stage, I think I became Sally.'

The young hack was scribbling away and on the verge of his next question, when she saw her father fighting his way through the throng to get to her.

Nicholas deliberately stood in front of the reporter,

much to Lucinda's delight. 'Are all first nights going to be like this,' he asked her.

Lucinda was amused. 'Probably. Hey, you look like you've been pulled through a hedge backwards.'

'You try fighting that mob,' he retorted, looking ruefully across the busy room, adjusting his black tie and smoothing the front of his jacket. 'Who invited them all?'

'Peter's PR people, I assume,' she shrugged.

'Lucinda darling, you look ravishing!'

There was no mistaking the Amazonian figure who now approached Lucinda, and who was encased in a peacock-green velvet dress that was almost too short.

'Rachel!' squealed Lucinda, visibly sparkling. 'How wonderful! Mummy didn't tell me you were coming. When did you get here?'

'Just, darling. Your mother doesn't know. How could I miss such a momentous occasion? When I heard about tonight I was busy working on Saul's New Age poetry tour. Detroit cancelled, thank God. Who needs Detroit? So I literally hot-footed it to JFK, on to the first available flight to London, and here I am . . . Saul's holding the fort out there on his own.'

Rachel smothered Lucinda in an extravagant hug, 'You were something else up there on that stage tonight, Lindy.'

'Rachel darling, how good to see you . . .' Nicholas accompanied his greeting with a perfunctory kiss on one cheek.

Lucinda saw Rachel stiffen. She had never been able to understand why her father and her mother's best friend didn't get on. Rachel was, after all, so witty and affable.

'Serena, darling!'

Serena turned round on hearing her name, and then looked bowled over as she saw her old friend. She was at Rachel's side in a trice, kissing and congratulating her daughter on the way.

'I can't believe you're here! Were you in the theatre?'

'Yes, I sneaked my way into the gods, and stood at the back.'

'Why didn't you tell us? You could have sat with us.'

At this, Nicholas looked transparently pleased that she had not.

'And is Saul with you?' Serena enquired, secretly hoping the reply would be negative.

'No darling, he'll be in Alaska by now.' Rachel gulped champagne, 'Gone up there for inspiration.'

Nicholas was looking as if he thought this was the best place for Rachel's husband, when they were all distracted by Peter Ruddock who was waving from the other side of the room.

Gesturing with her eyes in his direction, Lucinda spoke. 'Will you excuse me for a few minutes, my director wants me. Lovely to see you Rachel, thanks for coming.'

They all watched Lucinda negotiate a path across the crowded room, forced to stop politely to accept praise and admiration from almost everyone she passed.

She was a few feet from Peter's table when a man of strong build stepped sideways, treading on the long fishtail at the back of her dress.

'Careful,' she urged, holding her dress protectively.

He was laughing at something the woman next to him was saying, and had obviously not heard the warning.

Letting her dress fall, Lucinda tapped him on the shoulder.

He swung around abruptly, and the trapped hem caught in a buckle on the side of his shoe. Lucinda tugged at her dress. At the same time he tried to free his foot, ripping a huge hole in the sheer fabric, sending its white, pearlized beads rolling across the floor. Lucinda gasped in horror as her sphagetti-string shoulder straps also snapped under the strain.

The front of her dress fell down to reveal a deep cleavage piled into a specially designed strapless bra.

173

'Oh, I'm so sorry, I didn't see you . . .'

He was staring at her breasts.

Lucinda, face bright scarlet, retrieved the front of her doomed dress, holding it modestly across her exposed bosom.

'Well, it seems that you're having no trouble seeing me now,' she snapped, her eyes flashing in anger.

Then, looking at her torn dress with dismay, she went on, 'Look what you've done, you clumsy oaf. You should be more careful.'

A few people turned to watch the scene with obvious interest, and this upset her even more.

'Thanks for ruining my dress,' she told the stricken man in front of her.

'Please let me help you,' he offered earnestly, taking a step towards her with outstretched hands.

But someone had whispered quietly in Peter Ruddock's ear and, freeing himself from a gaggle of people, he was at her side in seconds. The presence of his intelligent face and concerned eyes, behind tortoiseshell glasses, made Lucinda feel slightly better.

'What's going on?'

'My fault entirely,' Ryan announced.

Instant recognition sparked in Peter's eyes as he looked at him. 'Ryan Scott Tyler, long time no see. I thought you were living in LA.'

'I was for a while. I'm between LA and London at the moment, working on a movie project to be shot in England. Actually, Lucinda here would be perfect for the leading role of Nancy. It's a wonderful part.'

Peter curtly interrupted his flow, 'Lucinda will be playing Sally for quite some time, we expect a long run. And then, who knows? Broadway beckons perhaps.'

'Who knows anything in this business?' Ryan reacted quickly. 'We're all slaves to an increasingly capricious box office.'

Unwilling to become embroiled especially while his actress was still *in extremis*, Peter merely smiled politely.

Ryan had already turned to Lucinda. 'Please accept my apologies Miss West.'

He *wanted* to add that the brief glimpse he'd had of her ample cleavage had been a pleasure he wouldn't have missed for the world. And if Peter Ruddock had not been standing over her like a bloody sentinel he would have told her so.

'Don't worry about it, Mr—' she paused.

'Tyler,' Peter supplied.

'I'll send you the bill for a new dress,' was her tart reply.

Ryan handed her a card. 'Be my guest.'

She took the card, but didn't bother to look at it. He was just another sophisticated man in elegant black tie. Even if he did have a pair of gypsy eyes.

'Come along Lucinda, I'm sure we can find something to patch you up for the remainder of the evening.'

Peter manoeuvred her to one side. With his arm encircling her waist protectively, he led her across the room.

Ryan watched her go.

All evening he had been desperate for an introduction to Lucinda West. It had not been quite how he had envisioned it, but there was one thing he could be sure of now.

She would certainly remember who he was when he called her.

And he intended to do so, soon . . . very soon.

Chapter Fifteen

Ryan called Lucinda's agent, Lou Goldstein, the following morning.

'Good morning Mr Goldstein, Ryan Scott Tyler.'

Lou Goldstein had heard of the young director, very vaguely. 'Good morning,' he responded with practised caution.

Ryan detected it. 'I'm a film director.'

'I know,' Lou interrupted quickly.

'I'm looking for a young, English actress to play the part of Nancy Mitford in a movie I'm co-producing and directing, called *The Mitford Papers*. I saw Lucinda West last night in *Burden* and thought she would be perfect for the role.'

Lou replied in his East End accent, 'Lucinda's committed to *Burden* for six months, with an option to continue for at least a year. The reviews this morning look good and Ruddock's talking about taking it to Broadway next . . .'

'I'd like to talk to her about it anyway.'

'Send me the script, and we'll take a look.'

'Why don't I send it direct to Miss West?' Ryan suggested.

'Because I'm her agent, that's why! Come on Mr Tyler, you know the score.'

Ryan decided to appeal to him, it was a long shot but worth a try.

'Listen Mr Goldstein, I'm the jerk who ripped Miss West's dress at the first-night party last night, and I want to send her some flowers. Can you give me her address?'

He went on before Lou had a chance to reply.

'I'm desperate to make amends, particularly since I want her for the part of Nancy.'

Lou sighed down the phone. He had heard hundreds, nay thousands, of similar stories in the twenty-five years he had been a theatrical agent. He told Ryan what he told everyone, in his indifferent 'Don't bother to argue with me' tone.

'I'll pass the message on to her. If you wanna send her flowers, there's no problem. Send them to my office, and I'll make sure she gets them.'

'OK, I get the message,' Ryan surrendered. 'I'll send you the script, Mr Goldstein, thanks for your help.'

If nothing else, Ryan was tenacious. Determined to see Lucinda West again, he set about trying to find out where she lived. It proved easier than he expected.

A call to Rod Swallow, a celebrity photographer friend of his, gave him the address of Amanda Wakeley, a dress designer where Lucinda bought a lot of her clothes.

Next, Ryan took a cab to the shop on Fulham road, instructing the driver to wait for him. Inside, he bought a black velvet evening scarf from a pretty young girl, who wrapped it in embossed matt brown paper and grosgain ribbon. Applying his most disarming smile, he made his move.

'The stole is a gift for Miss Lucinda West. I wonder if you could give me her address, so I can deliver it personally.'

The assistant looked unsure. 'We aren't allowed to give out addresses, but if it's really important I can ask Miss Wakeley.'

'Thank you,' he said, the charming smile still fixed, but doubting Miss Wakeley would divulge her client's address.

'If you can just wait a few minutes, I'll check.'

She disappeared into the back of the elegant shop just

as a grey-suited chauffeur came in, with an evening dress wrapped in a polythene bag draped sloppily over his arm.

'Anyone at home?' he asked chirpily, glancing around the shop.

'There's a girl here, but she's gone to speak to her boss, she should be back soon.'

The driver dropped the dress on to the counter.

Ryan recognized it instantly as Lucinda's.

'Listen, do me a favour mate, tell them this is Miss West's dress, it got ripped or something last night. Anyway she's going to call later to explain.'

The driver's eyes shot towards the shop door, 'I'm on double yellows, see. I got clamped last week. Can't afford that, it's more than my job's worth.'

'Don't worry, I'll tell her.' Ryan smiled reassuringly, hoping he looked suitably convincing.

He must have done.

'Cheers mate,' the driver walked briskly out of the door.

Not waiting for the girl to return, Ryan grabbed the gift he'd bought and left the shop.

He jumped into the waiting cab, pointing to where a dark blue Mercedes was signalling, pulling slowly away from the kerb a few hundred yards in front.

'Can you follow that Mercedes?'

The cab driver laughed. 'Just like in the movies, eh mate.'

'Yeah, like the movies, but in real life you don't get paid if you lose him.'

The cab driver laughed again and, putting his foot down, shot through a set of lights on amber, following the Mercedes into Sloane Avenue, turning right into Sprimont Place, leading to Elystan Place, stopping the car halfway down the road outside a small Victorian house, prettily clad in ivy.

Ryan instructed the driver to pass the house, and got

out at the end of the street. He gave the cabbie a fiver tip, receiving a broad grin in return.

He had a fifteen-minute wait before the Mercedes drove slowly out of the street, turning left towards Kings Road. After that he walked briskly to the house, and a quick glance at his watch told him it was almost twelve-thirty. Rapping smartly on the green painted door, he waited patiently for a few moments. When there was no reply, he tried again.

A hollow 'Who is it?' came out of an intercom located on the wall to his left. The voice sounded muffled, sleepy almost; deeper than Lucinda's.

Ryan imitated a cockney accent. 'I've a delivery for Miss West. It's to be signed for.'

An exasperated sigh followed. 'Hang on, I'll be there in a moment.'

Expecting a housekeeper or a secretary to answer the door, surprise registered on Ryan's face when Lucinda opened it herself.

Her long hair was tied back in a messy ponytail and her face, bare of make-up, looked younger. He thought that she looked much more attractive this morning than she had last night.

'Good morning Miss West, I come bearing . . .' he coughed, slightly embarrassed, '. . . a hope-you'll-forgive-me gift. You see, I don't think I can afford a new dress at the moment, so I thought this might compensate.'

She looked hesitantly at the package he thrust in front of her. 'Beware of strangers bearing gifts, my mother always told me.'

She recognized the familiar wrapping paper, and made the incorrect assumption that the new assistant at Amanda's had been responsible for telling Ryan where she lived.

'But I'm not a stranger,' he said with a sanguine smile.

The dark gypsy eyes she had seen last night now held a playfulness that she found extremely appealing. Relaxing a little, she felt herself responding to him, fascinated by his hypnotic gaze and unusual lilting voice; positive she could detect an Irish accent.

'So it's you, the ripper.' She smiled in spite of herself. 'How did you get my address?'

'I was a detective in a former life,' he quipped, ready for a little repartee.

And there it was again, the soft intonation as he had said 'life'.

'Are you Irish?' she asked.

'Half Paddy, half American. My mother was from Kildare. I lived there for ten years. And my father was a Yankee, from God knows where.'

A hard light entered his eyes fleetingly, yet long enough for her to notice. Then the charming smile was there again, lighting up his attractive face.

A chill breeze blew up the path.

She shivered as the neck of her long cotton bathrobe fell open a little. Crossing her hands over her chest, grasping the lapels, she began to laugh.

'I've only met you twice Mr Tyler, and both times I find myself having to cover my breasts.'

He winked mischievously, fixing her with a bold stare. 'You don't have to cover them on my account, and please call me Ryan.'

Her laughter increased, a tinkling jaunty sound, full of merriment.

'I never could resist a persistent man, so since you've been so diligent in finding me and I'm sick of reading the morning reviews, I think the least I can do is offer you a coffee.'

'I'd be delighted,' he said, smiling.

She thought he looked a bit like a naughty boy who'd been rewarded for doing something good for a change.

Ryan was still clutching the present as he followed Lucinda into her house. He was feeling incredibly pleased with himself.

Chapter Sixteen

PELHAM CRESCENT, SW7, 1994

'What do you think of Ryan Scott Tyler,' Serena asked casually as she stepped out of her midnight-blue cocktail dress. She hung it carefully on a padded hanger, before putting it away in her wardrobe.

'Sorry Serena, I didn't hear what you said,' called Nicholas from the depths of the large bathroom.

She waited patiently until he had finished cleaning his teeth. Then, sticking her head around the bathroom door, repeated her question.

'What do you think of Ryan Tyler?'

Nicholas wiped his mouth with the back of a monogrammed face towel, before he replied.

'I'm not sure, haven't really thought about it. We've got nothing much in common. According to Lucinda he's very talented, won an Emmy last year for a TV film. I think he's ambitious, and he seems to make Lucinda laugh.'

Serena didn't reply immediately. She was studying the rear view of Nicholas's body, clad in plain white boxer shorts as he faced the mirror. He had never been fat, but recently he had put it on a little. And the skin covering his back had gone flaccid, losing its youthful tone. He was fifty-four, and beginning to look it.

'I don't trust him. There's something shifty about him. Half Irish, half American, doesn't even know where his father is.'

An image of Ryan's sallow-skinned face entered her

head. 'I really don't understand what she sees in him; those wild eyes of his, looking right through you,' she sighed. 'Don't ask me why, but I have an uncanny feeling he's courting Lucinda for all the wrong reasons.'

Nicholas was tired. They had spent a delightful evening at Bibendum, one of his favourite restaurants. Ryan had generously paid the bill, Lucinda had looked radiant; they had all relaxed, and Nicholas had enjoyed himself immensely.

A rare event these days.

Their eyes met in the mirror.

'I think you're overreacting darling, as usual. He seems harmless enough.' Nicholas flicked a wayward strand of hair out of his eyes. 'Can we resume this conversation some other time, I have a very early meeting in the morning and I'm dog-tired.'

'Lucinda's in love with him,' Serena announced, before walking back into her dressing room.

She was pulling a silk nightdress over her head when Nicholas appeared, leaning against the door, openly admiring his wife's body.

The sheer fabric revealed all her smooth contours. Apart from the inevitable slackening of her thigh and tummy muscles she was in good shape, and looked at least ten years younger than her forty-nine.

He felt a stirring in him, but quickly crushed the desire. They had not made love for more than two years. He remembered the last time with unfortunate clarity. He had run, and rerun it in his mind a million times.

Serena had been drunk, very drunk, and in an expansive mood. They'd been to a party, where she had spent most of the evening flirting with a man young enough to be her son.

Nicholas had insisted on leaving early and, to his surprise, Serena had virtually seduced him in the back of the car on the way home. Shortly afterwards they had fallen into bed together, ripping each other's clothes off, laughing and frolicking like a couple of teenagers.

It was then she had done it.

She had shouted another man's name.

Daniel . . . Daniel . . . Daniel, repeating it over and over again, her eyes squeezed shut, tangled hair falling across her flushed face. Her teeth bared in animal lust, she'd pleaded, 'Fuck me hard Daniel, I want you to fuck me hard.'

Nicholas would never forget his immediate hot rage. Or the physical ache that had lasted for days, eventually being swallowed up by a great sadness and a feeling of desolation. He blamed himself. Blamed himself for his preoccupation with his business. Then there was his repressive personality.

The 'Daniel' incident was Serena's way of punishing him, he knew that. For a long time afterwards he considered asking her for a divorce, but his courage failed him. He not only harboured a profound love for his wife, he was also terrified of being alone.

The name 'Daniel' was never mentioned again.

Nicholas's compulsion to keep things to himself had escalated over the years and he had characteristically refused to be drawn into a discussion about the incident, even though that was what Serena had needed more than anything else. Instead he had simply moved into the spare room. Serena had expected him to stay for a few weeks, then return. After two years he was still there.

'What did you say, Serena?'

'I *said* Lucinda's in love with Ryan Tyler. Why is it, Nicholas, I have to constantly repeat myself?'

He ignored her barbed comment. 'Are you sure?'

Concern was beginning to overcome his fatigue. This Tyler chap might be charming, bright and ambitious, but he was certainly not son-in-law material. Nicholas had much higher hopes for Lucinda than a struggling movie director of dubious background. She was his only child, and would no doubt bear him grandchildren. The thought of Ryan Tyler being their father was not on.

'Absolutely,' Serena replied emphatically, a frown creasing her brow. 'The problem is, I don't think for one moment that he's in love with her.'

Serena was right, Lucinda was in love with Ryan Tyler.

To the point of insanity.

It had happened so quickly, sweeping her off her feet at such a rate, that not even the adulation she received for her part in *Burden* could compare with the euphoria that now seemed to inhabit her whole being at the thought of Ryan.

Every sensation was heightened.

If it was a pleasant day, to Lucinda it was glorious. If the birds sang at dawn outside her bedroom window, it was like a chorus of nightingales. Whining cab drivers no longer irritated her. She even smiled sweetly at bad-tempered shop assistants.

Life was good, she was in love.

That's how she was feeling late one Sunday morning, busily preparing a roast-beef lunch in her cluttered pine kitchen and musing over the last few months spent with Ryan.

At first he had been reticent, shy almost, not wanting to talk about his past; but slowly and surely she had learnt of his devotion to his mother and three sisters, still living in Rathangan, Kildare.

Only last week, he'd recalled the pain he had endured at his father's desertion, two days before his eighth birthday. For a long time he had blamed himself, because he had cried for a bicycle which his father had said they couldn't afford. Six months later the family had left New York, to live in Ireland.

Lucinda's heart had gone out to him as he described

arriving in Dublin, shabby and exhausted, terrified of meeting his grandfather. But things had changed since those days . . .

She was so happy he was directing *The Mitford Papers*. It was his first full-length feature film; it had brought him to England and to her.

She was also happy because there was no performance at the theatre on Sundays, and the afternoon stretched out lazily in front of her. She had refused lunch with her grandparents at their stuffy apartment on Eaton Square, opting instead for a quiet time with Ryan.

Her father had given her six bottles from his celler: a very special Château Lafite, vintage red Bordeaux, and she had decanted one precisely how he had instructed – leaving it to breathe.

Thoughts of Ryan dominated all of her waking hours, and most of her nights as well. She carried his image in her head wherever she went. She allowed her mind to stray briefly to Peter Ruddock who had already warned her that she was looking tired, advising her sternly to take more beauty sleep.

He didn't understand.

How could she sleep with Ryan's hungry lips on her body; his skilful hands gently probing, stroking, stimulating her almost to the point of orgasm; then teasing, holding back, until she was literally begging him to enter her.

Their lovemaking was passionate and noisy, exactly the way she liked it. Whenever he was inside her, Lucinda felt she was possessed by a kindred spirit.

She heard a key turn in the lock, interrupting her reverie.

Wiping her hands swiftly on the backside of her faded jeans, and fixing a warm smile on her face, she emerged into the narrow hall to greet Ryan.

As soon as she saw him, she knew something was wrong.

'Ryan what is it?'

He struggled out of his overcoat, hanging it on the newel post at the foot of the pine staircase.

'I could use a drink,' he said through clenched teeth.

'Of course. Sit in the drawing room, I'll bring us both a glass of wine.'

Her use of the word 'drawing room' for the tiny front room never failed to amuse him, and he managed a smile.

'I'd like a real drink, Scotch on the rocks if you've got it.

Her eyebrows raised in surprise, and she instantly regretted opening the Château Lafite.

'I'll see if I've got any. I'd no idea you liked whisky, or I'd have got some in.'

'My father lived on it. He didn't know when to stop, so I usually avoid it. But today I feel like a stiff drink.'

She nodded, returning to the kitchen where she found an old bottle of Johnnie Walker in the cupboard. There were a couple of measures left in the bottom. She emptied them into a tumbler, then poured herself a glass of wine, going back to join Ryan.

He took the glass from her outstretched hand, and she sat next to him on the huge sofa.

It had been a house-warming present from her mother and father when she'd moved in a year ago.

Ryan gulped his Scotch, staring straight ahead into nothingness.

'The finance has fallen through for the movie, Lu.'

Lucinda experienced a pang of dismay on hearing his usually effervescent voice so flat and defeated. She could almost touch his despair.

'But surely there are other investors. It's a great project, it'll make a wonderful movie. Is there nowhere else you can go?'

He seemed not to hear her. 'I really thought it was in the bag. I thought this time, at last, I had the green light.'

His voice dropped even lower. 'I was a fool to believe in Rick Aronson. That bastard is the same as all the rest of the fucking suits, so full of bullshit I'm surprised it's not flowing out of his ears.'

Lucinda had never seen him like this before. She could feel his anger taking over, with a life force of its own.

'It's not the end of the world Ryan, there'll be lots of other movies. You're only thirty-five.'

It was a lame attempt at trying to lift the gloom that seemed to cling to him.

'You just don't get it, do you Lucinda. I thought you of all people would understand. I've been working on this for almost two years, right from conception. I've been to more meetings than the chairman of Paramount. But above all, I haven't worked properly for the last year – apart from a couple of small promos that wouldn't even pay for a good night out at Spagos.'

He sighed deeply, then dropped his head into his hands.

'I'm heavily in debt. The bank put up two million dollars for my company, Scottsdale Productions, against some property I own in LA, and now I'm struggling to service the loan. Well, to be absolutely honest, I can't pay the interest at all at the moment.'

Lucinda stroked his head. 'I'm so sorry Ryan,' she said softly, deeply saddened.

He looked up.

'I'll have to go back to Los Angeles as soon as possible, that's where the work is. I'm sorry Lu, but I can't exist on fresh air and empty promises any longer. I've got to earn some real money.'

She was shocked. Losing him had not even entered her head. But LA was the other side of the world, they would never see each other. The thought made her feel physically ill.

Her mind began to race like a computer processing the names of people who might be able to help financially.

'But, Ryan, we'll never see each other.'

'Well, we'd better start saving now for all the flights and telephone bills.'

She studied his strong profile, clearly etched in the sunlight streaming through the open window. She was fighting to overcome her panic as she thought about losing him. Oh, there'd probably be the token couple of trips to LA, but then it was inevitable they would begin to drift apart. Ryan would become involved in some other project, and would most certainly meet someone else.

Suddenly a thought struck her.

Her father had deposits all over the world. His money, her mother had often hinted, was lying idle most of the time, just gathering dust. And interest of course.

Perhaps he would consider investing in the film? It was risky, but she might be able to persuade him that it could be fun, particularly as she was committed to playing the female lead.

Stubborn and fractious Nicholas might be with her mother; hard-headed and shrewd to his business associates; but with her he was indulgent, sensitive to her needs, attentive and affectionate.

He adored her.

Not daring to build Ryan's hopes, Lucinda decided not to mention her plan. If it worked, telling him would give her the greatest pleasure. If it failed, he would never know.

'You expect me to invest ten million dollars?' Nicholas paused, calculating in his head. 'That's approximately six million and eight hundred thousand pounds. All for a film about a couple of ridiculous debutantes.'

'The Mitford sisters weren't just a couple of debs, Daddy. They knew Hitler, they had fascinating lives; it's a very compelling story.'

'Have you gone completely mad, Lucinda?'

Lucinda was sitting opposite her father at his large desk,

feeling slightly vulnerable in the hushed comfort of his elegant office. It was like being a little girl again, reprimanded for a prank. But she had insisted on meeting him in business surroundings.

When he had asked her why, she had answered that it was the best place to discuss business.

'I know it sounds like a lot of money,' she ventured slowly.

Nicholas interrupted, abruptly. 'It not only *sounds* like a lot, Lucinda, it *is*.'

She sighed impatiently. 'OK, OK, it is. But I'm not asking you to invest in something frivolous like a yacht, or a fashionable work of art.'

Nicholas was tempted to inform his daughter, in no uncertain terms, that both those items were saleable. But he let her go on.

'This is a viable business deal; movies do make money you know, Father. The script is brilliant and Ryan's a talented director. It'll take multi-millions at the box office. You won't be sorry, believe me.'

Nicholas glanced down at a set of profit and loss accounts he'd been studying, his hand was shaking a little. When he looked up he seemed slightly less hostile, yet his voice was still stern and unyielding. Levelling his eyes, he fixed them on her. He was thinking how thin she had become over the last few months since she'd started to play Sally Lawrence. She was a grown woman, but he still worried about her.

'Why has Ryan been unable to raise the finance to date, if it's such a brilliant project?'

Lucinda chose her words very carefully. 'Ryan has been let down by a syndicate of investors in Los Angeles, he's raised two million dollars himself but needs the remainder to put the deal to bed.'

Nicholas groaned inwardly at her use of American business slang.

'There are several people interested, I just thought I'd give you first opportunity. You'd get a major share of the profits for your investment. Mummy says you've got money lying all over the place doing nothing, I thought you might like to invest some of it wisely. It's going to be a breakthrough film.'

Now Nicholas was angry.

'Your mother is talking complete nonsense.' His tone was emphatic. 'I do *not* have money "lying all over the place".'

He took a deep breath, clearly resenting the fact that Serena had talked about his finances with their daughter.

'And I know exactly how to invest any money I do have, thank you very much Lucinda.'

'Will you at least look at the proposal?' she urged.

Nicholas felt himself weakening in the light of her pleading gaze; forgetting that she was a brilliant actress.

'What do I know about films? I'm a property man. The movies are notoriously risky, there's been more money lost than made.'

Lucinda sat on the edge of his desk, a petulant look on her face. She reminded him of times past, when she'd sat on his knee, cajoling him for some treat or other. Which she invariably got.

'I know it's a lot to ask Daddy, but I thought it was worth a try. Ryan is so desperate, and I'm down for the female lead.'

'What about *Burden of Deceit*? I thought you were heading for Broadway?'

'Lou doubts whether I'll be able to play Sally in New York, the backers are demanding an American actress. So, by the time Ryan gets through pre-production and starts shooting, I can be available.'

She watched him write something on a piece of paper, noticing for the first time how prominent the veins on the back of his hand had become, clearly visible under his wafer-thin skin.

'I understand you being wary, Daddy. Films are not exactly gilt-edge stuff, but they can sometimes . . . often . . . make a lot of money.'

She was unprepared for his next question, and looked slightly startled when he asked it.

'Are you in love with Ryan Tyler?'

Unable to avoid his scrutiny, she replied in a steady voice. 'Yes I am, and I want to marry him. If he doesn't get this movie deal he'll have to go back to LA, and I intend to go with him.'

There was no mistaking the hint of emotional blackmail.

Nicholas disguised his inner turmoil, but Lucinda could almost hear the cogs turning in his brain as he considered what she'd just said.

'OK, I'll look at the proposal; take a little advice, see what I can do.'

She moved towards him, smiling. 'Thank you Daddy, thank you so much.'

Holding up his hand, he leaned back in his leather chair. 'Don't thank me prematurely, I haven't decided to invest yet.'

She leant forward to plant a kiss on his brow, deciding to make one final appeal.

'But you're the sweetest man in the world. And I know you'll do this one favour for me, Pops.'

At that moment Nicholas made an impetuous decision, something he never did usually. Even as he made it, he felt sure he would live to regret it.

Grabbing her hand, he held it tightly, and told her, 'I will invest in Ryan Tyler's film on one condition, and one condition only; that you promise not to marry him for at least two years.'

A sharp intake of breath was the only indication of Lucinda's surprise. Slipping her hand out of her father's, she walked slowly around his desk. Leaning forward, she announced her reply.

'You've got a deal.'

Lucinda left her father's office in a state of euphoric anticipation. She couldn't wait to tell Ryan.

She had agreed to Nicholas's condition lightly, thinking that he would change his mind once he got to know Ryan better, and realized how much in love they were. Anyway, she was convinced she could easily persuade him to change it, if and when the time came.

She told Ryan that evening. He had popped into her house for a drink, as he usually did before she went to the theatre. She was pouring wine, chatting amicably, she dropped it into the conversation in a deliberately nonchalant voice.

'By the way, I went to see my father today. He's agreed to put up the finance for your movie.'

Ryan was leaning against the fridge. She handed him a glass of wine, taking a sip of her own.

He couldn't believe his ears. 'What did you say?'

She was enjoying herself immensely, and wanted to savour the moment. She was smiling triumphantly over the rim of the glass.

'I said that I went to see Daddy this morning and he's agreed to finance your movie.'

He was looking at her rather sceptically. 'This isn't some horrible joke, is it?'

She shook her head adamantly. 'I couldn't bear the thought of you going back to LA, just when I've found you, so I had a brainwave. He wasn't keen at first, but I managed to talk him round.'

'It's fan-fucking-tastic,' his black eyes were gleaming.

'Why do you always swear when you're excited?' she asked, laughing, thinking of his noisy cursing during love-making.

Inclining his head slightly, he looked shyly up at her from under thick, sooty eyelashes.

'The first time I had sex, I was so excited, I could think of nothing to say to the hapless, young female involved. So I shouted "Fan-fucking-tastic" over and over again. It kind of stuck with me. So, every time I'm really excited . . .'

She was laughing uproariously now, tears filling her eyes as he grabbed her by the waist.

'Seriously Lucinda, this is the most brilliant news you've given me,' his voice deepened as he pulled her into him.

She could taste his energy, smell his passion.

'I love you,' Ryan heard himself telling her.

He wasn't sure he did, but it seemed the most appropriate thing to say. 'I love you,' he repeated.

His mouth sought hers, smothering her endearments in a hard, potent kiss, squeezing her so tightly she cried out.

'Put me down, Ryan!'

He released her, breathless and panting. Then he punched the air, yelling. 'Yes! Yes! Yes! I think this calls for a celebration.'

'Great. Where to?' Lucinda looked at him expectantly.

'To bed first. I'll go and buy a bottle of good bubbly, while you warm the bed. Then, after the show, our favourite restaurant. And then . . . bed again.'

He pecked the end of her nose. 'Don't expect any sleep tonight, Miss West, you're going to lose count of how many times you come.'

A thrill of anticipation shot through her.

'Then why waste time eating Ryan, we can grab a pizza after the show.'

'You're quite right, why waste time in a restaurant when I can eat you.'

His voice sunk to a low carnal growl, as he pretended to savage her neck.

All her senses were heightened, and a wanton look

entered her eyes as she pushed him gently towards the door.

'Go and get the champagne, we haven't got long. I'm due at the theatre in less than an hour.'

He grabbed her chin, covering her mouth with a wet, hungry kiss before dashing out of the room, shouting. 'Back soon.'

She was laughing deliriously as she ran upstairs, frantically ripping her clothes off, leaving them where they fell, before jumping into bed.

Chapter Seventeen

NEW YORK CITY

Luna felt sick. She always felt physically sick when she was nervous.

This time she'd been that way ever since Brad Coleman had breezed into her office the previous day, informing her in his cheerful voice that the big man wanted to see her.

'Tomorrow at ten-thirty prompt. Don't be late, he's a stickler for punctuality.'

'Why, what have I done?' had been her immediate reaction.

She had no idea why Clayton D. Spencer II wanted to see her. He was the senior vice-president of Spencer Howard and Franklyn, Bank and Trust; a large private bank founded in 1896 by his great-grandfather's brother, Randolph B. Spencer, with branches in London, Hong Kong and Tokyo.

She had been working at the bank for the last ten months as an assistant to Brad Coleman, vice-president in charge of the Special Finance department; that meant high risk loans, usually in default or slipping into in-solvency.

By way of explanation Brad had merely shrugged, then winked at her.

'He's heard how beautiful you are, and wants to check you out himself.'

Luna had blushed.

Bradley was always teasing her. Sometimes she wasn't sure if he was joking or not.

'He's a ladies' man, our Mr Spencer, the stories are legendary.'

Leaning forward to where she was sitting at her desk, he whispered into her ear. 'I even heard he did it with Marilyn Monroe, when he was about eighteen.'

'He was in good company.' Luna was smiling.

Bradley, standing up to his full height of six foot three, reminded her of a footballer. The type all the girls had hankered after at college. With the clean-cut good looks that had been popular on screen in the fifties; the archetypal all-American boy. Now he pointed an accusing finger in her direction.

'Just remember you're far too young for him, he's much older than your daddy. You're more my age.'

'And you, Bradley Coleman, are married.'

He pulled a long face. 'I know, all the good guys get snapped up first.'

She laughed, and he threw a file on to the desk in front of her.

'Look at that Luna. Let me have your comments later today. It's a construction company. They've got into massive debt during the recession; heavy borrowing on expansion, the usual. They want to defer their capital repayments for six months. I personally don't think they'll hang on for that long.

'I think we should get the president in and start turning the thumbscrews. Anyway, let me have your opinion. Actually . . . I'm getting worried; you're so damn good, old man Spencer is probably going to promote you to my job.'

'No way Brad, you're so damn good yourself.'

'Heh, what is this, a mutual appreciation society?'

She joined him in his laughter, white teeth gleaming against her dark beige skin.

But she worked hard that night, returning late to her small loft conversion in Tribeca; a surprise gift from her father when she had started her job on Wall Street.

Luna would always remember with fondness the wonderful two weeks she had spent with him, scouring stores to choose fabrics and furniture; long hours spent browsing through antique shops; and, on the final day, arguing over an expensive French armoire which she had thought was wildly extravagant and he had insisted on buying for her.

Now she made herself a sandwich in her cosy, narrow kitchen, and drank two Diet Cokes before going to bed at ten-thirty, determined to have an early night.

She fell instantly into a deep sleep, only to wake a couple of hours later, thoughts of the impending meeting racing around her head. Sleep eluded her after that, and she was pleased when she finally heard the news vendor shouting on the street corner opposite, which meant it was seven a.m.

She dressed carefully in a sedate black suit and simple white shirt; her long, wavy black hair, braided in a thick plait, hung halfway down her back. As a finishing touch she clipped the diamond pin her father had given her on her graduation day into the lapel of her jacket.

Leaving her apartment on Franklin Street, she caught a cab to 120 Wall Street.

It was a few minutes after nine when she reached the forty-two-storey bank building. Once inside, she went straight to her office on the twelfth floor, where she tried to work on some accounts but was unable to concentrate.

At ten-twenty she took the elevator to Mr Clayton Spencer's office on the top floor, striding up to his secretary with more confidence than she actually felt.

'I've got an appointment with Mr Spencer at ten-thirty.' She glanced at her watch, pleased to be a few minutes early.

'He's on a conference call right now, I've just put it through. Take a seat, I don't think he'll be too long Miss Fergusson.'

Connie had a slow, drawling Alabama accent that Luna found very attractive.

'Thanks, but I prefer to stand. I sit for such long hours all the time.'

She started to chew her bottom lip when the president's voice bellowed through the intercom.

'Connie, I asked for coffee over half an hour ago.'

Connie looked unconcerned, as she answered brightly, 'Ah did order it sir, coming right up. I have Miss Fergusson here, she has an appointment with you at ten-thirty.'

'Send her right in, and chase the coffee. I think they must have gone to Colombia for it,' he growled.

Connie raised arched brows. 'Men, all the same. Ain't got no patience. Go right in Miss Fergusson. I'll be following you with the coffee real soon.'

Luna's gaze shot towards Clayton Spencer's office. 'To be honest, I could do with a stiff drink, never mind coffee.'

'I know what you mean.'

The women shared a brief moment of understanding, before Luna walked, tall, straight-backed and with an elegant poise that Connie envied, towards Mr Spencer's office door.

Clayton Spencer II greeted her ebulliently as she entered his huge office.

'Good morning, Miss Fergusson.'

With her feet sinking into the thick, wool carpet, Luna crossed the vast room. The president was much smaller than she had previously thought, and his immaculately coiffured white hair framed his face like a silver halo. He looked tanned and fit. She had heard that he ran five miles every day.

'Sit,' he commanded, pointing to an impossibly big chair. She did as she was told.

Sitting upright on the edge of the seat, Luna crossed her long, shapely legs, encased in sheer black stockings, careful to replace her skirt to a decent length.

Beautiful legs, Clayton thought.

Remarkable-looking woman, such unusual eyes. For some reason they looked familiar. A few seconds later it came to him; they were exactly the same green as his wife's . . . Siamese cat.

The door opened.

Connie walked in carrying a tray containing coffee and macaroons. She placed it on the desk, before quietly leaving the room.

Luna had used that interruption to take in every detail of the minimalist office.

Blond wood panelling lined the walls, bare of books or ornaments of any kind, except for a beautiful Hopper painting lit by a single halogen spotlight. She also noted a pristine white sofa; two chairs that looked as if they'd never been used; and an unusual glass and iron contraption that Luna assumed was a coffee table.

Mr Spencer's enormous maple-wood desk dominated the room; meticulously free of papers or mess, unadorned by the usual family photographs.

'You're not taking coffee.'

It was a comment in retrospect to a question.

She shook her head as he poured himself a cup.

'So Miss Fergusson, you've been with the bank for ten months. Why haven't we met?' He grinned impishly. 'I think they've been keeping you away from me deliberately.'

He was teasing. His old eyes twinkled, giving them a youthful glow.

In response Luna's face broke out into the brightest smile he had ever had the pleasure to behold.

'Wow, that's some smile you've got there Miss Fergusson. You should be on the screen, not sitting behind a desk looking at lines of figures all day. Boring old stuff . . . What's a young beauty like you doing in this business?'

Luna accepted the flattery lightly. She knew that his genial manner concealed a ruthless business brain, and that he had been married for forty-two years to the same long-suffering wife, had five sons, and was credited with countless affairs. Some of them scandalous.

She was beginning to understand how he had got his reputation. Even at seventy-four, he still had the ability to make a woman feel special.

'I've wanted to be a banker ever since I was about ten years old. In school vacations I used to accompany my father to his bank, to help.' She chuckled. 'In hindsight I was probably hindering the poor girls in the accounts office, where I spent most of my time.'

She paused and uncrossed her legs.

Clayton looked for a brief glimpse of stocking top, but was disappointed.

'Anyway, it fascinated me, the whole system. I've never wanted to do anything else.'

'*My* father did very much the same thing with me, only I was younger than you, five to be precise. I was the only son, and I hated banking.'

He looked wistful for a moment.

'I wanted to be a baseball player.'

'Well, now you own a whole team,' she commented.

'Ah, but to play is something quite different.'

She felt an unexpected twinge of sympathy for him.

'Your father is in off-shore banking Luna, is that correct?'

'Yes, that's right. He started his own bank in 1970, when I was a child. First in St Vincent in the Eastern Caribbean, very small; then he moved to the Cayman Islands. He now owns one of the biggest private banks in Grand Cayman.

And half the Island, Clayton Spencer could have added.

Instead, he said, 'Well Luna, you've made quite an impact here, becoming something of a star in the short time you've been with us.'

She blushed modestly as he glanced at a file in front of him. It contained her CV.

'You graduated from Harvard Business School cum laude. Very impressive,' he commented, with just the right amount of practised approval.

Luna had the distinct feeling that she was being tested, interviewed for something. She waited with bated breath, not daring to hope for promotion so soon.

He was drumming his short fingers rhythmically on the desk top.

'Have you ever been to Europe, Luna?'

Her heart skipped a beat. 'Yes, once. My father took me to Venice and Rome for my eighteenth birthday. It was wonderful.'

'How about London?'

She shook her head, the long plait falling over her shoulder. 'No.'

'Well, it rains most of the time; the local transport is inefficient; you can't get a cold beer; the natives are hostile, and they don't speak American.'

She laughed ruefully.

'All absolutely true.'

Her voice, when she replied, literally simmered with enthusiasm. 'I'd still love to go, I've read and heard so much about England.'

Her youthful exuberance was infectious and spoke of the joy of discovery. It was not lost on Clayton Spencer.

He threw a file across his desk, towards her. 'As the good fairy said to Cinderella, *You shall go to the ball*. So say I to you, Luna Fergusson. *You shall go to London*.'

She was surprised, but kept her reaction calm.

He admired her cool. Instinctively he knew that David Cahn, his PA, had made the correct choice.

'We'd like you to work in our City branch. The post is for one year. Unfortunately the young man who was to take this job has just been diagnosed HIV positive. We don't think it would be wise to send him under the circumstances.'

He might as well have been talking about a bad dose of the flu, but she felt it inappropriate to comment.

'What will I be doing?'

'You'll be handling our Special Finance accounts; high risk investments, much as you do now. We need someone young, enthusiastic, willing. Someone who can deal with artistic types who haven't got a goddamned clue about business. Those guys get into cost overruns as often as you and I go to the john.

'If you do get any difficult clients, you can always turn on that radiant Fergusson smile. You'll probably have them running into the bank with interest and capital repayments posthaste.'

He drank the remainder of his coffee, then set the cup down.

'David Cahn will brief you in full about the job; incidentally it was David who suggested you for the post. If you accept, we'd like you to start the beginning of June, six weeks from now.'

So it was all David Cahn's scheming, Luna thought happily. He'd never mentioned a thing to her, but she knew he was aware of how ambitious she was.

She couldn't wait to see him, to thank him. She had liked David from the first moment she'd met him, on her second day at the bank. She had been in the elevator when he'd dashed in, bumping into her, causing her to drop the files in her hand. He was so apologetic, offering to buy her a coffee or a drink to compensate. She'd accepted, eager to get to know people and that date had been the beginning of a firm friendship. She'd spent several hectic weekends out at his home in New Jersey, with his talkative wife Penny and their three young sons.

'How much time do I have to think about it?'

'Forty-eight hours,' the president replied sharply, before standing up.

The meeting was clearly over.

Luna rose. Her legs felt weightless, and her head was spinning as if she'd just stepped off a merry-go-round.

Clayton Spencer extended a broad hand.

'I accept,' Luna announced emphatically.

He looked genuinely pleased. 'Good! I like decisive people, got no time for all these wishy-washy folk,' he grunted, then smiled.

She could see how handsome he must have been when he was younger.

'I wish you every success in London, Luna. I'm sure you'll do a great job.'

She took his hand, shaking his firm grip vigorously.

'I promise I will. Thank you for considering me.'

Looking into her beautiful, flashing eyes, so resolute and determined, there was no doubt in Clayton Spencer's mind that she would not let him down.

Luna could hear the phone ringing as she turned the key in the door of her apartment.

She ran to pick it up, recognizing her father's deep voice at once.

'Luna, baby, how are you? I've been trying to reach you for the last few days.'

'Hi Dad, I'm fine! Great to hear from you. This is a good line, where are you?'

She thought she could detect a low ripple of laughter.

'I'm on my second martini in the bar at the Carlyle, want to join me for the third?'

'You're in town!' Luna squealed.

She was thrilled that today, of all days, her father should decide to come to New York and surprise her. She couldn't wait to see him and share her news about going to London.

'I'll be right there. I'd like a glass of my favourite chilled Chardonnay please.'

'Coming up.'

She could hear his laughter clearly now.

'Don't be too long,' he added.

'Don't eat all the nibbles,' she replied, smiling as she replaced the telephone.

She was still smiling when she left her apartment a few minutes later to catch a cab to the Carlyle Hotel.

Royole Fergusson was sitting in a corner of the Café Carlyle, facing the door, when she entered the room.

He stood up, a smile literally filling his entire face. And several heads turned as the tall, striking young woman crossed the room and nestled into his open arms.

'Luna, so good to see you!'

They embraced.

Luna breathed deeply, filling her nostrils with the smell of him; his slightly musky body odour, mixed with Polo, her favourite aftershave, the one she had bought him for Christmas last year.

'Let me look at you,' Royole said, holding her at arm's length.

'You saw me six weeks ago, Dad,' she laughed, pushing a stray hair out of her eyes. 'I haven't changed much since then, have I?'

'I know, but every time I see you I think that you've become just a tiny little bit more beautiful.'

He indicated a small amount with his thumb and forefinger.

Luna pinched his cheek. 'You always say that.'

'Because it's true.'

He sat down, patting the seat next to him, as the waiter approached the table with a glass of white wine and a vodka martini.

'Good to see you, baby,' Royole repeated, lifting his glass and chinking it against hers.

A warm glow filled her, it was good to see him too. 'Funny, but I was only thinking about you on my way home from the office today.'

'And *what* were you thinking? Good stuff I hope.'

'I was thinking that I miss you and, since I'm due for a few days' leave, that I'd like to come home and spend it with you. I thought we might get up to some of the old stuff we used to do a few years back. You know, mess about on the boat, a couple of barbecues in the backyard, beating you at Scrabble, the usual. I was going to ring the travel agent tomorrow and make the flight reservations. I'd intended to surprise you.'

'Instead I surprised you.'

He seemed pleased with himself, relaxed and comfortable in his daughter's company.

'It's wonderful, I'm delighted you did. Anyway, I can still come home for a few days next week. Depending on how long you're staying in New York, I may be able to travel back with you.'

Luna looked at him expectantly.

'I'm only in town for a couple of days, then I have to get back for an important meeting on Monday morning. Why don't you come down for the weekend, I'd really like that.'

It was Thursday, and she had a lot of work to do; work she had intended to take home at the weekend.

She had also accepted an invitation to the theatre and dinner on Saturday night with the extremely attractive Mark Cobain, a brilliant young lawyer she'd met at party at her friend Zoe's house three weeks ago. He'd recently split up from his steady girlfriend, and several predatory single girls were already pursuing him. She liked him a lot, and was afraid if she cancelled he might not call again.

'I'm sorry Dad, I can't make it this weekend; but the next one should be OK.'

Disappointment filled his voice. 'Oh, I am sorry. Weekends are not the same any more without Caron.'

His eyes had suddenly clouded over and she tried to make him feel better.

'Come on Dad, stop feeling sorry for yourself. You've got your golf, your tennis and lots of friends. I really don't know why you won't live with Christy. She's crazy for you.'

She had broached this subject several times before and he always replied the same way. Tonight was no exception.

'I don't want to live with Christy, or anyone else for that matter. Your mother and I built Whispering Cay together. Caron is everywhere in that house, I can feel her presence so strongly it's almost tangible, even though she's been dead eighteen months.'

Luna sighed.

She would have liked to remind her father that whilst her mother was alive he hadn't exactly been passionately in love with her. It was only now after her death, perversely in her opinion, that he wanted people to think he had been totally devoted to Caron.

'Our marriage was a good partnership, it's not easy to replace.'

She had to suppress her real opinion, that her mother had adored him, sacrificing everything herself to make him happy, and now it was difficult for him to find anyone else prepared to do the same.

She admired her father, and respected the way he had nursed her mother through a harrowing year of bowel cancer; an experience that had robbed him, for a while, of his own zest for life. But sometimes he tried her patience when he tortured himself with the same interminable questions: if he had loved Caron more – cared for himself less, taken her to the doctor when she'd first complained of stomach pains – might she have survived? Could she have lived longer?

Just then, a tall, attractive woman with long, red hair and huge breasts came into the bar. She smiled and waved at Royole, who waved back.

'Who's that?' Luna quizzed, watching the leggy redhead take a seat opposite.

From the familiarity in her body language it was clear that she knew Royole well. As she looked blatantly in his direction, Luna felt slightly embarrassed. She always found it difficult when women were attracted to her father.

There had been so many.

She looked at him now, assessing his face; she saw a very good-looking, middle-aged man with a warm smile and unusual, sensitive eyes.

What she failed to see was the powerful sexuality Royole Fergusson possessed. He would be fifty-four in three months' time, and still attracted women of all ages with magnetic force.

'Her name is Monique, she works here. We often chat.'

Royole wouldn't have dreamt of telling Luna the truth, that he had slept with her several times.

'I think she likes you, Dad,' Luna grinned.

'What, an old man like me, course not!'

He laughed easily, dismissing this suggestion with an indifferent wave of his hand, popping a couple of peanuts into his mouth. Then wiping salt off his hands with a paper napkin, his expression changing subtly, he became serious.

'I have a proposition for you, Luna.' The tone of his voice matched his face.

Luna waited silently for him to continue.

'I want to offer you a partnership in the bank. Ever since Caron died I've been thinking about it. I need some fresh, young blood; you would be ideal. Of course it'll all be yours one day anyway. Meanwhile there's plenty of room for you at home, and you've got lots of friends there . . .'

'I've only just got settled here,' Luna interrupted quickly. 'I like Spencer Howard, and I'm doing well.'

Ignoring her, Royole continued, 'I would offer you eighty-five thousand dollars a year, plus perks; a new BMW convertible and a full partnership.'

Luna grappled with her thoughts.

'It's a great offer, and I really do appreciate it Dad, but—' she hesitated, uncertain as to whether she should say what was on her mind. She finally decided to be totally frank.

'I'm twenty-seven Dad, I really don't think I could live at home any more; and to be perfectly honest . . .'

She took a deep breath.

'. . . I really don't feel like replacing Mummy, nor could I do such a good job as she did.'

There was a long pause. She could see Royole was upset, by the slight tightening of his mouth; but it had to be said. Luna knew he wanted her there for purely selfish reasons, to fill the void left after Caron's death. He had, after all, used his wife as a sounding board for his ideas. She had been his confidante and business adviser, always there for him.

Luna could never fill her shoes, nor did she want to.

'I have to live my own life Dad, just as you have to.' Unable to suppress her excitement any longer, she explained,

'I've been offered a post at the London branch of Spencer Howard. A promotion to assistant vice-president, with a substantial salary raise. I start in June.'

Royole stared at her, disbelieving.

'What did you say Luna?' He sounded shocked.

'I said I'm going to work in London; isn't it exciting?'

Luna found her father's anxious expression disconcerting. If she hadn't known him better, she would have thought he was afraid.

'When did all this happen?' he asked sharply.

'This morning. Clayton Spencer offered me the post, I was stunned. He gave me forty-eight hours to think about it.'

She didn't tell him about the young man with Aids, whose job she had taken.

'It took me about forty-eight seconds to accept. I've always wanted to go to London, I can't wait! Don't you think it's great news to get promotion so quickly, after only ten months? And as soon as I get settled, Dad, you must come to stay; for as long as you like.'

Royole cast his mind back to the last and only time he had been to London, and the colour drained slowly out of his cheeks.

'That's great news Luna, I'm really happy for you.'

He didn't sound very happy, she thought.

'But do you think it's the right thing to do just at this point? Like you said, you're settled in New York, you've made quite a few friends and you love your apartment. I think you're being very hasty, Luna. You don't know anyone in London. It's a big city, and it can be a very lonely place. Why not wait another year at least?'

'I may not get another opportunity like this in a year's time, Dad. If I refuse, they may overlook me for promotion in the future. The contract is only for a year, I can let my apartment.

'I think the timing's OK; I'm single, no ties. I'm absolutely thrilled. I've had a raise in salary to seventy-five thousand dollars, plus bonus incentives. It's great!'

Her lovely face was infused with vivacity as she stuck her elbow gently into his ribs.

'Come on, lighten up Dad. By the look on your face you'd think I'd just told you I was going to Cambodia to work for the Khmer Rouge.'

When he didn't reply she assumed his taciturn attitude was a direct consequence of her refusal to work at Fergusson.

'Are you upset because I won't be joining you in the bank? Listen, there'll be plenty of time for that in the future, Dad. You have to understand that I need to establish myself first. I couldn't bear to don the cloak of nepotism, as Brad calls it, just yet. There are such a lot of Daddy's boys . . . and girls . . . in Wall Street who struggle to add up a column of figures, let alone run a bank.'

Luna lifted her father's hand from his lap, and held it in both of hers. Dropping her head to one side, she said: 'You *do* understand, don't you?'

'Of course I understand Luna, and I'm very proud of you.'

He tried to give a smile, but it was tentative and forced.

'You know me, I've always worried about you. The first time you fell and cut your leg, aged three, I made such a fuss, insisting on taking you to the hospital. You only had two stitches, but I was convinced you needed major surgery. I'm an old fusspot of a father who adores his daughter and only wants the best for her.'

Luna was overcome with a surge of love for him.

'His daughter adores him too, and wouldn't want it any other way. Believe me Pa, I'm going to be fine.'

He nodded reassuringly, yet could not expel the apprehensions from his mind. Nor could he explain that his disappointment at her not joining Fergusson Bank was nothing compared with his disquiet about what she might encounter in England.

Royole tried to convince himself. London was a big city, and the chances of her bumping into any of the Frazer-West family were pretty remote.

Raising his glass, he made a concentrated effort to lighten the mood. 'Here's to Luna Fergusson's assault on

London, they won't know what's hit them.'

Yet, even as he uttered the words, he was thinking of a phrase his own father had often used.

Remember, what goes around comes around.

It filled him with a deepening sense of unease.

Chapter Eighteen

JUNE 1994

'This flat is available, fully furnished and ready for immediate occupation,' Charles Hammond informed her in his clipped vowels.

It amused Luna how the English called apartments 'flats'. Elevators were 'lifts', sidewalks were 'pavements', and so on. Clayton Spencer had been right when he'd said that they didn't speak American.

The young estate agent had messy blond hair that kept falling in his face, and curious eyes which he had been unable to take off her all morning.

He rang the bell. There was no sound.

'The owner did say he would be here to show us around.'

He sounded a little unsure.

They waited a few more seconds then he rang the bell again, more urgently this time.

'How long have you been in London, Miss Fergusson?' he enquired pleasantly whilst they waited.

'Ten days.'

'And how are you finding it?'

He was genuinely interested. He had been born and lived in London all his life, and in his opinion it was the most civilized city in the world.

'A culture shock. I miss New York,' she replied, as a voice came from the intercom.

'Who is it?'

'Charles Hammond, from Winkworth. We arranged a

viewing for twelve-thirty, sorry we're a little late.'

'I thought you weren't coming, I was in the shower. Hang on, I'll be right there.'

Charles Hammond licked his lips. 'Flats in The Belvedere are very sought after, and this one has a particularly beautiful view of the river. It's available either on a six-month let or annually.'

'I hope it's nicer than the last one,' she commented, thinking about the shabby basement they'd just left; it had been described in the letting brochure as 'luxury accommodation in an unrivalled position in Chelsea'.

A moment later the door opened, and a man appeared.

For as long as she lived Luna would never forget her first sight of Ryan Scott Tyler.

He was wearing a short, white towelling bathrobe, with the name of a hotel she didn't recognize on the breast pocket. It barely skimmed his knees, revealing strong muscular legs, tanned and covered in thick dark hair.

But it was his eyes she noticed instantly, and felt compelled to look at. There was something almost sinful in their hypnotic gaze.

Disconcerted by the sudden rush of heat flooding her body, Luna focused her attention on what Charles Hammond was saying.

'Sorry to disturb your shower. We'll be very quick, we have a busy schedule.'

'No problem,' said Ryan easily, opening the door wider and standing to one side as Charles ushered Luna into the large, square hall.

'You carry on Mr Scott, I'll show Miss Fergusson around,' the estate agent trilled.

'Tyler,' Ryan commented.

The agent looked blank. 'Excuse me?'

'My name is Ryan Scott Tyler,' he explained, extending a hand in Luna's direction. 'And you are?'

She gulped, not trusting her own voice, wondering why

on earth she felt so nervous, and chiding herself for being so foolish.

'Luna Fergusson, pleased to meet you.'

She took his hand. Hers was clammy in contrast.

Then she smiled.

Ryan thought that he had rarely, if ever, seen such radiance.

It wasn't only warm and inviting, it had an extra quality. He searched his mind for the correct description, finally settling for 'benevolent'. Not happy with that, he changed it to 'pure magic' a second later. She ought to be in the movies, he thought. She could convince even the worst cynic to believe in that smile.

Ryan let go of her hand.

'Luna, what an unusual name. It suits you.'

Feeling herself blush, she lowered her eyelids shyly.

'Come along then Miss Fergusson, we're late. We're late, we're late for a very important date.'

The estate agent recited the lines from *Alice*, like the white rabbit leading her through Wonderland.

'I've got a lunch appointment, so I'll leave you guys.' Having said this, Ryan then seemed reluctant to move.

'Unless you need me to show you round?' he offered.

'Only if you've got the time,' Charles Hammond replied.

'No really, we don't want to hold you up. We'll be fine, you carry on.' Luna was dismissive, hoping he would go so that she could feel normal again.

'Just one thing, a question if I may.'

Ryan was looking directly at Luna.

'Are you American? You have a very unusual accent.'

'It matches my name,' she smiled again.

Ryan struggled to concentrate on anything other than the fact that he found her strangely familiar, as if he had met her somewhere before.

'It's a long, boring story. I'm a mixed-up West Indian

215

who went to school in America from the age of thirteen, hence this confusing accent.'

'Don't ever change it. It's charming, so melodic.'

'And yours, I'm almost certain, is Southern Irish. From . . . County Wicklow?' she guessed.

He looked amazed.

'Very close; Kildare actually. I'm impressed, you must have spent time in Ireland.'

'No such luck. Instead I spent a lot of time with an Irish housemother in Highclaire Academy, Vermont, who sounded exactly like you. She was from Ballyconnell.'

Charles Hammond gave an impatient little click with his finger on the brochure, then pointed at a door to their left.

'I believe the drawing room is this way.'

Ryan nodded. 'Straight through, go ahead; I'll catch you guys later.'

He turned and walked towards his bedroom, as Hammond propelled Luna into the drawing room, instantly adopting his trade jargon.

'Wonderful proportions, amazing views of the Thames; ideal for entertaining.'

Luna followed him to the terrace. French windows ran the full length of one wall, affording panoramic views of the river. They led on to a spacious terrace, where a table and four tired-looking chairs stood next to a big terracotta pot, holding a half-dead plant. Luna couldn't recognize what it was, or had been.

The river was busy. She watched a ferry and a pleasure boat ply slowly past, only half listening to Charles Hammond. She was still shaken from her encounter with Ryan Tyler.

'. . . the view is wonderful at night. In summer one can sit out on the terrace and eat al fresco, watching the sunset.

'So romantic. We have several clients in Chelsea

Harbour, they're all very happy. It's convenient for Fulham and Chelsea, shops and restaurants, et cetera, and not too far from the City for you. The best of both worlds actually.'

She didn't reply.

After a few moments the agent continued briskly.

'Shall we look at the rest of the flat, Miss Fergusson?'

Luna stared at him blankly. 'Sorry, what did you say? I was miles away.'

That was patently obvious, but he was too polite to mention so.

'I said, shall we look at the rest of the flat?'

'Yes, of course,' answered Luna, immediately looking around the sparsely furnished room, then following him into the kitchen, thinking that it was the best apartment she had seen so far. With a little love and attention she could make it home.

'Big enough, don't you think?' he asked brightly about the tiny room.

'For a very large cupboard, yes,' Luna replied, teasing him.

Running her hands across the smooth work surface, she noticed a half-empty bottle of Château Latour, one of her father's favourite wines.

'Well, I suppose it depends how much time one spends in the kitchen. I imagine, with your lifestyle, not a lot.'

Hammond shot her a quizzical glance, before leading her back across the hall.

He was poised to knock on the bedroom door as Ryan walked out, dressed in a stylishly cut black suit with a white, round-necked tee-shirt underneath.

Using his thumb, Ryan indicated over his shoulder towards the bedroom. 'I must apologize for the mess in there. My indispensable Portuguese help, Inez, doesn't come in on Tuesdays.'

He winked and grinned. 'I was brought up with a house

full of women, who did everything for me. That's my excuse, I'm afraid housework is not my strong point.'

'Is it anyone's?' Luna enquired in response. 'I was brought up surrounded by servants, so I'm equally spoilt.'

Charles Hammond was hungry. He had reserved Deals Restaurant for lunch, and was eager to get his client out as soon as possible. Anticipating another discourse on similarities in their respective backgrounds, he cut sharply into the conversation, looking at his watch with deliberate implication.

'Miss Fergusson, we really must get on.'

'And I must go, I'm already late for lunch.'

Ryan held out his hand again, focusing his full attention on Luna.

A distinctly impatient sigh escaped Charles Hammond's lips as he turned and marched into the bedroom.

Ryan ignored him. 'Nice to have met you Luna. By the way, this is a great apartment for a single person, and that's not just sales talk. There's plenty of security if you're living alone. Are you living alone?'

He was fishing.

'Yes I am,' she supplied, wanting him to know.

'Anyway, like they say in LA, it's got good vibes.'

'I'll take your word for it.'

A long lock of hair fell from the chignon that she had hastily tied at the back of her head that morning.

She fiddled with it unsuccessfully, then took the slide out. Holding it and shaking her head, she let her long hair fall. It tumbled down her back, almost to her waist, in an abundant mane of black spirals attractively streaked with dark gold; sun-bleached from a weekend spent on the boat in Cayman with her father two weeks before.

Amazing, Ryan thought. From the depths of his imagination rose a vision of her naked, her hair falling over her breasts.

'The bedroom, Miss Fergusson.'

The estate agent's voice had lost its earlier polite tone, and he was making no attempt to disguise his impatience now.

Luna glanced briefly in his direction, then back to Ryan.

'Nice to have met you.'

'Same here. Please call me if you want a second viewing, I'd be happy to show you around.' He slipped a card into her hand.

'And now I really must go.'

She sensed that he was as reluctant to leave, as she was keen for him to stay.

He walked towards the door, while she stepped the few feet into the bedroom.

They both turned simultaneously, she waved and he smiled.

'Ciao,' he called, then added spontaneously, 'I do hope you take the apartment. I'm not quite sure why, but I think you'll be very happy here.'

The door shut quietly behind him, and at last Luna concentrated on the bedroom. She liked it immediately. It was messy and masculine, holding a strong aura of Ryan Tyler.

There were books and newspapers piled by the side of the bed. And a huge, black and white Annie Leibovitz framed image of John Lennon and Yoko Ono hung above an armchair.

Idly she picked up a silver-framed photograph. It showed Ryan with an attractive blonde girl, they were both smiling. She, in profile, was staring adoringly into his eyes.

With a jolt, Luna realized they looked very much in love.

A stack of letters lay on top of a small desk, next to a thick Filofax. And she noticed a tiny teddy bear, with the words 'I love you' blazoned across its chest in red lettering. It was resting on the handlebars of an exercise bike, positioned in front of a set of sliding doors.

The room told Luna a lot about the occupant: he was untidy, artistic, sentimental, health conscious, had a sense of humour and was well read.

A small dressing room, with open hanging space, adjoined the bedroom and a large bathroom with a big, walk-in shower cabinet. There was one other small guest bedroom that Ryan was using for storage. It was stacked to shoulder height with brown boxes and masses of books.

'Well Miss Fergusson, what do you think?' asked Charles Hammond when they'd seen it all and were walking out through the front door.

'I like it very much, it's the best so far.'

Luna was thinking that whatever she saw later that afternoon would make no difference, her heart was set on Ryan Tyler's flat.

Nicholas Frazer-West was on his second gin and tonic when Ryan was shown to his table in the Connaught restaurant. Ryan was fifteen minutes late.

Nicholas was annoyed, but feigned politeness as he rose to greet him.

'Ryan old chap, nice to see you.'

Ryan had suffered his fair share of insincere greetings in his time, but this one from Nicholas Frazer-West had to be the best; or the worst, depending on how you looked at it.

'Sorry to be late. I'm letting my apartment. Someone came to look round this morning but didn't get there on time, so I had to wait for them and that delayed me.'

Ryan wasn't good at apologies, and it showed in his indifferent body language.

This served to irritate Nicholas further and they faced each other more like opponents than business partners.

Ryan glanced swiftly around the dark, panelled room before sitting down. It reminded him of Frazer-West's club where he'd first met him, all hushed gentility and condescending staff.

Nicholas lifted a hand to the maître d'. 'Jacques, menus please. What would you like to drink Ryan?'

'I'll have a vodka martini with a twist, thanks.' He thought he might need a stiff drink to help him get through lunch smoothly.

Nicholas waited until Ryan had his drink in front of him before speaking.

'I didn't know you were moving.'

Ryan took a sip of his martini. 'Well, I'm moving in with Lu, didn't she tell you?'

'No, she did not,' was the curt reply.

Ryan watched Nicholas's reaction closely, it was evident he disapproved. He felt a renewal of the tension that occurred whenever he met Lord Frazer-West. But determined not to be intimidated, he defended himself.

'She *asked* me to move in with her, Mr Frazer-West.'

He couldn't bring himself to call Lucinda's father either 'Lord' or 'Nicholas'.

'I see,' was all Nicholas said, from out of tight lips.

But it was enough to make Ryan mad as hell. He was about to confront him with the old line 'I suppose you don't think I'm good enough for your daughter', when the waiter arrived to take their order, and the moment passed.

Ryan bit his tongue. This guy was financing his movie he reminded himself, he had to play the game for the sake of the deal.

Nicholas ordered Dover Sole, but Ryan loved fast food. He would have given anything for pizza Margarita, with a side order of French fries and an ice-cold beer. He scanned the menu.

'I'll take the roast beef from the trolley, and some vegetables.'

'Fresh vegetables of the day come with it, sir.'

The waiter had a crisp, cultured voice, not dissimilar to Lord Frazer-West's.

'Yeah, great,' he handed the menu back.

'So, how is my wonderful daughter? We don't get to see her much these days, she's either working or busy with you. We invited her to have lunch with us last Sunday. My mother was in town from the country; she's almost eighty, and has always adored Lucinda. But apparently you were going to Stratford for the day.

'We were all very disappointed. She hasn't seen her grandmother for months.'

'Yeah, we had a ball. Went to see *Twelfth Night*. Lu loved the play and I loved the place, so between us we had a great time.'

Ryan gulped the remainder of his cocktail, fervently wishing Frazer-West would cut the pleasantries and get down to the nitty gritty.

As if he had read his mind, Nicholas broached the real subject.

'So, how is our movie going?'

'Fine. We've just about finished pre-production and we'll start to shoot in two weeks' time,' Ryan answered with a wide, confident smile.

'But that isn't on time, is it Ryan? As I recall, in the schedule you gave me, you should've started to shoot three weeks ago.'

Nicholas pushed his unfinished drink to one side and laid both his hands flat on the table, contemplating his long fingers.

'I'm aware of that. I did write to you explaining the reason for the delay.'

Nicholas did not look up.

'You're correct when you say you wrote to me, but I understood from the letter that there was to be a delay of no more than ten days. By my reckoning, if you start work in two weeks' time, you'll be precisely five weeks late.'

Nicholas lifted his head only when the food arrived at the table.

'How do you like your beef, sir?' The waiter looked at Ryan.

'Medium rare,' he replied, his attention never leaving Nicholas. 'Listen, this happens all the time in pre-production – technical problems, last-minute script changes, costume hold-ups. I can't always prevent these things.'

Nicholas held up his forefinger and pointed it directly at Ryan, who felt his hackles rise. He resented being treated like an errant schoolboy.

'But if you can't prevent these delays, then who can?'

'Yorkshire pudding, sir?'

Ryan nodded, and the plate was placed in front of him. Nicholas's fish followed.

The waiter backed discreetly away as Nicholas continued.

'Every hour, of every day, of every week that you delay, it eats into the budget. You have a deadline, Ryan. You said in April, when I agreed to finance the film, that pre-production would take no longer than eight weeks. It's now the tenth of June and shooting still hasn't begun. Distributors are not known for their patience. If the film isn't ready on time, they'll have your guts for garters, and my investment will be travelling very quickly down the proverbial.'

Nicholas cut a slice of fish. 'So, for God's sake, don't sound so blasé.'

The ability to inject just the right amount of positive aggression into his tone, without sounding angry, had taken Nicholas many years to perfect. Yet it had little effect on Ryan, who merely shrugged, stabbing his fork into a piece of beef.

He disliked Frazer-West with a passion.

On more than one occasion he'd wished he had not

accepted his investment. Arrogant bastard, Ryan thought; the type who enjoyed inspiring fear rather than admiration.

'If I sound blasé, it's not intentional. And, I'm sorry, but I do know more about the movie business than you, if you don't mind me saying. I can assure you that this delay will not affect the final wrap. I've allowed enough injury time.'

Nicholas placed his knife and fork deliberately on the side of his plate before fixing Ryan with an unnerving gaze.

'I may not know a bloody thing about making films, young man, but I do know about making money. And that's the bottom line. I can see that you believe in yourself, a quality I admire, and your talent speaks for itself; but I have a lot at stake here, not least my daughter's reputation as an actress.

'I want to see this film finished on time, and on budget.'

He gesticulated to a passing waiter to refill his empty wine glass.

'Mr Frazer-West, you want exactly the same things as me. Believe me when I say I can deliver.'

Nicholas was not convinced. 'I do hope so, because I'm afraid I can get very tetchy when I lose money, particularly this amount.'

'You're not going to lose your money, you have my word.'

Nicholas wanted to laugh out loud; how could he accept the word of a maverick film director?

'I'll feel a lot more reassured when the film actually starts shooting. You do have a definite date, I assume?'

'June twenty-first, my mother's birthday; and bar fire, plague or famine we begin on that day. The studio is booked, locations, everything in place. Believe me, Mr Frazer—'

'Please don't ask me to believe you again Ryan, it's making me extremely nervous.'

Nicholas wiped his mouth with the back of a napkin, and Ryan decided to change the subject.

'How's Lady Serena, is she well?'

The question was intended to keep the conversation going, rather than out of genuine interest.

Nicholas replied with a resigned lift of his shoulders. 'As always, driving me to distraction.'

'Don't all women? If they didn't keep us guys in line, I think the world would be a very boring place, don't you?'

Nicholas grinned, 'You've got a point there,' he agreed.

It was the first time Ryan had ever seen him look even remotely amused, but it was not to last.

The smile left Nicholas's face as quickly as it had appeared, and his next remark was given a deadpan delivery.

'Tell me, are you in love with my daughter?'

Caught off guard, yet instinctively alert, Ryan responded at once.

'Yes, I am.'

His tone was assured but nevertheless there was a flicker in his eyes and, ever perceptive, Nicholas spotted it and identified it as doubt.

It was slight, but enough to confirm his fears. He resolved again that once the film was finished, he would get Ryan Scott Tyler out of Lucinda's life.

Even if it was the last thing he did.

'You're late,' Lucinda greeted him in the hallway of her house, hardly letting Ryan plant a quick kiss on her cheek.

'Sorry Lu, but the meeting with Bev Benson went on longer than anticipated. You know how it is.'

'I know how it should be, but I'm not sure I know how it is. We were supposed to be going to Poppy's drinks party, remember?'

Ryan had completely forgotten about the birthday bash of Lucinda's best friend.

'You could've gone alone Lu, I would have joined you later.'

She shook her head.

'I was waiting for you, I didn't know where you were. I was worried, why didn't you call?'

'What can I say? I . . . forgot, I'm sorry.'

It was a lame offering that did nothing to soothe her temper. Lucinda's mouth set in a petulant line as she walked into the drawing room without saying another word.

He followed.

'Heh come on, I said I was sorry Lu. What more do you want? Missing Poppy's party isn't exactly the end of the world.'

'That's not the point. It's you Ryan, you've changed.

'I feel like I don't know you any more. You say you're sorry, but it's so obvious you're not really; it's like you don't give a damn.'

He was tired, he had a headache starting, and the last thing he felt like now was a quarrel.

'Anyway, you look tired baby, you could use an early night.'

'Thanks Ryan, you can say the sweetest things when you try.'

Picking up a magazine and flopping on to the sofa, she began to flick through it. He sat down opposite, observing her.

Lucinda was dressed in a black tuxedo and a white shirt. Her long hair had been hastily tied back with a ebony comb. It made her face look gaunt and waif-like, and she was wearing only a dusting of blusher and a little mascara.

Ryan pointed at her.

'You're getting too thin, but then I've told you that before. You should eat more.'

'You can never be too rich or too thin,' Lucinda commented drily, 'to quote the Duchess of Windsor.'

'Well, I personally think Wallis Simpson was wrong. I believe you can be both.' He closed his eyes and rested his head on the back of his chair.

'Oh shut up Ryan, who cares anyway! Nancy Mitford was like a bloody willow tree; you should be grateful, I resemble her in that respect at least.'

'In others too,' he mumbled under his breath, but it was loud enough for her to hear.

'Just what do you mean by that?' Lucinda snapped.

'She was a privileged, spoilt, upper-class, rich bitch.'

Ryan had kept his eyes shut. When he opened them he remained unperturbed by the look of shock on Lucinda's face.

'Ryan, how dare you, I'm not a bitch. The other things yes, through no fault of my own. But . . . a bitch?'

Now she looked hurt, and he was instantly sorry.

'I'm only joking. Come on Lu, chill out. I have had a bad day, then as soon as I walk through the door I'm greeted by your miserable face because I'm late and we've missed one of your friend's boring parties.'

She was seething again.

'It didn't sound like a joke, and my friends are *not* boring. Sometimes, Ryan, you are so fucking Irish it makes me sick.'

'And what's that supposed to mean?' It was his turn to be angry.

'I think you know exactly what I mean.'

'No, I'm not sure that I do Lucinda. Tell me, I'm fascinated.'

She dropped the magazine a few inches and spoke over the top.

'Arrogant, insular, with an underlying yet well-camouflaged hatred of the English, particularly my type of English; *upper-class twits*, as you refer to them.'

His eyes hardened, and he gave a short callous laugh.

'You have no idea do you, growing up in your own safe

227

little world, completely cocooned from reality.'

Her mouth curled down at the edges. 'No Ryan, but that's not my fault. Why do you resent me for it?'

She was right, it wasn't her fault; so he decided to placate her. Joining her on the sofa, he tried to prise the magazine she was pretending to read out of her grip, but she stubbornly refused to let go.

He gave up after a couple of minutes.

'Most of your friends I find boring Lu, OK. It's not the end of the world, we've just got no background in common. For instance, you tell me what I can talk about to that stupid wimp who's engaged to Poppy? Rupert or Robin, whatever his name is.

'Robin,' she muttered.

He lifted her chin, forcing her to look at him.

'And I want you to know that I don't really think you're a bitch; but all actresses as talented as you are, how shall we say, *temperamental*.'

He'd tried to make amends, but to no avail.

'I think the best idea would be for you go out, Ryan, and come back in. Then perhaps we can start again. First you're late, and then you start insulting me.'

'Sure I can go if you like, and not bother to come back at all,' Ryan retorted hotly, surprising himself with a display of quick temper.

It also surprised Lucinda. He was normally infuriatingly passive and detested arguments.

Ryan admonished himself inwardly, he should have known better. Lucinda couldn't cope with criticism in any shape or form. She was highly talented, and with that came all the related insecurity.

'If that's what you want,' Lucinda was yelling, 'just do it. Just go.'

'If you're going to spend all evening in a foul mood, I think I might as well.'

She looked at him in stony silence.

His head was hammering relentlessly now, and he felt slightly nauseous as if he had a migraine coming on.

'Come on Lu, let's not argue, it's a complete waste of time.'

She ignored him. Bending her head, she stared at the print in the magazine, without seeing a single word.

Stubborn silence was her way of punishing him, he knew that. She had done it all her life with her father, and Nicholas had always capitulated.

She obviously fully expected him to do the same, and was visibly shaken when he stood up, and stormed towards the door.

'I'll see you later when we're both in a better mood.'

He left the house quietly and caught a cab back to his own apartment.

He went straight to his bathroom, frantically searching for his migraine medication, relieved to find four pills left in the bottle. Clutching two in the palm of his hand, he went to the kitchen for a glass of mineral water.

As he passed the answering machine in the hall, he noticed the message light flashing. When he returned a few minutes later, carrying a bottle of Evian and a glass, he clicked the switch to play, and leaned against the wall, listening with his eyes shut.

'Hi Ryan, this is Steve Watts, warm and sunny in Santa Monica. Important news man, I'm getting married. To Susie . . . who else? Anyway, we'd love you to make the wedding bash. Call me as soon as you get in.' *Bleep* . . .

'Bev Benson calling, it's eight-thirty p.m., just got word from New York that Marek Beard is on for Hitler in the movie. Good news huh, hope you'll get some shut-eye now.' *Bleep* . . .

'Ryan . . . oh, it's the answering machine . . . it's Mum calling, you know how I hate using these things. Please call me as soon as possible.'

There was a long pause, then she spoke again. 'It's not urgent.' *Bleep* . . .

Ryan smiled, same old Mum.

Then a strange voice, one he didn't recognize at first.

'Mr Tyler, it's Charles Hammond, from Winkworth. I thought you'd like to know that Miss Fergusson, the lady who looked around your flat earlier today, has rented it for a year. I'll call you in the morning to discuss details.' *Bleep* . . .

It was the final message.

He flicked the switch to rewind, and walked towards the bedroom, taking his clothes off en route. He draped them over a chair, and slid between the cool sheets, letting his head sink on to the soft duck-down pillows.

His last thoughts, before he slipped into a deep sleep, were that he was pleased Marek had agreed to play Hitler, and that the gorgeous Luna would be living in his flat. He might even get to see her again.

Nicholas Frazer-West was also late home that evening.

But he had had the courtesy to call Serena, telling her to start dinner without him.

When he eventually arrived at nine-thirty he found her in the breakfast room, eating from a tray on her lap. She was avidly watching television as she forked linguine into her mouth with one hand, and stroked the head of her pet British Blue, Merlin, with the other.

'Evening darling,' Nicholas said, joining her on the sofa.

He patted the cat's back. It stretched and yawned, snuggling closer to Serena, whose eyes had not left the television set.

'Evening Nicholas,' Serena replied absently, her eyes flitting in his direction for a second before darting back to the screen.

'What are you watching?' he asked with little interest.

'It's fascinating. A documentary about the plight of homeless children in Brazil who are being killed in their hundreds by vicious street gangs.'

'It sounds frightfully depressing to me,' Nicholas commented, standing up to take his jacket off.

'I think I'll go and take a bath. Could you fix me a gin and tonic in the meantime, darling?'

'Hmm, hmm,' she answered idly, wondering why on earth he couldn't get his own drink.

She supposed it was because it was something she had always done for him, and she imagined herself still mixing gin and tonics for Nicholas when they were in their dotage. That thought was infinitely more depressing than the documentary.

'Of course, I'll bring it up as soon as this is finished.'

'Thanks.'

Nicholas slipped quietly out of the room.

He climbed the stairs wearily, thinking of Ryan Tyler and his movie. It was extremely worrying. Never having speculated so rashly before, he feared he was going to live to regret it.

Serena brought his drink whilst he was still in the bath. She handed him the glass and, turning to face the mirror, she studied the tiny bags under her eyes, plucking critically at the loose skin.

'I saw Jane Edwards yesterday for lunch, she's had her eyes done. They look wonderful, she looks at least ten years younger. I think I might go for a consultation, to the same man who did hers.'

'I've never heard of anything so absurd! Your eyes are fine.'

She spun round.

'I *knew* you'd say that Nicholas; you may not be bothered about ageing, but I am.'

'I think one should have surgery purely for medical reasons, it's quite appalling to do it for vanity. Look at

231

the mess that Michael Jackson has made of his face. I'm totally opposed to it.'

'Oh, for once in your life think a little bit frivolous can't you? You're always so serious. What's wrong with wanting to look younger or better?'

He was about to retort that few people actually did look better, when she left the bathroom.

His ears pricked up a few minutes later as he heard her shouting from the bedroom.

'Nicholas . . . ! Quick, your pal Jeremy Gray's on television.'

A moment later Nicholas appeared at the doorway. He was still dripping wet, a towel wrapped hastily around his waist.

'Turn the volume up will you, Serena.'

She did as he asked, and the newscaster's voice rang throughout the room.

'It was officially confirmed today that Sir Jeremy Gray, Minister for Trade and Industry, has secured an important aerospace contract with the Kuwaiti government. The contract is estimated to be worth tens of billions, and will provide much needed employment for a new plant soon to be opened at British Aerospace.'

A quick newsflash showed Jeremy shaking hands with the Kuwaiti Foreign Minister.

Serena turned to face Nicholas. 'Good for Jeremy!'

'He's done bloody well,' Nicholas nodded, 'First a knighthood, and now this.'

Drying his back vigorously, he went on. 'I know he's been working on that contract for a long time, and against stiff competition from the Americans. I must call immediately and congratulate him.'

Serena was still watching the television when Nicholas emerged from his dressing room a few minutes later, wearing a bathrobe and slippers. She gave him a sideways glance as he slipped through. He looked pleased with himself, like the proverbial cat who has got more than his fair share of the cream.

She watched the end of the news, undressed, then crept quietly downstairs to make herself a cup of tea. She could hear Nicholas's voice as she reached the landing outside the study. Normally she was uninterested in his telephone conversations, they were invariably boring business discussions.

But tonight, for whatever reason, she felt compelled to listen. Placing her ear close to the door, she could hear him speaking.

'I've just spoken to Jeremy and he suggests a meeting in London; not too soon, perhaps in about six weeks. I thought you should know, it couldn't be better news.'

Nicholas abruptly stopped talking, except for the occasional *mmm* or *yes*. Then, very distinctly, she heard him again.

'Don't worry Nabil, I'll keep you posted about any further developments on the Eurasian contract. I'm looking forward to seeing you in London, be well my friend.'

Serena continued mouse-like downstairs.

She was in the kitchen before Nicholas came out of the study, and she breathed a sigh of relief on hearing the stairs creaking under his feet as he climbed back up to his bedroom.

Whilst she waited for the kettle to boil, she filled the cat's bowl with fresh milk and placed it next to his food on the floor.

More and more, Serena began to feel a distinct unease. It deepened gradually, until a distant memory stirred itself into life in her mind.

The letter.

The one she had found in Nicholas's study years ago, that time that he had gone secretly to the Cayman Islands.

233

She was unable to recall the exact contents now.

Yet she remembered, with vivid clarity, that the letter had involved Nicholas, Nabil Khoorey and Jeremy Gray.

Chapter Nineteen

THREE MONTHS LATER

'I need you to check out this account Luna, it looks a bit precarious. God only knows why we ever lend anybody money for a film.

'One of our valued clients, Lord Frazer-West, a successful property developer who's been with the bank for several years, put up the money initially. The loan was secured against Frazer-West collateral, an office building he owns in the City; it's valued at seven point two million pounds, and is fully let at the moment. All the details are in there.

'Anyway the movie, need I say, has gone over-budget and they need a further two million to complete it. Frazer-West is not prepared to put up any more money or collateral.' He sighed. 'Give me nice, easy corporate or retailing loans any day of the week.'

Luna took the file from the outstretched hand of Jeff Milne, director of the Special Finance department and her immediate boss.

She read the heading on the top left-hand corner. 'Scottsdale Productions.'

The name rang a bell.

'As you know, I'm going on holiday tomorrow for two weeks, and the big man', Jeff pointed to the ceiling above his head, 'is screaming. He wants it sorted out. I mentioned that I'd pass it on to you. So, here it is, your big chance to impress him.'

Luna was angry. She could feel a hot flush entering her

cheeks, and tried unsuccessfully to compose her face.

'What's wrong?' questioned Jeff, walking round her desk, his handsome face scrutinizing hers.

'I think you know what's wrong,' she said through clenched teeth. 'I refuse to continue to work all hours that God sends on your goddamn files, whilst you get all the credit. I've had it . . .' she pointed to an imaginary space above her head, 'Up to here.'

Jeff, seemingly unaffected by her outburst, leaned forward, his face almost touching hers. She could smell his warm breath, it smelt vaguely of peppermint.

'I love you when you're angry Luna, all flashing eyes and flushed cheeks. So bloody attractive.'

He grabbed her hand which was lying across the top of the desk, and forced it down on to his flies.

She could feel his erection stirring and, hating herself for the desire she felt, she ripped her hand away sharply.

'I want to give it to you up to here,' he said, and before she could stop him his hand slipped up her skirt.

She crossed her legs quickly, trapping his hand before it reached its destination. She squeezed harder, leaving nothing to chance.

'Well you can't Jeff, because you're going away with your nice, tolerant wife and two point four kids, whilst I work on your fucking accounts.'

Glaring at him, Luna released his hand and stood up. She walked around her desk, not stopping until she reached the window. Looking down on to Austin Friars, she felt deeply disturbed by the fact that she was jealous.

Her affair with Jeff Milne had started casually. She'd been lonely in London and grateful to have a drink after work, and the odd dinner, with the affable Jeff. It had got out of hand when she'd asked him to help her install some new furniture in her apartment. He'd been happy to oblige, almost too eager. She should have heard warning bells then.

He'd brought wine and take-away Chinese, which they'd eaten in her tiny kitchen. His wife and children had been away at his mother-in-law's in Scotland that week, far enough to put them out of mind whilst he made passionate love to Luna in virtually every part of the flat.

Jeff had stayed with her that night, and several subsequent nights. He was good in bed and great fun.

Luna at that time had no intention of becoming heavily involved with him. Married men, and certainly not her boss, were not on her agenda. Yet, slowly and insidiously, the charming Mr Milne had crept into her life and now, damnit, she needed him.

And he was patently aware of it.

Placing his hands tenderly on her shoulders, Jeff made her face him.

'Heh, come on, I'm going away for two weeks; fourteen days, that's all Luna. You knew all about me when we met. I've never lied to you, never made any false promises have I?'

Luna was forced to agree.

'No Jeff, you haven't. That's the problem I suppose, in my naivety I thought that you might.'

'What can I say?' He lifted his hands, opening them in a gesture of hopelessness.

'You don't have to say a thing,' she said, picking up the file, shaking it at him.

'I'll do this one for you Jeff, but only on the premise that I get the credit. Have I got your word?'

'You've got it,' he grinned, and took a couple of long strides towards the door.

'By the way, I want you to know that you've got the best legs I've ever had the pleasure to be wrapped inside.'

'Is that all you think about, Jeff?'

The grin was still on his face, as if fixed with glue. 'Can you think of anything better?'

'Yes, as a matter of fact I can.'

237

He detected the slight irritation in her reply and decided not to antagonize her any further. The last thing he wanted was a nasty scene.

'You know how I feel about you, Luna.' His voice had adopted a syrupy smooth tone.

Her only reply was an indifferent shrug.

He opened the door. 'Aren't you going to wish me a good hol?'

Luna was smiling. 'Happy holidays, Jeff. Enjoy . . . as the Americans say. Enjoy your fourteen precious days in Tuscany. And if you do get an opportunity to think of me, though that's doubtful, try and remember how I looked when you were last screwing me. Lock the image in your mind, because from now on it's history.'

The smile slipped from his face. 'Are you serious Luna?' he asked, incredulous. Rejection was a new experience for him.

She enjoyed her brief moment of triumph, before replying, 'Absolutely, never more so in my entire life.'

'I believe you,' he whispered, and left the office in a state of shock.

Luna went home an hour later feigning a migraine; back in her flat in Chelsea Harbour, she drank a full bottle of white wine and went to bed crying.

Waking up four hours later, with a genuine headache and an intense sense of isolation, she recalled the last time she'd felt like this. It had been on the day her father had left her at Highclaire Academy, when she was thirteen.

But Luna was resourceful. She did what she always did when she was depressed, she made herself tons of junk food and absorbed herself in work. She sat up in bed, feeling marginally better, surrounded by several plates: one full of crisps and nuts, a Big Mac burger and chips, two cans of Coke, a bowlful of chocolate buttons and a tub of Häagen-Dazs.

Opening the Scottsdale file, she studied the account.

Immediately she experienced a slight tremor of anticipation when she read the names of the two directors; one was a Lord Frazer-West, whom she had never heard of, but the other was Ryan Scott Tyler, the film director.

Her memory jogged. '*That's* where I'd heard of Scottsdale Productions!'

Ryan had given her his card on the day she'd first looked at the apartment, but she'd subsequently lost it when moving. For a while she had secretly harboured the hope that he might call her, had resisted changing the telephone number for several weeks, eventually accepting defeat and registering her new number as ex-directory.

An image of Ryan as she had first seen him, fresh from the shower, flashed through her mind.

She bit deeply into the burger, sending mustard trickling down her chin. Roughly wiping it off with a paper napkin, she savoured the flavour, and realized that her next meeting with Ryan Scott Tyler was going to be a professional one.

Luna stood up as Ryan was shown into her office.

'Mr Scott Tyler, pleased to meet you again.'

Ryan studied the exotic face in front of him.

Recognition slowly registered as light from the window behind her illuminated the perfect contours of her high cheekbones. He was struck, as he had been on their first meeting, by a nagging sense of familiarity.

When he had called the bank to make an appointment, he hadn't at first made any association with the name 'Fergusson'.

'Luna! How are you finding my apartment?'

She was flattered that he'd remembered her name, then reminded herself that it was a difficult one to forget.

'It's my apartment now,' she replied brightly. 'I'm afraid I've made quite a few changes, you wouldn't recognize it.'

'It always did need a woman's touch,' he agreed.

She indicated a chair in front of her large teak desk, and they sat down simultaneously.

'I do miss the river,' he told her. 'There's definitely something about living near the water. I have a small house on Malibu Beach in LA, right on the ocean; there's nothing to compare with waking up to the sound of the waves, and a fresh sea breeze to blow away all the cobwebs.'

'So, where do *you* live now?' Luna enquired, smoothing her wayward hair down with the flat of her hand. It was tied back from her face, giving her almond-shaped eyes a distinctly feline quality.

'I live at Elystan Place, SW3, in a very pretty Victorian cottage,' he said without much enthusiasm. 'I preferred the Harbour.'

She was tempted to ask why he'd moved in that case, but didn't want to look prying. Nevertheless, the urge to know more about him was overpowering, so she risked him telling her to mind her own business.

'Why did you move?'

'It's a long story, I'm sure you'd be bored.'

Ryan had no inclination to discuss the fact that he'd needed money, and his girlfriend had been insistent that he move in with her. He changed the subject.

'So, how are you enjoying living in London, Miss Executive Banker?'

'It's a culture shock; takes a bit of getting used to. There's lots of stuff I miss about New York.'

'Like what?'

She thought about his question, noting at the same time that he was wearing the identical black suit she had seen him in on the day they'd met.

'. . . Like efficiency, great service, my apartment in Tribeca, the view down the East River from my office, eating the best damn burgers in the world, and going down the Village on Monday nights to hear amazing jazz. It's a different buzz here that's all; calmer, slower, less frenetic. I'll get used to it in time, I suppose.'

'Maybe not. Some people get off on that fast-track life. Me, I like a bit of both.'

Luna suspected she could detect a hint of ridicule in his dark eyes, but wasn't sure. She was feeling the same hot flush and confusion his presence had caused on their first meeting. She struggled to concentrate.

'We've asked you here today to answer questions regarding the movie you're co-producing and directing.' She glanced down at the file on her desk. '*The Mitford Papers*.'

'Yes, we're in the process of completing the shooting.'

His deliberate choice of the word 'completing' did not escape Luna.

'As I understand from the loan agreement, Lord Frazer-West owns sixty-five per cent of Scottsdale Productions, and you own the other thirty-five.'

'That's correct,' confirmed Ryan. 'I had a two-million-dollar loan from Bank of America. He did a deal with you guys for the remaining ten million dollars, against some property he owns in London. I can't remember where it is.'

'Throgmorton Avenue, in the City,' she supplied. Then she went on to give the bank's perspective.

'Scottsdale Productions have applied for a further two million dollars to finish the movie. As you're no doubt aware, Lord Frazer-West is reluctant to offer any further property as collateral to increase the loan, or any further finance for this project. He may be persuaded, but I need to be certain that you can complete the movie in a maximum of four weeks, and that the distributors are comfortable with the delay.'

Ryan breathed deeply. He was aware that it was crucial to be convincing.

'All the interest has been paid during production, so why the hassle now? I don't understand why the bank can't just increase the loan, or extend it with a higher interest rate. The movie will be wrapped up one month from now, on that you have my word.

'I spoke to the American distributors yesterday, and they're putting something in writing to the bank to assure you that they're prepared to re-schedule.

'The movie was due for general release in December, they've re-scheduled it for late spring. There's really no sweat.'

'But, Ryan, you don't seem to understand. You won't be able to finish your movie without the remainder of the finance. If Lord Frazer-West is not prepared to advance the loan personally, or come up with more collateral, and Spencer Howard refuse to extend their loan, then we'll be forced to foreclose. And there'll be no *Mitford Papers*.'

Luna leaned back in her chair.

'I really don't know how to convince you that I *can* finish my movie on time, Luna. I think the best solution would be for you to come down to the set, see how a movie's made, and talk to some of the production team. It might give you a greater insight into the industry.'

He gave her a cool smile.

'You don't seem particularly concerned about this finance,' she ventured. 'I must remind you that it's extremely crucial.'

Ryan answered truthfully.

'Look, I'm a movie-maker, right? It's all I've ever wanted to do since I was given my first camera at eight years old. I spent all my spare time in flea-infested cinemas, lost in a world of images and camera angles. By my own admission I'm no businessman, nor would I ever want to be, but I *am* passionate about this movie. It's late, sure; but only because I'm a perfectionist. And if I can't get the additional finance from Spencer Howard, then I'll beg, steal and borrow until I get it someplace. Believe me when I say *The Mitford Papers* will be made, and distributed worldwide. It's going to be a great movie.'

Luna gently clapped her hands a couple of times.

'Pretty speech, and very well delivered. However, passionate oratory is not what banking is about. I'm a banker, that's all *I've* ever wanted to be, and banking is about money: hard cash, the nitty gritty, the bottom line. I'm afraid it's no place for idealists.'

He laughed sarcastically.

'How right you are, and you could say the same about the film world. I told you, it's dog eat dog out there and I wouldn't have got this far if I didn't know the way to turn in a commercial package.'

'I grant you that, but you have no real understanding of commerce, without which there'd be no film world at all.'

She closed the file, placing her hands on top. He noticed how tiny her fingers were.

'I would like to come down to the set, if I may. When would be convenient?' Her tone was brisk and businesslike.

'Tomorrow or Friday, we're on location in Gloucestershire. It's a particularly beautiful part of the county, you should enjoy the scenery.'

'I'm not on a sightseeing trip,' she said curtly, consulting a small black diary.

'I can't do tomorrow, but Friday would be fine. Shall we say ten-thirty in the morning?'

'Ten-thirty, it is . . . if you want to get up very early and fight the traffic out of London.'

'What do you mean?' She looked vague.

'The village of Stow on the Wold, where we're filming, is a good two hours' drive from London. That's if you know the way.'

He took a pen out of his inside pocket and began writing something on the loose-leaf pad on top of her desk. She could see he was drawing a rough map.

'My geography of England is a little rusty, so perhaps we'd better make it eleven-thirty to be on the safe side,' she amended.

'This is the address, and directions.' He stood up, passing her the slip of paper.

Her hand quivered slightly as she accepted it. 'Nice to have met you again, Ryan.'

'By the way, you don't look like a banker.'

In fact in that instant she reminded him of a young Sophia Loren, but with much darker skin.

'And what do I look like?' Luna could not resist asking him, disturbed by his penetrating gaze.

'A fucking goddess.'

He replied with easy candour, before leaving her office without a backward glance.

'Cut! That was great,' Ryan shouted, addressing the film crew gathered in the dining room of Langton Hall. The large manor house, built of Cotswold stone in 1658, was set in fifty-five acres of rolling countryside, seven miles from the picturesque market town of Stow on the Wold.

Lucinda picked her way across the set, holding her long, elegant evening dress above her knees as she stepped gingerly through thick wiring, ducking under camera equipment, careful not to catch her perfectly set hair.

Ryan was talking to a cameraman when she reached him. She rudely interrupted.

'Ryan, why is it that we have to do so many takes of every single scene? In my opinion it was fine on the third and fourth take.'

Trying to ignore her, but distinctly peeved, Ryan continued, 'Excuse me Danny, I'll get back to you later.'

He then yelled over the top of her head. 'Everyone take a break for lunch.'

The cameraman stepped to one side with an understanding nod. He had worked with fractious prima donna types for the last fifteen years. In his opinion Lucinda West was better than most, at least she turned up on time and worked bloody hard.

As soon as Danny was out of earshot Ryan turned to Lucinda, his dark eyes flashing angrily.

'I would appreciate it if you didn't interrupt me when I'm discussing technical problems with crew, and please do not question my authority as director.'

Her bottom lip curled, a habit that irritated him acutely. He suspected she had developed it when she was a child, to cajole her indulgent father.

'I know you're a perfectionist Ryan, but the film *is* already four weeks over schedule.'

An exasperated sigh exploded from his lips. 'I don't need to be reminded of that, Lucinda. You know, as well as I do, why. I want this film to be right, the best. It's looking great, I can't rush it now.'

'I understand, I'm merely concerned. I spoke to Daddy last night, he's getting pressure from the bank. They want him to put up more collateral to guarantee a further loan. I warn you Ryan, he's very reluctant to do so.'

'I already know that, I went to Spencer Howard the day before yesterday to discuss the loan. Banks, investors, moneymen; the whole lot are a fucking nightmare.'

Lucinda could feel his frustration, and felt sorry for him.

'But you can't make movies without them,' she reminded him. 'But, hey, you didn't tell me you had had a meeting with the bank. What did they say?'

Some of his anger was ebbing away as he looked into her face; so grave and serious, full of concern for him and for the movie.

'I didn't want to worry you Lu. They're looking into the loan agreement, trying to sort something out. I'm sure it's going to be OK,' he told her, with more confidence than he felt.

As she fiddled nervously with the string of pearls around her throat, he touched the side of her bare arm reassuringly, stroking the smooth skin below her shoulder.

'I haven't exactly been the perfect person to live with lately, have I?'

'I understand, Ryan,' she stated simply, 'We're all under a lot of pressure, you particularly with this bank thing hanging over your head. What will happen if they won't extend the loan?'

Ryan slid his forefinger across his throat. Spotting Luna speaking to a technician at the far side of the room at the same time, he had the grace to look a bit sheepish and said, 'Can you excuse me for a moment Lu, but Miss Fergusson has just arrived.'

Lucinda shrugged, wondering who 'Miss Fergusson' was. Glancing after Ryan, she saw him approach a tall dark girl from the back and tap her on the shoulder.

As the girl turned round, long black hair flying, Lucinda was momentarily stunned by her beautiful face. She stood rooted to the spot in reaction. There was something familiar about the girl. Like people you meet in dreams Lucinda thought, real, but not real. It was almost scary.

Ryan must have said something funny, as a moment later she could hear the girl's throaty laughter. Deliberately she began to pick her way in their direction. But then she realized that Ryan and his Miss Fergusson were already walking across the set, towards her. Lucinda's heart began to beat faster.

'Lu, I'd like you to meet Miss Fergusson,' Ryan introduced them.

For a split second the two women's eyes met, Luna's open and inquisitive, Lucinda's half closed and wary.

'I think we've met,' Luna smiled, with a knowing look.

'No, I don't think so,' Lucinda was shaking her head.

Luna laughed lightly, adding in a soft voice, 'Perhaps not in this life.'

For some strange reason, Lucinda found the innocent comment disconcerting. She was saved from having to make a reply when Ryan spoke.

'Miss Fergusson is here from the bank. Late I might add, but better late than never.'

Luna groaned, 'I'm sorry, I should have been here an hour ago, but I must admit I've been hopelessly lost. This country is such a maze of tiny, twisting lanes, I don't suppose I'll ever get used to it.'

She was wearing a pair of casual, navy blue cords and a crisp, white cotton shirt. Her hair was caught loosely halfway down her back in a tortoiseshell slide, several wayward strands fanning across her shoulders. She was carrying a soft, leather briefcase and held a blazer, draped over her arm.

'I'm very lucky to have Lucinda playing the lead in *The Mitford Papers*. She's a brilliant actress and a rising star.'

Lucinda looked at Ryan fondly. It was at that point that Luna recognized her as the girl in the photograph she had seen in Ryan's bedroom, when she'd first viewed his apartment.

'Sorry, I'm a new girl in town, should I have heard of you?'

Lucinda shrugged, her scarlet lips parting in a thin smile. 'No reason, unless you've seen *Burden of Deceit*.'

'Of course, now I know who you are! How stupid of me.' Luna smiled warmly. 'You play Sally Lawrence. I've heard you're marvellous. I've been so busy since I've been in London there's been no opportunity to catch up with the theatre. But I did see a big piece on you in *Vanity Fair*, that's obviously where I know you from.'

Lucinda shrugged again, still gripped by the unexplained feeling of intimacy Luna's presence had engendered in her.

'Perhaps' she commented quietly, and then let Ryan speak again.

'Miss Fergusson is a banker. She's here to check us out, to decide whether or not she makes a recommendation to her credit committee for an extension of our loan. We're in her hands,' he sneered slightly. 'That's correct, isn't it Miss Fergusson?'

Luna noticed that he had not once referred to her by her first name, and she was irritated by his flippant attitude.

'That's quite correct Mr Tyler, but it's not quite as simple as you make it sound.'

'Ryan finds it hard to be interested in anything other than movies I'm afraid, Miss Fergusson.' Lucinda interrupted quickly to dispel any wrong impression.

Luna nodded emphatically. 'I think I've already gathered that.'

The two women looked directly at each other, smiling in mutual accord. At any moment Ryan expected them to say in exasperated unison, '*Men.*'

They were standing very close, and were exactly the same height. Ryan stared at their faces in profile. He observed them intently, suddenly realizing why he found Luna so familiar; she looked amazingly like Lucinda.

Ridiculous, he thought, but they looked so much alike they could almost be sisters.

Chapter Twenty

Luna spent all day on the set.

She watched Lucinda West, enthralled by her talent.

She also admired Ryan. The air of nonchalant indifference he normally wore was replaced by a vitality and command of the situation that reminded her of how her father had been when she was a young girl.

She met some of the other actors and several technicians, and left at seven in the evening to drive back to London.

Impressed by what she had seen, she was determined to try and get Ryan the extra money needed to finish his film. Her first job the following morning was to call Lord Frazer-West.

'Good morning sir, my name is Luna Fergusson.'

She heard his sharp intake of breath at the mention of her name, and wondered why.

'I'm assistant vice-president of Spencer Howard Franklyn, and I've taken over the Scottsdale loan from Jeff Milne.

'I wonder if it would be possible for us to meet to discuss the current situation?'

'I don't think there is anything to discuss, Miss Fergusson. I've already informed the bank, both verbally and in writing, that I'm not prepared to offer any further collateral or finance. I warned Mr Scott Tyler about his inability to complete this film on time and within budget weeks ago. The man is a law unto himself, I'm afraid I find him very difficult to deal with. Mr Milne and Peter McLaughlin both know my feelings.'

'But you own sixty-five per cent of the company; the shoot is almost finished, a month at the most.'

Lord Frazer-West sighed audibly. 'I'm patently aware of that, young lady.'

She would have loved to ask him how he knew she was young, but resisted.

'You have a huge portfolio of property, Lord Frazer-West, I'm certain the bank would look favourably on—'

He interjected, not letting her finish.

'I repeat, I'm not prepared to put up any more collateral. I've been banking with Spencer Howard for more than twenty years and I am, as you are no doubt aware, a valued client.

'I think, under the circumstances, that the bank should look favourably upon this loan. It's the first time I've ever speculated, how shall I put it, in a high risk venture, and I've decided it's high time the bank took a risk on *my* behalf. If they are unprepared to do so, I may have to take my business elsewhere.

'I can afford, as they say, to bite the bullet on this one. Do you understand Miss Fergusson?'

'Of course sir, I understand perfectly, and I appreciate what you are saying. Thank you very much for talking to me, I'll be in touch. Goodbye.'

He offered her a curt 'Goodbye' in return; Luna waited for the click on the line.

'Fuck you.'

She cursed down the telephone, before slamming it back into the cradle. Arrogant bastard, she thought as she studied a file in front of her. It contained an impressive list of the Frazer-West properties, and he was right when he said he was a valued client.

Peter McLaughlin, the Chief Executive, had warned her

that Lord Frazer-West could be very tricky; and under no circumstances must she upset him.

She closed the file, tapping it with her fingertip. The property Frazer-West had put up as collateral was located in the City, it was a small office building, fully let. She flicked an intercom switch through to her secretary.

'Yes, Miss Fergusson?'

'Find me the deeds and valuation on 47 Throgmorton Avenue, please Susan.'

'Right away.'

The secretary entered her office five minutes later carrying a file.

'Thanks,' Luna took the file.

Flicking through it, her eyes scanning the details, she discovered that it was a listed building. Number 47 was in fact a gilt-edge property, fully let to several small accountancy companies and loss adjusters. Her heart skipped a beat as she read that the lease was coming to an end in six months. She called the estate agents Healy Baker and was put through to a Tim Picton-Jones.

'Hi, I'm Luna Fergusson from Franklyn Spencer Howard' she said brightly.

The estate agent replied with a bored-sounding, 'Good morning, how can I help?'

'I believe you handle property for a client of ours, forty-seven Throgmorton Ave.'

'Can you hang on while I locate the file.'

Luna heard a dull thud as Tim placed the telephone on his desk, this was followed by a rustle of papers, and the voice of a girl in the background.

'Got it, Forty-seven Throgmorton, very fine property, perfect location.'

Luna could not resist a slight smile, as the agent's voice was suddenly filled with enthusiasm.

'I believe the head lease is due for renewal soon?' she asked, holding her breath as she waited for the reply.

'You're quite right Miss Fergusson. There is a twenty-year lease coming to an end, in . . .' He paused, 'March twenty-sixth to be precise, my birthday in fact,' he chirped.

'Can you give me some indication of the increase in value, for collateral purposes?'

Luna felt a warm surge of triumph as she heard Tim's next words.

'I would predict at least twenty-five per cent uplift on the old rent, so,' he did a rough calculation, 'that would value the property at approx nine million pounds, give or take a few quid.'

'Great, that's exactly what I wanted to hear. Can I have that in writing please, Mr Picton-Jones?'

'For a small fee, certainly,' he retorted.

Nothing for nothing, Luna thought ruefully as she agreed.

'I'll fax it over today,' the agent said.

Smiling triumphantly, she replaced the telephone, thinking as she did so that the revaluation would just about cover the extra finance Ryan needed to complete his movie.

'Yes!' shouted Luna and punched the air. With her heart beating fast, she rang Peter McLaughlin on his private line. He answered immediately.

'I think I've come up with a solution to the Scottsdale problem sir, can you spare me a moment?' Her cool voice belied her inner excitement.

'Of course Miss Fergusson, come right up.'

All day Nicholas had been nagged by Luna Fergusson's telephone call, unable to banish it from his mind.

He was positive that she was Royole Fergusson's daughter.

He was certain the banker had said his daughter's name was Luna. It was an extremely unusual name, he doubted there was another one.

Nicholas had disliked her waspish tone, and found the fact that she was working for Spencer Howard disconcerting. He had been considering moving his account for some time, and the unwelcome telephone call that morning had finally made up his mind.

He considered the possibility of also changing his bank in Grand Cayman, taking his money out of Fergusson hands altogether. But, thinking that he was being ridiculously paranoid, he decided to leave well alone. His account was very healthy and the off-shore company had proved invaluable. There were no problems. A phrase his late father had frequently used came into his mind.

'If it works, don't change it.'

This thought served to confirm his decision, and he left his office with a satisfied smile. It was a balmy September evening, and a warm blast of air greeted him as he stepped on to Curzon Street. The chauffeur was holding open the back door of the Bentley. Nicholas glanced up at his office before he slid into the cool, air-conditioned interior.

Frazer-West Properties had long since outgrown the building, and he knew that he must think seriously about moving into bigger premises soon. Serena always accused him of procrastinating. She was right, but he hated change.

'Home, José,' he said to the Portuguese driver, as the car slipped silently down Curzon Street and into Mayfair.

Nicholas stared out of the front window, thinking of the evening ahead. Lucinda and Ryan were coming for dinner, but he knew it was not a social call.

They obviously intended to mount a joint attack, to persuade him to invest more money or put up more collateral for the bank loan. Ryan could go to hell as far as he was concerned, but he hated upsetting Lucinda.

The thought troubled him for the entire twenty-minute journey home.

Serena let him into the house.

She was dressed for dinner in a chic, black evening suit, styled like a man's with a flimsy, white silk bodice underneath.

'Umm, you look nice,' he commented as he walked into the hall.

She accepted the compliment with a wide smile. 'Thank you, sir.'

There was a teasing tone in her voice, something he hadn't heard for years. His nostrils pricked up.

'You smell nice as well, what is it?'

'Hah, you noticed. It's a new fragrance called Passion.'

'Very alluring,' he commented.

Nicholas coughed, slightly embarrassed as he detected what he thought was desire in her sparkling eyes. He looked down, surveying his feet, afraid to catch her eye for fear he might have been mistaken. He could never be completely sure with Serena.

'Sorry I'm late darling, but my meeting this afternoon with Anthony Black went on and on. That man is a human dynamo. I thought I was a manic workaholic until I met him, he makes me look positively laid back.'

Serena propelled her husband towards the foot of the stairs, where she pushed him gently.

'Go on, you've got fifteen minutes to wash and change.'

'What's for supper?' he called, as he went up.

'Your favourite, grouse; just came in this morning from Scotland.'

'Mmm, wonderful,' he mumbled, thinking with malicious glee that Ryan Scott Tyler would probably hate grouse.

If he'd ever heard of it.

Lucinda's girlish giggles and Serena's peals of laughter greeted him as he entered the drawing room a little later.

'Evening,' Nicholas said, striding to the centre of the room where his wife and daughter were sitting on the sofa, studying a pile of photographs.

Ryan was nowhere in sight.

Both women looked up.

'You must look at these snaps taken on the set at Langton Hall, some of them are hilarious,' suggested Serena, taking the bundle from Lucinda's hands as she jumped up to greet her father.

'Daddy darling, long time no see. I missed you.'

Lucinda snuggled into his neck. Her perfume was much stronger than Serena's, and not as fragrant. He didn't like it.

'I've missed you too, poppet.' Using his pet name for her, he placed a warm kiss on her cheek.

'Drink,' Serena handed him his usual large gin and tonic.

'Thanks,' he took it from her.

Looking around the room, he spoke to Lucinda. 'Isn't Ryan with you?'

Lucinda pulled a long face. 'He's been delayed, I'm afraid. The bank called him urgently this afternoon, asking him to go in for an emergency meeting.'

Lucinda averted her eyes, whilst Nicholas raised his.

'You see, he can't pay the wages next week. Things are very critical. We're going to have to stop production if he doesn't get something sorted out soon.'

'I'm fully aware of the situation, Lucinda. I do own equity in Scottsdale Productions, and I haven't been entirely inactive myself. I've been exerting my own kind of pressure on the bank to come up with the finance, and I think I'm nearly there. They're beginning to cave in.'

There was a long silence, the only sound their respective breathing, finally broken by Lucinda who spoke in a deliberately impassioned voice.

'The film is wonderful Daddy, it's Academy material.

255

We all believe that. If it falls through now, I think it'll break my heart, not to mention Ryan's.'

'I don't give a damn about Ryan Tyler, his heart, or his reputation for that matter, but I do care about you.'

He placed his hands on her arms, and was at once reminded of the way she had looked the day she had left home for Hastings School.

'This film really is very important to you, isn't it Lucinda?'

Her voice was small as she said simply, 'Yes, it is.'

Father and daughter shared a few seconds of subtle understanding before Nicholas spoke again.

'I'll call the bank first thing in the morning and negotiate a further loan agreement.'

'Mr Tyler, did you hear what I just said?' Luna asked. There was still no reply. She considered his face, usually so dark but ashen now, and frozen in shock.

She repeated herself. 'The bank have approved the loan . . . in theory . . . and subject to a revaluation of the property on Frogmorton Avenue. But I doubt there'll be a problem.'

There was still no reply. But gradually the colour returned to his face and then she heard his deep voice booming across her desk.

'That is fan-fucking-tastic! Miss Fergusson, you're a genius.'

'I'm no genius, just an efficient banker,' she corrected him candidly.

'If *I* say you're a genius, then believe me you are. You've saved my movie, you've saved my life. I really thought I was in for the chop.' His voice lightened as he slid his finger across his throat.

'Tell me, how did you do it?'

Not waiting for her reply, he went on, totally excited.

'Listen, this calls for a celebration. You can tell me all about it over dinner.'

'I'm not sure Mr Tyler,' she hesitated.

'For Christ's sake call me Ryan like before. Why the hell not? Come on, loosen up Miss Lady Banker. What harm can it do?'

His ebullience was infectious, and she found herself replying with equal enthusiasm.

'Why not? Yes, why not indeed!'

It was eight-thirty, and she would only have been going home to an empty apartment.

Ryan thought quickly. 'I need to make one phone call, then we can go. What kind of food do you like?'

'Actually, I'm no fancy food freak. All that French stuff doesn't interest me, but I adore Italian.'

'Well, at least we have something in common. I could live on fast food and my favourite is Italian. I know just the place.'

He was grinning broadly as he picked up the telephone.

'Great I'll just use the bathroom before we go.'

Leaving her office, closing the door quietly behind her, she felt sudden misgivings as she overheard Ryan speaking on the phone.

'Lu, I'm really sorry, but I'm tied up in a meeting at the bank and it's going to go on for some time. It looks very positive. Don't wait for me to start dinner, God knows what time I'll be through here.'

'No problem Ryan, I understand, and Mummy and Daddy will too. In fact Daddy's just agreed to go into the bank tomorrow to sort out a new package with them. I think he's willing to put up further collateral.'

Ryan felt a sharp pang of guilt as he listened to her, knowing she had been instrumental in Frazer-West's decision.

'He may not have to do that, I think they're going to

257

extend the loan anyway. I'll tell you all about it later, OK?'

He was eager to ring off before Luna returned.

'I've got everything crossed for you here, Ryan.'

'Well, don't uncross any of it till I get home, and I'll do it for you.'

He heard her chuckle.

'Promises, promises, that's all I get from you these days.'

'This is no empty promise, trust me.'

He replaced the telephone just as Luna opened the door.

'Ready?' she enquired, her hand poised on the light switch.

'As ready as I'll ever be,' Ryan replied, following her out of the office.

He was pleased not to be eating in the stultifying atmosphere of the Frazer-Wests' elegant town house, and ecstatic that he now had his extra finance. More so, because it had been achieved without further input from Lucinda's imperious father.

At that very moment Nicholas was actually talking about Ryan.

'Is he going back to live in Los Angeles after the film, Lucinda?'

They were eating at the huge, twelve-seater table in the formal dining room, on the ground floor. Lucinda had suggested eating in the breakfast room, but her father wouldn't hear of it.

His question instantly put her on guard.

'To be honest, we haven't really discussed it much Daddy. All we seem to do these days is work, talk about work, then fall into an exhausted sleep; only to awake the next day to start the whole process all over again.'

She helped herself to a bread roll as the cook served hot celery soup.

'Had you any idea when you started all this that making a film would be such hard work?' Serena enquired, dipping her spoon into the soup.

'Yes, I had some idea, but one's never absolutely certain about anything until it actually happens.

'I suppose I thought it couldn't be tougher than going on stage every night, but it's so different. With live theatre your applause is immediate and you have constant audience commitment, it's almost like a rapport. Whereas with a film you only have a camera and a demanding, or in my case fractious, director.'

Sighing, she tore her bread savagely.

Serena thought how drained she looked. 'Is Ryan that difficult, darling?'

It was a casual question yet, for some reason, Lucinda felt she was being drawn.

'He's a brilliant director Mummy, all genius has temperament.'

And you're no exception, Serena thought. Aloud she said, 'That's not quite what I meant.'

Nicholas tilted his soup plate to scoop up the last spoonful. He drank it, placing his spoon carefully on the side of the plate, before wiping his mouth slowly with the side of a starched, white linen napkin.

'What exactly do you mean, Mother?'

Serena's mouth was full of soup, so Nicholas replied for her.

'I may as well be frank, your mother and I are concerned.'

'Concerned about what?'

Lucinda searched both of their faces, resting on her father's as he carried on talking.

'Your on-going relationship with Ryan Tyler. Do you remember what I said when I agreed to finance *The Mitford Papers*?'

259

Lucinda dropped her spoon noisily so that it splashed, spotting the lace tablecloth.

'Yes Father, I remember it well. So?'

'I'm merely refreshing your memory, that you promised not to marry for at least two years. I wondered if you had given our agreement any further thought?'

Serena took up the conversation.

'We're worried about you, Lucinda, you must understand that. Both of us think that Ryan is totally unsuitable and would only make you very unhappy in the long term. Fine to have fun with for now, but don't make a silly mis—'

She didn't finish.

Lucinda flung her napkin down, smacking the table top.

'All my life, the pair of you have been telling me what's right and what's wrong for me. For God's sake, I'm twenty-seven now! Don't you think it's time you stopped? Can't you respect the fact that I've a mind of my own. I'm a successful actress, which I achieved without help from either of you.'

'That's not entirely fair, or true.' Nicholas cut in. 'We supported you through RADA after Hastings, or have you forgotten that?'

Lucinda expressed her mounting frustration, 'How on earth could I forget, Daddy, when you won't let me? Have either of you ever stopped to think for a moment about what I want, how I feel, what makes me happy?'

'Of course. We think about it all the time Lucinda, you are our only daughter.' Serena paused for Nicholas to speak.

'We have no son, and when you marry I would like to think of your husband in that vein. Ryan Scott Tyler, for all his charm and charisma, is not of our class Lucinda. You must realize that. His values, his background are not yours. Marriage to him would be a disaster, and would never have my blessing.'

'I don't need your blessing, or your consent. What you're trying to say is that Ryan isn't good enough for me. Worse than that, you think he's not good enough for *you*. Your values stink. You can't even see reality because of your own hypocritical snobbery.'

Lucinda spoke in a voice that shocked both her parents. Serena blanched as Nicholas shouted, 'How dare you!'

Lucinda pushed her chair back, her voice getting louder as she stood.

'I dare because I want happiness, true happiness. Something you two seem to have overlooked. It's not about money, position or class; it's about laughter, sharing, and . . . love.'

Serena lost patience.

'Oh for God's sake Lucinda, you're not on stage now, spare us the sentimental dramatics. You know as well as I do that what your father has said is true.'

Fuelled by her mother's harsh words and her father's smug attitude, she gave way completely to her impetuous anger. Realizing, even as she did it, that she was overstepping the mark she counterattacked.

'I really don't know how either of you has the gall to tell me about love and marriage. Have you looked at your own lately, it's a fucking sham.'

Staring at her parents' stricken faces, she stated her own position.

'I love Ryan and I intend to marry him, with or without your consent.'

Nobody spoke as Lucinda stormed out of the room, fighting hard to stem the tears. She almost knocked over June who was coming out of the kitchen with a tray containing roast grouse and game chips.

'Not staying for dinner, Miss Lucinda?'

'I hate bloody grouse!' she shouted, slamming the door as she left the house.

Serena left most of her food. Nicholas merely picked at his, eating only a meagre amount.

They had both lost their appetite.

Neither of them discussed what had happened until later in the drawing room when coffee was served.

'I shouldn't have brought up the subject of Ryan Tyler, it was my fault entirely,' Nicholas admitted with an exasperated sigh.

'She's in love, Nicholas. Hopelessly, passionately in love with him,' Serena commented with an air of resignation.

'Nothing either of us says will make her see sense.'

'We both know how much she likes her own way, and how hot-headed she is when she doesn't get it. But she'll be full of remorse tomorrow, and no doubt calling to offer her apologies.'

'I'm not so sure Serena, but I hope you're right. I just know that this man is no good for her.'

'But, as she's just reminded us Nicky, she's twenty-seven and a grown woman. I think she's made it very plain that she resents our intrusion. I really think we have to let Lucinda get on with her own life.'

Serena stood up and stretched, giving Nicholas the same look he'd seen earlier, when he'd first arrived home. Certain, now, that what he read in her eyes was desire, he was seized with nerves.

'I'm going to bed darling, I feel exhausted. Probably too much red wine and not enough food.'

He held up his brandy goblet. 'Thanks for your support down there with Lucinda. I don't deserve it, so often in the past I've taken her side against you.'

'The past, who cares about the past? It's gone, let's try and live for now, and the future. Do you think that just for tonight we could bury it?'

There was a definite implication in her question, and he understood precisely what it meant.

'I'll try Serena,' he promised in a very hushed voice.

'Will you, please.' She held out her hand to him.

He gripped it tightly and they walked upstairs together, stopping on the landing outside Serena's bedroom.

'Do you know what day it is today, Nicky?'

He racked his brain for a special event that he might have overlooked.

'I know it's Wednesday.' He raised his eyebrows. 'Have I forgotten something?'

'It's exactly two years to the day, since you left this bedroom to sleep in that one.' She pointed to the door opposite. 'Don't you think that's a long enough punishment for both of us?'

'I suppose so Serena, but it's difficult for me to forgive.'

He desperately wanted to ask if she loved him, but couldn't; she might hesitate or, worse, say no.

'Try Nicholas, life is much too short. You and I are running out of time . . . we're not getting any younger.'

Not letting go of his hand, she opened the door to her bedroom and pulled him gently inside.

Lucinda lay awake waiting for Ryan's return, glancing at the digital clock on the bedside table every few minutes. It was gone one when she heard the door close, and his footsteps mounting the stairs.

He opened the bedroom door with infinite care and crept into the adjoining bathroom, slipping out of his clothes as quickly and quietly as possible, before padding across the carpeted floor towards the bed.

Ryan stopped dead in his tracks as the room was suddenly flooded with light.

Lucinda was sitting bolt upright in bed.

'Where on earth have you been?'

'Told you, the meeting went on late,' he was dismissive. 'And, by the way, we've got the extra finance. Great news eh?'

He sat on the edge of the bed close to her, noticing her eyes were red and swollen. She looked as if she'd been crying.

'It's ten past one Ryan, how long can a meeting go on for?'

He raised a hand. He was tired, it had been a long day, and he'd had far too much to drink.

'OK, OK, I don't need an inquisition. The meeting did finish late, but not that late. I was hungry, so were Miss Fergusson and her boss, Peter McLaughlin,' he lied. 'So, I took them both to Scalini's to celebrate. The time flew, you know how it is.'

'Yes, I know how it is Ryan,' she said sadly, clicking out the light.

He felt his way around the bed in the dark, and slipped in beside her. Snuggling up to her rigid back, he tried to slide his arm around her waist, whispering into her ear.

'I'm sorry Lu, it was just one of those things.'

'I want to go to sleep, if you don't mind.'

He rolled over with a deep sigh. 'OK I get the message, I've been a naughty boy for not coming home on time. I've said I'm sorry, what more do you want?'

Her only reply was to slide further away from him.

Exasperated, he jumped out of bed and left the room, slamming the door behind him.

He spent a restless night in the spare room, feeling guilty about Lucinda, and concerned about his growing interest in Luna. He was inexplicably drawn to her, frighteningly so. She was exceptionally beautiful, but it was more than that. He had met many beautiful women.

He tried to analyse why Luna was different, and could come up with no plausible answer. He realized that the kind of magnetic force he felt when she was near him had been there the very first time he'd met her.

It was a new experience for him, one which made him feel out of control, and he wasn't sure he liked it.

He fell asleep eventually, after making several mental vows: to placate Lucinda first thing in the morning; to exert every ounce of energy and motivation to finish the movie in the next few weeks; and to avoid Luna Fergusson . . . all in that order.

Chapter Twenty-One

'It's a wrap.'

Ryan's voice reverberated around the vast studio lot at Shepperton. All the cast and crew of *The Mitford Papers* cheered, several turning to kiss and embrace.

Lucinda pushed her way past a burly cameraman to reach Ryan. He opened his arms and she fell into them, tears of emotion and relief pricking the back of her eyes.

He hugged her tightly.

'We made it Lu, we fucking made it, and it's good.'

'It's more than good Ryan, it's great.'

His body was hot and taut with contained tension. Kissing him full on the lips, she stepped back, grabbing his hands.

'I don't think I've told you lately that I love you.'

'I don't think either of us has had a lot of time to tell each other anything lately, and I haven't exactly been the easiest person in the world to live with over the last three months.'

'Congratulations!'

They both turned at the unmistakable sound of Lord Frazer-West's impeccable diction.

'Well done, my boy,' he patted Ryan on the back, a wide jocular grin lighting his face.

It was obvious he was genuinely pleased.

Gathering Lucinda in his arms he kissed her warmly on both cheeks. 'Well done, poppet!'

Then, holding her at arm's length, he added, 'You could

do with a holiday now, you look exhausted.'

'I'm taking one, Daddy. Ryan's going to LA in a couple of weeks to start editing, so I thought I'd hitch a ride. I've never been to Hollywood, and I hear the shopping's great on Rodeo Drive.'

She looked directly at Ryan.

It was the first he'd heard of her plans to accompany him to LA. He looked as surprised as Nicholas.

They were both saved the necessity of a reply when loud music suddenly drowned out every other sound, except for someone shouting above the din: 'It's a wrap party!'

The popping of champagne corks followed, as caterers began to file in carrying large platters of food.

'Come on Miss Frazer-West, I think we both deserve a drink.'

Ryan took her hand, then turned to Nicholas. 'Champagne?'

'I'm not a champagne man as a rule, but since this is a special occasion . . .'

Ryan crossed the room to where a large trestle table had been set up as a bar. He grabbed a bottle of Pol Roger and three glasses, returning to Lucinda and her father, standing slightly apart from the rest of the crew.

'Is it tradition to do this when you finish shooting?' Nicholas asked.

Ryan poured the champagne, laughing as it bubbled over the rim of the glasses.

'Yes, having a wrap party is a kind of tradition I suppose. There's so much tension involved in making a movie. We all spend a lot of time together during the shoot, it's a very intense gig. So, the party . . .' He held up his glass, '. . . is kind of like a coming-down process, getting back to normal life. You know, getting drunk, relaxing.'

Ryan stopped speaking as he saw Luna Fergusson out of the corner of his eye.

She was walking towards him, a tall, very handsome older man by her side. As she approached he couldn't help thinking how wonderful she looked. Her hair, a mass of tangled waves, fell halfway down her back. She was dressed in a garnet red, high-necked short dress, cut to reveal part of her shoulders. The outfit was unadorned except for a chunky gold necklace, and several gold bangles that chinked together as she walked. He wondered who had invited her, he found out moments later.

'Hi, everyone,' Luna said brightly, seemingly oblivious to the three blank faces in front of her.

Ryan recovered first.

'Welcome to the wrap party, Miss Fergusson.'

Luna stifled the urge to say that there might not have been one without her, and to ask why he insisted on calling her 'Miss Fergusson' in front of his girlfriend.

'Thanks Mr Tyler, Peter McLaughlin sends his apologies. He's unable to attend this evening, his wife is ill. So I hope you guys don't mind, he passed his invite on to me.'

Nicholas was bristling, and attempting a lame smile.

Lucinda looked sullen.

Ryan was nonplussed.

'I'd like to introduce my father, Royole Fergusson.'

Royole stepped forward on cue. As he smiled, Ryan was instantly reminded of Luna.

Surprise registered on all faces when Nicholas laboriously acknowledged Royole.

'No need for introductions, we know each other. We met many years ago in Jamaica before you were born, Lucinda.'

Royole looked at Lucinda for the first time, struck as Ryan had been by the subtle similarities between her and Luna. He decided that it was not so obvious, more to do with expression and bone structure than actual features.

He was surprised to find Nicholas Frazer-West in such

incongruous circumstances, but disguised it well with another one of his easy smiles.

'I'll never forget how we met. It was in 1966 in Port Antonio; I was caught out in a violent storm and the Frazer-Wests kindly sheltered me for the evening. We saw each other once more after that, then I left Jamaica a few months later.'

Royole chose not to mention their business dealings out of professional respect for his client's privacy.

Ryan had noticed a visible change in Nicholas since Royole Fergusson had joined them. His eyes had narrowed and there was a rigidity in his stance that had not been there before.

'Where do you live now?' Lucinda asked politely.

'I live in Grand Cayman. I'm a banker, and for my sins I've sired another banker.'

He grinned in Luna's direction, before facing Nicholas to ask, 'So, how is Lady Frazer-West?'

'You can ask her yourself,' Nicholas replied coldly, glancing over Royole's shoulder as Serena glided towards the small group. Royole waited until he heard her footsteps stop behind his back and Nicholas's voice, seeming to come from a long way off, saying, 'Serena darling, I don't know if you remember . . .'

Royole turned before Nicholas had a chance to say his name.

'Royole Fergusson the second, at your service.'

He swept a hand in front of himself, bowing his head; it was more to avoid her eyes than to remind her of their first meeting.

Serena thought she might faint. Taking a very long, deep breath she willed her face into the semblance of a smile.

'Of course I remember. Mr Fergusson, how nice to see you again.'

She would like to have screamed that hardly a day had passed for the last twenty-seven years when she had not thought about him. Her bottom lip was quivering uncontrollably. Luna watched the beautiful woman fascinated, recognizing her very own mannerism.

Serena knew she had sounded ridiculously polite. She lowered her eyes, afraid to look at Royole as he gazed at her in blatant admiration. For a moment she looked as if she was about to crumple.

Nicholas held out his arm, so did Royole.

She took Nicholas's gratefully, looking at Ryan who was still holding the champagne bottle. 'I could certainly use a glass of that.'

Serena deliberately had to turn her back on both Luna and Royole, doubting her ability to stay in control if she was introduced to the stunning, dark-skinned girl standing next to him; who she knew, without any question, was her daughter.

Ryan got another glass, filled it and handed it to Serena, who was focusing on Lucinda, her heart beating loudly in her own ears. It was like a jungle war-drum, fast and incessant.

'Lucinda darling, you look very pale.'

'So do you, Mummy.'

Lucinda had been watching her mother closely when she was re-introduced to Royole Fergusson, having never seen anyone have such an impact on her. Curious to find out why, she resolved to ask her mother at the first opportunity.

Nor had Serena's thinly disguised shock gone unnoticed by Nicholas, now gripped by the same violent jealousy he had experienced the very first time he'd met Royole Fergusson.

The tension was so thick, Ryan thought that he could have cut it with a knife. He raised his glass in a desperate effort to lighten the mood.

'Well, here's to *The Mitford Papers*.'

'I'd drink to it if I had a drink,' Luna commented.

'So would I,' added Royole.

Ryan laughed lightly. 'Sorry you guys, in all the excitement I forgot my manners, you know how it is.'

He sounded uneasy. Taking the opportunity to break up the stilted atmosphere, he steered Luna and her father away from the Frazer-Wests, towards the bar.

The champagne had all gone.

Royole had a vodka and tonic, and Luna a glass of white wine.

Suddenly the music stopped.

Patrick Lerner, the assistant director, stepped into the centre of the set, clapping his hands a couple of times and shouting.

'Hush everybody, quiet please! Thank you. I thought a few words would be appropriate.'

'Make it a few Patrick, we haven't got all night.'

A titter rippled through the crew.

He grinned. 'OK, don't worry, I get the message. I just wanted to say, on behalf of the cast and crew, a big thank you to our director, Ryan Tyler. He's put us through unmitigated hell for the last few months, but without him we wouldn't have made this great movie. Ryan, come here.'

Patrick held out his arm, throwing it around Ryan's broad shoulder when he stood next to him.

'Speech, speech,' several voices shouted in unison.

Ryan held up his hand, and coughed to clear his throat.

'It's always difficult to know what to say at times like this. The simplest, most sincere thing I can think of is "thank you". Thank you everybody for all your hard work. It's been extremely tough at times. I know I can be a hard taskmaster, but I think you're all well aware that it's for the good of the movie. I believe we all agree that *The Mitford Papers* is a great movie, let's hope the Academy think so too.'

'To *The Mitford Papers*!' someone shouted from the other side of the room.

Ryan raised his glass, searching the sea of faces directly in front of him for Lucinda. She was nowhere to be seen.

It was Luna's gaze he caught.

She was staring at him, completely unabashed.

And in that precise moment Ryan knew that he wanted her more than he had ever wanted any other woman in his life. He was sure that she knew how he felt, and he sensed that she felt exactly the same way too. It was only the sight of Lucinda pushing her way through the crowd towards him that broke the spell. Laughing nervously he took her hand, pulling her very close to him, Luna watching all the while.

'I have something I'd like to say, it won't take long,' she muttered.

'Go ahead,' Ryan encouraged, pushing her forward. She started to speak to the crowd.

'Tonight we have given birth to a new movie, and we're all in a celebratory mood. Therefore I thought this was the appropriate time to announce that, in approximately seven months' time, I will be giving birth to Ryan Tyler's baby.'

Her voice dropped to a whisper, 'God willing.'

'Congratulations.'

Patrick Lerner, who was closest to Lucinda, planted a wet kiss on her cheek, before turning to shake Ryan's hand. Ryan responded, trying hard to look pleased.

Actually he was extremely angry that Lucinda had chosen a public social occasion to announce such highly intimate and staggering news.

Several people noticed his dazed expression and they fell away, leaving Ryan and Lucinda alone.

'You're going to be a daddy Ryan, aren't you happy?'

'I just wish you'd told me when we were alone, Lucinda. Did you have to do it now, in front of all these people?'

How could she say that she had been planning to tell him later that very night, when they were together, over a bottle of their favourite champagne . . . but that the sight of his impassioned face, when he'd looked at Luna Fergusson, had ignited such violent emotions that she'd have done anything to reclaim his attention.

'I'm sorry Ryan, I thought you'd be pleased.'

'I'm shocked Lucinda. I had no idea.'

'But, you are pleased?'

She placed his hand on her flat stomach, insisting. 'Tell me you're happy.'

Despite her pleading eyes he pulled his hand away sharply, repeating what he'd already said.

'I wish you'd told me when we were alone, that's all.'

He turned away from her anxious expression to be confronted by Nicholas, who looked like he'd seen a ghost.

'Your mother isn't feeling too good Lucinda, I'm taking her home.'

Lucinda nodded. 'She doesn't look too good.'

'No,' he replied, his lips tight.

He didn't mention the pregnancy, nor did she. Nor did he say goodnight to either of them, as he turned and walked across the crowded set, a defeated slump to his shoulders. Like an old man, Ryan thought, and felt an unexpected flash of sympathy for him.

Lucinda was close to tears. What should have been such a happy moment had turned into a nightmare. All through her own impulsive stupidity.

'I want to go home Ryan.'

'Yeah, I think it's time to go now. The party's over, at least for me.'

His words stung.

His reaction had dulled the sweet anticipation she'd been savouring for the last week, ever since finding out she was pregnant. She felt a bitter taste in her mouth.

Ryan quickly scanned the room. There were several clumps of people deep in conversation, punctuated by the

273

odd burst of laughter. A lone couple were dancing to the rhythmic beat of Bob Marley's 'Is This Love?'.

He was looking for Luna and her father, but they were nowhere in sight. They'd left immediately after Lucinda had made her announcement.

Taking Lucinda by the arm, he propelled her out of the lot. 'Come on, let's escape while we can.'

A deepening sense of anticlimax descended on Ryan as he drove back into central London. He barely spoke, answering any attempts at conversation in monosyllables. He was relieved when she eventually gave up, and they endured the journey in awkward silence.

He stopped the car outside her house, and was about to climb out when Lucinda spoke.

'I want this baby, Ryan. And I intend to have it, with or without you.'

Staring straight ahead, he startled her with his emotive reply.

'No child of mine is going to be born without a father, and no child of mine is going to be illegitimate.'

'I must see you,' Royole demanded.

Serena was gripping the telephone tightly, her knuckles showing white through her lightly tanned skin.

'I don't think that'll be possible.'

She sounded dismissive, as if she were talking to one of her staff.

'Serena, please, I'm flying back to the Caribbean tomorrow. I have to see you before I go, it's important. Just a few minutes of your time . . . I promise that's all.'

Her grip slackened, and she felt herself weaken.

'OK Royole, but I can't stay long. I've got a very busy day.'

Before she could change her mind he told her, 'I'm at Luna's apartment and she's at work, so come over now. It's not far, Chelsea Harbour.'

'OK, whereabouts?'

'Flat forty-three, it's on the seventh floor of the Belvedere, Chelsea Harbour.'

'I'll be there in half an hour.'

'I'm not sure I can wait that long, Serena.'

There was a spark of amusement in his deep voice, and she pictured him smiling as she replaced the telephone. Then she ran upstairs to her bedroom, where she changed from a smart suit into faded denim jeans and a sweatshirt. She quickly wet her short hair, raked her fingers through it, pulling several jagged strands on to her brow. Her flushed cheeks didn't need blusher, so she just applied a thin coat of lip gloss.

Allowing herself one last lingering glance in the mirror, she spoke to her image. 'You don't look too bad for almost fifty.'

Hoping that Royole would agree, she bounded down the stairs two at a time, like a teenager. She caught a cab five minutes later on Fulham Road. It was a glorious September morning; brilliant sunshine streaming out of a cloudless sky, the air warm but not too hot. Traffic was congested on the King's Road, and she arrived at Chelsea Harbour at a quarter to twelve.

Royole opened the door of the apartment.

'You're fifteen minutes late, Lady Frazer-West.'

He tapped his watch face, pretending to admonish her. 'I've been counting.'

She started to apologize as he pulled her into the hall, then he winked and she knew he was teasing. Serena took a deep breath. She was having difficulty harnessing the mixture of emotions that were threatening her usual unflappable self-control. She wasn't sure what to do, or what to say.

'Come on through to the living room,' Royole suggested, gently touching her arm.

Serena flinched. It was like an electric shock.

'Are you OK, Serena?'

'No, I'm not actually. I feel like a terrified young girl. I could use a drink.'

She strode ahead of him, into the large room. It was bathed in bright sunlight. Her roaming eyes took in every detail. Silently she admired the bold Designers Guild fabric, which she recognized immediately, on the sofas and chairs; the neat French Empire side table; and an interesting set of prints lining the walls. Luna had good taste, she was pleased. Serena stopped by the open window, staring out across a choppy Thames. She could see the river activity, but none of it registered in her mind. All she could think about were the powerful feelings that this man Royole Fergusson aroused in her after all these years.

'What would you like to drink?' he asked from the far side of the room.

'Something strong, whisky . . . with a little water.'

His eyes raised, but he said nothing as he poured a Scotch, then excused himself to go to the kitchen for ice and water. Returning moments later, he joined her by the window and handed over the drink. It was full to the top with ice, Caribbean fashion. They both stood side by side for what seemed to Serena a very long time. She sipped her drink nervously, afraid to look at him. He broke the silence.

'Tell me, how did you feel when you saw me yesterday? And, please, I need to know the truth.'

Her gaze never left the river.

'I thought that you looked great, still very attractive for your age.'

Royole laughed. 'Thanks! I like the "for your age" bit. But I want to know how you felt, not just an opinion on how I looked . . .' he grinned, repeating, '. . . for my age.'

Then the laughter left his voice.

'By the way, you look very beautiful for any age.'

'Thank you,' she said between mouthfuls of whisky.

'So Serena, tell me honestly, how did you feel?'

She inclined her head slightly, then lifted her chin until their eyes were level; hers glittering like newly polished sapphires, his searching.

'I need to know.'

She bit into a lump of ice, it shattered in her mouth. Swallowing the cold fragments, she shook her head at the same time.

'I knew you for one day, one amazing day, and you walk back into my life, with my daughter, after twenty-seven years. How the hell do you think I feel Royole? I'm shocked, disturbed, threatened . . . confused.'

Her voice faltered and she began to cry. 'Shit,' she spat out, hating herself for the tears she could not hold back.

Shading her eyes with a shaking hand, she pushed Royole roughly away as he tried to take her into his arms. She sniffed, and wiped a tear from her cheek with the back of her hand.

'Leave me Royole, please, I'll be OK in a moment.'

'I'm sorry Serena, but I had no idea you were going to be at the party last night. It was a hell of a shock for me too. I wouldn't have planned to meet you again quite like that.'

'I know it wasn't your fault. But seeing you again after all this time, with Luna by your side, like ghosts from a past that I believed buried, it was difficult to cope with.'

She took a slug of her drink. 'Luna's exceptionally beautiful Royole, she looks like you.'

'She looks like both of us, and not unlike Lucinda.'

Serena found talking about Luna painful, and she changed the subject abruptly.

'Anyway, how are you, Mr Royole Fergusson the second?'

She tried to make light of the situation, desperate to

bring a little normality into the conversation.

'I'm fine. Lonely . . . Caron died two years ago . . . cancer.'

'I'm sorry.'

It was perfunctory sympathy, and Royole understood.

'Are you happy Serena?'

She thought about the question carefully.

'Nicholas has been a good husband. I've had a wonderful, privileged life with him. Yes, I suppose I'm as happy as the next person.'

Friends' failed marriages and subsequent acrimonious divorces flashed through her mind.

'It could be much worse.'

'That reeks of compromise Serena, making do—'

'Oh, come on Royole,' she interrupted, 'I'm sure your marriage was much the same. Aren't they all after a certain length of time?'

He didn't want to discuss Caron or his marriage, and she saw him stiffen.

'There could be something else, something more. I've spent a sleepless night thinking about it.'

Instinctively she knew what he was going to suggest, and she wasn't sure how to confront it.

'I really will have to go now, Royole. I did say I couldn't stay long. I've got lunch with friends, and a meeting this afternoon. I do interior design you know.'

She stuttered. 'Well, you didn't know. Anyway I do. And then I have some people coming for dinner this evening.'

'Spare me the banal chatter, please. This is serious.'

She felt slightly affronted. 'Banal it may be to you, but it's my life.'

Taking a step back, she walked away from the window, dropping her glass on to the top of the coffee table as she passed. He made no attempt to follow her.

She stopped at the door.

'It was nice seeing you again, Royole. Take care of yourself, and don't forget our promise about Luna. Please don't feel tempted to tell her about me, it would only harm her.'

He stayed where he was, staring out of the window with his back to her. But when he spoke, his voice was loud and very clear.

'Leave him.'

'I can't, it would kill him.'

'Think about yourself Serena . . . please. You know it's what you really want.'

'How could you possibly know what I really want?' she shouted across the room, irritated by his irrepressible ego. Yet, at the same time, she had to fight an urge to run into his arms. Gripping the door handle to stop herself from doing just that, she heard her own voice telling him something.

'Yes, I'll think about it Royole.'

'Is that a promise?'

'That's a promise.'

Chapter Twenty-Two

'I'm sorry to disturb you Miss Fergusson, but the lady insists on speaking to your father. Will you talk to her, please?'

The secretary's voice was apologetic.

Luna was exasperated.

'I thought I left explicit instructions, no calls. Tell her he's away on business; tell her anything, apart from the truth.'

'I already have, but then she asked where she could contact him. She says it's a matter of the utmost urgency, she's most persistent.'

'OK, put her through,' Luna instructed.

There was a short pause, then a cultured English voice came on the phone.

'Is that Luna Fergusson?'

'Yes it is. Who is this?'

'Lady Serena Frazer-West, I'm calling to speak to your father. They said you could help me get in touch with him.'

'I think the only person who can do that for you now would be a medium, Lady Frazer-West.'

Luna heard a discernible gasp, followed immediately by a hushed 'Oh, my God.'

'I buried him yesterday,' Luna said, instantly regretting the flippancy of her earlier remark.

There was a long silence, before Serena mumbled, 'I'm

so terribly sorry. So young, what a waste. I'm so terribly sorry. So sorry,' she repeated.

There was something in the woman's voice that Luna understood, a kind of anguish and deep sadness. It made her think that Royole had meant more to this woman than a passing acquaintance met a couple of times in Jamaica.

'He died suddenly, eight days ago, a massive coronary. There was no pain, no suffering.'

That's the legacy he left behind for *me*, Luna thought bitterly. There was another long pause before she continued, her tone cooling to a businesslike detachment.

'If it was business you wanted to discuss with my father, perhaps I can help.'

'No. No, I just wanted to have a chat with him. You see, I was thinking about coming out to the Cayman Islands for a holiday and, obviously, if he'd been there it would've been nice for us to get together.'

She's regained her composure, Luna thought; back to being polite, like nothing has happened. She would never be able to understand the stiff upper-lip attitude of the English.

Luna was polite in return.

'Well, if there's nothing else, you must excuse me Lady Frazer-West.'

It was clear she wanted to end the conversation.

'Of course, absolutely. Just one question before I go. Have you any other family?'

Luna found this question intrusive. 'Why do you ask?'

'I just wondered, that's all,' Serena responded absently.

'Well, I've got an aunt, my father's sister. She's a widow and lives alone in Philadelphia. An uncle whom Dad lost touch with years ago. And a couple of cousins I haven't seen since we were kids.'

'Oh, I see . . . I met your father very briefly, but I want you to know that I liked him very much. It's a sad loss. Goodbye Luna.'

'Goodbye.'

Luna dropped the telephone on to the desk, and her head into her hands, aware only of a dull ache in the pit of her stomach. She was trying to work, making an attempt at coping, but she knew she wasn't functioning correctly. How could she?

'Why Dad, why? How could you leave me like this?'

Her mind ran riot with images of him; some from childhood, others as recently as two weeks previously when he'd been in London. When at last she lifted her head, her neck ached and her throat was dry. Glancing at a small clock on the desk she was surprised to see it was after two. She had been slumped in the same position for over an hour.

Luna stayed at the office late. Working was therapy, she told herself, unable to face the real truth; that going home to Whispering Cay, with echoes of her father's voice following her through every room, was too painful. That night, on her way home, she stopped at the Hog Sty Bay Café, a waterside bar in Georgetown. She drank rum and soda continually for three hours, until she slipped off the bar stool and staggered out to her car. Laughing maniacally when she almost careered off the road twice, and hardly noticing the bump as she hit the side of the wall turning into the drive of the house, she somehow got home in one piece. Not bothering to switch on the lights, she dragged herself upstairs, holding on to the banister for balance.

She banged her shoulder on the door frame as she walked into her father's bedroom.

Switching on the lights at last, Luna almost fell as she pulled open his wardrobe doors. She flicked through his clothes, until her hand rested on his old, grey dressing gown.

She stroked it lovingly, then very carefully lifted it out of the wardrobe. Tearing her own clothes off, she slipped the gown over her naked body, tying the belt tightly

282

around her waist. Then, falling to her hands and knees, she searched for his slippers.

Sitting on the floor, she pulled them on to her small feet. They were huge, and her feet kept slipping out as she tried to walk towards the bed. Tripping up before she got there, she crawled the remainder of the way.

She wrapped her slim arms around her body, and began to rock. She rocked to and fro, crying, 'Come home Daddy, please come home,' until she eventually fell into an exhausted sleep.

Luna awoke the following morning with a thundering headache and a stiff neck, disturbed by the insistent ring of what she thought at first was the telephone.

As she began to surface, she realized that it was in fact the doorbell.

'OK, OK, I'm coming,' she shouted, stepping gingerly down the stairs.

Easing open the door, she was greeted by the anxious face of Chris Johnson, her father's old friend and chief executive at the bank.

'Are you all right, Luna? We were all worried about you; no show at the office, no reply on the telephone.'

She was holding her head with one hand, and steadying herself with the other.

'No Chris, I'm not. I've got a self-inflicted disease, I'm afraid. I don't think I'll make it to the office today. Come in.' She tried to smile, but it hurt.

He stepped into the hall, looking concerned and a little sheepish.

'I wouldn't have bothered you at all, my dear, but I thought that what with all the trauma you may have forgotten . . . it's the reading of your father's will today.'

She fell against the door, her tangled hair covering most of her face. Several strands rose and fell as she spoke through it.

'How could I have forgotten that! I must be going mad.

What time's the meeting?' She pushed her hair roughly behind her ears.

'*Now*. You're already fifteen minutes late, but everyone's waiting for you.'

'I'll be two minutes.'

She raced upstairs, the hurried activity causing her head to pound harder. Chris made himself a cup of coffee while she showered and dressed. He was washing up the cup and saucer as she ran back downstairs.

'I'm ready.'

He joined her in the hall. 'Wow, some transformation.'

Chris admired her choice of a simple, short-sleeved black dress and the single row of pearls that Royole had given to Caron on their tenth wedding anniversary.

She had tied her hair into a chignon and it sat neatly on her crown.

'You look a lot better.'

'Believe me, I don't feel it. Thank God for make-up.'

Chris opened the door, and she followed him to his car, noticing a big dent in the wing of her own as she slid into the passenger seat. Bodden Thompson and Bush, the attorney's office, was on Harbour Drive in Georgetown. Chris drove as fast as he could, pulling up in front of the building in under fifteen minutes.

'I'll park the car, see you up there Luna.'

She jumped out, with a halting smile and a quick wave.

Frank Bodden's office was located on the second floor. Luna bounded up the stairs two at a time, almost bumping into a young man coming down.

She rapped on the door, and entered as the lawyer shouted, 'Come in.'

Luna marched into the office, apologies spilling out of her mouth.

'I'm terrible sorry to be so late, but my alarm didn't go off this morning and I've been under sedation. Well, you know how it is.'

Frank Bodden looked at her out of watery eyes, full of understanding and sympathy.

'Of course we do, Luna, we understand perfectly. You know how I felt about your father. Everyone here is in deep shock and mourning.'

He stood up, and led her gently to a chair. As she sat down Chris strode into the room, closely followed by Royole's secretary, Dawn, and a woman Luna barely recognized as her father's sister, Elouise. Elouise took a step towards her, and Luna felt a rush of rage.

'How are you Elouise? I must say you were noticeable by your absence at the funeral.'

The woman bent her grey head 'I'm sorry about that Luna. I tried to get down, but it was such short notice, and Charles had a terrible bout of asthma. I couldn't leave him. You understand don't you?'

Luna turned away in disgust, refusing to accept pathetic excuses which reeked of lies.

'You should've been there,' she said flatly, thinking that Elouise could evidently make the effort to come down to Cayman to find out how much money her brother had left her, but not to pay her last respects.

'Would you like a drink of anything Luna?' Mr Bodden asked kindly.

'I'd love a Diet Coke, please Frank.'

It was Luna's tried and tested remedy for hangovers. Everyone else was already drinking coffee.

Mr Bodden waited until his secretary had provided the Coke. Then, settling down in a huge armchair that almost dwarfed him, and focusing on Luna, he began to speak.

'This won't take very long. Miss Luna here is the main beneficiary of Royole Fergusson's will.'

He put on his spectacles and read aloud, 'This is the last will and testament of Royole Fergusson the second, of Whispering Cay, South Sound Road, South Sound, Grand Cayman, West Indies.

'I, Royole Fergusson, bequeath all my worldly goods and chattels to my next of kin and only daughter Luna Josephine Fergusson.

'They include:

'All equity in Fergusson Bank and Trust.

'All equity in freehold and leasehold properties (see enclosed list).

'Fifty per cent hold in Telfax.

'Forty per cent holding in Palm Court Apartments, Cayman Brac.

'Whispering Cay. (And all its contents.)

' "Luna's Dream" the fifty-foot off-shore cruiser.

'I bequeath forty thousand dollars to Chris Johnson, a great friend and even better banker, and I hope he buys the boat he's been promising himself since I met him. I bequeath ten thousand dollars to my long-suffering secretary Dawn, which I hope will enable her to take the European tour she has been talking about for years.

'I leave a property in Miami, an apartment in Coconut Grove, (deeds with Mr Frank Bodden) to my sister Elouise, and a pension fund, details of which are enclosed. I bequeath twenty thousand pounds to each of my nephews, in the hope that they spend it wisely; and a further twenty thousand dollars to my brother Robert, if anyone can find him. If not, I would like it to go to a charity of my sister's choice. Lastly, I bequeath a diamond and emerald necklace to my daughter Luna. This is a gift from her mother, and must be worn on her wedding day. She will find it in the safe deposit box, number 514174, at the bank. "I'm sorry I will never see you wear it, Luna. All my love, Pa."'

Mr Bodden looked up, oblivious to Luna's taut face.

'There's a list of charities that Royole Fergusson supported, he has made bequests to all of them.'

He handed everyone present a photostated copy.

But Luna had stood up shakily, 'I think I'm going to . . .'

Unable to finish, she fainted, hitting the side of her head on Mr Bodden's desk as she slumped from her chair.

It was Chris Johnson's concerned features she saw first as she regained consciousness. She shut her eyes again as Elouise's head appeared to be swimming over his shoulder. A glass of water was thrust in front of her face.

'Drink this.'

She wasn't sure who said it, but she did as she was told, sipping the water slowly. Mr Bodden was patting the side of her head and fussing.

'I'm going to be fine,' she told him as she struggled to sit up, aided by three sets of arms.

Chris helped her back into a chair and she rested her head on her lap, beginning to feel a little better.

Chris leaned forward, 'Are you sure you're OK, Luna. You gave us all a bit of a fright.'

'I feel bloody stupid.' She spoke out of the side of her mouth. 'I'm sorry folks, it's just that I haven't been eating much lately and I'm very tired.'

'We understand,' Mr Bodden consoled her. 'I think you should go home to bed. I'll talk to you later. We can set a meeting up when you're feeling better.'

'I'll take her home,' Chris offered.

She leant heavily on Chris's arm as he half carried her out of the office, down two flights of stairs and on to Harbour Drive. There was a fresh breeze coming off the sea and she breathed deeply, suddenly feeling better than she had for days. And Luna realized that she felt hungry for the first time since her father's death. But her appetite would have to wait.

'I feel fine now Chris, and I want to see what's in that safe deposit. I can't understand why my mother left a necklace with my father. Why didn't she leave it to me when she died? Damn, I don't know the number of the box, and I don't feel like going back in there.'

Chris took her by the arm protectively. 'I know exactly where it is.'

She was smiling. 'Well done, Mr Johnson. Want to come and see what my mother wanted me to wear on my wedding day?'

'Are you sure? It might be personal.'

'It's probably a piece of costume jewellery, something of sentimental value that's all.'

'Well, yes OK, if you don't mind.'

Chris took her to the bank where they descended one floor to the basement and the vaults. He found number 514174 easily, and he opened it using a master key and the secondary key.

Luna pulled the long steel box out of its compartment. At first she thought it was empty, until she slid her hand inside to pull out a faded, square jewellery box. Despite herself, a thrill of anticipation seized her as she slowly opened the lid.

'Holy shit!' she squealed, as the lid dropped fully open and her eyes rested on the most exquisite necklace they had ever seen. Chris stared at it too, mesmerised by the glittering facets of one hundred and thirty diamonds, and ninety-five emeralds.

'Holy shit is right Luna! That's some piece of jewellery.'

She pressed one of the diamonds with her fingertip. 'Do you think it's real?'

He looked closely. 'It's real all right. I'm almost scared to touch it.'

Then, looking at the base of the old box, Luna announced. 'It was bought from Garrard, in London.'

'Perhaps. It could just be a Garrard's box,' Chris suggested.

'Yeah, maybe,' Luna agreed, bewildered. 'But how on

earth did my mother come by something like this?'

She gazed at the necklace again, before snapping the box shut and holding it against her chest.

'It's really strange, because my mother and I were never particularly close. As you know, she worshipped my father, to an unhealthy degree. But in retrospect I think that she harboured some kind of resentment for me. You see, she never told me that she loved me, not once. So, perhaps this was her way of telling me.'

Chris thought about the elegant, self-assured Caron Fergusson whom he had always found to be quietly aggressive and exacting, with a chronic obsession for her husband.

'Perhaps,' he said, not wanting to disillusion Luna.

In truth he doubted that her mother was capable of a romantic, sentimental gesture such as this. Royole yes, but never Caron.

'Let me have another look,' he said.

Luna opened the box, and he peered again at the necklace, his nose almost touching the gleaming stones.

'It's obviously old, you can tell that by the settings. My brother works for Christie's in London, why don't I call him? Jewellery's his thing. You could always send him a photo and perhaps he'd do a little research for you. It won't do any harm.'

'That's a good idea. I'd love to find out its origins. In any case, I've got to go back to London in a couple of weeks, to serve my notice with the bank and pack up my apartment.'

It was the first time she'd mentioned a subject he had been reluctant to broach.

Seizing his opportunity, Chris asked her warily, 'Have you decided to come back to live in Cayman?'

'Yes, I made up my mind last night. I want to run my father's bank.'

'It's your bank now,' Chris cut in, unable to hide his

obvious delight. She didn't notice the ardent look on his face as he continued.

'It's what Royole would have wanted.'

Chapter Twenty-Three

Lucinda groaned as she staggered to the bathroom.

Dropping to her knees, she gripped the side of the toilet bowl and retched violently several times. Coming up for air a few minutes later, she thought that surely her insides must be empty by now. Then she felt the familiar rise of nausea yet again. Dropping her head once more, her stomach contracted as she vomited for the sixth time that morning. Panting, she pulled herself to her feet and flushed the toilet before staggering to the sink where she splashed her face with cold water, silently cursing her gynaecologist who had told her only yesterday that the morning sickness was due to cease.

Her sunken face, the colour of faded notepaper, stared back at her from the mirror. It made her think how much she hated pregnancy. Her breasts resembled cows' udders, her ankles had swollen like she had elephantiasis, and she had never felt so ill. Lucinda wondered how she would ever get through the next six months. She heard Ryan moving around in the bedroom, and a moment later saw his face at the door.

He waited for her to finish gargling mouthwash.

'Are you all right?'

'I am now, but I hope this sickness stops soon. I really don't think I can cope with much more.'

Ryan grimaced, he doubted he could either.

'I thought Mr Mortimer told you it would stop soon.'

'He did, but he was wrong. I can't believe I feel so ill.

Whatever happened to this pregnant bloom everyone talks about? Poppy sailed through her time, looking and feeling wonderful.'

'Perhaps it's just the first three months,' Ryan ventured hopefully, standing back as she walked through the door.

She pulled a long face. 'Mummy was sick for most of her pregnancy, so I'm probably going to be like her.'

Lucinda sat on the edge of the bed, looking mournfully into Ryan's open suitcase. Two new shirts she had bought him last week were neatly folded on the top.

'I wish I was going with you Ryan, I would've been able to see my friend Sally in New York.'

He came out of the bathroom, carrying a small towel bag which he pushed down the side of his case.

'I wish you were coming with me too.'

Ryan told her what she wanted to hear, but was secretly pleased she couldn't go. He had a lot of work to do, and Lucinda would be an unwelcome distraction.

'I'm only in New York for a couple of days Lu, and you have to be here for the scan, it's important. Anyway, I'm going to be so busy I would've had very little time to spend with you.'

He closed the lid of the suitcase and fastened the locks. Then, sitting down next to her, he placed his hand tenderly on her stomach.

'Look after junior whilst I'm away, and more importantly look after yourself.'

'I'll try,' she said weakly. 'But I feel so ill all the time. I really wish you weren't going away at all Ryan.'

In an effort to suppress his mounting irritation he kissed her swiftly on the lips, only to feel slightly repulsed by the offensive smell of bile on her breath.

'It's not for long, the time will fly.'

'Not for me,' she muttered forlornly, biting her nails. 'What will I do with myself whilst you're away?'

This time he let out an exasperated sigh. 'I don't know, what do other pregnant woman do? Buy baby clothes, go for lunches with other pregnant friends and swap morning-sickness stories, start decorating the back room as a nursery, attend antenatal classes, knit—'

This last suggestion produced a wan smile. 'I've never knitted a thing in my life.'

'Well try baby bootees, I hear they're quite a challenge.'

He lifted his case off the bed. Lucinda was laughing now as she stood up.

'I promise to knit at least four sets of bootees whilst you're gone, that's a pair a week, if you'll promise to be good in New York and LA.'

As she took a step closer to him, the doorbell rang.

'That's my car Lu, I have to go.'

She held on to the lapels of his jacket. 'You haven't promised you'll be good yet.'

Ryan pecked the end of her upturned nose, once more telling her what she wanted to hear.

'I'll be good Lucinda, how could I be anything else?'

Due to strong tailwinds across the Atlantic, Ryan's flight into JFK landed at four-thirty that afternoon, twenty minutes earlier than scheduled.

He had no luggage and he cleared Immigration and customs fairly quickly, checking into the Carlyle Hotel, on Madison, at a few minutes to six. He was in New York for three days, to talk to Trevor Gould about the musical score for *The Mitford Papers*. Then he was going to LA. Normally he would have stayed at the Peninsular Hotel, on 55th and 5th, but when he'd called they were already fully booked.

Remembering a conversation he'd had with one of his actors a few months before, Ryan recalled that he'd been staying at the Carlyle at the time, happily singing its praises. So he'd decided to give it a try himself. And he was impressed with his room. It was fairly small, but what it lacked in size it made up for in style. He showered, and changed from jeans and a sweater into black trousers and a casual, open-necked shirt. Carrying his jacket, he left the room.

Stepping out of the elevator on the ground floor, Ryan caught the eye of a bellboy.

'Could you direct me to the Café Carlyle.'

The boy pointed across the lobby, chirping in a bright voice. 'Right over there sir.'

'Thanks.'

He walked towards the bar. It was busy, mostly men, and he rightly assumed they were business types having a pre-dinner cocktail. He sat at the bar and ordered a beer. He drank thirstily, thinking how good it was to have a really cold beer again. Ryan didn't see her walk across the room, and jumped as a hand rested on his shoulder. However, he recognized the voice instantly.

'Well, fancy seeing you here Mr Tyler.'

Ryan spun round, almost spilling his beer

'I could say the same to you, Miss Fergusson.' Recovering, he offered, 'Can I get you a drink?'

'Yes please. I'd like a glass of Diamond Mountain Chardonnay, it's my favourite Californian wine. I always drink it when I'm here.'

'So you come here often, do you? If you'll excuse the cliché.'

His casual enquiry produced a strange reaction. Luna's face at once became detached, and a faraway gaze entered her eyes. She waited until the barman had served her wine before she answered.

'This was my father's favourite hotel. We always met here for drinks, whenever he was in town. It was a kind of ritual, he'd have a vodka martini and I'd have one of these.'

She lifted her glass and held it to her lips. Ryan was

perceptive enough to sense a profound sadness emanating from her.

'Is there something wrong, Luna?'

Opening her eyes wide, she stared, without really seeing him. It was her father's face she could see; he was laughing and throwing peanuts into his open mouth.

'No, there's nothing wrong Ryan, nothing wrong at all. I just miss him.'

'Miss who? Sorry if I sound a little confused, but I don't know what you're talking about.'

Shaking her head, as if to dispel the image of her father, she looked at his puzzled face.

'It's my father, he's left me . . . he died less than a month ago.'

An image of the tall, handsome man with her at the wrap party flashed into his head.

'I'm so sorry, I had no idea. Christ, that must have been a shock. How old was he?'

'He would've been fifty-five next week. We were going to New Orleans, him and I, to celebrate his birthday. He loved jazz you see, well . . . so do I.'

She looked distracted for a moment. 'That reminds me, I must cancel our hotel reservations. I'd forgotten all about that.'

Deciding he needed a real drink, Ryan called the barman.

'Can I have a whisky and water,' then, pointing to Luna's half-full glass, 'And another one for the lady.'

Ryan was reluctant to dwell on the subject of her father's death, but instinct told him that she needed to talk about it.

'I assume you were very close to your father.'

'He was my whole world, ever since I was this high.'

With the flat of her hand she indicated a couple of feet from the floor.

'It's strange coming to terms with the fact that I'll never

speak to him again. You know, never see his face, hear his voice, share my trials and tribulations. He was my best friend.'

'What about your mother?'

Her face paled.

'Dead.'

Ryan was consumed with a desire to comfort her.

'Look, it must be hell. All I can offer you is the lame consolation that time is a great healer, and it does seem to work. Everyone says the same, but I don't suppose hearing stuff like that helps you much at the moment. It's too soon.'

Luna nodded her silent agreement, then finished her wine in one gulp and slid the second glass in front of her.

'Thanks for the drink Ryan, I'm not great company at the moment. By the way, how long are you going to be in New York?'

'Just a few days, I'm here to talk with Trevor Gould about the music score for *The Mitford Papers*.'

She whistled.

'Wow, you should have one great score! He's a very talented composer.'

'And you, staying in town long?'

Ryan asked the question eagerly, hoping he could ask her out for dinner the following evening.

'I leave for London tomorrow night. I came up for a meeting with the big man, my ex-boss Spencer Clayton. I've given notice to the bank. He's asked me to stay on for a month until they can find a replacement. It suits me, as it gives me the opportunity to tie up any loose ends in London. The bank will keep the apartment, so you won't have to worry about sub-letting.'

'So what will you do now?'

'I'm going to run my father's bank. He started it from nothing, and it was always his wish that I'd take it over

one day. It's just happened a bit sooner than anticipated.'

She pushed her half-empty glass across the bar top and
stood up.

'Thanks again Ryan, it was nice talking to you.'

Ryan also stood up.

'I don't know about you, but I'm starving. I've just got
in from London, all I've had all day is a bowl of Cornflakes
and airline food. How about we grab something to eat, I
hate eating alone.'

Luna thought about the empty apartment she was staying in courtesy of the bank, the inevitable lonely burger
and the bottle of wine she seemed to be drinking most
nights. She kept telling herself it was to help her sleep,
afraid to face the truth.

'Yeah, OK, I'd like that. But I can't promise I'm going
to be a lot of fun.'

Ryan paid the check. 'Nobody laughs at my jokes
anyway.'

Luna laughed. Ryan took her to Fusillo, a fun Italian
restaurant he knew, located on 3rd Avenue between 75th
and 76th. They ate wonderful pizza, with everything on;
two side orders of french fries and lashings of ketchup;
polished off two bottles of an excellent Valpolicella
between them; and drank three cups of cappuccino each.

'That was good,' Ryan commented as they rolled out
of the restaurant, giggling at nothing in particular.

'It was great, thanks Ryan, I feel better than I've felt
for weeks. It's good to have a drink for social reasons,
instead of using it to blot out reality.'

'Is it that bad?'

He knew by the look on her face that it was.

'Sometimes.'

They fell into step walking down the street in comfortable silence. A silence suddenly broken by Ryan's voice,
charged with anger.

'Life! It makes me so fucking mad sometimes. Why is it that bad things happen to good people, and good things happen to bad people?'

'I can't solve that one, Ryan.'

He stopped walking. Pulling her round to face him, he stood so close to her that she could feel his hot breath on her mouth.

'Well someone should, look what's happened to you.'

As usual, strongly affected by his nearness, she was overcome by the need to get away from him. Looking over his head to the street beyond, she spotted a yellow cab. She waved and it crawled into the kerb next to them.

'Thanks again for the pizza Ryan, hope everything goes well with the movie score.'

She was at the taxi door, yet seemed rooted to the spot. He didn't want her to go, and racked his brain for an excuse to stay with her a little longer.

'Hey, I've never seen the East River at night, would you like to show me?'

'Come off it, Ryan Tyler. You lived in New York, so how come you haven't seen the East River at night?'

'Well, I fibbed. What I meant to say was I've never seen it with you.'

She was chuckling as she opened the car door. 'Come on then, let's go look at the river.'

He got into the taxi and sat next to her, giving a wide, boyish grin. She responded with a girlish one of her own, and when they got to the river bank, they walked along arm in arm.

Luna pointed out the bank building where she worked, and talked about her first months in New York and how impressionable she had been. Ryan told her his life story in minute detail. He missed nothing out, telling her things he had never told anyone before. Luna listened, picturing the small farm in County Kildare where he'd spent ten formative years. She was genuinely interested, she wanted to know everything about this man.

They both smiled when he ran out of life history and reached the present.

'I think it's home time, don't you?' Luna suggested.

'Whenever. The way I feel at the moment I could stay out all night.'

They crossed the street, hailing an oncoming cab. 'TriBeCa,' Luna said through the thick bullet-proof glass inside the taxi.

As soon as the taxi came to a halt outside the apartment on Franklin Street, Ryan quickly paid the driver and let it go.

'Don't tell me . . . you've never seen a loft conversion in TriBeCa,' she said grinning.

She would have invited him up, if it were not for the spectre of a pregnant Lucinda constantly looming in her mind. Luna had deliberately not mentioned it, nor had he.

'Well, as it happens, I haven't actually. But I'd never presume to suggest anything so contrived.'

'Ryan Tyler, you're incorrigible.'

He took a step closer to her, longing to stretch his hand across the few inches that separated his fingers from her face and hair. He could almost taste her breath, and he could actually smell her body, a delightful mixture of musk and flowers. But it was Luna who made the first move.

Her fingertips found his mouth, so gently they felt like a feather brushing across his lips. He grabbed her wrist and licked each of her fingers in turn. Then, with a violence that alarmed her, he pulled her towards him, covering her mouth with his. It was a hard kiss, forcing her lips open. She could feel his deeply probing tongue.

Finally he stopped. Pushing her roughly away, as if he'd been burnt, he struggled to speak.

'Jesus, Mother of Mary . . . Luna.'

Luna was gasping and holding her bruised mouth, she took a step back, afraid of what she could see on his face. It was the same stunned expression from the night of the wrap party. She held up her hands, as if to ward off his next words, but he just stood perfectly still, staring at her for a very long time. At last he spoke.

'Goodbye Luna, take care.'

He started to walk down the street.

'Bye Ryan,' she called after him, watching his back, half expecting him to turn.

But he didn't and she let herself into the empty apartment, with more than a hint of regret.

Chapter Twenty-Four

'It's a very important piece. I need to do a little more research, but I believe it's French, early nineteenth century. A necklace of this calibre would certainly have been made for an aristocrat, or even royalty.'

Simon Johnson held the necklace by the clasp. It dangled over his hand, the light from a single spotlight on his desk bouncing off the flawless jewels.

Luna could not take her eyes off the piece.

'Valuation is difficult until we find out its exact origins; but to give you a ballpark figure, you're looking at half a million pounds. If not more.'

'*How much*?' Luna was visibly shocked.

'This is a very rare antique necklace Miss Fergusson, in perfect condition. There are collectors who would pay almost anything to have something like this.'

With the utmost care, he replaced the necklace in its box, lining the stones up neatly.

'It's an exquisite bijou, one of the most beautiful I've come across since I've been working at Christie's.'

'And how long is that?' she asked with interest.

'Coming up for twelve years next month.'

She looked at his cherubic face, thinking how different he was from his rugged, good-looking brother Chris, who was ten years older.

'You must've been a baby.'

'Not quite, I started at seventeen.'

He switched the conversation back to business.

'Miss Fergusson, may I suggest that we do a special feature on the necklace for next month's catalogue. After the list of goods for sale we include a rarity item or two as a set piece. This creates interest among the punters and perhaps it will help you find out how your mother came by your legacy.'

He looked at a large calendar on the wall.

'The catalogue's due out in ten days' time. Our copy date has expired, but I'm sure we can rush something through. Unless you want to wait until next month.'

'No, I'm not planning to spend that long in London. I've got a lot to sort out in Cayman. Your brother's very capable, I hasten to add, but I need to get settled.'

'I'm really sorry about your father. I know Chris thought the world of him; I'm sure he'll be sorely missed.'

Simon Johnson's brief speech sounded just a little bit too rehearsed to Luna, and she muttered a quick 'Thank you' before reverting to the necklace.

'I really am very puzzled as to how the necklace came to be in my parents' possession, they weren't even particularly interested in antiques, let alone jewellery. Would it have been possible for it to have made its way to the West Indies, and for them to have acquired it there?'

He thought about her question.

'It's possible, anything's possible, but improbable. A piece of this sort would most definitely have been worn for state occasions or important balls. I'm going to contact several people I know in Paris and London, they'll get back to me *asap*. I'll obviously call you as soon as I have any news.'

He closed the lid of the box, and handed it to her. 'Keep it safe.'

'Don't worry, it's going into the bank vault. Thanks a lot, Simon. Nice to have met you.'

Luna shook his hand.

'Same here. And it's my pleasure, believe me. It's not

every day of the week I get the opportunity to work with such a beautiful piece. Don't ask me why, but I have a gut feeling that this is a very important find.'

'Nicholas dear, have you seen Christie's catalogue this month?'

Nicholas had more on his mind than antiques, but he humoured his mother, patiently.

'No Mother, I haven't. Don't tell me you've found another rare piece of eighteenth-century Sèvres. I really don't think you've got room for any more.'

He heard her sigh loudly down the telephone.

'It's nothing to do with porcelain, this is much more interesting. And I quote . . .'

She began to read from the catalogue.

'Are you listening, Nicholas?'

'Yes, Mother,' he groaned, only half attending.

'"An extremely rare and important necklace. French, circa 1809, believed to have been commissioned by Napoleon for the Empress Josephine. Exceptionally fine, in perfect condition, with two hundred and twenty-five flawless diamonds and emeralds."'

'Very nice Mother, but what's so special about that?'

'Don't get snappy with me,' his mother admonished. 'I'm merely trying to tell you that the necklace in the catalogue is the same necklace that Serena thought she had lost in Port Antonio. I'd recognize it anywhere.'

'What,' he gasped, at once alert. 'Are you sure?'

'As sure as I know your name is Nicholas Edward Frazer-West.'

Nicholas promised to call his mother later, after he had been down to Christie's. He then called home, only to be told by the housekeeper that Serena had gone out for the day. Unable to concentrate in his meeting, he was pleased when it drew to a quick conclusion, and he was free to take a taxi to the Old Brompton Road, demanding to speak to Christie's chairman, Andrew Broomfield, whom he vaguely knew.

Broomfield was away on holiday and Nicholas spent a frustrating fifteen minutes trying to locate someone who could help him with information regarding the Empress necklace, as the auctioneers had dubbed it.

At last he was taken to Simon Johnson, who was busy examining a diamond tiara.

'My name is Frazer-West, and I've just seen this in your catalogue.'

Nicholas was waving the catalogue in front of him and pointing to the photograph of the necklace.

'That necklace belongs to my wife, Lady Serena West. It was a family heirloom she inherited on the death of her grandmother.'

Simon at once gave Nicholas his full attention.

'Do you have proof to substantiate your claim, sir?'

'Of course, I've got photos of my wife wearing it on our wedding day. I tell you, it's one and the same.'

Nicholas went on to say. 'It disappeared when we were living in Jamaica more than twenty-five years ago. I told her at the time not to take it, but we'd been invited to a big fancy-dress ball in Port Antonio, and she was going as a French courtesan. I must add that my wife had no idea of its value, she thought it was a very good imitation.'

'Hardly an imitation. I think sir, that you'd better come with me.'

Simon led Nicholas away from the main showroom. Not until they were in the privacy of his office did Simon speak.

'The present owner of the necklace brought it in a couple of weeks ago. It was given to me for authentication and assessment. It has a tiny jeweller's mark on the underside of the clasp.

'I did a little research and discovered that it was made by a famous French jeweller Etienne Nitot in the early 1800s for the Empress Josephine. After the Revolution

Nitot and Sons reset and remodelled several pieces of the crown jewels. I believe this was such a piece. The necklace is in perfect condition, extremely rare and historically important. In short a priceless antique.'

'We, that is my wife and I, had no idea it was so valuable. We'd have never taken it to the West Indies had we known. So, as you can appreciate, I would be very interested to know who claims to own it now.'

'As you must realize Lord Frazer-West, I'm not in a position to disclose the name of the owner.'

'Why not, man? It must have been stolen that night in Port Antonio; there's no other explanation.'

'I only have your word for that, I'm afraid sir. I think the best thing would be for you to come back when you have proof that the necklace did belong to your wife. Then we can investigate further.'

'Come along man, I'm telling the truth. Just tell me who brought the necklace in, and I'll have a quiet chat with them. Perhaps they acquired it in all innocence. Andrew Broomfield is an old friend of my late father's, I'm certain he would approve of you telling me.'

Simon, not wavering, responded briskly.

'Mr Broomfield is back from holiday in two days, sir, so I suggest you contact him then.'

Nicholas decided he was wasting his time and would have to try another route. He left Christie's and returned to his own office, trying to think of a way to find out the identity of the owner of the necklace. He considered placing an ad in *The Times*, then changed his mind, eventually planning to wait until Andrew Broomfield came back from holiday.

As it happened, he didn't have to wait. Later that day he received a telephone call from Luna Fergusson, telling him that she had information regarding the necklace. They arranged to meet for drinks at six that evening, in the Savoy cocktail bar. Nicholas arrived at a few minutes after six, and ordered a large gin and tonic. Luna appeared at his side as the barman was serving him.

'Good evening, Miss Fergusson,' Nicholas greeted her.

'Hi, Nicholas,' she said cheerfully, irritating him with the use of his Christian name.

Stuffing a handful of peanuts into her mouth, she spoke to the barman through them, ordering a Diet Coke. Nicholas found her manners extremely sloppy, and thought it was quite evident that she had been schooled in America.

'So, you have information regarding the necklace. How did you know I was interested in it?' Nicholas asked, as she sat down next to him.

'I had a call from Simon Johnson at Christie's, you see the necklace belongs to me.'

Luna looked directly into Nicholas's eyes, seeing a flash of amazement first, quickly replaced by a look of comprehension.

'Did Mr Johnson also tell you that the necklace in question once belonged to my wife, and that it disappeared after a party in Jamaica?'

It was Luna's turn to be visibly astounded, and she made no pretence at hiding it.

'No, he didn't. He simply said that you had some information that might be relevant to my quest.'

'And what quest is that, Miss Fergusson?'

'My mother left the necklace to me, with the express wish that I was to wear it on my wedding day. I have no idea how she came by such a piece of jewellery, I was intrigued and wanted to find out.'

Nicholas took a sip of his drink.

'I believe it was stolen, Miss Fergusson, by someone who saw my wife wearing it in Port Antonio as part of her fancy-dress costume during the party I mentioned.

He paused to inject just the right nuance into his tone.

'Your father was there the night of the party.'

Luna's voice rose. 'How *dare* you suggest my father

had anything to do with it! He was a man of the utmost integrity.'

Nicholas raised his eyes. '*Was*?'

Luna was shaking. 'Yes, he died less than a month ago.'

Nicholas paled. 'I had no idea, but please keep your voice down young lady.'

'I will not!' she said angrily.

Nicholas gave an embarrassed little cough, looking around the bar, hoping that there was no one there who knew him.

'I repeat, how dare you intimate that my father was involved in a crime. Tell me what proof do you have?'

'None, but he had the opportunity and the motive.'

'What motive?' she screeched.

'Money,' Nicholas replied calmly.

'Money! Well, if that was the case, why didn't he sell the necklace?'

She was yelling at the top of her voice now, several people were gawping in their direction.

Nicholas stood up. 'I refuse to continue this conversation if you insist on acting like a delinquent. Really Miss Fergusson, control yourself. Outbursts like this will not achieve anything.'

He was right, she knew that, but he had pushed her too far. Seething, she stood in front of him, feet slightly apart, chewing her bottom lip.

'My father was not a criminal, Lord Frazer-West. He was good, honest and kind. I have no idea how the necklace came to be in his possession, but I intend to find out. I know he would never have stolen it.'

'How can you be so sure? How do you know what was going through your father's head at the time, you weren't even born. Has the possibility entered your mind that your mother might have stolen it? She was around then as well.'

The Coca-Cola hit Nicholas full on the temple, then trickled into his astonished eyes. He spluttered, fumbling for a handkerchief, as she glared at him, formidable in her rage.

He backed off.

'I'll fight you on this Lord Frazer-West. I couldn't give a fuck about the money, but there's no way you're going to sully my family's good name.'

Wiping his mouth, he opened it and was about to retort when she turned on her heel and strode out of the bar. Nicholas finished his drink with as much dignity as he could muster and left the Savoy. Instructing José to drive directly home, he was pleased to see lights on in the drawing room as the chauffeur turned smoothly into Pelham Crescent and stopped in front of the house. He could hear Lucinda's voice as he climbed the flight of stairs to the first floor and walked in to join her, carrying the Christie's catalogue.

'Evening darling,' Serena welcomed him, as he crossed the room, stooping to plant a light kiss on her brow. Lucinda rose from the sofa to kiss her father warmly on both cheeks.

'So, how is my grandchild doing?'

He regarded her rounded stomach, thinking at the same time how frail she looked. Pregnancy did not suit her at all.

'Fine. I had a scan today and all's well.' She crossed her fingers on both hands. 'I haven't had any morning sickness for the last three days.'

'That's great news, darling. You've been looking a little peeky to say the least. Your mother and I have been extremely worried about you.'

'Daddy, I really believe you think I'm still about eight.'

Serena stood up, crossing the room to the drinks trolley.

'He does, I'm afraid. You're still your Daddy's little girl Lucinda, and nothing will change that.'

Serena looked at Nicholas. His brow was furrowed, and he looked perturbed about something.

'Drink darling?'

'No thanks, I had one at the Savoy.'

He was flicking through the Christie's catalogue and had found the page he wanted.

'Come here Serena, I've got something to show you.'

Sitting on the arm of the sofa, she handed Lucinda a soda water, whilst glancing casually at the colour photograph Nicholas was holding towards her. The thumping in her temple and left eye started as soon as she recognized the necklace . . . Luna's necklace.

Serena reprimanded herself inwardly for having acted so impetuously all those years ago. *Be sure your sins will find you out*, she thought ironically.

'It's my necklace. The one I thought I'd lost in Jamaica.'

'Exactly! It's worth a fortune Serena, it's a priceless antique. Read this.'

Nicholas slapped the photograph and passed her the catalogue.

'And you'll never guess who owns it now.'

With supreme effort Serena adopted an astonished expression when Nicholas went on to make his announcement.

'Luna Fergusson! Can you believe it, Royole Fergusson's daughter. He must have stolen it at that party or afterwards from Mango Bay.'

'That's incredible, Nicholas. How do you know that this girl, what's her name, has the necklace?'

'*Luna Fergusson*,' Lucinda said to herself with venom, an image of Ryan looking at the exotic Luna at the wrap party blotting out all other thoughts.

Nicholas answered his wife's question. 'I've just had drinks with her.'

The memory of Luna's violent outburst was still fresh in his mind.

'She's a very odd girl, and obviously convinced that her

father is no thief; but I intend to get to the bottom of this if it's the last thing I do.'

An involuntary shudder ran through Serena. She felt an icy chill, in spite of the warmth of the room.

'I tend to agree with the girl Luna, I think that Royole Fergusson was an honest man. He may have done a lot of things in his life, but I don't believe being a thief was one of them.'

Lucinda didn't notice her mother's use of the past tense when referring to Royole Fergusson, but Nicholas did. He asked himself how could Serena possibly know the man was dead. He was about to question her when the telephone rang.

'I'm expecting a call from Rachel,' Serena said far too quickly, escaping to the study before anyone could reply.

It wasn't Rachel, but Ryan. After exchanging a few pleasantries with him, Serena called her daughter. An elated Lucinda rushed to the study, eagerly taking the telephone from her mother's hands.

'Ryan! How are you?'

Serena climbed the stairs wearily, with Lucinda's excited chatter about the baby filling her ears. She had been shaken by this new turn of events. But now, for the sake of her daughters, she steeled herself to put a stop to it all.

Two days later a Fed Ex envelope landed on Luna's desk. It was from Chris Johnson, and she knew what it contained even before she opened it.

She had called Chris after her argument with Nicholas, asking him if her father had ever mentioned the Frazer-Wests, or his time with them in Jamaica. Luna had been unprepared for Chris's reply, that Lord Frazer-West was a client of the bank and had been for more than ten years. He warned her that he was a difficult man, urging her to proceed with the utmost caution.

Pulling out the file, she placed it on her desk. A company name was typed on the left-hand corner, with a code number next to it. She read out loud, 'Halcyon Corps . . . 4125,' then continued to read silently. She discovered that Nicholas Frazer-West had deposited three million dollars in cash, and formed an off-shore company at Fergusson Bank in 1980. Subsequent deposits had been made on specific dates over the ensuing years. Each and every one of them, she noticed, had been transferred from the same account at the Mercurial Bank in Beirut.

She had a call to make.

'Chris. Hi, it's Luna.'

'How are you?' he asked.

'I'm fine. Listen, I need a favour. Can you fax the Mercurial Bank in Beirut and try to wheedle some info out of them re account number 809 422 4111.'

'That's the account used for Halcyon transactions and deposits.'

'Exactly. Please find out anything you can, and get back to me *asap*.'

'Will do. Incidentally, I've had a fax from Frazer-West this morning. He's planning a trip out here next week, so you haven't got much time. Take care Luna, do you hear me.'

'Yeah, sure.' Heedless to his warning, she replaced the telephone, deep in thought.

Luna stayed at the office late, hoping for word from Chris. She checked the fax machine every few minutes, eventually giving up at eight o'clock and going home.

The message light on her telephone was flashing as she entered her apartment. She flicked the switch, hoping to hear Chris, but it was his brother instead. Asking her to call him urgently as soon as she got in, he had left a home number. She scribbled Simon Johnson's number on a pad, then called.

'Shit!' she swore as she heard his answering machine.

She left a message and clicked her own machine off.

A second later she jumped as the shrill tone of the telephone rang unexpectedly.

'Hi Luna, it's Chris. Sorry I didn't get back to you sooner, but I've got the information you need. The account holder is one Nabil Khoorey; he's Lebanese, living in Paris. Hope that helps?'

'Well, it doesn't mean a thing to me, but it sure as hell will to Frazer-West. Thanks Chris.'

He repeated his earlier warning.

'Don't worry about me Chris. I'm a big girl, I can look after myself.'

'I do worry, and I think you know that.'

She had always considered Chris Johnson to be like a big brother, he'd been around since she was a young girl. Yet she'd heard something in his 'I think you know that' which transcended brotherly affection. She wasn't absolutely sure, but as she walked towards her kitchen she had the strongest instinct that Chris Johnson was in love with her.

At seven-thirty the following morning she awoke to a persistent ringing. It was Simon Johnson on the phone.

'I thought you should know, Miss Fergusson, that Lord Frazer-West intends to press charges. He claims to have proof that the necklace was stolen and he's pointing the finger at your mother and father. It's out of my hands now I'm afraid.'

He sounded relieved.

'If you need to speak to anyone here about it, I think you should call Mr Broomfield, the company chairman. However, I must warn you he's a family friend of Frazer-West.'

'Thanks for the warning Simon, I appreciate it.'

'No problem, and good luck.'

'I think I might need it,' she added ruefully, before

saying goodbye and jumping out of bed. She showered quickly, then dressed in a pin-striped trouser suit and plain, white tee-shirt. Picking up the newspaper on her way through the hall, she dropped it on to the dining table as she passed by, then continued through to the kitchen where she made herself a strong, black coffee and two slices of wholemeal toast. Luna spread them thickly with lots of butter and black cherry jam. She had developed a passion for English conserves. Sitting at the table, she had an unobstructed view across the terrace. A few drops of rain spattered the window, falling from ominous black clouds suspended like a tarpaulin over the murky Thames. Her thoughts drifted to Cayman – taking breakfast on the terrace of Whispering Cay, dappled with sunlight and fanned by a warm Caribbean breeze. It crossed her mind that if there was one thing she was not going to miss about London it was the bloody awful climate. The incredible unpredictability of it infuriated her more than the actual weather. Biting into a slice of toast, she glanced at the headlines in *The Times*.

'Sir Jeremy Gray denies serious corruption and bribery allegations.'

She read on, not particularly interested, but welcoming any distraction from her own problems for a while. The report claimed that Sir Jeremy Gray, cabinet minister for Trade and Industry, had been conducting a year-long affair with Nadia Michaelis, who was also having an affair with another man called . . . Luna gasped as she read the name . . . Nabil Khoorey. The police were anxious to talk to Nabil Khoorey, who had been involved with corruption and bribery at a high governmental level. There was a photograph of a tall, attractive brunette, who looked Anglo-Indian, but was in fact half Iranian Luna learnt as she read on. Another photograph showed Sir Jeremy in the garden of his country house, smiling confidently amidst his cosy family and prize azaleas. He was quoted as saying the whole thing was farcical, he had never heard of this Nadia woman or Nabil Khoorey.

As Luna stared at the assured face of the peer, something about the dogmatic look of him reminded her of Lord Frazer-West.

'What's the matter Serena darling? You look like you've seen a ghost.'

Nicholas joined his wife as she was sitting and reading the morning newspaper.

She handed it to him silently, watching his reaction closely. Nicholas blanched as he saw the headlines.

He blinked rapidly as he continued to read before throwing the paper on to the sofa with a disgusted grunt.

'I don't believe a bloody word of it!'

His blustering anger failed to hide from Serena his obvious fear. 'Don't you, Nicholas?'

'Of course not, it's utter nonsense. Jeremy is a happily married man. He adores his family, he wouldn't be mixed up with trash like that.'

He pointed to the photograph of the woman.

'I think that "trash", as you put it, is the whole point,' said Serena.

'What the devil do you mean?'

'Oh, come on, you know as well as I do that men like Jeremy Gray get off on women like that. Need I elaborate?'

'I really don't think Jeremy's that kind.'

'He's the classic stereotype; upper crust, repressed childhood, public school, plain wife. Say no more. The press will make mincemeat of him.'

She sighed.

'Actually I think you know a lot more about Sir Jeremy Gray, and Nabil Khoorey, than you care to admit. I seem to remember Nabil was one of your closest friends at Eton.'

314

'What on earth are you talking about, Serena? As usual you're making mountains out of molehills; I haven't seen or heard from Nabil in years. In fact I think the last time was on our wedding day.'

'You're lying, Nicholas.'

His face infused with a rush of anger. 'How dare you accuse me of deliberate lying?'

She stood up to face him. 'I dare, because I know the truth.'

When she spoke again there was a cautionary note in her voice.

'I don't intend to mention it to anyone Nicholas, and I suggest you do whatever is necessary to cover your tracks.'

He didn't reply, so she went on more urgently.

'I'm warning you, be very careful. There's never any smoke without fire, and once the press get their dirty little paws on something like this they'll never let go. Not until there's been sufficient blood-letting. Whatever your involvement, make damn sure they don't find out.'

It was evident from his haunted expression that her words had hit home. Without a word he left the room. She heard him run upstairs, then a little later the door slammed as he left the house.

Nicholas went straight to his office and, locking himself in, he shredded every file appertaining to Nabil Khoorey or Jeremy Gray. He did exactly the same with all correspondence relating to his off-shore accounts and companies in the Cayman Islands. Satisfied that he'd done everything he could for the time being, he rang Jeremy Gray. All he got was an answering machine. He slammed the phone down, cursing, unable to understand why Jeremy hadn't rung him. Then he tried Nabil, whom no one had seen for weeks.

No success again. Taking no chances, he collected the shredded evidence into a plastic bag, and then dumped it into a garbage bin at the back of the Hilton Hotel before returning to his office.

There was a call for Nicholas later that night from a telephone box. Serena answered initially.

'Serena, darling, It's Jeremy Gray. How are you?'

'How are you, is more to the point Jeremy.'

'Absolutely fine, couldn't be better. Don't believe everything you read in the newspapers.'

'I don't usually, but that woman's allegations do seem pretty damning.'

'It's all utter nonsense Serena, I've never met her before. I've already instigated libel proceedings.'

'Well, I'm sure it'll all blow over very soon,' she said, with more reassurance than she felt. 'I'll get Nicholas for you.'

Pressing the hold button she shouted upstairs towards the study, where Nicholas was working. After putting the call through, she ran upstairs to the drawing room and carefully picked up the receiver of an extension telephone. She could hear Jeremy's voice as she held it to her ear.

'Don't worry old chap, I've got everything under control. Nabil's taken a much needed, long holiday, and the woman will be taken care of.'

'What do you mean?' Nicholas hissed.

Serena could almost smell her husband's fear.

'I mean she'll be retracting that nonsense she told the press very soon. Like I said, it's all under control. I don't want you to worry about a thing old boy.'

There was a short pause, then Jeremy's soothing voice continued, with just a hint of a threat beneath the calm veneer.

'It is of course a time for extreme caution, I'm sure you appreciate that. I know I can rely on your discretion, Nicholas.'

'That goes without saying.'

'I thought so. I'll keep you posted with developments as and when they occur, and I'd advise you not to ring me until this whole nasty business blows over.'

'I understand.'

Jeremy put the telephone down and the line went dead. Serena waited for Nicholas to replace his receiver, hardly daring to breathe.

'Serena, is that you?'

She jumped, startled by his voice.

'Yes, it is,' she replied softly.

'Stay where you are, I'm coming up.'

She heard his footsteps on the stairs, a moment later the door was flung open, and Nicholas walked into the drawing room.

'Nicholas, I'm sorry for eavesdropping . . . but I had to know.'

Ignoring her, he began to pace the room. Back and forth he marched, like a caged animal. When he eventually stopped, Serena could see that he was close to tears.

'As they say in the movies Nicholas, the shit has hit the fan. I think it's high time you and I had a long chat.'

Chapter Twenty-Five

'Please take a seat Miss Fergusson, Chief Inspector Bush will be with you right away.'

'Thanks,' Luna said quietly as the secretary left her in a small dark office. Sitting down on an uncomfortable bentwood chair, she looked around with interest. It was her first visit to Scotland Yard. She wasn't sure what she expected, but it certainly wasn't her present austere surroundings.

Chief Inspector Bush joined her a few minutes later with an ebullient 'Good morning, Miss Fergusson' and a warm, beaming smile. He was very attractive in an ugly sort of way. And Luna suspected he laughed a lot from the network of laughter lines surrounding his dark grey eyes. She began to get up.

'Stay where you are Miss Fergusson, please.'

He walked around the desk and sat down, focusing his full attention on her. He thought she looked like she had just jumped off the cover of some expensive glossy. Straight into his drab office. He shook his head at the incongruity of it and started to speak in his soft Welsh accent.

'I believe you have information regarding bribery allegations concerning Sir Jeremy Gray.'

Luna fished in her briefcase, pulling out the Halcyon file.

'I know nothing about Sir Jeremy Gray, it's Lord Frazer-West I have information about.'

She searched his face, it was inscrutable.

'Go on,' he prompted.

'I'm a merchant banker. My father, until his death a few weeks ago, owned an off-shore bank called Fergusson Bank and Trust. It's located in Grand Cayman. Anyway, to cut a long story short, I have recently had dealings with a client called Lord Nicholas Frazer-West who has been banking with us since the early eighties. He made a deposit of three million dollars in cash in 1980, and subsequent large deposits over the years. The last one was made eight months ago, for six hundred thousand pounds.'

'So, what are you getting at Miss Fergusson?' the policeman asked. Lord Nicholas Frazer-West had been seen with Jeremy Gray on several occasions, but so far they had been unable to come up with any evidence to suspect him of anything other than friendship. And the Nadia woman claimed that she had never seen or heard of him.

'Well, I wouldn't have thought anything about it if I hadn't read the story about Jeremy Gray in *The Times* this morning. You see, apart from the original deposit made by Lord Frazer-West in 1980, all the subsequent ones have been paid from a bank in Beirut. The account is in the name of Nabil Khoorey.'

Nicholas was drinking his third glass of neat gin when his secretary called through on the intercom.

'There's a Chief Inspector Bush in reception to see you, sir.'

'What does he want?' he slurred, 'I'm about to leave for lunch.'

'He says he's from the Serious Fraud Squad, sir.' She hesitated. 'Shall I send him up?'

'In a few minutes,' Nicholas said sharply.

Flicking the intercom off, he whispered to himself. 'I need a few minutes to compose myself.'

He hid the glass and the gin bottle in his desk drawer. Running trembling fingers through his hair and down the front of his suit, he stood up shakily as he heard a sharp rap on his office door.

'Chief Inspector Bush, sir.' The policeman took one long stride forward. 'So sorry to disturb you, I'm sure you're a busy man.'

'Not at all, always delighted to assist the police in their enquiries. Please take a seat.'

The sight of his visitor had a sobering effect on Nicholas. He gathered his thoughts, reminding himself of what Jeremy had said. The police had no real evidence, apart from the story Nadia Michaelis had given them. He steeled himself to keep calm and stay in control whatever happened.

'Are you acquainted with Sir Jeremy Gray, sir?'

The question was expected, and Nicholas answered easily.

'Yes I am, he's been a friend for many years. Our respective families were very friendly when we were young. Jeremy and I virtually grew up together.'

'Well then, I assume you're aware that he's under investigation for serious bribery and corruption charges against the state.'

Nicholas took a deep breath and lowered his eyes.

'Yes, I am aware, but I refuse to believe the allegations of some cheap prostitute, Chief Inspector.'

Michael Bush declined to comment. Whilst admiring the photograph of Serena on Nicholas's desk, he changed the subject adeptly.

'This is a beautiful office, if I may say so. Puts mine to shame. How long have you been here?'

Nicholas thought back to the day he'd purchased the leasehold.

'Since 1978.'

'Did you know Nabil Khoorey then?'

Nicholas's throat had gone very dry and he longed for a glass of water.

'I'm so sorry Chief Inspector, I didn't offer you any refreshment. Would you like some tea? Or coffee perhaps?'

With a wave of his hand the policeman declined. He smiled easily and looked like a friendly shopkeeper. Nevertheless Nicholas warned himself to stay on his guard.

'Well, you don't mind if I do.'

'No, not at all.'

Nicholas sent for a glass of mineral water.

'So, Lord Frazer-West, could you please tell me when you first met Nabil Khoorey?'

'Yes, I met him when I was ten years old, at prep school. We both went up to Eton together, and became friends. He came to my wedding in the mid-sixties, then we lost touch after that I'm afraid.'

'Was that the last time you saw or heard from him, sir?'

A knock on the door interrupted them, and Nicholas's secretary entered with a glass of sparkling water. He drank thirstily, the word *deny, deny, deny*, running through his head. Standing the empty glass on his desk, he smacked his lips decisively.

'Like I said, the last time I saw Nabil Khoorey was in 1964 at my wedding.'

There seemed to be a glimmer of triumph in the policeman's eyes as he stood up, holding the large brown envelope he'd been carrying. It scared Nicholas. His heart began to pound frantically, he could feel it thumping against his chest and thundering in his own ears.

Michael Bush opened the envelope, pulling out a file which he dropped on to Nicholas's desk. It bore the words 'Halcyon Corp'. Nicholas tried to look at the file, but the code numbers were a complete blur.

'Since you haven't seen or heard of Nabil Khoorey since

1964, can you explain why he's been depositing vast sums of money into your account in the Cayman Islands for the last twelve years? One made only eight months ago for six hundred thousand pounds to be precise.'

The policeman knew he had him.

'I can explain, Chief Inspector, I really can explain. I can. Nabil was . . . is . . . you see . . . I know where he is. He's gone away on holiday, by the seaside, where Robbie used to take me.'

Nicholas was muttering incoherently, trying desperately to be plausible.

'You'd better come down to Scotland Yard with me sir, if you don't mind, I think my commander would like to talk to you. Just a routine chat, you know. You can explain everything to us there.'

Serena had been waiting for over an hour outside the Spencer Howard Bank when she finally spotted Luna coming out.

'At last,' she whispered to herself, starting the ignition. Pulling away from the kerb, she had to slow down as Luna hailed a cab. She followed the cab down the Embankment, hoping that Luna was going straight home. She was. Serena kept her distance as she drove into the entrance to Chelsea Harbour, and waited until the cab had left before she parked her car.

She went up to Luna's front door.

'Who is it?' Luna's voice came through the intercom.

'It's Lady Serena Frazer-West; may I have a few words with you?'

The door opened whilst Serena was still waiting for a response from the machine.

'Come in Lady Frazer-West. I was wondering how long it would be before you turned up.'

Luna stepped to one side and Serena walked into the brightly lit hall. She immediately thought about the day she had come to see Royole, not quite able to grasp that it had only been a few weeks before.

The two woman faced each other. It was the first time Serena had really looked closely at her daughter. There was a remarkable resemblance not only to Lucinda and herself, but also her own grandmother. Ironically that was whom the necklace had belonged to.

'I suppose you've come about the necklace. If you intend to accuse my father too, Lady Serena, you might as well leave right now. I do not, and will not, believe that he was a thief.'

'Your father was not a thief, far from it Luna. He was the wonderful, sensitive man I fell in love with when I wasn't much younger than you.'

Serena had expected Luna to be shocked and was surprised by her cool reaction.

'I thought there was something going on between you guys; I noticed my father's face when he met you at Ryan's wrap party. I've never seen him look at anybody like that before, not even my mother. And when you rang after his death, I detected something in your voice. I couldn't put my finger on it right away, but I knew it was more than plain old-fashioned sympathy.'

'You're very perceptive Luna, and you're right, it was a lot more than that. I was devastated. You see, your father had asked me to join him, after all these years. And I had decided to leave Nicholas, to be with him.'

Luna, rarely stuck for words, could think of nothing appropriate to say. She was saved from uttering the obvious clichés because Serena spoke again.

'I wonder if we could sit down, there's something else I want to say to you.'

'Sure, come through.'

Serena followed Luna into the living room. It was in total darkness, lights from the South Bank and the river twinkling brightly in the window frame. Luna flicked a switch and the room was flooded in harsh, white light. They sat opposite each other on two huge sofas.

'Would you like a drink?' Luna offered.

'No, thanks. I would rather do this stone-cold sober I think,' Serena replied, biting the corner of her bottom lip.

'You know, it's really strange Lady Frazer-West, but I have exactly the same habit as you. I always chew my lip when I'm nervous.'

'Well, it's actually not that strange Luna, considering you're my daughter.'

At first a deadly silence followed Serena's admission.

Luna glared at the stiff, elegant woman opposite, poised and serene. So Caucasian, so English . . . so *different*.

'Sorry if I'm not jumping for joy or anything like that, but what you've just told me is going to take a while to absorb. I mean apart from being in shock, there are a hundred questions racing round my head. The one that springs immediately to mind is why did you give me up?'

'I can explain. It was very difficult—' Serena started to answer.

But Luna interrupted. 'This explains a lot of things! My mother's . . . Caron's . . . attitude towards me. All my life, I've wondered why she resented me. I thought it was because my father loved me so much and showered me with all the attention, but now I know she had good reason . . . I remember, when I was about thirteen, witnessing a terrible row between my parents. My mother was shouting something about a love-child.

'Jesus, it must have been dreadful for her to see me every day of her life, knowing that you and Dad had . . .'

She dropped her head as her voice broke, and she had to stop herself biting her lower lip. Serena wanted to approach her daughter, this exceptional-looking woman that she and Royole had made, but she held back, afraid of rejection.

'There's something else you should know Luna, you have a twin sister.'

Luna's head was still down, and there was no sound save her loud expulsion of breath. Serena continued in the same controlled voice.

'Lucinda was conceived within hours of you. I had intercourse with Nicholas in the morning, when presumably Lucinda was conceived; then I made love with your father the same afternoon, when you were conceived. You were born within minutes of each other, on the night of the twenty-eighth of March, 1967, in a midwife's cottage in Gloucestershire.'

Even now Serena shuddered at the memory.

'I loved your father, and would've given everything up for him, even Lucinda . . . but he didn't want me at that point in his life. He felt there was no room for a spoilt, little rich girl from England, who would be dependent upon him. In retrospect he was probably right. Anyway, after you were born, I contacted him and asked if he would have you. Bring you up as his own, and never disclose who your real mother was.'

For the first time since she had come into the flat, Serena felt her steely control falter. She blinked rapidly, clearing her eyes of a thin film of tears.

'That was the deal. He agreed, and came to London for you. He fell in love with you on sight, I might add. I never saw him again until the night of the wrap party. It was a terrible shock, seeing you both again after twenty-seven years.'

She wrung her hands together. 'Are you aware that Lucinda is pregnant?'

Luna nodded.

'Well, bearing that in mind, I think it would be unwise to tell her any of this. At least for the moment.'

'What's the matter Lady Serena, are you afraid she'll disapprove? We can't upset the golden girl now can we?

Too much for her to cope with I suppose, her mother fucking a black man and having his mulatto love-child, her half-caste twin. Ha, Ryan would love it! Make a great story for his next movie.'

Luna began to laugh, a harsh, hollow sound.

'I intend to tell her at some point, but not yet. I understand your anger Luna, but can you forget that for the moment, and think only of Lucinda's unborn child. She came close to a miscarriage only last week. So, a shock like this, well anything could happen.'

'To be perfectly honest with you, I don't give a damn about Lucinda or her baby, or you for that matter. You sit there talking about your love for my father, yet you never called to see how he was, or to ask just once if I was OK. Not a letter, a card, a few scribbled words; not even a five-minute telephone call. Nothing . . . in twenty-seven years. I could've been dead! So don't talk to me about understanding, and Lucinda's unborn child.'

Serena spread her arms wide, in a gesture of hopelessness. It spoke more than a million words. Tears slipped from the corners of her eyes.

'I'm sorry Luna, I thought it was for the best.'

'I'm sure you did. I'm sure you thought it was the best for *you*.'

Both women simultaneously looked directly at each other.

'And the necklace, Lady Serena? How did my mother come to have your necklace?'

'Oh yes, the necklace. I did that in an impetuous moment. I rang virtually every hotel in London till I found out where your father was registered, then sent my nanny round to his room with the necklace and a letter, asking that it be given to you on your wedding day. I doubt Caron even knew of its existence. I was as shocked as you to learn of its origins, and value; in all honesty I thought it was a very good imitation.'

Luna's tone was resigned then biting. 'I can't imagine wanting to wear it on my wedding day . . . under the circumstances. I intend to loan it to a French museum for a while at least.'

'I can appreciate how you feel Luna, but what you must also understand is that I gave your father the necklace as a gesture of the love I felt for you both at the time. So that there was something from me for you. It was very difficult for me, please try to understand, I was very young and caught up in the kind of emotion that breeds madness.'

Personally Luna thought that emotion bred compassion, sympathy, mercy and love, and would have liked to have told Serena so. But she declined from getting into an argument with someone who she doubted would understand such sentiments.

'Does Lord Frazer-West know all this?'

'He does now, I told him last night.'

She didn't add that he had asked her for a divorce.

Luna suddenly leapt to her feet. Clamping a hand to her mouth, she muttered through her fingers.

'Oh no, if I'd known all of this sooner things might have been different. I wanted to punish him for what he'd said about my father, you see, so I took the file to Scotland Yard.'

Serena looked bewildered. 'What has Scotland Yard got to do with this?'

'Everything now, I'm afraid.'

Ryan had been trying unsuccessfully to contact Lucinda for most of the day. He had left several messages on the answering machine, but to no avail. He was beginning to get worried, perhaps something had happened to the baby. Eventually he rang her parents' number. It was answered by one of the staff, he thought it sounded like the housekeeper.

'Ryan Tyler speaking, is that June?'

'It is sir.'

Her usually cheery voice sounded flat, and he felt a stirring of unease.

'I'm trying to contact Lucinda, do you know if she's there?'

'She's here, with her mother, but . . .' she hesitated.

His unease deepened. 'Is there something wrong June?'

'Yes, there is, but I think you'd better speak to Lady Lucinda.'

There was a click and the phone went dead. A moment later he heard Lucinda's tremulous voice.

'Ryan, is that you?'

He felt a lump in his throat. Holding his breath, he asked, 'Are you all right, Lu? The baby?'

'The baby's fine, but I'm not. Oh, Ryan!'

He could tell she was close to tears.

'My father committed suicide last night. The chauffeur found him in the garage this morning. He did it in his car, carbon-monoxide poisoning. There's going to be an inquest.'

It was at this point she broke down completely.

'Don't try to talk now, sweetheart. I'll be on the next plane back to London tonight. I'll see you in the morning.'

Luna was never able to explain, even to herself, why she went to Nicholas Frazer-West's funeral. Out of guilt, for the part she believed she had played in his downfall? To have a glimpse of Ryan Tyler?

Or was it simply that she felt compelled to pay her last respects, and see her mother and half-twin for the final time? Since Serena's visit, Luna had steadfastly blocked out all thought of the Frazer-Wests, concentrating only on herself and her plans for returning to the Caribbean. It was only after hearing of Nicholas's suicide that she

328

allowed herself to think of 'Them' . . . as she referred to her mother and Lucinda.

Nicholas was to be buried next to his father in the family grave at the chapel at Redby Hall, which Luna learned had once been the Frazer-West ancestral seat. Boarding the train at Paddington, she had second thoughts and almost turned back. It was a glorious day, sunlight streaming into the carriage as it sped out of London, deep into the country.

The service had begun when she crept into the tiny chapel. She took a seat at the back, squeezing into a pew tightly packed with family and mourners.

Luna mouthed the words to three unfamiliar hymns, then sang at the top of her voice for 'Jerusalem'. Spotting Ryan's dark head, she stared affectionately at his profile as he turned to whisper something in Lucinda's ear. For the first time, she noticed how curly his long, thick eyelashes were.

'Let us pray.'

Luna dropped to her knees, reciting the Lord's Prayer. She found herself thinking only of her own father, and ended up wishing she hadn't come after all. She could hardly wait for the last words of the final blessing, so that she could leave the church . . .

'Luna.'

Serena was panting as she caught up with her after the service. 'I saw you at the back, then you were gone. Won't you stay for the burial?'

Luna looked over Serena's shoulder to where the congregation were streaming out of the church. She could see Lucinda, her head bent, talking to Ryan.

'No, I think I'd better go. I've done what I came to do.'

'And what was that?' Serena's eyes were expressionless.

'To pay my last respects of course.'

Luna was seized with a terrible sense of isolation.

'And to say I'm sorry, and goodbye.'

Serena's hand reached out tentatively. Luna hesitated, then gripped it firmly. The two women stood very still for several long moments, their eyes unwavering, their hands locked.

'I'll be thinking about you Luna, take care.'

'I will, I promise. And you take care of yourself . . . Mother.'

March 1996.

Chris Johnson was annoyed.

'I thought we were going out to dinner, Luna.'

Detecting his transparent irritation, she drowned his words with a kiss on the mouth.

'I want to watch the Oscars, we can go out tomorrow night. Now be a good boy, go get some pizza and fries, and I'll open some good claret.'

'Who cares about the Academy awards anyway,' he was muttering as he walked out of the kitchen.

'You could always watch the highlights tomorrow on CNN,' he added hopefully.

'I want to watch it live Chris, now go.'

She heard the door slam, and went back to pouring a bottle of '83 Château Giscours. If there was one thing her father had taught her it was to appreciate good red wine. She was soon slumped in front of the television with her glass, her long legs curled under her body.

Moments later Luna was transfixed. She was watching Lucinda West walk up the red carpet, towards the entrance to the Dorothy Chandler Pavilion. She looked elegant in a simple, ivory slip dress, with a dazzling six-row choker of diamonds and pearls at her neck.

To Luna's surprise, Lucinda was not escorted by Ryan, as she had anticipated, but by a heavily built man with a blond ponytail. Standing a few feet from him was a much older man. He was well preserved in a Hollywood sort of way, lightly tanned with his fashionably long hair streaked with grey, and he had piercing blue eyes. Luna reckoned he was in his early sixties.

He was gripping the slim waist of an elegant blonde woman who was looking with adoration into his face. She wore a long black silk gown. The woman was Serena Frazer-West.

A television reporter had stopped Lucinda.

'Miss West, how do you feel about your nomination for Best Actress? You've got some stiff competition.'

Lucinda looked into the camera with a dazzling smile.

'I'm thrilled to be nominated. *The Mitford Papers* is a great movie.'

Luna was busy looking at Lucinda's face, trying to notice if motherhood had changed her. She made a rapid calculation. By her reckoning the baby would've been born last May.

Chris had returned and laid down two trays, joining her on the sofa, yet she barely noticed his presence as she watched, fascinated. Instead she listened avidly as the reporter turned to the attractive man still holding Serena protectively close.

'Mr Negretti, is it true that you're going to direct Lucinda West in her next movie?'

Mark Negretti smiled benignly, 'Well, we're still in negotiation, you know how it is.'

He spoke in a gravelly voice, and Luna thought it matched his craggy features.

Stepping to one side the film director began to manoeuvre Serena away from the cameras, but he wasn't quick enough. The reporter had pushed in front of him, intent on his next question.

'Is it true Lady Frazer-West, that you and Mark Negretti have enjoyed a whirlwind romance and intend to get married later this year – when Mr Negretti's divorce is finalized?'

Serena blushed attractively. Her face glowing, she said clearly, 'Well, we're still in negotiation, you know how it is . . .'

There was a final shot of Serena being led by the hand of her escort towards the entrance to the Pavilion. Then an endless stream of film stars and media celebrities followed.

Chris was chattering incessantly, bored by the repetitive comments and fabricated smiles. Luna stayed glued to the screen, scanning the mass of faces for Ryan Tyler every time the camera swept around the packed tables. Just before the Best Actress category was announced, she had to hold her breath.

'And the winner is . . . Lucinda West, for *The Mitford Papers*.'

Luna watched Lucinda stand up, envy burning into her like a white hot iron. Then she saw him.

He was smiling and clapping, moving towards Lucinda, placing a kiss on her ecstatic, upturned face. She couldn't watch any longer. Excusing herself, she fled to the bathroom where she threw up.

The letter arrived six weeks later. The address was incomplete, and she wondered how it had ever found her.

Luna Fergusson,
Fergusson Bank,
Cayman Islands,
West Indies.

She didn't recognize the big, untidy scrawl. Then, examining the envelope, she saw that it had an Irish postmark. Tearing it open, she was still unprepared for the heady surge of adrenaline when she looked at the end of the short letter and saw the name 'Ryan'.

Hi Luna,

I don't know whether this letter will find you, I never did get your correct address. If it does, I hope you're well.

As you can see, I'm in Tipperary, Ireland. (I suppose you've heard the song 'It's a long way to Tipperary'?)

Anyway, I'm here casting for my next movie – about a prominent American Irish politician who is funding the IRA, and who gets himself into no end of trouble. It feels good to be home, after all the razzmatazz of Hollywood. I guess you know that Lucinda picked up Best Actress for *The Mitford Papers*. She acted brilliantly, and I'm sure you'd agree she deserved it. But she's not in this movie, she's too busy papering her walls in Los Angeles with the scripts that pour through her door every day. By the way, we lost the baby. Lucinda had a miscarriage. And, to cut a very long story short, it all turned to shit after that.

Luna was hyperventilating as she read on, and had to stop to take a few deep breaths.

It's pissing down with rain here at the moment, but when it stops, which isn't very often, and the mist clears, there is a view from my bedroom window across the valley that fair takes yer breath away. I'll be here for at least six weeks, possibly longer. So, if you fancy a pint of best draught Guinness and an Irish whiskey chaser with me and old Danny O'Farrell (the publican at The Old Boot, in the village), then we would both make a fair lass like you most welcome.

All my love,
Ryan.

Luna read and reread the letter a dozen times, before picking up the telephone. She spoke to her secretary in a rapid voice overflowing with excitement.

'Call the travel agency, and get me details on flights from here to Dublin. Yes Carolyn, that's right . . . Dublin, Ireland.'

These books are available from your local bookseller or can be
ordered direct from the publishers.

To order direct just tick the titles you want and fill in the form
below:

☐ THE SEVENTH WAVE Emma Sinclair	0-00-647294-X	£4.99
☐ THE LIVERPOOL BASQUE Helen Forrester	0-00-647334-2	£4.99
☐ AN OLDER WOMAN Alison Scott Skelton	0-586-21508-5	£5.99
☐ WILLIAM'S WIFE Jean Plaidy	0-00-647299-0	£4.99
☐ THE RED SHAWL Jessica Blair	0-586-21857-2	£3.99
☐ LONG, HOT SUMMER Betty Burton	0-00-647635-X	£4.99

Name:
_____

Address:
_____

_____

Postcode:
_____

Send to: HarperCollins Mail Order, Dept 8, HarperCollins
Publishers, Westerhill Road, Bishopbriggs, Glasgow G64 2QT.

Please enclose a cheque or postal order or authority to debit
your Visa/Access account –

Credit card no:
_____

Expiry date:
_____

Signature:
_____

– to the value of the cover price plus:

UK & BFPO: Add £1.00 for the first and 25p for each additional
book ordered.

Overseas orders including Eire, please add £2.95 service charge.
Books will be sent by surface mail but quotes for airmail
despatches will be given on request.

**24 HOUR TELEPHONE ORDERING SERVICE FOR
ACCESS/VISA CARDHOLDERS –
TEL: GLASGOW 041-772 2281 or LONDON 081-307 4052**